PR… …NT

“Grant’s powerful, emotionally intense and highly sensual romance will mesmerize readers yearning for an unconventional story and dynamic characters. The driven prot… …ils of a Regency worl… …marriage mart lure re…

“Exquisite . . . …hor’s voice and look forward to more.”

—MANDI SCHREINER, *USA Today*

“With her second impeccably written, exquisitely sensual historical, Grant proves she suffers from no sophomore slump as she once again shakes up the staid Regency historical world with her refreshingly unconventional, multilayered characters and richly emotional storytelling style.”

—*Booklist* (starred review)

“With exquisite prose, breathtaking sensuality, and stunning emotional insight, Grant spins a poignant, compelling story of two deeply troubled protagonists who need to come to terms with who they are, forgive themselves, and learn to love. A brilliant addition to the growing number of romances featuring uncommon characters, this story takes fans for a walk on the wilder side of Regency London and will have fans anxious for the next series installment.”

—*Library Journal*

"A charmingly risqué protagonist . . . begs the reader to turn the page."

—*Publishers Weekly*

"Luscious, erotic, and emotionally intense . . . Cecilia Grant is a fresh, unforgettable voice in historical romance."

—MADELINE HUNTER,
New York Times bestselling author

A Lady Awakened

"Elegantly written, emotionally powerful . . . with a compelling combination of exquisitely nuanced characters and lusciously sensual romance. Sweet, poignant, and completely satisfying, *A Lady Awakened* is a romance to treasure."

—*Booklist* (starred review)

"Grant details Regency country life beautifully, with a firm and respectful hand, and the subtle yet engrossing courtship is enchanting and gratifying as it transforms these two strong-minded and very unlikely lovers."

—*Publishers Weekly*

"This intriguing debut blends erotic themes into a plotline that has been used before, but never in this way. A desperate heroine, a wickedly sexy hero, an unexpected passion and strong storytelling along with compelling characterization mark Grant as one to watch."

—*RT Book Reviews*

"From the characters to the language to the love scenes to the plot, so much came together unexpectedly and beautifully. I loved this novel."

—JANINE, Dear Author

"I'm in love with this author's voice. It is hard to explain why I love her style of writing so much, but as I read I didn't want to miss a single word."

—*USA Today*

"A marvelous gem of a book . . . I loved it!"

— MARY BALOGH,
New York Times bestselling author

"If you only read one debut this year, this is the one to read. Incredibly sexy, surprisingly sweet. I loved *A Lady Awakened*!"

—ELOISA JAMES,
New York Times bestselling author

By Cecilia Grant

A Lady Awakened
A Gentleman Undone
A Woman Entangled

A Woman Entangled

CECILIA GRANT

BANTAM BOOKS
NEW YORK

A Woman Entangled is a work of fiction. Names, characters, places, and incidents are the products of the author's imagination or are used fictitiously. Any resemblance to actual events, locales, or persons, living or dead, is entirely coincidental.

A Bantam Books Mass Market Original

Published in the United States by Bantam Books, an imprint of The Random House Publishing Group, a division of Random House, Inc., New York.

BANTAM BOOKS and the rooster colophon are registered trademarks of Random House, Inc.

ISBN 978-0-345-53256-5
eISBN 978-0-345-53257-2

Cover design: Lynn Andreozzi
Cover photograph © George Kerrigan

Printed in the United States of America

www.bantamdell.com

9 8 7 6 5 4 3 2 1

Bantam Books mass market edition: June 2013

For my agent, Emmanuelle Morgen,
who knows the right thing to say
and the right time to say it

A Woman Entangled

Chapter One

London, February 1817

DISCOMFITURE, FOR all that it felt like a constant companion, never failed to find new and inventive guises in which to appear.

"I'd like to take out *A Vindication of the Rights of Woman*, the first volume." Her sister's voice soared into every corner of the lending library, all but rattling the bay window in whose alcove Kate had taken refuge. "I'm engaged at present in a work of my own that will build on Miss Wollstonecraft's foundation. Where she restricted herself to theory, however, and broad societal prescription, I address myself directly to the individual woman of today, arming her with practical methods by which she may begin even now to assert her rights."

She wouldn't speak of *bodily emancipation* in such a setting, would she? Kate held her breath. Surely even Viola had better sense than to—

"In particular I introduce the idea that women will never achieve true emancipation until we have absolute governance of our own persons, within marriage as well as without."

A stout young man, sitting at the long table nearest

Kate's alcove, looked up sharply from his book. An elderly woman seated on the opposite side of the room did the same. So, no doubt, did every peacefully reading patron in this establishment. Vi's was a voice that commanded attention, all crisp consonants and breath support, exactly the voice you'd expect from the granddaughter of an earl.

Or the daughter of an actress.

The young man's table was scattered with volumes, all perused and discarded by patrons who hadn't bothered to return them to the desk. Kate swiped one up and bent her head over a random page, to avoid meeting anyone's eyes. *To Elizabeth it appeared that had her family made an agreement to expose themselves as much as they could during the evening, it would have been impossible for them to play their parts with more spirit or finer success . . .*

Pride and Prejudice. That single line was enough to set Kate's bones vibrating like a struck tuning fork. Surely it had been written for her, this tale of a young woman struggling under the incessant mortifications thrust upon her by a family that did not know the meaning of discretion.

She turned a page. No more sound from the library's other end; the clerk must have gone to fetch the requested volume, and to escape any more discussion of practical methods for asserting a woman's rights. In the book, meanwhile, the party at Netherfield dragged dismally on, plaguing Elizabeth with the disagreeable attentions of Mr. Collins and the cold silence of the Bingley sisters and Mr. Darcy.

Of course Mr. Darcy had already begun to take note of Elizabeth's fine eyes by this point in the story, and Mr. Bingley was so smitten with Jane that he never noticed half the graceless things the Bennet family did. Could there really be such men in the world? And if so, where did they reside?

"There you are." Viola stood at the other side of the book-scattered table, *Vindication* volume in hand, peering at her through those plain glass spectacles she always insisted on wearing in public. "Are you ready to go?"

The stout man glanced up again, no doubt recognizing Vi's voice. He sent a quick look from one lady to the other, piecing together their relation.

And then he saw Kate, properly. Though he'd been sitting no great distance away, a mere half turn of his head necessary to bring her into view, his eyes apparently had not landed on her until now.

A dozen or more variations she'd seen of this response, on too many occasions to count. Some men managed it without looking witless. Most, unfortunately, did not.

The man's features stalled, then veered away from the jolly smirk they'd been forming in favor of a glazed-eyed reverence. He blushed, and bowed his head once more over his book.

Not terribly useful, the admiration of such a man. Still, it gave a girl hope. If she could one day drive a marquess, for example, into a like slack-jawed stupor—and why should she not? Title notwithstanding, a marquess was a man with the same susceptibilities as any other—then she might make something of the triumph.

"Novels and more novels." Her sister, indifferent to such small drama, had begun turning over the discarded volumes on the table. "I suppose nobody wants to read what might actually improve his mind." The man abruptly closed his book—doubtless a novel—and shoved it away as though he'd only just noticed its offending presence in his hands. His gaze averted, his cheeks pink as fresh-butchered pork, he pushed to his feet and fled to some other sector of the room.

"Yes, I'm ready." Kate's own voice had all the patrician clarity of Viola's, though she aimed it for shorter distances and always took care to stir in a bit of sugar. "Help me gather up these books. They oughtn't to be left lying about."

How long could a marquess, once stunned, be counted on to remain in that state? Could he procure a special license and marry her that same day, before his first rabid infatuation receded to the point where he might think of meeting her family? Or maybe she'd do better to get him out of London altogether, that he might not encounter any friends who would feel it their duty to knock him back to his senses. She'd have to count on sustaining his state of stupefaction, in that case, for the length of the journey from Mayfair to Gretna Green.

Difficult and unlikely. But not impossible, necessarily; at least not for her. Stupefaction was her stock-in-trade, and she would not stoop to the tedious false modesty of pretending not to know it.

The library clerk, when she stopped at his desk, accepted her armload of stray books with an effusion of gratitude such as no plain-faced lady would ever have received for the same task, and fetched her the other two volumes of *Pride and Prejudice.* She signed her name, paid her pennies, and emerged with her sister into the chill February afternoon.

"You've read that already" was Viola's pronouncement on ascertaining what books she held.

"Indeed I have. But you *own* that volume of the *Vindication of Women,* and every other volume, too. Surely you're the last person who ought to be questioning someone else's borrowing habits."

"*A Vindication of the Rights of Woman*, it's called. The meaning is entirely different. And my purpose wasn't to borrow a book, but to begin making myself known." She drummed her gloved fingers on the volume's binding, a rhythmic accompaniment to the ring of their heels on the pavement. "The more library clerks and booksellers I make aware of my project, the more likely it is that they'll mention me in discussions with one another—perhaps even in discussions with publishers. In fact, I think it very likely that publishers spend time in just such establishments. One day I may well be overheard, and approached by some enterprising man who sees that the time is ripe for a book like mine."

Oh, she'd be approached, certainly enough. Behind those false spectacles and taut-pinned hair and the sensible Quakerish garments she favored, Vi had her share of the Westbrook beauty. One day some man would see past her brusque manners to notice the fact, and if he was enterprising, it would surely occur to him to feign an interest in her book, perhaps even to present himself in the guise of a publisher.

That was why Kate could not allow her to undertake these errands alone. For a young lady of intellect, Viola was shockingly ignorant in some matters.

"I wonder, though, if a more gradual kind of persuasion might be to your benefit." At the corner she turned east, steering her sister along. "If perhaps you concentrated your efforts at first on pleasantries—on asking the clerk to recommend an interesting book, for example, or even speaking on commonplace topics such as the weather or an amusing print you recently saw—then by the time you introduced the subject of your own book, you might have a reservoir of goodwill already in place. Even a clerk who doesn't necessarily subscribe to your book's ideas might be disposed to advance your cause with his publisher friends, simply as a favor to a charming customer."

"But I don't want to be a charming customer." Viola's voice sank into the low passionate chords of the instrument with which she shared a name. "I want to be taken seriously. I want to know my book is appreciated on its own merits—not because the reader finds me sufficiently *charming*. I'm sure Thomas Paine never concerned himself with whether or not he was *charming*." The word apparently furnished endless fuel for disgust. She jabbed at *Pride and Prejudice*. "Your Mr. Darcy isn't the least bit charming, and yet everyone tiptoes about him in awe."

It's different for women. She needn't say it aloud. Vi knew well enough.

Kate shifted the volumes to the crook of her other arm, and fished in her reticule for a penny as they approached the street crossing. She wasn't without sympathy for her sister. The constraints of a lady's life could be exceedingly trying. Demoralizing, if one allowed them to be.

The trick was not to allow them to be.

"Lord help us all if you mean to pattern yourself after Thomas Paine. Perhaps he wouldn't have got into such trouble if he'd spent a little effort on charm." She paid the crossing sweep, a ragged dark boy, with the penny and her sweetest smile. "And Mr. Darcy had ten thousand a year and a grand house to his name. Much will be forgiven in the manners of such a man." She caught up her skirts and stepped into the street, sister alongside.

"What of his Elizabeth, then?" The unavoidable legacy of a barrister father: progeny always on the lookout for an argument. "*She* never takes pains to charm anyone, least of all Mr. Darcy, and yet— Where are we going?" She halted, abrupt as a fickle cart horse. "We ought to have turned north by now."

"The girls won't be through with lessons for nearly an hour." Kate took her sister's elbow to usher her the rest of the way across. "That gives us time to go by way of Berkeley Square."

"Berkeley Square?" The way Vi pronounced it, you'd

think she was naming the alley where the meanest residents of St. Giles went to empty their chamber pots.

"Berkeley Square, indeed. I have a letter for Lady Harringdon." Might as well serve up the objectionable news all at once, rather than by spoonfuls.

"On what possible subject can you be writing to that . . . woman?" She knew how to pack inordinate amounts of meaning into a pause, Viola did, this time suggesting she'd groped for a word suited to Lady Harringdon's perfidy and found none strong enough.

"She's just married off the last of her daughters this week. I'm offering my congratulations, as civil people do on such occasions to their kin."

"*Kin,* do you call her?"

Yes, she'd known that word wouldn't pass without remark. "She's married to our father's elder brother. That makes her our aunt."

"Well, somebody ought to tell that to her. Her and Lord Harringdon and whatever mean-spirited offspring they spawned." Viola walked faster, swinging *Vindication,* volume one, in a pendulum motion as though she were winding up to brain one of that family with it. "Good lord, Kate, do you secretly correspond with the dowager Lady Harringdon as well? With all the aunts and uncles who refuse to know us? I would have thought you had more pride than to truckle to such people."

"I don't secretly correspond with anyone. I've already told you the occasion for this note, and I hardly think a word of congratulations can be construed as truckling." To keep her voice light and unruffled required a conscious effort, but she had plenty of practice in the art. "Indeed I should think it will provide an instructive example of proper manners to Lady Harringdon, while proving that her own lapses in civility do not guide the behavior of Charles Westbrook's children. You see, I'm partly motivated by pride after all."

Partly. But in truth she had grander ambitions than to simply make a show of unbowed civility to her aunt.

They weren't really so unlike, she and her sister. She, too, intended to be known. One day the door to that glittering world of champagne and consequence—the world that ought to have been her birthright—would crack open just long enough to admit a girl who'd spent every day since the age of thirteen watching for that chance, readying herself to slip through. Even at two and twenty, she hadn't given up hope. Enough attentions to people like Lady Harringdon, and *something* must finally happen. *Someone* must recognize the aristocratic blood that ran through her veins, and the manners and accomplishments worthy of a nobleman's bride. Then she'd dart through that open door, take her place among her own kind, and single-handedly haul her family back into respectability.

"Do what you must." Viola's shoulders flexed, as though the insult of a trip to Berkeley Square had an actual physical weight that wanted preparation to bear. "*My* pride shall take the form of waiting across the street while you go about your errand. Anyone looking out the window may see that *I* am not ashamed of our mother."

That was petty; the argumental equivalent of jabbing her with a sewing pin. And it smarted every bit as much. "Neither am I ashamed of her. Only I'm not willing to dismiss Papa's family as a lot of villains because they objected to his marrying an actress. No family of good name would desire such a union for one of their sons."

"'Such a union?' To a woman of character and intelligence, you mean, daughter of a proud theatrical family, who studied Sophocles and spat on indecent offers from gentleman admirers? Yes, doubtless any reasonable family must abhor that match, and strive instead to get their son shackled to some insipid chit who hasn't any interests or passions of her own and whose talents extend only to a few polite pluckings on the harp. *There* is a recipe for conjugal felicity, to be sure."

Kate made no answer, beyond a small inward sigh. Really, it must be very pleasant to live in Viola's world, with everything drawn in such broad strokes. People and actions easily classified as righteous or knavish; no margin granted for human fallibility or the claims of society. No energies squandered in pondering extenuating circumstances. No time wasted on doubt.

One of the *Pride and Prejudice* volumes was pressing a sharp edge into her forearm, so she switched to a one-handed grip, like Viola with her *Vindication*. Conjugal felicity, indeed. That came in several guises, surely, or at least you might get there by more than one path. If Mr. Darcy, for example, had come to *her* with that first grudging proposal, openly acknowledging his abhorrence at so lowering himself, she would have swallowed her pride long enough to choke out a *yes*. Affection and understanding could come afterward—or if they never came at all, she would have a good name and the grounds at Pemberley on which to build all the felicity she required.

As they made their way into the residential streets of Mayfair, she tipped back her head for a view of remote upper windows. Surely somewhere in London was a gentleman who would suit her needs. Surely some aristocrat—some marquess ripe for stupefaction—must appreciate a beautiful bride with such pragmatic expectations of the wedded state. Surely someone, someday, could be brought to lower himself as Mr. Darcy had, and spirit her out of that middling class in which she had never truly belonged.

Surely that man did walk and breathe. The trick was only to find him.

* * *

ROUND THE landing, down the stairs, and through the heavy oak front door, Nicholas Blackshear spilled out into the cold sunlight of Brick Court, black robes billowing in his wake. TIME AND TIDE TARRY FOR NO MAN, warned the inscription on the sundial where he paused to confirm the hour. It told the truth, that inscription, but far from heeding its exhortation to haste, he always seemed to stop here an extra moment, reflecting on the hallowed figures who must have consulted this same timepiece as they'd gone about their business in the Middle Temple.

William Blackstone and Oliver Goldsmith had each surely stood here—he had only to glance up at Number Two Brick Court to see where the jurist and the writer had slept and studied a few generations ago.

But so it was throughout the Inns of Court. Just as he always had to stop at the sundial, so must he quietly marvel, every time he took a meal in the Middle Temple Hall, at the serving table whose wood came from the hull of Sir Francis Drake's *Golden Hind*. So must he always attempt, mid-meal, to picture all the details of the evening, some two hundred years ago, when the benchers and students had been privileged to witness the very first performance of *Twelfth Night* in that same room.

To be a London barrister was to live surrounded by the best of everything England had to offer, all from men who'd charted their own courses to greatness. A fellow might end up anywhere, who began here. If he was literarily inclined, he could look not only to the example of Goldsmith but also to the poet Donne, the satirist Fielding, the playwrights Webster and Congreve—onetime barristers all. If he aspired to etch his name in big bold letters upon the pages of English history, there were Francis Bacon's footsteps to follow in, or, more recently, William Pitt's.

And if his ambitions ran to the idealistic, he might

pattern himself after William Garrow, reforming the practice of courtroom law before gaining a seat in Parliament, and a role in all the glorious wrangling through which the nation's daily business was managed. One day, if he, Nick Blackshear, was scrupulous in both personal and professional conduct, he might restore the family name to such respectability as would make any ambition possible. In the meantime, the law itself must be his purpose, a fit exercise for his faculties, a consolation for disappointments old and new.

Nick swung out from Brick Court into Middle Temple Lane and headed north. Bewigged, black-robed gentlemen made a steady traffic both ways in the lane. His tribe. His species, with all their quirks and crotchets. Some argued as they went along in twos and threes, sawing at the air or jabbing with peremptory fingers. Some presented a hazard to their fellows as they barreled blindly ahead, never looking up from the pages of a brief. He wove through their ranks, long legs and five years of practice steering him clear of collisions while his robes whipped with each sharp turn. At the end of the lane stood the gatehouse, with the Old Bailey looming on the far side of Fleet Street, and—

"Blackshear!"

He'd know that voice in his sleep. Partly because he'd spent a good year studying with the man; partly on the merits of the voice itself. Most barristers made an effort to speak well, and almost all had the genteel accents of the well-born, but few could spit a word like Westbrook. His consonants snapped like a flag in high winds; his vowels poured out in measures as precise as medicine into a spoon.

Nick pivoted, finding the man and stepping clear of traffic in one economical move. He liked to be early to court, and he'd tarried a bit too long already at the sundial. Never mind. Westbrook had hailed him, and there was not much he wouldn't do for Westbrook.

"Walk on, walk on, I wouldn't dream of making you late." The man was grinning as he pulled even with him, wheeling one hand in a move-along motion, because in the course of that year he'd so graciously taken him on, he'd learned Nick's habits well enough to understand the importance of punctuality. "In the criminal courts today, are you?"

"Stubbs means to keep me busy with desperate cases all this session. Beginning today with an incident of pickpocketry in Whitechapel." He gave one smart rap to the bag in which he carried his brief. "I'm to spare a wretched young man from transportation, if all goes well."

"Stubbs, to be sure. A well-meaning man, but his head's nearly as soft as his heart. See that he's prompt with your gratuity this time." Westbrook gave a nod and half-salute to a passing gentleman in the silk robes of King's Counsel. Burnham. Nick knew the name of every KC.

"Indeed I took a lesson from the last time, and collected in advance. Mind you, I suspect it's out of his own pocket. From what I've read of the boy I doubt he has either means or connections sufficient to engage a barrister. But you know how Stubbs is."

They both did. To rail at the eccentricities of this or that solicitor was a barrister's pleasure and privilege, though he would never go too far in mocking Stubbs. Other solicitors, after all, had ceased to bring him clients since the events that had blemished his family name. Stubbs continued undeterred.

"Well, I know you'll give the client a fine, spirited defense." The older man clapped him on the shoulder. Father had done that a very few times—he'd been a cerebral man, not much given to such displays—and to this day the action loosed a melancholy that went trickling through his veins. "Indeed that brings me to my purpose in seeking you. An opportunity has arisen that I think may suit your talents and inclinations. I won't delay your arrival in court by telling you all about it now, but I wonder if you might come to the house for dinner. Mrs. Westbrook and the family would be glad to see you, and we could speak on my subject over a glass of port."

"I'd like that very much. It's been too long since I've seen them. Let me bring the port. I just bought a new bottle of something fine." He got the words out rapidly as they approached the gatehouse into Fleet Street. Westbrook, like any barrister, knew the value of efficient speech and wouldn't think it brusque.

They parted at the street and Nick made a mental note to buy port. And to ask one of his neighbors which sort was fine. He had better uses for his money than to be frittering it away on transitory luxuries, but hanged if he'd turn up empty-handed to dinner. Not when his host had four daughters to dower, and a son still living with him as well.

Ah, the daughters. His pulse swung into a foolish little jig at the prospect of seeing Miss Westbrook. His pulse would never learn.

The rest of him had learned all too well. It hadn't wanted any scandal on his side to put Kate Westbrook beyond his reach—she'd put herself there from the beginning, and kindly left him in no doubt of the fact. His pride still smarted sometimes at the memory, when he allowed himself to dwell.

So he would not dwell. Certainly not when there was an opportunity to be thought of. He'd turn his pondering there instead.

What sort of opportunity? He wound through the usual crowd loitering outside the bail dock's brick wall, curiosity kindling steadily as he went. Westbrook knew every detail of his circumstances; knew how heavily his practice depended, these days, on the sorts of clients who couldn't afford to be fastidious in choosing their representation; knew how the work dwindled during those periods when the criminal court was not in session. Maybe the opportunity had to do with a good long case in Chancery, or the Court of Common Pleas?

The gate, the bail dock, the great courthouse door, and the corridors all went by in a pleasant blur, mere background to the question of what news he'd learn tonight over a glass of fine port. When he crossed the threshold into the courtroom, though, he put that question away. A client and his soft-hearted solicitor were depending on him, and until he left this room again he was entirely at their service.

TRUE TO her word, Viola stationed herself under one of the great maples in Berkeley Square's center, the very picture of righteous disapproval with her back turned to Harringdon House and her arms folded tight about all the borrowed books.

Not that she had much to disapprove. Kate stood ready with her letter, and when the butler answered her knock she bid him carry the note, with Miss Westbrook's regards, to the countess. That was that.

"Shall I announce you to her ladyship?" The butler opened the door three or four inches wider.

Something swift and predatory uncoiled in her middle, awakened by that motion of the door easing open; by the glimpse of patterned carpet and gleaming oiled woodwork within. Eleven such notes she'd delivered here, one for each marriage or birth or younger son turned ashore triumphant, and she'd never in five years met with the opportunity to be announced.

But a girl of grand ambition prepared herself for every

possible windfall, and she had in fact rehearsed this moment before her mirror once or twice.

She took a half-step back, clutching her cloak together and lowering her lashes in a pretty show of confusion. "Oh, no. I have no thought of troubling her ladyship. She can read the note at her leisure."

In her private rehearsals she'd always imagined a look of august yet deferential approval on the butler's face; an unspoken assurance that he would tell Lady Harringdon of her caller's impeccable manners and modesty, with perhaps a mention of the beauty that rendered such diffidence all the more becoming.

But he wasn't even looking at her. His gaze had gone beyond her to the street, and he was once again pulling the door open, all the way this time.

She turned. At the end of the walk, clearly waiting for her to pass, stood a tall gentleman of late-middle years, ebony walking stick in one hand, the other hand reaching for his hat. And all of a sudden she felt every ounce of the confusion she'd been feigning but an instant before.

He looked so much like Papa. Not about the face, entirely—or rather, the chin and cheeks and jawline might all be the same, but a thick brush of blond whiskers prevented her discerning this—rather it was his stature, and a certain quality in his posture, and other things beyond her ability to name. Without intervention from her brain, her blood knew him. Or knew his blood, to be more exact, as like must recognize like.

He doffed his hat and nodded, his smile showing the same impersonal politeness with which he would doubtless greet any woman, young or old, high or low, fair or plain, who stood impeding his way on his own doorstep.

Kate curtsied as she passed him, and came up in time

to see a quizzical look in his eyes; then a startled awareness.

Her heart thudded and her face flushed warm. He knew her. Without, to her knowledge, his ever having seen her before, he must have detected the traces of Papa in her person, just as she'd done with him.

Neither she nor the gentleman spoke. Just as well, because she could think only of the most injudicious things to say. *Good afternoon, my lord. I'm a daughter of the man you ceased to call* brother *three and twenty years ago.*

Yes, Mother used to be an actress. But if you'd met her even once, you'd see that she's a woman of the highest moral character.

He kept your letters. He has a stack of them, years and years old, that he never threw away. She'd found them once, by accident. In Father's study, in the older writing desk he never used. She'd meant to take it for her own use, but she'd opened the lid to find letter upon letter, most of them from when he'd been at Rugby. Affectionate notes from his mother. Carefully lettered missives from younger sisters who were still mastering the proper use of a pen. And from this brother—Viscount Melford at the time—dense, cross-written pages recounting his adventures at university and encouraging young Charles in his studies. She oughtn't to have read them but she had.

I know what he meant to you once, and you to him. Do you never think of him? She couldn't say that. She couldn't say any of these things. And she'd been standing too long staring in silence at this man to whom she was both a blood relation, and nothing at all.

She scuttled away—in her rehearsals she'd always glided, swanlike, employing every air she'd acquired from the dancing master at Miss Lowell's—and across the street to where Viola waited. A glance, when she dared risk it, confirmed that the man had gone inside. Whatever disturbance he'd felt at the sight of her, it had apparently been but a hiccup in his lordly routine.

"Well, that was quick, at least." Vi greeted her with a grudging approval, and with the *Pride and Prejudice* volumes held out at arm's length for her to reclaim. "I feared you might persuade the butler to admit you to her ladyship's presence."

"No, I merely left my note, as I told you I would do." She took back her books. She had news to confide, and no one to confide it in. Viola would care nothing for the opportunity to be announced to their aunt, and to the report of encountering their uncle she would probably respond with withering contempt.

"You might have posted the letter, then, and saved us this march across town. Lord knows anyone living in Berkeley Square can afford the two pennies."

Kate made no reply. She loved her sister. Indeed she loved her whole family. But was it so unreasonable of her to crave a life in which people valued courtesy, consideration, and etiquette, and recognized that there was more to be thought of, when delivering a letter, than whether the person on the other end could afford to pay the postage? Was it so wrong for her to want to not be *nothing* to people who shared her name and her blood?

The mile and a half from Berkeley Square to their Bloomsbury destination provided ample time for reliving that brief drama on the doorstep—it could scarcely have been a minute, altogether, from her lifting of the knocker to her flush-faced retreat—and wondering at the import of each twist and turn. The butler would not have decided on his own to announce her. Lady Harringdon must have instructed him to do so the next time Miss Westbrook called, but why?

She's bored, came the suggestion from the most audacious corner of her brain. *Her daughters are all gone and she doesn't know what to do beyond making matches for young ladies. She'd like someone new to bring out.*

Even if that were true—and Kate would not let herself presume that it was—Lord Harringdon, from his obvious surprise at encountering her, would appear to have not been in on the plan. He'd probably marched straight upstairs to find his wife and demanded to know why one of the Misses Westbrook had been on his doorstep, and then dissuaded the countess from any charitable impulses she might have entertained.

Or, no, he wouldn't have had to. Because when he'd asked his wife to account for the presence of Miss Westbrook, Lady Harringdon would have said, *Oh, that poor girl. She insists on coming by with her little notes on every occasion, and I meant to finally bring her in and tell her plainly that she must give up hoping for our notice.*

Kate squirmed, deep under her skin where neither her sister nor any passerby would see. Usually that audacious corner of her brain would put up a fight against the part that wanted to deal in measly expectations and self-doubt. Today it slunk back into silence, content to leave her with the construction of events most unflattering to her hopes.

And matters only got grimmer when she and Viola reached Queen Square, and Miss Lowell's Seminary for Young Ladies. In the parlor where the day pupils waited to be fetched home, a clutch of girls gathered at the fireplace, chatting like convivial magpies. Bea and Rose stood by the window at the opposite end of the room.

Kate's fists clenched; she had to will the fingers loose again. With every bit of her body she remembered that feeling of standing apart, shut out from the jokes and the gossip and the giggling over this or that girl's handsome elder brother.

"It's not right that they should be so excluded." The words forced themselves out in an urgent undertone, even as she felt all the futility of this conversation. "On balance they're of better birth than any girls here."

"Of better brains, more to the point, and better character." Viola didn't trouble to keep her voice low. "So why on earth would they desire the approval of this lot? I had much rather be excluded."

Yes, that had been perfectly plain during their own years at Miss Lowell's. While Kate had waged a meticulous and dogged campaign to work her way into, and eventually to the head of, the ruling group of girls, her sister had gone her own way, clad as always in the convenient armor of indifference to the judgment of others.

"They're not like you. Well, Rose isn't." Bea had her own kind of protection, a single-minded devotion to music that left her little spare attention for taking note of how she was snubbed. She might well come through unscathed. But Rose was different. "A fifteen-year-old girl ought to have friends. She oughtn't to have to try to convince herself she's better off without them. It taxes her spirit, I'm sure." Indeed their youngest sister looked a bit smaller every day when they came to collect her from Miss Lowell's, and every day her smile seemed more a product of effort.

She smiled now, catching sight of them, and the falseness of it, the strain in her undissembling blue eyes, made Kate's heart sink like a stone.

She returned the smile nevertheless. All the harder, in fact; all the brighter she beamed at both approaching sisters, that they might look only at her, and not turn to notice how several of the girls by the fireplace were watching their exit with a smirking exchange of whispers.

"How were your lessons today?" Kate ventured once the girls had their wraps and the footman had seen them all out the front door. "Did you make anything pretty to show us? Shall you be demonstrating the steps of the quadrille?" Even to her own ear, her good cheer rang hollow and inane, but what else could she do?

"Not today." Bea was the one to answer, while fastening up her cloak. "We didn't study the quadrille, and at all events, Rose missed the entire dancing lesson. I wish I'd been so lucky."

Rose's smile collapsed. She threw a single wounded look at her sister, then spun and started down the walk to the gate.

"What is it?" Bea followed, the two older girls falling in behind. "I didn't say anything about *why* you missed the lesson."

"Yes, but now they'll ask, won't they, and they're liable to make a to-do of everything, when it was nothing at all and I wish it could just have been forgotten." At the gate she fumbled with the latch for a second. "Someone tied knots in my embroidery silk," she said without looking up. "A knot every inch. Miss Riggle wouldn't let me go until I'd undone them all, and so I missed the dancing lesson." She pulled the gate open and walked through without waiting for a response. Her cheeks had gone red.

"What a lot of stupid cows." Viola was not taken aback for even a second. "Whatever satisfaction they got from the prank could hardly have been worth the time and effort on their part."

Vi didn't understand. The time and effort were precisely what made the prank so breathtakingly cruel. Whoever had done it must have told herself—probably more than once—*Yes, this drudgery is worthwhile. I will persist in this tedious task because that is just how much I'm willing to do, how far I will go, to hurt Miss Rosalind Westbrook.* And depend upon it, that detail wasn't lost on Rose.

Kate slipped through the gate and caught up to her

sister's vehemently striding form. "I'll say something to Miss Lowell if you like. About Miss Riggle, at least. It was wrong of her to—"

But Rose was shaking her head, hard. "I beg you won't. It was of no consequence. And please not to mention it to our mother and father." Beneath her brusque dismissal was such desperation, such raw, heart-piercing humiliation, as made Kate want to seize something and tear it to pieces.

All she had for that was *Pride and Prejudice*, still clutched in one hand. The volumes felt awkward now, unwieldy. Heavy and sharp cornered and crammed full of wishful fancy.

She would not tear them. A lady didn't destroy library property. But if *she* were ever to write a novel, it would be the opposite of a love story. Her hero and heroine would choose duty over their hearts' desire, that their children need never be taxed for a romantic indulgence that was none of their own.

A cold wind rushed down from the late-afternoon sky, and Kate caught her cloak edges together with her free hand. Yes, the very opposite of a romance would be the story to warm her heart. Something full of prudent choices and practical considerations. Something where people consulted their heads and kept a tight rein on their sentiments.

She huddled deeper into her cloak. Men thought her unfeeling, she knew. *Heartless*, Mr. Blackshear had pronounced her, the last time he'd come to call. Of course he'd laughed as he'd said it, good-natured and brotherly, though they both knew he had reason to mean it.

Well, be that as it would. She carried enough already, what with worrying for her younger sisters' welfare, scheming to make connections that could better all their prospects, and striving to somehow mend the great rift in Papa's family. She had neither time nor energy enough to feel guilty for every young man she'd disappointed. They'd surely all go on to find girls who could afford the luxury of marrying for love, and they'd be happier than they ever could have been with her.

Beauty faded, after all, and with it, the love it had inspired. A beautiful woman did well to be heartless. And if she hadn't quite attained the state herself, at least she could make such a show as would convince all the rest of the world.

Chapter Two

THE NEWS of opportunity did not wait for port. That was the way at the Westbrook table. As in the dining halls at the Inns of Court, spirited conversation must accompany the meal, and business, not the mundane niceties of a dinner party, must be the consuming topic.

"Barclay is the fellow's name, and his title now as well." Mr. Westbrook went right on carving up his cutlet while delivering this, the intelligence that had warranted Nick's invitation. "He means to turn his seat in the House to some purpose, one can see. No gradually learning the lay of the land, and certainly no giving his votes to a proxy. He's resolved to attend regularly, and to argue bills and even introduce them, just as soon as he's acquired a tolerable proficiency in the requisite skills."

Here was everything to awaken his approval. There *were* skills pertinent to the responsibilities of a parliamentary seat, and precious few men, from what he'd heard and occasionally observed, ever troubled to improve their mastery of those skills. Lord Barclay showed promise already.

"Is he Tory or Whig, this baron?" Across the table,

Miss Viola inclined slightly forward in her chair, the merest accent of distaste on the word *baron*. Miss Viola had opinions about rank and privilege, and no hesitation in making those opinions known. "What sorts of bills does he mean to introduce?"

"His letter did not disclose a party affiliation, but he seems to take a particular interest in matters of public welfare. Especially—as might be expected from a former military man—the welfare of returned soldiers." Westbrook nodded down the table at Nick. "You shall see the letter for yourself, over our port, and glean what you can of his political leanings."

"I would think his affiliation might be the same as his brother's." The eldest Miss Westbrook usually kept silent, with a look of graceful forbearance, when the conversation turned to politics. She sat at his right hand tonight and he could feel her delicate air of triumph at having this knowledge to contribute. "Unless there's more than one Major Barclay, recently created baron, he's the younger brother of the Marquess of Astley."

Perhaps he took a small fortifying breath before turning to face her directly. Even after three years of acquaintance, with all the accompanying disillusion, with witnessing the mundane flaws and pettiness to which any mortal must be prone, the sight of her could still hit him like strong sunlight after a day spent in windowless rooms.

Of course they were a handsome family altogether, the Westbrooks. Handsome parents did generally tend to produce handsome children. The middle three—Viola, Sebastian, Beatrice; such was the consequence of marriage to an actress—took after their mother, fair-skinned and auburn-haired with heart-shaped, piquant faces. The youngest, Miss Rosalind, had her father's pale hair and expressive blue eyes. But in the eldest, Katherina, mother's and father's looks had mingled to downright alchemical effect: her beauty somehow exceeded what she'd gotten from both parents combined.

He couldn't much blame himself for the folly of three years since. Probably every man who met her fell a little in love, at least in the beginning.

"What have you done, committed all of *Debrett's* to memory?" He teased her because everyone in the family teased her. And because teasing required a certain nimbleness of his brain, and prevented him from sinking into a languid contemplation of her eyes, or her hair, or the precise curve and color of her lips.

"Not all of it, I'll wager." Her brother, seated on her other side, leaned forward to speak past her. "Our Kate is particular. She confines her notice to earls and above."

"My interests are not so narrow as that." She spoke with a playful, arch quality, presenting Nick with her profile as she went back to carving tiny bites of her own meal. "I also take note of new creations, and of second sons in the case where the first has produced no heirs. Your Lord Barclay happens to be both of those. His brother the marquess has been married over a dozen years and hasn't any children at all."

Mrs. Westbrook frowned across the table at her daughter. "I know you speak flippantly, dear, and mostly in jest." For all the scandal of her former profession, she had an air of moral authority that would do any jurist proud. "But we oughtn't to take pleasure in a childless marriage. I'm sure there's a deal of sorrow behind what you see on that page of *Debrett's*."

"Must there be sorrow?" Miss Viola seized at this point like a terrier snatching a veal chop from an unattended plate. "Is it not possible that Lord and Lady Astley themselves take pleasure in their childless marriage? I can well imagine that the lady, at least, might welcome the freedom to pursue other interests and occupations."

The first time he'd dined at this house, and witnessed

this style of conversation, his jaw had nearly hit the tabletop. If either of his sisters had ever dared to address their mother the way Miss Viola spoke to hers . . . well, there'd really been scant opportunity for that. Mother had so seldom felt well enough to appear at the dinner table, and was gone altogether by the time Kitty reached the age of sixteen, and Martha eight.

Score a point for Miss Viola, by the way. Mother might have been better off, and might even be alive today, without the dubious blessing of fecundity.

"It's possible." Mrs. Westbrook answered her daughter with the graciousness of a barrister who held better arguments up her sleeve. "However, I think it unlikely that a husband and wife would both have wished for childlessness, particularly in the case where there's a title and estate and the consequent need for an heir."

"I hope my husband would wish for childlessness, for my sake." Miss Beatrice was one of several artistically inclined Westbrooks, not so forward with her opinions as Miss Viola, though she might well get there given time. "I hope he would value my dedication to the study of music, and not wish to see me give it up."

"I might have expressed that same sentiment when I was seventeen." The Westbrook matriarch directed a nod at her second-youngest daughter. "But feelings can change, sometimes in ways you would never expect. I passionately loved the theater, and I have not the smallest regret over leaving it to marry your father and bring you all into the world."

"Well said." Mr. Westbrook raised his wineglass to his wife, and grinned a challenge at Miss Viola. "Does the counsel for the prosecution care to make a response?"

The truth was, the Blackshear dinner table had been a sad, staid, lifeless affair in comparison to the Westbrooks' argumentative warmth. Father, on those occasions when he'd emerged from his study like an owl venturing out from its hollow tree, had never goaded them in any way; never demanded to know the boys' opinions on any matter, let alone the girls'. Not that he'd meant to discount or discourage their thoughts. To be sure, it was more a matter of—

"Mr. Blackshear." The voice came from his right, soft enough to be confidential, and his thoughts pulled up hard, like a horse refusing a jump. Much as he might have believed himself absorbed in the conversation, or in his reflections on dinner tables gone by, some delicate spider-silk strands of awareness had run all the while to Miss Westbrook, and she need only make the slightest tug to have his full attention.

He turned. She was looking up at him, grave eyed, no trace visible of the flippant manner she'd worn a minute before. A single line of unease creased her brow. His thumb twitched, restless to reach out and smooth the worry away.

Hang his idiot body. His brain knew he'd never be anything to her; knew, moreover, that outward beauty was the shallowest of reasons for admiring a woman; the poorest signifier of her merit. And still his pulse *would* stutter when she spoke to him, and his thumb and every other fool part of him would poise themselves, puppet-like, to do her slightest bidding.

"I have a favor to ask of you." To her credit, she didn't look as though she expected him to dance on her string. She kept her voice low, and it occurred to him she'd been waiting to address him under cover of such energetic conversation as now occupied the others—Miss Viola having launched into an impassioned denunciation of all debaters who would employ "You'll understand when you're older" as a trump-card argument.

"I'd be glad to grant it, I'm sure." His words came out cordial but distant. The response of a man who didn't dance on strings, never mind the runaway thumping of his heart.

"When we're in the parlor after dinner, will you speak to Rose?" She sank her voice even lower. He had to lean in a bit to hear. She smelled faintly of some flower.

"To Rose? On some particular topic?"

She shook her head, flicking a glance to the end of the table where her youngest sister sat. "Any topic, excepting school if you please. Perhaps you might ask her to sing as well. She's had a difficult day, and I think the attention might be a comfort."

She *had* been very quiet through dinner, Miss Rosalind had. He inclined his head, suffused already with the warmth of a shared good deed. "You may rely on me. I shall make it my mission to cheer her, beginning by asking her to sing."

"Thank you." Her lashes swept down. "You're a good friend to this family."

To that he made no reply. This was their odd little charade, his and Miss Westbrook's; the pretense that there'd never been a time when he'd hoped to be more than a family friend.

But everything on that head had worked out for the best, really. Now that she'd turned back to her plate—and he wasn't confronted with the distraction of her looks—it was easier to recall that. If he'd succeeded in attaching her affections, then she, too, would now bear the stigma of a connection that made her own parentage look like the very pattern of propriety.

Or perhaps she wouldn't have borne it. A lady so concerned with social status might very well leave her husband's house, in such circumstances, and go back to the lesser evil of residing with her mother and father.

Nothing to the purpose, all this speculation. He hadn't won her affection, and he wouldn't repine. All scandal and stigma aside, a woman who thought herself too good to be a barrister's wife was a woman he could never make happy, nor ever quite fully respect.

Besides, he'd come here to learn about Lord Barclay and the opportunity. Not to covertly admire Miss Westbrook, not to fall into a melancholy reverie over respective family dinner tables, not to get caught up in a debate over other people's marriages and whether youthful feelings might change.

He bent his attention to his plate, and silently reckoned how many courses remained before he was left alone with Mr. Westbrook, a bottle of port, and the letter of opportunity.

THANK GOODNESS for steady, resilient Mr. Blackshear. If she'd disappointed his hopes three years ago—

No, that was disingenuous. She had disappointed his hopes. There was no *if* in the matter. She might not shuffle about feeling guilty for the fact, but she would at least face it honestly.

At all events, the important part was that he'd absorbed the disappointment quietly and then recognized his sentiment for the superficial infatuation it had been. No nursing his wounded pride, as so many men liked to do. No turning up his nose at the friendship that was all she could offer. He'd kept his connection to the family and now here he was, ready to show kindness to Rose for Rose's sake, not because he hoped to rise in her own estimation.

Kate climbed the stairs to the room she shared with Viola, skirts caught up in one hand, candle held steady in the other. Likely the gentlemen wouldn't appear in the parlor for some time, with Lord Barclay's letter to dissect and interpret like some exhibit admitted into evidence. She'd have a few minutes' respite from the chore of acting lighthearted. A few minutes to indulge her still-sagging spirits, and then she'd be fit for company once again.

The bedroom sat all in darkness, naturally. A barrister's income didn't provide for constant lamplight when the entire family was downstairs. A marquess's income, now . . .

She crossed to the dressing table and sat, setting the candle directly between herself and the mirror to cast the most merciless light on her reflection. A lady needed to be rigorous in her self-appraisal, when beauty was all the dowry she had.

One small section of her hair was not perfectly smooth; she adjusted the pin. If Mr. Blackshear entered into a professional association with this Lord Barclay, she would be but one friendly remove from the connection. If she could only prevail upon Mr. Blackshear to somehow bring her to the baron's notice, she would at least make the excellent first impression she always did with men.

And a marquess-to-be—was she tempting disappointment by daring to think of this?—might suit her purpose even better than a marquess. He would have grown up without expectations of inheriting, and thus he might have a broader conception of what kind of woman would make him a suitable wife. Too, if he interested himself, as Papa had said, in matters of public welfare, perhaps he was one of those modern sorts who argued for the dignity of all people and could easily be brought to see that the daughter of an actress might have every virtue that really mattered.

Altogether too many *mights* in that vision of events. In the mirror her mouth twisted with dissatisfaction; she huffed out a small breath that made the candle flame jump. Light skittered out to the edge of the dressing table's top, momentarily illuminating the tray where the maid always left her mail.

A letter sat there. The tray had been empty when she'd dressed for dinner; the letter must have come in the late post. It was, if she did not mistake—light had fallen on it so briefly and her heart was suddenly beating so hard she couldn't be sure of much—franked.

Franking privileges belonged to members of Parliament. An earl might frank a letter for his wife. Her hand reached carefully out, took up the letter by its corner, and brought it into the halo of candlelight.

For a moment she could do no more than look. And touch. The paper, a pristine ivory stock heavier than anything she'd ever been privileged to write upon, pleased her fingertips the same way starched linen did. The sealing wax gleamed a painfully elegant shade of gold. Her name, in an unfamiliar hand, had never looked so illustrious. And indeed the letter was franked, the date and signature scrawled with lordly disregard for legibility.

Her heart climbed up and up her throat as she slid her letter opener under the seal. The contents might poison all the pleasure she took in the letter's outside—this might be the rebuff she'd cheated Lady Harringdon of delivering in person—but better she should find out at once than delay and wonder.

The paper unfolded along its neat creases to reveal a very few lines of largely unremarkable text. *Thank you for your good wishes, &c, &c,* but the signature was all looping distinction and the postscript might as well have been written in letters of fire: *I am at home on Tuesdays and Fridays*.

Kate set the paper down, slowly raising her eyes to her reflection. She'd done it. She'd been wrong to doubt herself. Five years of patience and determination had finally, somehow, reaped their reward.

It's because she wants to bring you out. The audacious corner of her brain, silent since the trip to Miss Lowell's, lost no time in speaking up. Well, let it say its piece. Why *shouldn't* the countess wish to sponsor a girl whose beauty could take any ballroom by storm? The obstacle of her birth might even make the prospect more attractive to a lady who'd successfully married off half a dozen daughters and probably longed for a challenge of some sort.

She folded up the letter and put it away in the same drawer where she'd stowed the *Pride and Prejudice* volumes. The book recovered a bit of its luster, in such grand company. Behind the fanciful love story, after all, lurked an account of how a woman's prudent marriage might overcome all the mischief of her parents' incautious union.

The day after tomorrow was a Friday. Would so soon a call demonstrate an unbecoming eagerness, or fitting respect? Well, she had tonight and tomorrow to deliberate. She closed the drawer, gave one last appraising glance to the mirror, and rose from her chair to go down to the parlor.

LORD BARCLAY'S letter didn't tell a great deal more than what Westbrook had already related, but one thing it did tell—from the substandard hand and irregular spelling—was that he'd penned it himself. He didn't, then, have someone to manage that task for him.

Nick felt for his glass of port, still studying the letter. "He doesn't say he's in need of a secretary, I note. Just someone to train him in speech and argument."

"Indeed there's no explicit mention." They'd moved to one end of the table when the rest of the family had gone, and Westbrook now sat directly across from him. "I think we may assume, though, that if he did have a secretary, that man would be undertaking the speech training."

"Probably." He mustn't let his hopes run away with him. "Though I can see how a gentleman of discernment, even if he already had a secretary, would recognize that for those particular skills he could apply to no higher authority than a barrister."

"Without doubt. I'd only add that our presumptive sagacious gentleman would also recognize that the most valuable, most effective secretaries are those who begin with education and practice in the law. And that the best among these is the man with political aspirations of his own, who views the position as a kind of apprenticeship toward the day he's situated to stand for Parliament himself."

Nick drank, buying a moment to collect his thoughts. The fine port tasted remarkably like any other port he'd ever sent down his gullet, for all that Kersey across the hall had waxed rhapsodic over the vintage and over the time the stuff spent in wood barrels before bottling.

He set his glass down. "There's the matter of my family." Obviously there was. He could forget the Blackshear disgrace for long moments at a time in this house, where the Westbrooks' own outcast state, combined with their lack of interest in social scandal, kept them largely ignorant of these things. In his professional sphere, there was no chance of forgetting. "Do you not think it likely Lord Barclay would prefer to engage a gentleman who brought no whiff of unsavory connections with him?"

"No, in fact, I don't." Westbrook eyed him steadily, which was a trick a good barrister employed when he wanted his listener to believe he was telling the truth. "Recall to whom he wrote in the first place." He dipped his head in a cursory bow. "If he were truly put off by that sort of thing, he would have had nothing to do with me."

It wasn't quite the same, though. Westbrook had married a woman of virtue and integrity who happened to have worked on the stage. The resulting scandal had all to do with mistaken perception. With people refusing to see beyond that label of *actress*.

Too, so many years had passed since then. Nick shook his head. "I'm sure your professional reputation quite outweighs whatever traces of infamy might still cling to your name."

"You make my point for me." Triumph flickered in Westbrook's eyes before giving way to such fatherly gravity as compelled Nick to avert his own gaze to the letter once more. "People do forget, Blackshear." The kindness in his voice was nearly enough to make a man wince. "Another scandal comes along and displaces yours in the public imagination. Then another comes to eclipse that, and yet another to shoulder out the third. And all the while you toil on, building your good name in your profession and living a private life worthy of that good name, until finally the only people still inclined to shun you are those whose esteem really isn't worth much." He'd picked up his glass and was eddying its contents in small circles. "And I speak as the one who caused my family disgrace, mind. I expect your path back to respectability will be easier and shorter."

Nick smoothed the letter's folds, nodding in a style both thoughtful and noncommittal. *The path back to respectability,* he might say if he was in the mood for protracted debate, *was easier and shorter when your father was an earl.* Society hostesses had doubtless been quick in discovering they could overlook the one objectionable connection when it came to including the present Lord Harringdon on their guest lists. Sons and daughters of mere gentry weren't nearly so much in demand.

"I'll grant that it would have been ideal if this opportunity had come a year or so later, when you felt you'd got your good name back." The click of Westbrook's wedding ring against his still-circling glass marked off every few words. "However, it's come now. And you can't be sure of encountering another one like this. Besides, my credibility is somewhat at stake." Ah, here came the argument's death thrust. A shift in his voice, like a musical key change, signaled its approach. "The baron has asked if I know of a man with the skills and inclination to tutor him in speaking. I should like to be able to recommend the best such man I know. Not the second or third best."

He would have colored at the praise, were he not so aware of the scaffolding on which it rested. "Flattery *and* a tug on the bonds of gratitude." He lifted his port for another drink, partly to mask the smile he could not suppress. "Your tactics lack subtlety."

"They don't have to be subtle. They just have to work." Westbrook, in contrast, made no attempt to hide his smile. "Let me furnish Barclay with a date or two on which he can observe you in court. If he then wishes to meet with you, you can decide for yourself whether your circumstances are likely to make an impediment. I'll wager you ten shillings he won't care."

"A wager, now. Because flattery and the appeal to my sense of obligation were not manipulation enough." But he was going to say *yes* and they both knew it. Apart from the chance to make inroads on a political career, there was another advantage Westbrook had delicately refrained from invoking: the honorarium Barclay proposed to pay.

To stand for a seat in Parliament you needed land; land that could yield an income of six hundred pounds a year—three hundred if standing for a borough. To get that land, you needed money. Through diligent economy he'd managed to put some by, but not near enough, yet. And with so little income trickling in from court cases of late, he couldn't lightly toss aside the prospect of a few guineas honestly earned.

"Very well, you may send him my name." Equal parts foreboding and hopeful anticipation chased through him. "But if he doesn't like the name, and writes back to beg recommendation of another, I shall be calling at the first opportunity to collect my ten shillings."

"Naturally. We'll be delighted as always to see you." He hoisted his glass for what looked like a victory quaff. "Now, what days should I suggest he come watch you? Have you any particularly stirring cases in the remainder of this session?"

Coaxing Miss Rosalind to sing proved easy enough. She was already at the piano turning pages for Miss Beatrice when he entered the parlor. All he had to do was choose a seat near them, and, when the instrumental piece reached its end, request to hear something with words.

"A duet, if you please," he added, lest she think to leave the singing to her sister. "It's rare I visit a family with even one musical person to entertain me. Here I have an embarrassment of riches."

"It comes of their theatrical blood, I'm sure." Westbrook stood near the hearth, his elbow propped on the back of the armchair where his wife sat. "All of Mrs. Westbrook's family played singing roles from a young age. Myself, I expected all through my youth to be thrown out of church for desecrating the hymns."

"Some talent might come from the Westbrook side nevertheless." Miss Westbrook stood at the tea table, her hands moving lightly from pot to cup to sugar tongs. "Sometimes these things lie low in one generation and come out again in the next. Was our grandmother musical? Our grandfather, perhaps? We hear so many stories of our Stanley relations, and know almost nothing of the people with whom our father grew up."

Nick shifted a bit in his place on the sofa. He'd visited here long enough to see more than one of these uncomfortable little dialogues. In general Mr. Westbrook's relations were not spoken of at all, but every now and then Miss Westbrook must seize at some flimsy pretext to bring them into the conversation. Her father's family had cut him off before she was even born, and still she seemed to cherish hopes of seeing them all acknowledge one another again.

"Neither of my parents was musical, to my recollection." Westbrook accepted the cup his daughter carried to him, and took the seat on the hearth opposite his wife. "I suppose my sister Elizabeth played rather well. But I contend you all owe your talents to your mother."

Sometimes he detected a hint of disappointment in Miss Westbrook's aspect when one of these conversations failed to catch on. This time she merely arched her eyebrows and gave a philosophical tilt of the head before returning to the tea table.

The requested duet began, and a moment or so into it came Miss Westbrook with his tea. She crossed the carpet so smoothly that scarcely a ripple could be seen in his cup, when she lowered cup and saucer into his hand. She'd remembered how he liked the drink, pitch dark and unmarred by sugar, though it had been some time since his last visit and there were plenty of other barristers and law students who called here, too. *Thank you*, he mouthed, to not disturb the singers. She sent him a smile every bit as potent as the contents of his cup, and went back to busy herself with everyone else's tea.

The song proved to be a maudlin one, all about some noble lady wasting away for the love of some noble man, and the sisters sang it, so far as he could tell, quite prettily. He smiled whenever one of them glanced his way—or, more accurately, whenever Miss Rosalind did, Miss Beatrice being altogether engrossed by reading the music and playing—and idly followed their eldest sister's tea-serving circuit of the room.

If she were *only* a girl too keenly aware of her beauty, too concerned with class and consequence, he would never think of her at all. Not that he did think of her so very much. Certainly not the way he had in the beginning. He had the continuing study of law to keep him occupied, and agreeable colleagues, and now and then an adventurous woman with whom to dally, when he was in a dallying mood.

That he ever did think of Kate Westbrook had everything to do with those occasional glimpses of kindness and substance beneath the frivolous, self-satisfied mask. Her protective concern for her sister, to take one example. The guileless gravity with which she'd addressed him at dinner. Her consideration in serving everyone's tea exactly to taste. Even after three years, he sometimes wondered if he really knew her, and sometimes felt he knew her all too well.

Back and forth she went from the tea table to the sofa where Sebastian sat with a sketchbook on his knee, to the fireside armchairs where her parents held court, to a writing table on the other side of the room at which Miss Viola labored, no doubt on the same opus she'd been authoring since before he'd ever set foot in this house.

She walked as though on clouds, the eldest Westbrook daughter did, a beatific, almost secretive smile on her face. She'd seemed so little troubled by her failure to get her father talking about his family, too. Once or twice her glance connected with his and he felt her happiness like an electrical charge. What could have happened, in the half hour since dinner, to put her in this mood?

Enough of that. Here was Miss Rosalind looking his

way again, to see that the song was meeting with his approval, and *that* was the glance and *those* the spirits to which he ought to be paying attention, as indeed he ought to be paying attention to this dirge of a tune she and her sister were performing for his benefit.

And by the time the thing reached its fittingly dismal conclusion—the young lady succumbed to the ravages of her despair, leaving the young man to recognize, too late, the value of that devotion he'd so little regarded—he was ready with a good-natured jibe about the appetite for melancholy in modern young women. One or two teasing remarks more, concerning the feminine predilection for horrid novels, and Miss Rosalind settled on the end of the sofa nearest his chair, coaxed out of her diffidence into an earnest defense of the volume she presently had out from the lending library.

"I advise you to admit defeat now, Mr. Blackshear." Miss Westbrook slipped in from his left to hand her sister a cup of milky tea. "You may have studied disputation for four or five years, but she's had that many years at our family dinner table, and twice that many in the most contentious nursery you could ever hope to see."

"More to the point, Mr. Blackshear doesn't read novels." Miss Rose lobbed this intelligence to her sister. "So he's just said." With her mind occupied in organizing arguments, and her face aglow at the sense of carrying her point, the girl bore no resemblance to that muted creature who'd all but faded into the dining room wallpaper. "Therefore he has no grounds at all upon which to criticize them."

"Indeed he hasn't. The nerve of him." Miss Westbrook had pivoted round behind her sister and now threw him a look that stopped just short of a wink.

Without question something had happened to alter her spirits. He'd have to see whether he couldn't prize it out of her, later on. For now he shot her an answering smile and dove back into the argument, just for the pleasure of seeing how far he could debate a subject on which he was so utterly uninformed.

"WELL DONE," Kate said later, under her breath. She'd waited for this opportunity, watched Mr. Blackshear even while she'd drifted among siblings and parents, passing out cups and praising whatever creative endeavor engaged them; and when their caller had excused himself from a visibly revived Rose and gone to replenish his tea, she'd contrived to encounter him over the cream and sugar and cake. "I don't mind admitting you made a much better job of that than I would have done. No, this smaller pot has your murky devil's brew. The other is merely tea, such as refined people prefer."

"Refined people don't know what they're missing." Of all Father's young protégés, none sparred so readily, or with such good cheer, as Mr. Blackshear. He leaned in a bit, holding out his cup, and lowered his own voice. "You give me too much credit, though. I only followed your own instructions, asking her to sing and then engaging her in conversation."

"No, you did better." She refilled his cup and set down the pot. A little to the left was the bay window that overlooked Gower Street; she could draw him that way and then they'd have the piano between themselves and the rest of the room, and they wouldn't need to keep their voices quite so low. "You engaged her in argument. You didn't simply make her feel attended to, as I would have had you do. You made her feel clever and capable."

"She *is* clever and capable, and a seasoned disputer, as you said." He followed her to the window and took up a place on her right. "It's nothing to do with me."

"For Heaven's sake, take the compliment, Mr. Blackshear. If there's one thing I can't abide it's false modesty."

"Indeed." He eyed her sideways, one brow arching as he lifted his cup. "I hadn't noticed you to have much use for modesty of any kind."

So he was in that sort of mood, was he? Good. She could keep up with all the plaguing he cared to throw her way. "Ah, I take your meaning." She shaped all her features into an exaggerated show of comprehension. "You think me vain of my looks."

"No, Miss Westbrook. *Think* suggests an element of doubt. And that particular doubt, in my acquaintance with you, was long since done away with." He took another swallow of that disgusting double-strength tea he favored, this time angling to watch her over the rim of his cup. His eyes, dark and glossy as a dandy's polished boots, brimmed with mischief.

He was a decidedly handsome man. He always had been. His face had the excellent foundation of a strong chin, straight nose, and pronounced cheekbones, and his hair, though he unfortunately chose to wear it quite short, presumably to forego a cap under his barrister wig, was of an agreeable color. Under sunlight, and given a bit of length, the shade might be reminiscent of a much-handled guinea.

All that, however, was neither here nor there. Looks had never been the issue between them, unless you counted the bounty of her own looks that had justified setting her marital sights high.

"I must say, you gentlemen are very vexing in your expectations of us." A small toss of her head would not go amiss here, so she added it. "A man wants a lady to be beautiful, but to drift about in ignorance of the fact until the day he can come along and enlighten her. And all the while, a well-looking lady is subjected to such incessant attentions and courtesies from the lot of you as can leave her in no doubt of her appeal."

"*Subjected*, to be sure. I can see it must be excessively trying, to be constantly the recipient of flattering notice from men." He'd been shy of arguing with her, back in those days when he'd thought to court her, and in the succeeding period when mortification had kept him from speaking much to her at all. His society was infinitely more enjoyable now.

"The trying part is the inconsistency, the inherent contradiction in what gentlemen would like us to be. There's simply no such thing as a beautiful woman who's unaware of her beauty, unless she's monumentally oblivious. More likely she's feigning her ignorance in order to snare a credulous man in a web woven out of his own illogical expectations."

He grinned down at her from his superior height, cup arrested halfway to his mouth, eyes practically sparking with mirth. "You were on your way to a first-rate argument, up until that last bit." Oh, he was about to become pedantic. She'd seen this manner before. "Webs don't snare things, I'm afraid. *Snare* refers to a tightening action like that of a hangman's noose. Something caught in a web just sticks there. It may strike you as a fine distinction, but the last thing you want is to have a juror distracted by that detail when you're trying to drive your case home."

"Excellent advice. I'll be sure to remember it if I ever find myself arguing in a courtroom." She turned to look out the window, that no one in the room might glance over to find them facing one another with Mr. Blackshear smiling so. Mama and Papa, she knew, had never quite let go the hope that her heart might turn toward him, though the moment for that hope had long ago come and gone, even before there'd been any blot on his family name.

He turned, too, smoothly as though she'd given him a cue and he'd picked it up. In the window's many panes she could see their faint reflections. His eyes stayed on her and his head tilted to a quizzical angle. "What's happened to put you in such a fine contentious mood?" he said. "You were grave and solemn at dinner, and now you're pert and pleased as if you had a set of Almack's vouchers in your pocket."

All the triumph of Lady Harringdon's note went rippling through her again, not that it had subsided so very much in the minutes since she'd read those elegant words. "No vouchers quite yet." She hadn't meant to tell anyone, but his guess was so close to the truth, and her secret so deserving of congratulation, that to share the news seemed only right. "However, I received an equally gratifying item in the late post: an invitation to call on a grand lady in her Mayfair home."

"Did you, now?" He made no attempt to hide the fact that he was impressed. He might needle her as mercilessly as Viola on the subject of her preoccupation with society, but he understood ambition and he knew how to respect an unlikely goal achieved. "Then I don't suppose you'll have any need of my Lord Barclay after all. And here I was prepared to do what I could to flush him into your snare, or your web. But who is this grand lady, and how have you come to her notice?"

She truly hadn't meant to tell this part, but perhaps she could approach it as practice for when she must tell Papa and the others. She clasped her hands behind her back and lifted her chin. "The lady is my aunt, as it happens, and I expect she's been aware of my existence for years."

He twisted sharply left, frowning. "A Westbrook aunt?" Three words were enough to make his disapproval plain. You would think Mr. Blackshear of all people would have a bit of understanding for a family who'd chosen to cast out a brother upon his marriage. Of course she couldn't make any remark to that effect.

"A Westbrook aunt, indeed. Given that none of my Stanley aunts keeps a house in Mayfair, I should think that would be obvious." Her attempt at sauciness fell flat: the pique in her voice stood out like sharp notes on a wrongly tuned piano.

Not that he seemed to notice. "Why would a Westbrook aunt invite you to call, when there's been no intercourse between those families and yours since before you were born?"

"We haven't been entirely without communication." She stared out at the nearest streetlamp, to avoid his interrogating gaze.

"She's written to you before? Is your father aware of this?" He was so disagreeable all of a sudden; so peremptory and lawyer-like, and she could imagine all too well what would be his response if she admitted that the writing had been all on her side.

"With respect, Mr. Blackshear, those details are no concern of yours." She would not look at him. Not even at his reflection in the window. "I wouldn't have told you if I'd known you'd be so officious. You're not my elder brother, recall."

"Believe me, Miss Westbrook, I've never for a moment imagined I was." His reply came out so quickly, on the whiplash of his temper, and she knew if he'd taken time to think, he would never have said those words. He pivoted away, stepping nearer to the window and bringing the teacup to his mouth again.

Her face heated. Her stomach turned over. The bay in which they stood felt suddenly very small. The piano played on behind them, a Bach sinfonia whose cool precision only underscored her discomposure, and she could not for the life of her think of what to say.

She'd thought . . . well, in truth maybe she'd had some

inkling of his finding her attractive. Yes, of course she had. Men generally did find her attractive; there was nothing remarkable in that. She just hadn't imagined him to harbor, these three years later, any feelings as could spur him to speak so . . . pointedly.

Her hands were still clasped behind her back, and her nails were digging into her palm. How long had she been silent now? He'd been the last to speak; she ought to say something in answer.

But he spoke first. "Let me try again, without the officiousness." He frowned into his teacup as though the right words were floating there. Because he wanted to avoid looking at her. "As a friend to you and your father, I strongly recommend you confide in him. In your mother as well, for that matter. I'm sure they'd agree with me that it seems odd, this aunt wanting you to call now when she's had years to issue such an invitation."

"On the contrary, it's easily explained." All at once she couldn't seem to remember how to talk to him. His presence scrambled her thoughts and she could only spit them out as belligerence. "Lady Harringdon has heretofore chiefly occupied herself with making matches for her daughters. Now they're all married, I expect she's in want of something to do, and why shouldn't she like to repeat her success with another young relation?"

"Kate." Rarely, rarely did he call her by her Christian name, and she wished he hadn't done it now. The single syllable fairly dripped with pity. "Do you really think the countess intends to make a match for you? Has she said anything at all to support that notion?"

"I don't wait for her to say so." Now wounded pride leaped headlong into the whirlwind of mixed-up sentiments, making her more belligerent yet. "If she hasn't already formed the idea of sponsoring me into society, I shall have to form that idea for her."

"Such a thing isn't easily done." Said like a grown man lecturing patiently to an impetuous little girl.

"I never supposed it was. I don't limit myself to *easy* undertakings, you see. And you'll pardon me, I hope, for questioning the extent of your authority on the intricacies of better society." She knew perfectly well he'd always spent his evenings in study rather than going out to balls and card parties as other young men liked to do.

He blanched, and too late she heard the words she'd said, or rather, heard the insult he must have heard in them. For an instant his eyes widened, and flicked back and forth trying to read her, as if he couldn't believe the Miss Westbrook he knew would really say such a thing and he must make sure she was not some other woman in disguise. Then he shifted his gaze to a spot over her shoulder. "Quite right." His voice had gone crisp and remote. His posture was stiff as a soldier's. "I'm no expert in these things. I oughtn't to have taken up the subject at all." He made a partial bow, his eyes still not meeting hers. "I'll excuse myself now. Thank you for the tea. I wish you such success with your aunt as may render my concern laughable."

She nearly put out a hand to stop him from leaving. She'd meant to refer only to his retiring habits. He prided himself on those; she couldn't truly wound him with a jibe on the subject. She would never deliberately mention the scandal that had hurt his standing in society. Not once in the months since she'd learned of it had she given him the slightest indication that she knew.

But any explanation, now, must involve invoking that same set of events. And she was too agitated from their argument to find her way to a more circumspect apology. She could only watch as he withdrew from her company and made his way to the opposite side of the room.

He did not again address her for the remainder of his

call. He spent a good while speaking to Viola at her desk, and obligingly looked through some of Sebastian's innumerable drawings, and laughed with Mama and Papa by the fire. And when he took his leave it was with one bow to encompass all the Westbrooks, his glance skipping over her like a stone across the water in a game of ducks and drakes.

"What did you say to Mr. Blackshear tonight?" Vi asked her later, as they readied for bed. "Even I could see he was displeased with you." In the mirror, her blunt, guileless stare caused Kate to lower her own eyes to her hands.

"I don't remember quite what I said." She wove her sister's nighttime plait with a bit more concentration than usual, or at least the appearance of such. "Only it was in response to his presumption. He questioned my chances of making such connections as you know I am determined to make." Viola didn't know about Lady Harringdon's note, so Kate left that part vague. "I suppose I may have been a bit injudicious in my reply." Even the milder insult she'd intended was beginning to feel like the petty work of a schoolgirl at Miss Lowell's.

Vi shook her head—she could never remember to not do that when her hair was being plaited—and winced at the tug to her scalp. "You surprise me. For all the times I've had to hear you lecture on what courtesies are due to a guest, I should have thought you'd be the last among us to speak as carelessly to Mr. Blackshear as if he were but another sibling."

I've never for a moment imagined I was your brother. She ducked her head lower as heat crept into her cheeks. That had been the dropped stitch, the blotted word, the missed entrance; the point from which everything had gone completely off course. What did he mean, exhuming those sentiments and bringing all kinds of awkward consciousness into their relation? She would surely not have lost her temper, and would never have chosen her words so carelessly, if he hadn't said that to her.

"Really, it will be too bad of you if he keeps away from us now." Viola clearly took her silence as an invitation to further reproach. "He calls rarely enough as it is, and he's one of the few tolerable men among Papa's protégés."

"I'm sure that's not true. Papa knows any number of agreeable young men."

"Agreeable to you, I'll grant, since they spend the visit staring at you slack-jawed." Vi picked up her hair ribbon from the tabletop and wove it through her fingers as she spoke. "Mr. Blackshear has better sense. He remembers to ask after my book, and Sebastian's drawings, and what Mama thought of Mr. Kean's *Othello*. Did you not see how attentive he was to Rose? I would have thought you'd appreciate that."

"I did see. I did appreciate it. He was very good to her." She plucked the ribbon from her sister's fingers and wrapped it round the tail end of the plait. "I hope . . . if I've offended him, I hope he may not hold that against the rest of you."

If, again. She'd offended him. She hadn't meant to do so, at least not so deeply as she had, but she'd offended him all the same. He wouldn't hold it against the other Westbrooks, though, would he? He *did* have better sense, as Viola said. A brief squabble with her, and an accidental slight, couldn't put him off the household altogether.

Though it wasn't just the squabble and the slight. Too vividly she remembered the speed with which he'd turned from her and taken interest in his tea; the long, sinfonia-filled pause in which they'd stood there, the echoes of his rash utterance dancing circles round them both.

She tied the ribbon tight, measuring out the loops and

trailing ends to make a neat symmetrical bow. Vi was right. Mr. Blackshear *wasn't* like Papa's other young men who came to call. She could not permit her parents and siblings to lose his society merely because of some awkwardness or a misunderstanding between him and her.

She would apologize, in some way that wouldn't further pierce his pride. She wouldn't even wait for his next call—she could go to whatever court he was practicing in, and find a moment to tell him she was sorry. Perhaps he'd apologize, too, for having spoken indiscreetly. Or perhaps they'd simply pretend, both of them, that he never had. Either way, they would return to the easy cordiality that had been their habit, and they'd both be more careful with how they spoke, in the future. They would not again risk jeopardizing a friendship that affected more people than just themselves.

"Viola." She found her sister's eyes in the mirror. "Do you think our brother could be persuaded to chaperone us for an errand to one of the courts?"

Chapter Three

*Y*OU'LL PARDON *me, I hope, for questioning the extent of your authority on the intricacies of better society.* Well into the next day, he could remember her words verbatim. They'd burned themselves into the folds of his brain.

Nick flexed the fingers of his right hand one by one, a small, inconspicuous action that vented some of his bodily restlessness. A barrister couldn't, after all, give himself a quick shake while sitting at the courtroom table under the eyes of judges, jury, and opposing counsel. Possibly the eyes of Lord Barclay, too, but he'd forbidden himself to look.

The ridiculous part was that he couldn't even be sure whether she'd meant to make reference to the family scandal. She had a history of plaguing him for his habit of staying in and studying when other young men went out to balls. That might very well have been the target of her remark. He'd never seen any sign that she knew how his name had been tarnished.

Yet it certainly wasn't out of the question that she would know. She took a greater interest in these things than others in her household did. And if the subject should come up in passing between her mother and father—*Any day of the week will do for inviting Mr. Blackshear; he hasn't any cases of late to take up his time*—he could picture her inquiring, and her parents telling her, with an admonishment to allow no change in her manners with Mr. Blackshear.

Nick bent his head to the pages of his brief and pulled one back to frown at the second, though he knew precisely what was on each page. How could he expect to see no changes in her manner, when he'd committed a shameful change in his manner with her?

Believe me, Miss Westbrook, I've never for a moment imagined I was. He had to will himself to not visibly cringe in the courtroom. At least a dozen times since last night he'd relived the taste of those words on his tongue; seen her astonishment and dismay; felt all over again the self-disgust at his want of discretion, and worse, at his having such feelings to report in the first place.

He'd put a deal of effort, over the years, into shaping his affection along brotherly lines. He'd succeeded to a notable degree. Then there she'd been, incandescent with the triumph of her aunt's letter, bantering with him in her flirtatious style, and when they came to speaking in temper he simply lost his head.

It's done. You can't call back the words, either of you. She'll remain your friend, or she won't. She knows your secret, or she doesn't. Now is this really how you want to spend your courtroom time when that baron may be watching how you do? No. It wasn't. Enough woolgathering. He straightened the pages of his brief and sent his attention to the boxes where the witness and prisoner stood.

Lord only knew what Barclay would make of this case, if he'd never before experienced the criminal courts. A Miss Mary Watson stood accused of thievery from a Mr. Joseph Cutler, under circumstances that did credit to neither party. In such cases, he might tell the baron, a barrister's client must be Justice herself, and he always took care to picture her standing in the dock, blindfolded and regal, in place of, for example, the slatternly, fidgety woman who stood there now, periodically baring her unfortunate teeth in what seemed to be a smile. No doubt Stubbs had recommended she make some attempt to look amiable.

She looked about as amiable as a flea-ridden cur backed into a corner. Nick allowed one glance up to the gallery, to the place where Stubbs always sat. The solicitor had apparently known this glance was coming: he shrugged and shook his head, eyes big and plaintive behind his spectacles, hands helplessly half raised and lowered again.

Well, at least the accuser was no likelier than the prisoner to make a good impression with the jury. Mr. Cutler, perhaps striving for an air of sophistication, had no sooner taken his place in the witness box than he produced a silver toothpick and began to employ it, with an occasional flourish, in between giving his account of what had transpired.

"She took my ring, what had a value of three shilling." Cutler held up his denuded left hand as though to make a more emphatic proof. "Besides that, she took all the money I had on my person. Three pound in bank notes and eight shilling in coins."

"*All* the money you had." George Kersey, arguing for the prosecution today, was one of those barristers who believed every bit of testimony could be improved by a turn in his own voice. In this case, admittedly, he might be right.

"A ring, too, what were worth three shilling." The accuser now rested his ringless hand on the box's railing, where the jury might have a good view of it if they should need further reminding of that detail. "I woke to find all of it gone, and when I said I know she robbed me, she wouldn't give back but two shilling and sixpence."

"Two shillings and sixpence, which were taken from you, without your knowledge or consent." Kersey strode away from the witness box and spun to face Mr. Cutler again, the dramatic swirl of his robes coinciding with *knowledge or consent*. A hundred such frills and devices a barrister perfected, in order to frame pertinent points for the jury's benefit without addressing the men directly. Couldn't fault the fellow for that. If theatrics had no place, the jury would simply read over the briefs to arrive at a verdict.

"No, I never give my consent, nor give her any money, nor promised any neither. She stole it, without my knowledge, by thievery." He bit down on the toothpick and rocked his weight back onto his heels.

Here, indeed, was the crux of the case: Miss Watson claimed Mr. Cutler had paid six shillings for the pleasure of her company and then demanded his money back the next morning. Mr. Cutler maintained the company had been freely given. Miss Watson's seemed the more credible of the two tales, which point would, one hoped, help the jury to also credit her in the much murkier matter of the three pounds, some shillings, and vanished ring.

And he could do a bit to help with that, too.

"Mr. Cutler," he said when Kersey had concluded his questioning—with a fine, stylish stalking sort of return to the table and a fluid descent into his chair. "The arresting constable has stated that the prisoner had fourteen shillings and sixpence upon her at the time of apprehension, and no ring." He might have made a show of looking up the amount in his brief. He wasn't above the occasional flourish himself. But his opponent having so clearly staked out the theatrical territory today, he'd likely do better to adopt a contrasting style.

So he stood, hands clasped behind his back, at right angles to the witness box, all his attention presumably leveled on the man therein while still presenting a clear view of his profile to the rows where the jury sat. "In keeping with your allegations, oughtn't he to have reported three pounds, five shillings, and sixpence? And a ring?"

"Not if she hid all but the coins what were reported." Cutler saluted with his toothpick, in the manner of a fencer who'd just scored a hit.

"Indeed. But that seems an odd thing for her to do. To hide some of her ill-gotten gains, and keep the rest about her." A brief pause, for the jurors to consider this fact. "Also, the constable searched her room, according to his report, and didn't find any additional money. Nor any ring." Now came the time to dispense with scruple. He tilted his head. "A wedding ring, was it?"

On the left periphery, Kersey shot to his feet. As well he ought. "That point is not material to the issue at hand."

"Please confine yourself, Mr. Blackshear, to questions touching directly on the matter of whether or not the prosecutor was robbed by the prisoner. We are not here to consider his personal morality, or lack thereof." Nearly as good as a wink, the wry tone in which the honorable justice Scholyer delivered this reprimand. Surely some among the jury would read that for tacit approbation, and surely some would feel at liberty to pass private judgment on Cutler in consequence. Never mind that these men might pay but imperfect tribute to their own marriage vows. A seat in the jury box had a way of scrubbing a man's conscience clean, and leaving him free to condemn other men's lapses at will.

Nick bowed his head, half twisting to direct his acquiescence to the judges' bench, and maintained the posture until Kersey had sunk back into his seat.

He lifted his chin, none too hurriedly, and brought his gaze around to settle, for a thoughtful twelve seconds, on the prisoner in her box. She showed her teeth three times in that span: once to him, once to the judges, and once to the jury. He'd have a few words for Stubbs, when this was done.

A smart flick of attention back to the witness box. "Mr. Cutler, how much money do you have on your person at this moment?"

Up came Kersey again, but this time Nick didn't wait for him to speak. "I wish to examine the detail of Mr. Cutler's recalling, to the shilling, how much money he had on him on the night in question." He addressed the bench directly. Not so much as a glance at the opposing counsel. "If he demonstrates a like knowledge of what money he carries today, that will tell us one thing. If he cannot supply the figure, that may tell us something else."

It wouldn't, of course, tell them whether or not Miss Watson had committed the alleged crime. But in these cases—two conflicting stories and no real evidence to support either one—a scattershot attack on the prosecutor's credibility could tip the scales just the necessary amount.

"I'll allow the question. Be seated, please, Mr. Kersey." Justice Scholyer issued a curt nod. On the right periphery, one juror sat straighter and another edged forward in his seat.

You couldn't always pick out the precise point in a trial when momentum went one way or the other. But when you could—when you felt that first inkling that things hereafter were going to fall out in your favor; when you sensed the twining of luck with your own talent and preparation—a keen awareness vibrated straight through your frame, all the way out to your fingers and toes.

Nick angled his face again toward the witness box,

where the witness's knuckles stood out pale on the hand that now clutched at the railing. "If you please, Mr. Cutler." Calm, quiet, and matter-of-fact. No lilt of triumph. "How much money do you have?"

"Truly, I don't understand the wigs." Sebastian leaned near to mutter, since their neighbors in the gallery were all rapt and silent. "I suppose they think to look august, but instead they merely look quaint. As though they'd all been shut up in here for the past thirty or forty years and never knew the fashions had changed."

"It's a matter of tradition." Kate spoke behind her hand. "And I've always thought Papa looked distinguished in his wig."

"He's of an age to carry it off. A younger man cannot. Mr. Blackshear looks like a dandiprat."

Viola, at Sebastian's far side and happily engrossed in the trial, waved a hand to hush her too-talkative siblings.

So Kate said nothing more on the matter of wigs or who looked well in them. But the truth was that Mr. Blackshear on the courtroom floor had a way of making you forget to notice what he wore. He could be down there in a frock coat and red-heeled shoes, and you'd remark only his poise, his reined-in passion, his magnet-like gift for holding a whole room's attention in the palm of his hand. No wonder Papa had thought of him first, when the letter had come from Lord Barclay.

Another pinch of shame attending the memories of last night: she'd neglected to congratulate him. So eager had she been to bask in her own triumph that it hadn't even occurred to her to ask him what he'd learned from the baron's letter, over port, and what he thought might come of this opportunity. Probably he would have liked to tell all about it, if he'd had an interested listener instead of one so overwhelmingly concerned with herself.

"What a sordid case this is." Sebastian never could keep still for two minutes together. "It's a pity the accuser isn't someone of note. I could make a grand comical caricature of the robbery scene, and Tegg might buy it from me and sell prints."

Had her family made an agreement to be as conspicuous as possible . . . What was that line from *Pride and Prejudice?* A well-dressed man in the row ahead of theirs threw a look over his shoulder, his brow quirking in reprimand or perhaps disdain.

"Hush," she whispered to her brother. "Try to attend to the trial." No point in repeating, for the thousandth time, her wish that he'd aim his talents at some higher target than the front window of Tegg's. He'd shared a womb with Viola, after all, and absorbed his own dose of whatever queer political humor had infused his twin. Likely he was already thinking of ways he might represent the robbery tableau as a metaphor for some issue of the day.

She clasped her hands in her lap and inclined a degree forward, imitating Vi's posture that he might find proper examples of attention at both sides, and succumb to the influence. Down on the floor, Mr. Blackshear was giving way to the prosecutor's counsel as Mr. Cutler slunk out of the witness box and yet another colorful personage stepped in to tell what she knew of the disputed events.

Mr. Blackshear resumed his seat with the careless grace of a man who felt no need to make an impression. That was a calculated move, she knew—a working barrister's every breath and fidget had strategy behind it—but the attitude sat well on him. Even in the dandiprat wig, he projected a gravitas that must surely meet with many a lady's taste.

With her own taste, in fact, at least a little. She'd never

pretended to not find him handsome. Only he was something more than handsome, wasn't he, here in the courtroom. For the length of the proceedings, his social standing was beside the point. He fashioned his own consequence here, and she had to admit he did it so capably as to—

Her interlaced fingers tightened as his gaze lifted suddenly to the gallery—but he didn't see her. He exchanged some silent cryptic remark with the man over at the far left who must be the solicitor in the case, and cleanly retracted his glance to direct it toward the proceedings once more.

Well enough. His attention belonged on the courtroom floor. As did he. This was his sphere, and today's experience of observing him only emphasized what she already knew: that that sphere overlapped very little with the one around which all her own hopes traced their orbit.

She unclasped her hands, flexing the fingers one by one to let out their tension, and steered her thoughts back to the drama of Cutler versus Watson.

"An underhanded trick, that business of quizzing him on the contents of his pockets. I won't soon forget it." Kersey never took a defeat to heart, which was part of what made him a fine advocate, honorable opponent, and agreeable neighbor in Number Four Brick Court.

"To be sure, you won't. I expect you'll employ the trick yourself, now you've seen it so brilliantly executed." Nick wheeled round a corner, evading the good-natured blow aimed at his midsection and nearly colliding with a portly man bound in the other direction. The halls of the Old Bailey after a day's worth of trials could make Covent Garden look bucolic.

"Mind you, I still think your old girl did it." Kersey

had pulled off his wig and cap, and was raking his hair into romantic disarray as he walked. "My fellow was no saint, and it's a good bet he overstated the amount of his loss, but as to the question of whether she emptied his coat pockets while he slept, I'd say it's more than probable that— Good Lord." His voice changed, lowered, came out a half whisper. "What's a diamond like that doing in the criminal courts?"

Nick looked. There, descending the stairs from the upper gallery, was Miss Westbrook. And Miss Viola, he perceived a half second after, and the younger Mr. Westbrook, but she, inevitably, was the one who'd managed to step into that exact place where sunlight fell through the landing's window to wreath her uncovered hair in gold. She paused for a moment, hand resting daintily on the balustrade, as if she was aware of her light—aware of all her preposterous beauty—and wanting to give observers a chance to commit her image to memory for use in some later artistic endeavors.

"She's like a Botticelli angel, complete even to the halo," Kersey whispered, right on cue.

"The blond girl, do you mean?" As though there could be any doubt.

"Who else in here could you possibly compare to an angel?" Another raking of hand through hair, this time effecting a more deliberate arrangement. "Look at her, Blackshear. Poised above the teeming rabble. She'd make a fine Persephone, wouldn't she, pausing to pluck up her courage before her descent into the underworld."

Oh, good God. If she wasn't causing one man to forget himself and utter some foolish impropriety, she was reducing another to prating idiocy of this sort. "I think I shall break into your rooms and throw out whatever volumes of poetry you've been reading to tatters." He smacked Kersey's shoulder with the brief he still held. "I can assure you that's neither angel nor goddess, but

Charles Westbrook's daughter. As is the one beside her, with spectacles. The young man behind them is Westbrook's son. I suppose they must come and watch cases sometimes, since their father's in the profession." Though they'd never before come to see *him*. He'd got into a discussion last night with Miss Viola, however, over whether women oughtn't to sit on juries when one of their sex was on trial, and he'd talked a bit about today's case. She must have decided she'd like to see the proceedings for herself.

"A barrister's daughter? Never say so. She ought to be a viscountess, at least."

Trust me, she's entirely in accord with you there. He kept that thought to himself. There'd been slights and misunderstandings enough between them last night. He wouldn't go disparaging her to someone else.

Halfway down the stairs, they sighted him. Miss Westbrook did. Her gaze connected with his and he saw a mix of apprehension and purpose in her eyes. Ah, then, she'd come here with something to say to him. Apprehension kicked up in him, too. He didn't want an apology if it would mean open reference to what he'd rather leave unmentioned.

On the other hand, he owed her an apology in his turn, and perhaps he'd find an opportunity. And he was still in fine spirits from his time on the courtroom floor. And Kersey had never met any of the younger Westbrooks. He hauled the man with him and met the three of them at the bottom of the stairs.

"Let us have your verdict, Miss Viola," Nick said once he'd shepherded them all clear of the hallway traffic and done a round of introductions. "Would Miss Watson have been better served by a jury, perhaps even a judge and barristers, of her own sex?"

"You may be sure I pondered that very question throughout the trial." She straightened her spectacles, using a forefinger to reverse their creeping down the slope of her nose. "And although you did win the prisoner her freedom, I cannot help observing that it was done primarily through encouraging the jurors' predisposition to look with contempt upon a man of Mr. Cutler's class, rather than by making a clear case for Miss Watson's innocence. Not that you didn't execute it all quite cleverly. But in a truly just system, regardless the sex of the jury, your tactic couldn't succeed."

"Viola!" Miss Westbrook colored. She brought her eyes, apparently with some effort, to him. "You argued very well, Mr. Blackshear. We've seen enough of Papa's cases to know how barristers must attempt to influence a jury. We thought you gave your client a splendid defense."

"Didn't I just say so? I called him clever." Miss Viola scowled at her sister, who was now glancing about as if to take a count of all the people who might possibly be witnessing this latest example of unseemly Westbrook outspokenness. "I only mean to say that I begin to think the inclusion of women is but one in a whole host of reforms that must be brought to our jury system. Why should people like Mr. Cutler and Miss Watson be subjected to the judgment of those who view them as inferior, perhaps even comical creatures, and who can be easily swayed by a barrister's appeals to their sense of their own superiority?"

"I should say." Kersey was more than ready to approve these opinions of a lady he'd just met. "That trick with the wedding ring was particularly disgraceful, wasn't it?"

Westbrook the younger chimed in with an assertion that Mr. Cutler and Miss Watson were at least a *bit* comical, deserving of justice though they might be. Miss Viola accused him of missing the point, Kersey contributed such remarks as might best fan the flames of the dispute, and Nick found himself suddenly superfluous to the conversation. He caught Miss Westbrook's eye, through the vociferous knot of siblings and colleague, and shrugged one shoulder, smiling in what he hoped was a friendly but not overfamiliar manner.

She smiled back, with a long-suffering shake of her head, and the smile warmed him like a good swallow of brandy. Beneath the injudicious words and his doubts over what she knew of his circumstances, they did have a foundation of friendship that had persisted some years now. His earlier thoughts, as to her deliberate posing on the staircase, and her inflated opinion of her rightful station, felt more than ever unworthy of him.

And more unworthy yet, when, with an abruptness suggestive of hastily gathered courage, she wove around Miss Viola to stand at his side. "We thoroughly enjoyed watching you at trial. We thought you played your part impeccably." Color still sat high in her cheeks. "Viola forgets herself sometimes, but she means no offense."

"And I take none. I've been known to forget myself on occasion as well." He kept his voice light, and smiled as he said the words, but left a long enough pause that she could not miss his meaning. *Perhaps we can both simply forget the things we said last night, and be at ease with each other again?* "I'm honored the three of you should have come to observe, and I know how to value your praise. If you've seen your father try cases, you know the standard against which I must measure myself."

"My father will be pleased, I'm sure, to hear of the trial and all the various tactics you employed." Her head suddenly tilted a fraction, as if a new idea had occurred. "If you're at liberty Saturday, you might come to dinner and give your own account."

He bowed. Not for anything would he let her see he knew this was no spontaneous idea. The certainty that she'd come to the Old Bailey expressly to extend this peace offering, in its guise of casual invitation, rather woke every sympathy and protective instinct in regard to her pride. "I'm sure that would be everything delightful," he began, but her attention flicked elsewhere as he spoke. To his left and past him. A brief widening of her eyes, a flash of what looked like distaste, and then she was all polite composure once more.

He knew even before turning what he would see. Whom, rather. This wasn't the first time this had happened, with a client of Stubbs's.

Miss Mary Watson, freed woman, hovered uncertainly several feet away. On perceiving she'd caught his notice, she made a show of her teeth and looked as if she meant to approach him.

Damnation. With the hastiest of bows he pivoted away from Miss Westbrook, positioning himself to halt Miss Watson's advance. He was perfectly pleased to represent such people in their pursuit of justice. They were no less deserving of advocacy than the higher born. But he'd be hanged if he'd subject the Westbrooks, who'd ventured in here as polite observers, to a meeting with a woman who entertained men for money.

"Miss Watson." He put his hands behind his back lest she be tempted to seize one, as Stubbs's last presumptuous client had done. "I congratulate you on your freedom."

"It were owing to you, sir." She kneaded her hands before her, as if she had indeed intended to grasp one of his, and now must find another outlet for that impulse.

"The better part of your thanks must go to Mr. Stubbs. He prepared an excellent brief." The selfsame brief he now rolled up in his hands, to keep them busy behind his back.

"And picked an excellent man to argue for me. There's many as would look down on an unfortunate girl who lives by what means she must." Her eyes went past him, doubtless to Kersey, who'd done his best, in the questioning, to make her look like a woman thoroughly unacquainted with morality of any kind.

Nick set his mouth in a line. He couldn't join her in condemning Kersey, who'd pursued the obvious strategy for a barrister on the prosecution side. It must certainly have been unpleasant for her to hear, but Stubbs ought to have prepared her for that.

Dimly he registered that the conversation behind him had lapsed. Splendid. Kersey and the Westbrooks must be watching this exchange.

"He said you'd deal fairly with me, Mr. Stubbs did." She wrung her hands again and tottered a half step nearer, a tremor in her voice and—God, was she crying?—all manner of unconstrained emotion in her eyes.

"I hope I do so with every client brought to me by him or anyone else." A corresponding half step back would bring him nearer to the Westbrooks, whose proximity to this interview was already greater than he'd like. He put the distance in his voice instead. "I thank you for the compliment. Good luck to you."

But she didn't recognize the dismissal. "He said you were just the man to give me a fair defense, and not to judge me for a woman lost." Yes, they'd covered this point already, hadn't they? Nearer yet she edged, darting another glance beyond him to the others and dropping her voice to an ardent whisper. "Because of your own connections, I mean."

A spasm shot down his arm to his hand, crushing the brief he still clutched. For an instant he felt as if he'd thrust his head into a roaring furnace. His eyes hurt. His lungs hurt. His cheeks blazed with fury and shame, and for all his repeated blinking, he couldn't seem to see anything but hot light.

"I'm afraid your meaning is lost on me." The words practically cracked in his dry mouth. Where the devil was Stubbs, and why couldn't he keep a leash on his clients? "I haven't any but the most unremarkable connections."

The malevolent light subsided enough to give him a glimpse of her malevolent face wrinkling up its malevolent brow. "Mr. Stubbs, he said you had a brother as married a—" but these words, and whatever word followed, were audible only to him. Because as Miss Watson spoke, so did Miss Westbrook, in a fine, ringing voice that drowned out all else in the vicinity.

"We really must go now. Mr. Blackshear, I hope we may see you at dinner Saturday. Mr. Kersey, will you be so good as to show us out?"

Turn. Bow. Accept the invitation. Thank them for coming, and wish them good day. He couldn't. And after all he didn't have to, because even while speaking, Miss Westbrook was herding the others away. She must have perceived his mortification and come to his rescue.

He didn't feel rescued. He felt all the more mortified. She must have had an idea of what Miss Watson had been about to say, and wanted to spare him having it heard by others. She must know, then, and had simply feigned ignorance with him for the sake of politeness.

For how long had she known? And would he ever again be able to speak to her without feeling a suspicion of her pity or distaste?

"Miss Watson." The woman was perfectly visible now, the haze of shock and anger having dissipated. Her restless hands clasped and twisted as though she were scrubbing them under a pump. "I fear Mr. Stubbs has described my motivations inaccurately. I provide a petitioner with the best defense or prosecution I can because it is my job to do so. Any man who'd save his best efforts for the clients with whom he happened to feel some *affinity* has no place in the law."

What might be her response to this, he would never

know, because here, finally, came the architect of this embarrassment, hurrying down the gradually emptying hallway like a sheepdog after a runaway ewe. "My dear Miss Watson." Stubbs threw an anxious smile at Nick. "I'm sure I've told you Mr. Blackshear is a terribly busy man. Like all barristers. Indeed that's why clients must do their speaking to the solicitor, and trust him to pass any message along." His every glance and gesture spelled out an apology. It wasn't enough.

"A word, Mr. Stubbs." Nick waited until Miss Watson had been dispatched some distance away. He set a hand on the smaller man's shoulder and ushered him to the nearest wall, his other hand still tight about the crumpled up brief. When the solicitor raised his wary bespectacled eyes, Nick spoke. "You will please not to speak of my brother and his personal circumstances again. His marriage has been a cause of pain in our family. It's not to be bandied about to every Mary Watson I happen to represent."

Stubbs's mouth twitched with what was almost certainly dismay at Nick's tone; damn his naive, soft-hearted presumption. He inclined his head. "My humblest apologies. She was despondent when I visited her in prison, and fearful of being harshly judged by you—by any gentleman. I wished to reassure her. I didn't expect she would presume to broach the topic with you."

"I ask, Mr. Stubbs, that you refrain from sharing such details of my life story with *any* client, regardless your estimation of whether that person is likely to accost me in the hall."

"Of course. Forgive me. I won't so wrong you again." The solicitor was retreating already, preparing to shepherd Miss Watson to some place, it was to be hoped, where she would find no legal professionals to harass. He twisted away with a bow, and in the last instant before his back was turned, Nick would nearly swear a spark of pity had lit the man's eyes.

He leaned a shoulder into the wall, to take part of the burden off his suddenly unsteady knees, and watched the two figures until they'd disappeared around a corner. In his left hand the rolled brief crackled; he loosened his fingers and unrolled the pages to see what damage he'd done to some hardworking clerk's efforts.

Will toiled for money now, in an office on one of the docks. Speaking of clerks, and working. So Martha had informed them all, because she and her fool husband *would* insist on acknowledging the cast-off Blackshear brother and even invoking his name before those siblings who no longer saw him. According to her, he'd found employment in the timber trade, where apparently no one cared what sort of scandals you courted and married so long as you showed up at your desk at the appointed hour.

All down the left side of each page ran a chaos of puckers and furrows, mangling the clean, elegant letters Nick recognized as having come from the pen of Smithson. He set the pages to the wall and ran his free hand over them in a smoothing motion. Smithson took pride in his work—you could see it in the little loops and tails with which he embellished the first letter of each paragraph—and he deserved better than to have the product of his labor bear all the anger and frustration of a gentleman living out his own private nightmare of disgrace.

Heat rushed into his cheeks all over again at the memory. How much had the other Westbrooks overheard? Would he now have to contend with blunt questions from Miss Viola—who, for all he knew, might judge Will to be the wronged party in the whole affair—as well as a new awkwardness with Miss Westbrook? They'd invited him to dine there on Saturday. He couldn't imagine how he was to—

"Nicholas Blackshear?"

He twisted. An auburn-haired man of perhaps five and thirty stood a half-dozen feet away, eyebrows raised, head angled slightly forward, silk hat in one hand. Auburn-haired *gentleman,* rather. Five syllables, shaped into a polite inquiry, were enough to make the genteel accent clear, and, even with hat off and head bent, his air was one of consequence and command.

Nick's stomach lurched. He'd completely forgotten the possibility of—

"I take the liberty of presenting myself, though I believe my name has already been made known to you." The gentleman's head inclined a graceful few degrees more. "James Barclay, until recently Lord James Barclay; now simply Lord Barclay. Baron."

Chapter Four

NICK SEIZED his self-possession in fistfuls. Barclay wasn't the only man here who'd been raised as a gentleman. Regardless what one's wayward siblings might do, one did know how to behave. He rolled Smithson's mangled pages into one hand, and pushed off the wall to approach the man with his other hand held out.

"Ah, yes, Charles Westbrook prepared me for the possibility of this meeting. Was this your first experience of the Old Bailey?" His mind turned quickly. Barclay's being here at all probably meant he hadn't heard before of the Blackshear scandal. But how much of the exchange with Stubbs had he witnessed?

"I've never before had the privilege." He had a good, firm handshake, and eyes bright with interest. "I got here early and watched five cases. I was utterly transfixed, particularly by your own trial. Westbrook spoke most highly of you, and it's apparent to me he didn't exaggerate."

"I'm fortunate to have studied with him. He taught me much." His hands went behind his back again, that Lord Barclay not be distracted in his errand by the sight of the crumpled brief.

"I hope you speak the truth, and don't merely make a

show of modesty. I depend upon the notion that such skills can indeed be taught. If what I observed in the court today was rather a product of innate talent, then I fear it's all up with me." A dent appeared in one cheek as he grinned. A sort of incomplete dimple, halted halfway through by a scar.

"Nonsense." Probably one oughtn't to say *nonsense* to a lord. But the conversation had suddenly taken a turn into territory where Nick was most comfortable. So long as they spoke of trials and persuasion, he could bear himself with that ease conferred by perfect confidence in his own authority. "Diligence and a desire to succeed will get a man further than talent in most things. And if you've led men in the army it's likely you'll already possess some of the pertinent skills."

"I suspect your impressions of soldiering may be colored—as admittedly mine once were—by what you've seen in novels and plays. I assure you I never once had occasion to deliver a rallying speech in the manner of Henry the Fifth. A point for which my men were undoubtedly thankful." He would make an excellent pupil. That was already plain. He hadn't that tedious fragility of self-opinion so many men had. A teacher wouldn't have to tiptoe round his lordly dignity.

With effort, Nick kept his fingers from tightening on the already much-abused brief. He wanted this. The pleasure of imparting his expertise to someone so eager to learn; the chance to have influence with a member of Parliament; the myriad channels such a connection might offer for the industry of an ambitious man . . . Could he let himself hope Barclay had heard the conversation with Stubbs, or perhaps had even known all about the scandal beforehand, and thought it of no consequence? It wasn't completely out of the realm of possibility. Mr. Westbrook, to take one example, was of that mind.

"I shan't detain you any further." The baron glanced left and right, to acknowledge how the corridor had emptied about them. "But you're amenable, I hope, to discussing this at some greater length, and seeing whether you can't make a credible speaker of me?"

I'd like nothing better. However it's best we begin on a footing of honesty and therefore I cannot, in conscience, keep you ignorant of facts that could alter your own amenability to the arrangement. He could say that.

Before I answer, I feel I must disclose certain details connected with my family name, and give you a chance to honorably withdraw that invitation. That, too, would be a response of integrity.

May I ask whether you overheard the conversation I was having a minute or two before you first addressed me? Direct, scrupulous, and aboveboard. That was the tone he ought to take.

"Of course," he said, and bowed. "I'd be honored."

"THIS WAY, if you please, Miss Westbrook." The butler returned from putting away Kate's cloak and she followed him, finally, after years of wishing, through an archway to the main staircase of Harringdon House.

The main staircase alone was worth the wait.

Square in the middle of the room—not sidled up to one wall, as in Papa's house and every other she'd seen—the thing rose, a dark, polished, lacy-railinged work of art, its steps narrowing incrementally until the last step gave on to a landing all painted ivory-white. From there the staircase split into two staircases, *curved* staircases, doubling back above her at the left and right walls until they reached a second landing.

Wasteful, Viola would have said. *Why have two sets of stairs going to the same place? It's an ostentatious show of wealth and nothing more.* Her sister had accompanied her as far as Berkeley Square, but had gone off down the street to eat ices and, no doubt, make trenchant private observations about the fashionable people who were also eating ices.

She was glad Vi had declined to come in.

Her heart beat hard as she followed the butler up the stairs, and when she came to the landing and turned for her first look at what lay beyond, it seemed possible her knees would simply give way.

How had Papa never seen fit to mention that he'd grown up amid such splendor? Did people who lived in magnificent surroundings perhaps take the beauty for granted, and even cease to notice it? She never would. Even as a toddling child, she could never have looked on these soaring pale walls, this meticulous plasterwork, that overhead dome set with windows through which sunlight filtered down and not felt a bone-deep sense of wonder.

I ought to have been here as a child. Acquaintance with this house ought to have been my birthright. She'd meant to not have bitter thoughts on this visit. It was difficult, though, to keep from wondering how many ladies without even a drop of Westbrook blood had tripped unthinking up and down these stairs, coming to call on the countess or some other member of the family and never in doubt of a welcome.

She'd come to a stop, she realized, and was staring like some country bumpkin who'd never been inside a house before. She groped for the poise she'd practiced in front of the mirror at home. "It's very pretty." Graciousness, her last, best weapon—the dagger she'd whip out from her garter when all her armor had been stripped away—came readily to hand, and shaped her confusion of sentiment into a compliment to the butler. As if he'd personally overseen the scheme of ivory and gold, and wrought the next landing's Corinthian columns with his own bare hands.

He inclined his head from the step where he'd halted, the very picture of modest pride. "We're told it's some of William Kent's finest work." *We.* She would be jealous of a servant now, if she wasn't careful, for the unthinking ease with which he claimed a place in this house, this family.

"William Kent, of course. He brings such grandeur, doesn't he, such tasteful luxury to the public spaces in a house." She'd never heard of William Kent before this moment. No matter. The remark would serve for an architect or a plasterer. And she would file the name away, beside the Adam brothers and John Nash, for possible use on later occasions.

The butler led on and she followed, one covetous hand skimming along the iron balustrade. The fingers of her other hand felt through her reticule for the shape of her card case. She would not be ashamed of her card, fashioned as it was of the third-rate paper that had been all she could afford. If it sat among the other cards on Lady Harringdon's tray like a drab gray goose who'd stumbled into a flock of swans, well, that much of a contrast must she make to the rest of the company with her elegant manners and the swanlike grace of her person.

Let other ladies shine with their skill at the harp or their knowledge of current affairs. She knew her strengths.

Her heartbeat settled into a cadence of calm self-possession as she arrived at the first-floor landing. To the left and the right, broad doorways, each topped with an elaborately scrolled lintel, opened onto whatever triumphs of decoration lay beyond—but she would not again gape stupidly at the handiwork of Mr. Kent. She busied herself in drawing out a card, as she followed the butler through the left-hand doorway and a series of eminently gape-worthy rooms, and when they arrived at the double doors to the parlor, he took the card and read out her name to the four ladies seated within.

One thing to be said for growing up with an actress mother: a girl learned how to make a memorable curtsy. Kate sank straight down, dropping her eyelids and allowing the slightest inclination of her head, a blushing ingenue whose Ophelia had just stolen the show from Hamlet and the others. She could not hope to be grand enough for this room, with its imposing walls of red and gold climbing up and up to a coffered, decorated ceiling, but she could at least be the more striking in her simplicity.

She'd chosen her airiest muslin today, an unpatterned ivory whose tissue-light outermost layer followed her through the curtsy with tiny delays and hesitations, like a double handful of swansdown making its way to earth. When she rose, the lady seated on the sofa nearest the hearth—by age and bearing, almost certainly Lady Harringdon—was eyeing her with a faint smile of approval.

"She's pretty. What did your man give for her name?" This was a much older lady, in peacock colors with a turban, occupying a chair at the countess's left and peering at Kate through a quizzing glass. The youngest of the callers—seated on a sofa opposite Lady Harringdon's with a woman of the right age to be her mother—threw a smile to the new arrival, a certain rueful spark in her eye suggesting that she, too, had heard her person evaluated at a volume not so confidential as the speaker supposed.

Likely this visitor hadn't been called pretty. Her chin had a receding tendency and her forehead was overhigh. The smile bespoke an agreeable disposition, however, as well as suggesting the reconciliation to a want of beauty that one so often found in girls whom Nature had not conspicuously blessed.

Pity. If they'd met at Miss Lowell's, Kate would have seen to it that the girl made the most of those lively eyes. She'd prescribe the wearing of blue in proximity to the face, to begin. A rearrangement of the hair, allowing curls to fall across the forehead, would bring a better proportion to her features and almost entirely overshadow that shortcoming of chin.

But this was not her errand here, and her attention must rather go to her aunt.

"Miss Westbrook is her name," the countess repeated to the turbaned lady, who frowned and moved her glass from one eye to the other.

"Westbrook." She studied Kate fiercely. "Is she one of Richard's girls?"

"No, she's a Miss Westbrook who hasn't visited here before. Come and sit down, dear." Lady Harringdon patted the empty place beside her. "Miss Smith was just preparing to give us an amusing account of last Sunday, when Sir George Bigby took her driving in Hyde Park."

Miss Smith, the lady of faint chin, leaned a bit forward, her eyes crinkling at the corners. "Well, I cannot promise the story will be amusing—"

"No, it will. I insist upon it." Lady Harringdon delivered this edict in apparent earnestness, pointing at Miss Smith with her closed fan. "Miss Westbrook, it's my pleasure today to make you known to Mrs. Smith and Miss Smith, of South Audley Street, as well as to her ladyship the dowager countess of Harringdon."

Kate nearly stumbled as she took her place on the sofa. The lady with the quizzing glass was Papa's mother, and her own grandmother. Had it not occurred to her, when the young lady in ivory muslin proved not to be a daughter of Richard, that she might be a daughter of Charles?

Did she even know Charles had children? They hadn't spoken in many years, but it was the sort of thing Kate had always assumed a mother would want to know.

For the entirety of Miss Smith's tale—which, as she'd warned, did not prove amusing, the only twist in the narrative occurring when one of the horses halted to munch on a shrub on the side of the road and then showed a disinclination to move again—she stole sideways glances at the two ladies Harringdon. The countess, she could now see, had a small red-and-white spaniel on her lap and was using her fan to direct a gentle breeze upon the creature as she listened, all gratifying attention, to Miss Smith. She even laughed once or twice, with an unfeigned enjoyment that could be accounted for only by the fact that she'd resolved in advance to find the story amusing.

The dowager listened, too, the furrows in her brow deepening when Lady Harringdon laughed. "I fear I missed the joke," she leaned over to murmur, loudly, when Miss Smith's silence indicated there was no more story to come. "Was it to do with the horses, or with the gentleman himself?"

"There wasn't a joke, precisely." Lady Harringdon sent a kindly smile to Miss Smith, as if to reassure her that her tale had been a success. "Rather there was a general air of mishap attending the outing from start to finish. The humor was cumulative in nature, one might say. And so, Miss Smith." She plied her fan for a dramatic few beats, causing several of the spaniel's silky hairs to lift and fall again. "Having now spoken with Sir George at Lady Stapleton's ball, this drive of which you've told us, and, if I recall correctly, a pair of morning calls, what are your impressions of the man? Has he any qualities that particularly recommend him to a young lady's affections?"

In among Miss Smith's tactful answers, and the remarks of everyone else, a few things became clear. First, that Sir George was too old for a lady of Miss Smith's years: references to his being "worthy," "wise," and "distinguished" left little doubt of that. Second, that Mrs. Smith believed it an advantageous match.

And third, and most pertinent to Kate's errand here, was the fact that she'd guessed rightly at her aunt's fondness for matchmaking. Lady Harringdon entered into the matter of Sir George with all the authority of a woman who'd married off six daughters, one of them to a duke, and also with an obvious concern for the happiness of Miss Smith. If Kate was reading the situation correctly, the countess thought the man no great prospect for a young lady and meant to sow doubt among both Smith women as to the merits of the match.

Whether the dowager had any opinions on the subject, Kate could not say. The elder lady seemed often to not be following the conversation, despite her sedulous use of the quizzing glass. Once or twice she looked as though she was not altogether sure of who these people were, and how they'd come to be in her parlor. Which was no longer her parlor, after all, but Lady Harringdon's.

Sorrow stole in among Kate's thoughts like a blanket of fog. Papa, not having spoken to any of his family in so long, would have no way of knowing his mother had grown so frail. Maybe he wouldn't care by now. The dowager countess's confusion over the name Westbrook took on a new poignancy, too. What if the memory of her second son had faded away altogether?

"What would you say, Miss Westbrook?" Lady Harringdon's voice broke suddenly into her melancholy reverie.

Kate marshaled her attention on her aunt, groping for the most recent thread of discussion. This was why she'd come here. She had a clear purpose. Sentiment might lie somewhere behind that purpose, but she must not let sentiment deflect her from her course.

The countess had turned her head to speak, ending with an inquisitive tilt. She had a long, elegant neck, and one could easily imagine her perfecting this move before her dressing-table mirror in younger days. "Can a young lady be satisfied with a distinguished gentleman who is no capable whip?" her aunt went on. "Or do you demand a fellow whose skill with the ribbons must turn every lady's head in envy when he takes you for a drive?"

Now came her chance to impress Lady Harringdon with her good sense; that was to say, with her endorsement of the countess's opinions. She tilted her head in imitation of her aunt's posture—she, too, had a neck worth showing off, and a mirror to practice before—and pursed her lips, to look thoughtful. "Speaking only in the abstract, because I would not presume to venture an opinion on any person I haven't met, I must say I do give some weight to a gentleman's competence with the reins. Of course his character, his respectability, his conduct in society are all more important signifiers of his worth than whether he can drive four-in-hand." This for the benefit of Mrs. Smith, whose face had grown increasingly grave as Lady Harringdon had discounted the merits of Sir George.

She paused for breath, and also to let her listeners know a shift in tone was coming. "I cannot help wondering about a gentleman's diligence, however; about his capacity for application, when I hear he hasn't mastered one of these common masculine pursuits. Particularly in the case of an older man, who would have had ample time, one presumes, to practice. Any man, whether he begins with a natural talent or not, can become a competent driver with enough practice. Or so I've always believed." She turned her hands palm up where they lay in her lap, a kind of shrug in miniature. "Again,

I intend no reference to the recent example. A single incident of horses straying into the shrubbery tells us nothing, I'm sure. I don't doubt such mishaps occasionally befall even the most expert and experienced of drivers."

Thus did she neatly rake the soil over Lady Harringdon's sown doubts, and sprinkle a little water as well. Though if she were to hazard a guess, she'd say Miss Smith had already cultivated doubts of her own. The young lady was working to contain a smile, the glint in her eye suggesting she knew exactly what the countess and Miss Westbrook had been about.

"A girl with her beauty can afford to be particular about men." The dowager studied Kate through her glass, and apparently meant this observation for Lady Harringdon, though it carried to everyone in the room. "The other sort might not have that luxury."

Miss Smith lost the battle with her smile, and had to duck her head and feign an urgent interest in straightening her gloves. Really, there was no reason on earth for a lady with such merry spirits, and such fine eyes, to throw herself away on a stolid old man who didn't even know how to handle a horse. Someone ought to cut her hair and put her in a smart blue spencer, without delay.

"You speak well, Miss Westbrook." The countess, though not equipped with a glass, was considering her with a jewel buyer's shrewd gaze.

She bowed her head to accept the compliment. She *had* expressed her opinion rather artfully, if she did say so herself. Mr. Blackshear in his wig and robes could scarcely have done better. If he came to dinner tomorrow she would tell him all about it.

He probably wouldn't come, though. Just when she'd been hopeful of repairing the damage done by their careless tongues the night before, that impertinent Miss Watson had broached the topic of his brother's marriage, bold as could be. Kate had felt his mortification as though it had been her own. She'd like to assure him that Viola and Sebastian had paid little heed to the conversation and missed overhearing the damning part, but she had a feeling he'd rather she not speak of it at all.

And she oughtn't to be frittering away even a moment of her first call in Harringdon House by thinking distracted thoughts of Mr. Blackshear. Here was her aunt, eyeing her in a way that very much suggested she was imagining the impression Kate would make in a ton ballroom. Perhaps reflecting, as well, on how delightful it would be to screen out suitors for a lady who might attract them like bees to a blossom, once she was granted the proper patronage.

"Well, Miss Smith, and Mrs. Smith." That quickly, Lady Harringdon's attention had gone elsewhere. "I think the best thing for Sir George would be a rival or two. Do you know whether he'll be at Lady Astley's rout on Tuesday?"

Lady Astley! Kate's pulse thrummed at the mention, and a veritable crater of yearning opened up in the middle of her chest. That this name, of all names, should be brought up here, so soon after its appearance in Westbrook dinner table conversation, seemed so fortuitous as to possibly indicate the machinations of fate. Surely she was meant to go to this rout. Indeed perhaps that had been the plan taking shape in Lady Harringdon's mind, while she scrutinized her, and that explained her suddenly addressing the Smith ladies on this subject.

A bit was said about Sir George, whose attendance appeared to be in doubt, and a bit about Lady Astley's excellent table, and her obliging habit of inviting only as many people as would fit comfortably in the Cranbourne House ballroom and the adjacent room where cards were played. But before anything could be said of including Miss Westbrook in the party, a clock chimed, and Mrs. and Miss Smith rose to take their leave.

The dowager countess made to rise, too, slowly and with visible effort. Kate was on her feet and one step toward her grandmother before she caught herself. That wouldn't be done, in this house. It wouldn't be a young lady caller's place to help the dowager stand.

And indeed there were men coming in now for the purpose, and Lady Harringdon was touching the dowager's wrist. "Stay just a moment, your ladyship." The countess spoke kindly, gesturing toward the door. "Do you see, here is Lord Harringdon come to help you from your chair and to your room."

"Lord Harringdon. Very good." The dowager settled back down into her chair. She appeared a little unsure of who Lord Harringdon was. Even when he came to her chair, he at one side and a footman at the other, nothing passed on the old woman's face that would suggest she was looking at her son. So maybe Papa wasn't the only one who had lost the acquaintance of his mother.

Kate stood and waited, since the Smith ladies were doing so, for the dowager to precede them from the room. Once, the earl's glance connected with hers and he nodded. She dipped her chin and averted her eyes, suddenly shy of watching him support this unsteady parent who must have carried him about in her arms when he was small.

"Miss Westbrook, you will stay a bit longer, if you please." Lady Harringdon's quiet command recalled her to herself, and to her mission here. "You may be seated."

She sat. She and the countess would speak privately now. She must shake off the cobwebs of sentiment and have all her wits at the ready.

Mrs. and Miss Smith said their good-byes and made their exit through the double doors, Lady Harringdon nodding after them as they went. "Lovely girl," she said once they'd passed out of hearing. "A temperament beyond anything. It's a pity she isn't better looking."

For half an instant Kate was taken aback. But really, hadn't she herself made a similar judgment on Miss Smith's appearance, and lingered over the faults of her chin and forehead? She couldn't very well be appalled at her aunt for harboring like opinions and voicing them in private.

She, too, pointed her chin in the direction the Smiths had gone. "She has remarkably fine eyes." Three years at Miss Lowell's had made her fluent in this sort of discourse. The trick was to tread a tightrope, neither indulging in unbecoming criticism of another lady, nor seeming to reproach the other speaker for doing so. "And her manner, as your ladyship observes, is altogether congenial."

"Too congenial, if we're to be frank. She may think she's being kind to Sir George Bigby, but I'll wager he takes her good nature for personal encouragement. He'll be the more disappointed when she finally refuses him." She snapped her fan shut and let it dangle from her wrist, hoisting up the spaniel to direct her words to its indignant face. "Besides, her kindness teaches him to overestimate his own charms, and now he'll set his sights too high with the next young lady he courts. Ladies owe it to other ladies to help gentlemen to a more accurate valuation." She set the spaniel down. "Wouldn't you say so, Miss Westbrook?"

"I think I must defer to your ladyship's wisdom." A modest smile here, accompanied by a modest casting of her eyes toward the carpet. That the topic had moved so quickly to courtship was a very good sign. "Your success in matrimony, both in your own marriage and in the excellent matches of all your daughters, speaks for itself."

"You flatter me now. But you do so with a respectable

amount of skill." Unaffected good humor lit her eyes. "What of you, my dear? How does so beautiful and well-mannered a young lady come to be yet unmarried? Never tell me you haven't had offers."

She hadn't, in fact. It was a point of pride. She always watched out for any serious tendency in a man's attentions, and moved swiftly to discourage him before he could say or do such things as he might later have to remember with mortification.

This, Lady Harringdon didn't need to know. "I'm conscious of my Westbrook blood, and what is due to it." She held her head a little higher and felt her voice resonate under her ribs. "I had rather not marry at all than marry a person unworthy of my antecedents."

"A pity your father wasn't of like mind." The countess answered without hesitation. "Recall that only half your antecedents can be traced through him. The other half, we needn't speak of but to acknowledge that they render impossible any match worthy of the Westbrook name. A pity, as I said." She shook her head, all genteel regret. "You'd have been the diamond of your Season."

Kate sat perfectly still. She would not let her composure falter, for all that her aunt's speech hit her like a pail of cold water dumped over her head.

She'd been foolish. She'd been too sure of herself. Her overconfident imagination had credited Lady Harringdon with every plan and motive most flattering to herself, when she'd had not a scrap of evidence to support those fancies. Mr. Blackshear had warned her she was building cloud castles, and Mr. Blackshear had been right.

Deep within her, the very kernel of her pride rebelled. She hadn't planned so long for this chance only to admit defeat at the first reversal. If her cloud castles wouldn't support her, she would build the slower, more solid kind, one brick at a time.

"Without doubt life would be easier if I cared nothing for my better connections. To choose at every juncture the conduct and manners one knows to be right, brings little reward when society's perception of a lady begins and ends with the fact of her mother's having come from a family of actors." She lifted a shoulder, to show how utterly used to the condition she'd grown. "One does at least escape the vice of self-pity, encountering so ready a supply of it from other people—from other ladies, I should say. Gentlemen aren't so solicitous."

Gentlemen find nothing to pity in me. Let *that* truth ripple out in silence until it washed up against the William Kent walls. If she lagged behind her Westbrook cousins in every other worldly measure, she would cling the more ferociously to the one advantage she possessed. She knew very well, as must Lady Harringdon, that no daughter of this house had ever been called the diamond of her Season.

Her aunt considered her, lips pursed and eyelids half lowered. She might toss her out for impertinence now, or, if Kate had gambled correctly. . . .

"Proud as any Westbrook, aren't you?" One corner of her mouth twitched with the suggestion of a knowing smile. "But it's a becoming sort of pride, I'll grant. You may chafe at your misbegotten station—so would I, in your place—but you're scrupulous about staying within it. Your notes to me, over the years, have been everything correct. Never presumptuous or insinuating. That's not lost on me."

"Your ladyship is kind. I'm deeply sensible of the honor you've done me in inviting me here today." She fixed her attention on the spaniel and waited. Lady Harringdon had more to say. She could feel it. *That's not lost on me* was a beginning, a segue, a justification for something to follow, and shame on her if she now let a second pail of cold water catch her by surprise.

"I'm kind indeed to all who deserve it, I hope." Her aunt's voice held such cheerful purpose that Kate could not keep from looking up. "I have a proposal for you, my dear, and I shall begin by asking whether you're at liberty next Tuesday night."

Her heart beat hard in spite of her resolve to not hope. She'd known there must be some element of fate in the mention of Lady Astley's rout. "I'm quite at liberty, and at your service if you wish." That stubborn audacious corner of her brain lost no time in leaping to the question of what she might wear.

"That's precisely what I wish. I wonder if it might please you to accompany me to the rout you heard us speaking of." The countess beamed, looking for one perfect instant like a benevolent fairy in a fable.

Then she spoke on. "I've a mind to find you a post as companion to a grand lady, and what better way to begin than by taking you to a gathering where you can make an impression with your charming manners?"

Kate forced a smile, blinking several times. Dear Lord, how had she put herself in the path of disappointment *again*? And so soon after the first time, too?

"I hadn't . . ." She scrabbled after every bit of the poise that had run away like quicksilver dropped on the floor. "I'd had no thought of being a companion." *Companion.* The word had a sour taste in her mouth, and a desiccated feel. *Companion* was a sad parasitical existence borne by a lady who had absolutely no other options. A step above governess, perhaps, but not a great step. *Companion* was no life for a girl whose beauty would have made her the diamond of her Season.

"Indeed, with your parentage, you'd have had little chance of securing a post." Lady Harringdon scratched behind the spaniel's ears, the very picture of gracious condescencion. Clearly she thought Kate was overwhelmed by the generosity of the offer. "However I think my patronage may make all the difference. If you're seen attending me at this rout, there will be people who will accept you without question. My approval carries much weight among people of the ton."

Every sentence landed like a slap. *Yes,* her aunt's patronage could make all the difference. *Yes,* she could be accepted without question. *Yes,* she'd hoped to advance herself with the weight of Lady Harringdon's approval. All this, she'd dreamed of. Just not with the word *companion.* Would she even be welcome to call here anymore, once she'd been relegated to that lowly office?

Would she be welcome to call if she refused?

"I'm afraid I'm not familiar with the duties of a companion." The word's flavor didn't improve with repetition.

"Thus the rout. You can begin to learn."

"I shall have to ask my parents for permission." That would buy her time to decide what to do.

"By all means. I trust they'll see what a singular opportunity this is." Her aunt sat distant as a queen in her corner of the sofa. Beyond her was all the splendor of this room and the house's other rooms, the staircase, the columns, the lintels, and Kate could only feel that everything she wanted had moved further out of reach since she'd come to call.

Chapter Five

NICK WENT to the Westbrooks' for dinner on Saturday. To avoid the family would have been cowardice, and the half truths and misrepresentations he'd dealt to Lord Barclay had left him feeling quite cowardly enough. If Miss Westbrook or one of her siblings showed an inclination to broach uncomfortable subjects, he could firmly and politely decline that conversation. That was his right. And while he was about it, he could set the pattern for how he intended his relations with Miss Westbrook to go on: cordial, but with an appropriate degree of distance. If he was to make the advances he hoped for through this connection with Lord Barclay, he needed to conduct himself as became a distinguished gentleman of nine and twenty. It was well past time he curtailed those habits of familiarity and careless flirtation that had led him into trouble the last time he was here.

In the Gower Street entry hall he'd just handed off his hat and coat, and was preparing to follow the footman upstairs, when down came Miss Westbrook herself. She had no shaft of sunlight to pause in, as she'd had at the Old Bailey. Her gown was a plain one such as ladies wore for a morning at home. Some inward preoccupation had put a crease in her brow and pursed her lips, robbing them of their usual sweet fullness. No one catching a first glimpse of her in this moment would mistake her for an angel or a goddess.

And still, her beauty went through him like a fever chill, temporarily scattering his thoughts.

She glanced up and saw him. "Mr. Blackshear." Her face lit with surprise and pleasure. Two steps above the one where he stood, she halted. "I wasn't sure of your coming. I'm so pleased you did. I told Father all about the case you argued and I know he's eager to hear your account."

"Forgive my having left my attendance in doubt." He girded himself. If she was to speak of what had happened at the Old Bailey, she might well do it now.

"Oh, we're very informal on Saturdays, you know." She waved a hand, as if to dismiss his concerns. "Already there are two gentlemen in the drawing room who I don't believe were invited at all."

"I see. Are you going out?" He nodded toward the foot of the stairs, to remind her of her downward trajectory. "To call upon your countess aunt, perhaps?" That was probably a bit too teasing and familiar. With practice, he'd strike the right note.

"No." The pleasure in her face dimmed somewhat. "No, I'm absenting myself from the drawing room only for a little while." She studied the bottom-most stair but didn't move, save for one slight bounce on the balls of her feet. On a higher stair the footman stood still, waiting, with that patience common to servants, for this conversation to conclude.

Abruptly Miss Westbrook looked up. "I'm going to sit on the bench below for a few minutes. Might you like to bear me company?"

He really oughtn't. If he wanted to enforce a decorous distance in their relation, then certainly refusing to sit alone with her, away from the company, would make an excellent start.

He was curious, though, to know what accounted for that dimming he'd noted in her eyes, as well as to know why she'd forsaken the drawing room to sit on a bench in the entry hall. He bowed and took a step back down the stairs.

Miss Westbrook dismissed the footman and led the way to the bench. It stood at the back of the entry hall, halfway under the stairs, giving anyone who sat there a view of the front door. It wasn't secluded, really: between that front door and another set of stairs leading presumably down to the kitchen, the location assured intermittent traffic. Still, he preferred to stand against the wall and leave her the entirety of the seat.

"Why have we retreated to this hall?" He'd start with what he hoped was the easier subject. "Are you avoiding the young men who weren't invited?"

"Not altogether." She smoothed her skirts, looking slightly embarrassed. "It's been brought to my attention that I sometimes distract the young men who come to call here."

"Ah." He folded his arms and directed a solemn look to the floor. This would have been an ideal subject on which to plague her. Thus it made a good test of his resolve. "I collect, from your abandoning the drawing room, that you find the allegation to have merit."

"It's very tedious of them." She glanced overhead, as if she could see through the floor to the offending callers. "I expect to be noticed—it would be disingenuous of me to claim I did not—but I see no reason why they must continue to give their attention to me, as I'm told they do, when they ought to be listening to interesting and edifying things that other people have to say."

"I see." This sounded like the complaint of Miss Viola, who was certainly the Westbrook most likely to be desirous of an attentive audience at any time. "Do you believe they're being edified as we speak? Now that they don't have to contend with the distraction of your presence?"

She looked up at him and smiled, and he knew she was picturing, as was he, her sister delivering an oration to a group of befuddled young law students.

In spite of rigorous intentions he smiled back, and several seconds passed in which they shared the silent joke.

She was the first to look away. "I should mention that you were invoked as an exception, as a guest who pays proper attention to all the family." She folded her hands neatly in her lap. "No one thinks you foolish or tedious."

"I do try not to be tedious. But I'm afraid I'm not always above foolishness." He let those words stand. She would know to what he referred.

He'd said something similar when they'd seen each other at the courthouse. Some slender hint at an apology. For the sake of discretion, he ought really to have left it at that.

But the effects of her smile lingered, filling him with odd ideas. What if he owned the extent of his impropriety and made a full, frank apology? That might be the best insurance against his ever committing such a breach again. It might reassure her, too, in a way that vague remarks about foolishness and forgetting himself could not.

"Miss Westbrook." He stepped away from the wall, pivoting to face her. "I don't want you to think—that is, I don't want you ever to be uneasy in my presence, wondering at the turn of my thoughts. May I be perfectly candid, just for a moment?" So much for distance and reserve. But if this put them back on solid footing with each other, it would do just as well.

She nodded at him, her dark blue eyes wide with apprehension.

He took a breath. "The perfectly candid truth is that, like every other young man who visits this house, I notice your beauty. Sometimes to the point of distraction. Lord knows I'd like to be inured to it after three years, but I'm afraid I'm not."

"I see," she murmured. She studied her clasped hands, turning them over in her lap. Then her eyes, grave and luminous, rose once more to his. She was preparing, no doubt, to answer his candor with a frank reminder that he mustn't hope.

No need of that. "We wouldn't suit, I know." He half raised a hand to forestall her speaking. "Not only because you've set your sights on a more rarefied existence than I shall ever be able to provide, but because I have aspirations of my own. And—I trust this won't offend you—you're not the woman to enter into those hopes with me, and stand at my side through thick and thin, as I would desire a wife to do." That was important to remember. It wasn't just a matter of his not measuring up to her exacting standards: neither would she make a satisfactory partner for him. "I apologize for the impertinent familiarity with which I spoke that night, and I assure you it's no signifier of any sentiments or intentions that need cause you concern. Only the commonplace, graceless response of a susceptible man to an exceedingly beautiful girl."

There. He'd confessed what she'd surely already known. And now that he'd said it out loud, it seemed possible that even this much might cease to be true. He might yet become inured to her charms, just through the exercise of this unromantic bluntness.

"I don't think you're so very susceptible." She smoothed her skirts again, eyes averted. "We've already established that you're attentive to everyone in the family."

"Well, thank you for that defense of my dignity." Lord, he felt ten times better than he had when he'd walked in the door. He went to the bench and sat, at a good respectable distance from her. "Now let me be forward on another subject: why did your spirits sink when I asked if you were going to call on your aunt? Did your father forbid your going?"

She twisted to face him, no doubt startled that he should have perceived her mood. Then she frowned at the expanse of bench that divided him from her. "No, in fact I called on Lady Harringdon yesterday."

"She disappointed your hopes." He'd expected this. He'd even warned her of it. But he wouldn't feel any triumph if he'd been right.

"It was an enjoyable call and I made an excellent impression on the countess." She tilted her head, eyes still downcast. "So excellent, in fact, that she's proposed to help me to a post as a lady's companion."

"Ah. I'm sorry."

She smiled, bitterly, and now she met his eyes. "It was my own fault, at least in part. I had to go and say something about how I had rather never marry at all than marry a man unworthy of my better connections."

He could imagine that only too well. "And she, assuming you had no chance of that worthy match, concluded that a position as companion to some grand lady would best serve your pride and dignity."

"You were right at every turn. You tried to caution me against grandiose expectations, and I was too proud to listen."

He didn't like to see her so humbled. Her vanity might be an aggravation indeed, but it was hers, to be eschewed or moderated when the wisdom of age and experience prompted her to do so. It wasn't this aunt's place to rob her of her pride.

"This is a setback, to be sure." He leaned forward, propping his elbows on his knees and clasping his hands with steepled fingers. From this position he had to tilt his head to address her. "But if you will let it spell your defeat, I shall have to say I've misjudged you entirely. What answer did you give her, as to the offer to find you a position?"

Her chin lifted a fraction of an inch, and a slight catch came in her breathing. She hadn't had the smallest expectation of his responding so. Really, had she supposed he would gloat over the disappointment of her hopes?

"I told her I must speak to my mother and father. But I haven't spoken to them, because I cannot see . . ." She shook her head. "I confess it does feel very like a defeat. Taking a post as a lady's companion is as good as an admission to all the world that you've gone on the shelf. But declining the offer will almost certainly put an end to the connection. And the connection is important to me." Something new came into her voice, something low and ardent. "Not only for the reasons you're used to teasing me about. I want my family to—" She jumped as the door knocker sounded, a jarring cacophony from this distance. "Bother. More callers." In an instant she was on her feet, seizing his hand and tugging him after her while she ducked under the stairs and out of view of anyone standing in the front doorway.

A sense memory flared to life and went sizzling through his veins: a dinner party, some years ago at his eldest brother's house. He'd been seated beside a supposedly respectable widow, Mrs. Simcox, and halfway through the fish course her unshod foot had begun rubbing deliberately up and down the length of his boot.

Fresh out of Cambridge he'd been, serious and studious and very little experienced in these matters, but he'd known, at that first stroke of stockinged instep, what was his for the taking. With her ankle twined around his he'd consumed the mutton that followed the fish; with her knee hooked boldly over his own he'd downed two glasses of wine, nerves all alive in scandalized anticipation.

How exactly had the next part happened, after dinner? Had he gone out to use the necessary? Had she slipped from the company to lie in wait? At all events, they'd somehow or another been out in the same hallway, and the important point was that she'd grasped his hand, unspeaking, and whisked him to the wall, in a place where the stairs hid them from view.

The rest had been madness, imprudence, exquisite iniquity, right there in Andrew's house where a servant might have walked by. He'd had to completely revise all his notions of respectable widows that night.

"I'm sorry," hissed Miss Westbrook beside him, wiggling her fingers free of his. Sorry for taking that liberty with his hand and his person, she meant, and hauling him into this improper proximity. Side by side they stood, backs to the wall, his right knee flush against their erstwhile bench and her left foot toeing the top step of that flight down to the kitchens. Her right shoulder touched his bicep and her arm pressed against his, all the way down to the backs of their hands. He felt every fraction of an inch of the contact, his nerves as alive and awake as they'd been that night with Mrs. Simcox.

Damn his stupid susceptibility. He oughtn't to be having this response. He ought to be thinking disinterested, brotherly thoughts. Working up advice to give her about Lady Harringdon, or something of the sort.

Footsteps sounded right over their heads as a servant descended the stairs. Miss Westbrook's arm jostled against his as she threw him a glance. Her lips were twisted tight, keeping laughter in. She thought it a jolly predicament. She obviously had not the least idea of what went on between men and women who ducked into hiding under stairs.

If he were to steal a kiss . . . which he would not . . . all he'd require was a half twist of the upper body and an inclination of some eight or ten inches, down and across. Fingers under her chin, tipping her face to the proper angle.

He wouldn't do that. This was a test of his resolve, his self-command, his respect for Miss Westbrook, and his regard for her parents. He was not going to succumb.

Noises from outside intruded as the front door was presumably swung open. Carriage wheels. Distant voices. The clicking heels of whatever caller was now being admitted. A draft came, too, an outdoor breeze turning domestic and mundane. He felt a shiver run up the short-sleeved arm pressed against his before he felt the chill himself.

Quietly as he could, he unbuttoned his coat. This would be his response to the shiver of lovely Miss Katherina Westbrook's arm against his: not to seize her, but to stop her being cold.

He shrugged out of his coat. The kind of man who'd kiss an innocent under the staircase would wear a flawlessly tailored coat, with sleeves and shoulders so fitted that he must rustle a great deal in removing it. His own coat came off with scarcely a sound.

He pivoted halfway and set his free hand on her upper arm to pivot her, too, so they stood face-to-face. She'd succeeded in swallowing her laughter: her mouth was full and soft once more. She looked up at him, trusting, in perfect dependency on his honorable intentions.

The stair treads began creaking as the new caller made his way upward, and Nick swung his coat over Miss Westbrook's shoulders and settled it there. That would be the extent of intimacy between them. He'd been tested, and he'd prevailed.

He pivoted back and touched his shoulder blades to the wall. The footsteps had reached the next floor and gone off down the hall. They could speak again. "Did your aunt have a particular lady in mind, who would engage you as a companion?" He would never betray the least sign of having been tempted, that half minute or so.

"Not at present. She proposes to take me to some parties where I may meet grand ladies and presumably impress them with my manners, that they might mention me to any acquaintance who is in want of a companion." She huddled deeper into his coat, clutching at the buttons and buttonholes to wrap herself snug. She, too, put her back to the wall. With the caller gone upstairs there was no reason for them to remain there, shoulder to shoulder in the small shadowed space. But she didn't stir, so neither did he.

She cast her eyes to the floor. "It hurts my pride, Mr. Blackshear." Her voice, too, sank to somewhere near the level of their shoe soles. "And it doesn't serve my purpose. I'd thought of her taking me to balls and routs and making introductions, yes, but I'd supposed she'd be introducing me to gentlemen. I've pinned all my hopes on making a good marriage."

Yes. To think of and speak of her eventual marriage would reinforce his triumph over temptation. Already he was beginning to feel an appropriate friendly interest in her fortunes. "You have stringent ideas of what constitutes a good marriage. Myself, I know of no better union than the one to which you owe your existence."

"My parents have a happy marriage. That's not the same thing."

He tipped his head back, to frown up at the underside of the stairs. She was young, and full of feminine ambition, and she would doubtless learn in time how well her parents' marriage compared to many of those around her. He'd refrain from correcting her now.

Besides, he couldn't altogether condemn her unsentimental view. Will and his wife, after all, probably had a happy marriage. That didn't make it a good one.

Not that the two cases were comparable. In only one of them had the bridegroom wed a Cyprian after poaching her from another man.

"You may go ahead and call me heartless." She didn't look at him. She was misinterpreting his silence. "I know you think it."

"Not today." He folded his arms, careful not to dislodge his coat from her shoulder. "I think you ought to go to those parties, Miss Westbrook. You'd need practice, wouldn't you, before you were ready to assume a post? That would give you two or three parties, at least, in which to catch the eye of a marriage-minded duke."

She was smiling now, and beginning to look more like herself. "Are you the same man who warned me against hoping to be acknowledged by my own aunt? And now you would have me go into a ballroom as a companion-in-training and set my sights on a duke?"

"I grant it won't be as easy as it would if you were an invited guest, with her name announced." He could feel the tide turning, almost as if he argued before a jury. "But as I recall, you don't demand that things be easy before undertaking them. And if there's any lady in the world I'd wager on to capture a duke with only her personal charms for a lure, it's surely you." He'd been addressing her sidelong; now he turned his head, to send the conclusion of his argument by the shortest possible path. "I don't deny the odds against you are long. But the fact is, if you're in that ballroom, you have a chance. If you stay home, you haven't."

Gratitude flowed from her, filling the space between

them. "I don't need a duke, you know. I'm perfectly willing to settle for a marquess."

"Now, there's the brash, presumptuous Miss Westbrook I know." He brought his shoulders off the wall. He didn't have to be entirely reserved and distant, after all. Indeed why should he? She'd confided in him a deal today, and he'd made his bold confessions, too. Thus men and women might do, once youthful one-sided infatuation had bloomed and withered and been swept away into the gutter. "Now shall we go upstairs? I'd like to pay my respects to the rest of your family. And perhaps we'd better rescue the young men from their edification."

She half turned away, that he might slide his coat off her shoulders, and if he had a brief vision of leaning in to kiss the bare nape of her neck, well, it was no more than any man in his position would have done. The vision flitted through and past. By the time she'd turned back around to face him, he'd wiped all trace of its existence from his eyes and his thoughts alike.

AT DINNER she sat between a Mr. Sterling and a Mr. Green, both of them new to Papa's favor, both young enough for all manner of foolish fancy, both showing the usual, wearying signs of inclination to be smitten with her. Mr. Blackshear sat by Papa. They were speaking of barrister business, anyone could tell. Mr. Blackshear had a certain animation in his features—in his eyes, his mouth, the emphatic dive or arching of his brows—that appeared only when he got on that subject, which of course was the subject he liked best. His attention didn't wander her way.

She knew his scent now. A plain clean soap. His coat had brought it to her notice, and left traces on her shoulders. If she concentrated she could still catch the notes.

He didn't go in for fragrance, as some men did. Perhaps he followed Mr. Brummell's regimen of a daily bath, instead of the usual cloaking of one's odors in perfume. Though it was difficult to imagine he paid much heed to any of the Beau's dictums. Likely he disdained the man for living profligately and then fleeing his debts, if he hadn't already disdained him for an excessive preoccupation with the trivial matter of personal style. And that was presuming he even knew who Beau Brummell was. He very well might not.

In any event, Mr. Blackshear's coat had smelled of soap. So had he, in those few minutes she'd stood with her arm pressed to his, confined with him under the stairs. That was the nearest she'd ever been to a man. She'd heard his breaths, and felt them in the steady slight advance and retreat of his arm against hers.

"Are you fond of novels, Miss Westbrook?" Mr. Sterling, at her right, did use fragrance. Sandalwood. One didn't have to stand in contact with him to detect it. "My sisters are ferocious readers. Whenever I dine at home they must be telling me all about the latest volume they've taken out. I calculate within another three months they'll have read all that the subscription library has to offer."

"Not quite all, I should think." Viola, sitting directly across, was her usual impatient self. Unimpressed with these new visitors, but taking enough of an interest to point out their errors. "Most libraries of my experience offer books of history, philosophy, economic theory, all manner of topics, in addition to the surfeit of novels. Some ladies find these books make a welcome change from the lurid and fantastical tales they're expected to prefer."

"Novels aren't all lurid." Kate turned her smile, quick and warm, on Mr. Sterling before he could have time to absorb her sister's ungracious remarks. "I have *Pride and Prejudice* out just now. No crumbling castles or spirits wandering the moors, but a fine sketch of country village life, with many amusing parts. I'd recommend that to your sisters, if they haven't already read it."

"*Pride and Prejudice,*" Mr. Sterling repeated, before fishing a small book and pencil from one of his pockets and marking the title down. "*Pride and Prejudice,*" he said again.

"By the same accomplished lady who brought us *Sense and Sensibility.*" Mr. Green, on her left, contributed this to the proceedings, with an air of general authority and a faint aroma of lemon and cloves. "*Mansfield Park* as well, and then *Emma*. Beloved not only by gentlemen's sisters but by the Prince Regent himself. I commend your taste, Miss Westbrook." He raised his glass to her.

Viola's glance flicked from Kate to Mr. Green and his glass, to Mr. Sterling and his pencil, then back to Kate. She didn't roll or narrow her eyes, or put any particular twist in her mouth, but it was an eloquent look all the same.

Well, this was precisely why she'd spent that time downstairs in the entry hall. If Mr. Blackshear should glance this way they might share a second or two of recognition; of wry, private understanding.

He didn't, though. He was entirely occupied in relating something to Papa. He'd halted in the middle of cutting up his ham, and the knife in his right hand carved small circles in the air as he spoke, his wrist rotating as though he were physically reeling the story along.

She had some acquaintance with the knobby-boned contours of his left wrist. Not his right. They probably didn't differ in any way significant enough to note.

He'd seemed very little moved by his proximity with her, for all that he claimed to be susceptible. But then it wouldn't have been such a novelty to him as it had been to her. Doubtless he had acquaintance with women who would indulge him in all the proximity he'd like. Most men did, by the time they were approaching the age of thirty. For ladies it was different.

She ran her left hand up her right arm to the elbow and back. It had been an extraordinary conversation, really. Not only the part in which she'd stood with her arm pressed to his, but the earlier part that had begun with his asking permission to be candid.

A gentleman oughtn't to say those things to a lady and yet . . . such frankness proved unexpectedly reassuring. To suspect a man of harboring an attraction, and to be always weighing his words and looks for evidence, was after all a good deal more unsettling than simply to have it acknowledged. She would never wonder whether there was a secret subtext to his conversation now. They could speak openly, safe in the shared understanding that they did not suit.

She reached for her glass. "How many sisters do you have, Mr. Sterling? And are there brothers as well, or are you woefully outnumbered as our Sebastian is here?" There'd be time enough later for speaking with Mr. Blackshear. The task immediately before her was to make these new callers feel at ease. And when they'd taken their leave, all glutted with Westbrook hospitality, she would summon up her courage and talk to Mama and Papa about Lady Harringdon.

Chapter Six

"You're of age." Kate could tell Mama was piqued when she spoke in clipped, unmodulated syllables. "If you came to us and said you'd had an offer and meant to marry, we could not prevent the match, regardless our opinion of the man involved. I think the same rule must apply in the question of your taking a position." No hint of tension showed in her face, nor in her posture, nor in the grip of her fingers on the saucer holding her teacup. "Your father and I can express our reservations on the arrangement—and I assure you we will—but in the end I believe the decision must be yours."

Kate rested her hands on the arms of her chair and let her fingers tighten. A histrionic parent might have been easier to face, or else one who made a great show of her mild temper in hopes of inducing filial guilt—but Mama, for all her thespian experience, scorned such indulgences. No matter how she might be angered or offended, she consulted Reason above all else, and this, naturally, made a Westbrook child feel that much more reprehensible for having offended or angered her. "I'm not decided on taking a position. Only on going to some parties, if I may, and seeing to what sort of people I'm introduced." Better to leave out the part about charming a duke, for now.

"I don't understand, Kate." Papa leaned on the back of Mama's chair, as he always liked to do when they were all in the parlor together. All the guests had gone save for Mr. Blackshear, who was turning pages for Bea at the pianoforte. "You know what your Westbrook relations are. They made wrong, unjust judgments on your mother's character based solely on the fact of her having been on the stage, and they've chosen to sustain that insult to her for twenty-three years. Why would you court the notice of such people?"

She frowned down at her right hand, relaxing the fingers and tightening them again. *No, I don't know them, not at all. Because you've never told us anything about them beyond how unjust they were to Mama. And that's not the entirety of who they are. If it were, you wouldn't have kept those letters.*

And I court their notice because I cannot afford your kind of pride. None of your daughters can. Beyond the piano, Rose sat on the sofa, her teeth absently worrying her lower lip as she worked at her embroidery frame. She hadn't reported any more pranks since the day of the knotted silks, but perhaps that was only the sign of a stauncher secrecy.

Kate willed her spine stiffer. "I wish our Westbrook relations could have been so fair-minded as to see that a woman might be an actress and still be a lady of virtue. Their failure to do so indicates, to me, not malice or ill will but a want of imagination. A want of the courage that would allow them to slip the rigid grasp of convention and think for themselves." *And they are family.* She didn't know how to even begin to speak of Lord Harringdon and the dowager.

"Even if I were to concede that point, again I should have to ask what could compel you to seek a connection with them." Father, as always, was warming to the debate. "I'd hoped we had raised you to prize fair-mindedness, imagination, and independent thought above the purely superficial sort of consequence Lord and Lady Harringdon represent."

"Are you speaking of Lady Harringdon?" Viola swiveled to look over the back of the sofa where she sat and put aside her book. She'd shown very little interest in the descriptions of Harringdon House that were all Kate had disclosed of yesterday's call. Here, clearly, was a more promising subject. "What has she done; offered to nod at you when you pass on the street if you will repudiate our mother?"

And now every Westbrook in the room was privy to the conversation. Mr. Blackshear as well: he glanced over, his brow impressing itself with sympathetic concern. At least it looked like sympathetic concern; she would take it for that, and fortify her resolve with the idea of an understanding ally near at hand.

"She never asked me to repudiate anyone." She brought her attention back to her parents. "I sent her notes of congratulation on such occasions as seemed appropriate, and she invited me to call, and I think she'd like to do a service for our family. And so she's offered to bring me to some parties and introduce me to some of her acquaintance, that I can see what it would be like to be a lady's companion and decide whether such a position would suit me." That wasn't quite true. But if she said she was allowing Lady Harringdon to believe she'd made up her mind to take a companion post, she'd never be permitted to go.

"Companion? Good Lord." Vi folded her arms atop the sofa's back and rested her chin on one wrist, apparently settling in to watch the rest of this debased spectacle. "Mind you, I don't suppose a lady who takes a post as a companion really gives up much more of her autonomy than does a lady who marries. Where a wife has the advantage in consequence, the companion at least retains the integrity of her person."

This was what came of too little emphasis on narrow conventions, and too much encouragement given to imagination and independent thought: a daughter who felt free to spout off in mixed company about bodily integrity.

"I don't intend to give up any autonomy." Kate could feel a blush creeping from her cheeks to the tips of her ears. Studiously she kept her glance from the pianoforte. "As I said, I'm only accompanying my aunt to some social occasions. I'm not obliged to any more than that."

"What are these social occasions?" Mama's delicate brows drew a fraction of an inch nearer each other. "I'm not easy with the idea of your going into strange company—people whose names I'm sure I wouldn't even recognize—with a chaperone about whom we really know nothing at all."

"I wouldn't be doing anything that would require the services of a chaperone. I expect I would be at Lady Harringdon's side constantly. And the social occasions would be mostly private balls and card parties, all given by respectable people. I'm to go with her to a rout on Tuesday, if I might, at the home of that same Lord and Lady Astley whom we spoke about when Mr. Blackshear last came to dinner."

"Astley?" Mr. Blackshear still had one hand on the music book, though his attention had all gone this way. "Lord Barclay's brother and his wife, do you mean?"

She nodded. "It won't be a very large party. Just the marchioness and some of her friends. I'm sure they're all as respectable as can be." *And Mama said the decision was mine.* She thought those words but didn't speak them. She still had hope of gaining her point on more reasonable terms.

"Ah. I didn't realize there was to be a party." Mr. Blackshear looked at her parents. "I'll be there that same evening, meeting with Barclay. He invited me informally, so I didn't grasp the exact nature of the event."

"Indeed." Papa stepped away from Mama's chair. "Blackshear, will you grant me a word?" Mr. Blackshear left the piano, and a moment later both men were gone from the room.

"*That* can be nothing good." Viola twisted round and went back to her book. "If Mr. Blackshear knows his own interest he'll decline to be involved."

Decline to be involved in what, though? Kate watched the door through which the two men had gone, and wondered what Papa could possibly have in mind.

"I DON'T LIKE to ask this of you." Westbrook stood with his arms folded. They'd gone only to the end of the hall farthest from the parlor, so he must have had a brief conversation in mind. "I trust you won't hesitate to refuse, if it's too great an imposition."

Nick folded his arms, too. He had a fair idea of what was coming.

"The fact is I don't trust Lady Harringdon with my daughter's safety. I've been to ton parties, recall. Having grown up in that world, I can say with authority that *sir* or *lord* in front of a man's name is no guarantee of gentlemanly behavior. Unscrupulous men find great sport in preying on young girls of humbler station. And I fear a girl like my Kate, unworldly and dazzled by the trappings of high society, could be vulnerable to such predation."

"Of course. I'd be concerned, too, if I were her father." The words felt disingenuous. What had he been thinking, encouraging her to go and set her lures for a duke? He ought to have had Westbrook's perspective in mind.

"I don't want to forbid her going to this party. To be honest, I have hope that once she's seen the inside of a ballroom, and the sort of people one finds there, she'll begin to see it all falls a little short of what she's built up in her fancies."

Nick wouldn't hold his breath on that hope. But far be it from him to say so.

"Neither I nor Mrs. Westbrook, I'm sure, can countenance her going with only a stranger—as my brother's wife has been these twenty-three years—for protection. But if I knew there was a friend there, one as trustworthy as you, to keep watch of her, that would put a different complexion on things." He inclined his head, a mute apology for making this request.

There could be no question of saying *no*, and for that, Nick had only himself to blame. Little as he liked the idea of a rout, loath as he was to assume responsibility for Miss Westbrook, he was the one who'd goaded her into pursuing this scheme. He must be the one to see her safely through this one evening, at least. He owed her father that much.

"I'll keep watch of her." Unfurling in his stomach was a faint misapprehension: he might well live to regret this promise. But there was nothing to be done about that now. "I'll see what impressions I can form of the countess, too, that you'll have a better idea of whether she's a fit chaperone. Only send me word of what time she and her party plan to arrive, and you may trust her welfare to me."

THREE NIGHTS later he was at Cranbourne House, picking his way through the finely dressed, overperfumed ranks in search of Lord Barclay and regretting, just a little, that he'd promised to stay for the whole of this affair.

Miss Westbrook and the countess had come in a short while earlier. They'd taken seats among the matrons and wallflowers at one side of the room. She was in sublime looks, more so even than usual, and when she spied him and sent a smile his way he felt a pang of sorrow that he couldn't stroll over and wish her a good evening, let alone invite her to dance.

But an acknowledged acquaintance with him would do her no favors with Lady Harringdon—even if the Blackshear scandal should happen to have been beneath the countess's notice, the fact remained that he was the undistinguished second son of an untitled gentleman—so he restricted himself to keeping a surreptitious eye on the pair. And when several minutes passed without sign of any unscrupulous gentleman undertaking to approach her, he decided he could relax his vigilance long enough to locate the baron. The crowd was tolerable, and he ought to be able to glance through and around the forest of humanity to catch sight of her when he wished.

The *size* of the crowd was tolerable, rather. Of the crowd itself he could make no such assurance.

"Excuse me," he said, as he prodded his way past a knot of people who'd planted themselves in his path. He'd never liked this way of spending time, and since the business with Will, parties among fashionable strangers had become a downright torturous prospect.

Not that he had many invitations. In the past he'd gone mostly to gatherings hosted by a brother or sister, and there'd been none of that kind since spring of last year. Andrew and his wife, and Kitty and her husband, didn't care to see all their invitations politely declined.

The knot of people loosened to let him by. A lady in a feathered headpiece glanced over her shoulder at him, then leaned toward another lady and said something behind her fan.

She didn't know him. There was absolutely no reason she would. Still, he could never see such a response without imagining every unpleasant thing that might be whispered behind that fan. *Look there; do you remember when I told you of that family whose youngest son came back from the war so deranged that he . . . Yes, a courtesan, as I live and breathe, and the family could not prevent it . . . Oh, I'd never show my face at a party if my brother did such a thing. . . .*

Nonsense. He gave his head a quick shake to scatter those fancies. Even if the lady was such a zealous gossip as to be acquainted with Will's story, without Nick's name having been announced—he'd managed to escape that ceremony by explaining to the butler that he'd come for an appointment with Lord Barclay rather than as one of the revelers—she would have no reason to connect that story with him. She was probably only remarking on the lackluster arrangement of his cravat, if she was speaking of him at all.

And that was quite enough time given to contemplating the thoughts of a feather-headed stranger. Let her speak on what subject she wished. There was only one person at this gathering whose good opinion could be of any professional consequence to him. That person, therefore, would be the one on whom he'd concentrate all—

"Blackshear! Good Lord." The speaker stepped away from another conversation, eyes bright with curiosity, grin slicing across the aristocratic planes of his face. "Are you here of your own volition, or were you drugged and left on the doorstep?"

Well might Lord Cathcart ask. The last time the viscount had seen him, Nick had been dragging his heels through a progression of ever-more-sordid gaming establishments and regretting, with each step, that he'd allowed Cathcart to talk him into such a louche sort of evening.

Cathcart and Will, that was. It had taken his brother's and their old schoolfellow's cajolery combined to coax him out of his rooms and into that escapade.

And he was well shut of such capers. "You'll be relieved, I'm sure, to hear that I've come solely on a business matter." He performed a small, straightening adjustment to one kid glove. The viscount, as always, was meticulously tailored from head to toe, his own gloves pristine. Nick could never help feeling a bit shabby in his company. "Our host's brother has been made a baron and takes up his seat in the House this session. He'd like to learn what he can of public and persuasive speaking from someone with courtroom experience. I'm to meet with him here."

"Ah. Ambitious fellow. Just your sort. What's in it for you? I don't suppose a new title will come with any pocket boroughs to bestow."

"He'd hardly be bestowing them on me even if he had them. I don't meet the property qualification, recall."

"People get round that all the time." Cathcart gave a dismissive wave. "From what I hear, a good half the men in Commons had their land transferred to them by a patron, and taken back once the seat was secured."

"I consider that an argument for extending parliamentary eligibility to all men with a sufficient income, not only those who derive their money from the land." This was one of the liveliest mealtime topics among his fellows in the Middle Temple of late—but he must remember he was at a party, and speaking to a viscount who but irregularly attended sessions in the House of Lords. Cathcart wouldn't take much interest in the debate. "And even if I did wish to pursue a seat through adherence to the mere letter of the law, I haven't any patron willing to abet me with temporary ownership of land."

"You haven't a patron *yet.*" The viscount had a way of regarding all impediments as minor. "Perhaps this baron will be the man. And even if he hasn't got direct control of any seats in Commons, he might advance your interest with those who do. Don't tell me that hasn't entered your own thoughts."

"Entered? Yes." He fixed his gaze out over the ballroom. "However, the idea cannot progress very far, for reasons of which I'm sure I needn't remind you." Cathcart knew, better than almost anyone, of the constraints on Nick's professional hopes. He'd been Will's second, after all, in the duel by which the youngest of the Blackshear brothers had . . . avenged his ladylove's honor, or claimed her away from her protector, or whatever the object of that meeting had been.

"If you were hoping for an invitation to one of the better clubs, then yes, that matter might stand in your way. I cannot imagine the House of Commons is nearly so concerned with who a man's brother might have married."

Now the viscount was spouting nonsense just to cheer him. For all his political indifference, Cathcart knew perfectly well what sort of men filled the House of Commons. Country gentry. Second sons of peers. Heirs biding their time until they could assume the title, and take their fathers' vacated seats in Lords. A man's name counted for just as much in the House of Commons as in any refuge of the haut ton.

Little to be gained by arguing. Another subject had arisen and been openly recognized between them, and now Nick cleared his throat. "Do you hear anything of Will?" There was no good reason for him to ask. Martha had already told him all about their brother's basic circumstances, and was always willing to tell more if he would only inquire.

"I dined with him and his wife a fortnight ago. He's well. They both are." The viscount fixed his attention on the middle of the dance floor, recognizing the delicacy of the subject.

"Ah. I wasn't aware you'd kept up that level of intercourse." The knowledge stung, unaccountably.

"To a point. I don't care to impose the acquaintance on Lady Cathcart"—he nodded to where his wife, a shy, slender creature, was dancing with a man Nick didn't know—"so they don't dine at my house. But I do see them from time to time. Their circumstances are modest but Will seems content in the life he chose." He paused and turned his head to face Nick. "He doesn't reproach you, you know." His words came quickly, as though he half expected to be rebuked before he could get them all out. "No more do I. You chose the only possible course for a gentleman whose ambitions depend upon his good name. Even a trivial fellow like myself can see that."

Nick angled his face away, that the sentiments there not make a book for the viscount's perusal. Across the room a young lady had sat down by Miss Westbrook. The two were speaking, half turned toward one another, the very picture of happy conviviality.

"Thank you for saying so." He made a brief and slight bow, still not facing Lord Cathcart. "I appreciate your understanding."

"Think nothing of it. This is your pupil approaching now, isn't it? Astley's brother?"

Some distance to their right, the baron had indeed come into view, picking a path alongside the dancers. He raised a hand when Nick caught sight of him, and Nick greeted him in return.

Probably they'd want to confer in a room less noisy than this one. He'd have to abandon his watch of Miss

Westbrook. Not that she looked likely to get into any trouble, tucked away among the matrons and satisfied to be speaking with a friend, but he had taken her safety upon him and—

Inspiration struck. "Cathcart." He, too, had friends at this party, or at least one worthy friend who'd already proven his willingness to be cordial to people on the wrong side of a social fault line. He pivoted to address the viscount head-on. "Might I prevail upon you to do a service for a pretty girl?"

"BUT MR. Bingley is so much *kinder* a man." Miss Smith, who'd stopped by to greet Lady Harringdon and been commanded to join them, now occupied the chair at Kate's other side, absently twisting a corner of her shawl, not once glancing out at the spectacle of dancers and dance as she applied herself to articulating this opinion. "He defended Elizabeth and Jane against his sisters' criticism from the start. Mr. Darcy didn't come round until he'd been bewitched by Elizabeth's eyes."

"But he wasn't bewitched by her eyes, truly. He only thought them fine after he'd begun to admire her character and temperament," Kate said, clasping her hands in her lap and letting all energy flow into this unexpected and terribly welcome discussion. The friends to whom Lady Harringdon had presented her were impressive, to be sure, but their conversation had been strictly superficial. "Mr. Bingley approves everyone and everything indiscriminately. With Mr. Darcy, you know his good opinion, when it comes, is based upon his having perceived your particular merits."

"And I'm to be honored by that?" For a girl who'd grown up in a house without barristers, Miss Smith had an excellent disputing style, her thrusts and parries all delivered with such good nature as must blunt any sting of antagonism. "No, thank you; I prefer the generosity of a man who will credit me with every virtue, and leave me the burden of proving him wrong."

"What is all this talk of *I* and *you*?" Lady Harringdon, at Kate's right, had been content to fan herself and hum along with the violins, only intermittently attending the young ladies' conversation. Now she closed her fan with a smart snap. "You're not either of you in that story, and as I recall, those gentlemen both found brides who suited them very well. You must give up thinking of them, and pay some heed to unmarried gentlemen who actually walk among us."

That admonition, was meant for Miss Smith. At the moment of the young lady's sitting down, the countess had taken care to point out several gentlemen with whom it might behoove her to dance, if asked. None had yet approached.

Was there some residue of disappointment, still, that her aunt would not be pointing out such suitable prospects to her? To be sure. If she'd only had Lady Harringdon's proper patronage—if she'd entered the party as a guest, with her name announced, rather than trailing anonymously after the countess and sitting down among the matrons—she would have seen to it that every suitable man came near.

She would not dwell on disappointment, though. Not when she sat on a gilt-legged chair with a titled lady at her right and a congenial well-born girl at her left and a spectacle laid out before her of gentlemen in evening black dancing with ladies in gowns of every cut and color. She felt almost plain by comparison in her ivory muslin, despite having shortened the sleeves and trimmed the gown with pink ribbon that it might not look like the same one she'd worn to call at Harringdon House.

Almost plain. She'd drawn a few lingering glances already, even sitting off to the side as she was. Mr. Blackshear had smiled at her with undisguised admiration when they'd made their confidential across-the-room greeting. He looked rather impressive himself in evening clothes—his height and fine proportions were somehow more apparent in a crowd—even if he had come here only for business purposes instead of to dance.

"What can have become of your mother, my dear?" Again Lady Harringdon addressed Miss Smith, and made a show of craning to see past the dancers and into all corners of the room. "I declare she's nowhere to be seen."

"I expect she must still be in the card room. She'd only taken her place at a table a short time before I sat down here, you may recall."

"Ah, so you did tell us. I remember it now. I wish I knew how long she means to play, though." The countess's brow furrowed in a show of cogitative effort. "I might better plan out my evening if I knew when we could expect the pleasure of her company."

The hint was too plain for even a dullard to overlook. Miss Smith, no dullard, rose from her chair. "I'll go ask her, shall I?"

"That would be lovely, dear. But see that you come straight back to us. If a gentleman waylays you and asks for a dance, tell him you must seek my permission first, your mother being elsewhere engaged."

Miss Smith smiled—really, she looked a deal more radiant after a few minutes spent in energetic debate; you hardly noticed the forehead and chin—in a way that made clear she took no offense at being banished from the conversation to come. With a curtsy she turned and set off for the card room.

"What are we to do with her?" Lady Harringdon wanted to know as soon as she'd gone. "Here is a room full of eligible men and she'd rather sit and talk of made-up men in novels. She won't dance all the evening at this rate."

"I fear I'm to blame." Genuine guilt pinched at Kate. Miss Smith was supposed to be finding some alternatives to Sir George Bigby, not keeping her company. "She's so delightful a conversationalist that I kept her speaking on that topic. She ought rather to have been making conversation with some gentleman."

"She ought rather to be *dancing,* but no gentleman has asked." The countess tapped Kate's knee with the folded fan, in the manner of a judge certifying his words with a gavel. "I think we must take steps to make her more generally noticed."

The *we* was gratifying. That Lady Harringdon thought her a useful ally made up for a little of the indignity of sitting along the wall watching her own aunt working to make a match for someone else. "Ought we to move to a different side of the room?" It sounded a bit like fishing: you might have poor luck in one spot, then move downriver and meet with abundance.

"I think she'd do better to make a circuit." Again Lady Harringdon employed her fan in gavel fashion, this time upon her own knee. "What if you propose a turn about the room, and take special care to lead her past some of these groups of gentlemen, keeping her engaged all the while in such conversation as— But what can this rascal be wanting? You would think a viscount would know better than to march up and present himself when ladies are occupied in sorting out matters of great moment."

The viscount in question was a handsome man, impeccably turned out, with pale hair and high cheekbones and a cravat that combined a barrel knot with an intricate waterfall styling. "Lady Harringdon." He could not have failed to hear the countess's scolding words but he smiled, undeterred, and bowed over her hand. "I vow each of your daughters is more beautiful than the last." He nodded to Kate. "If you've any more to bring out in future Seasons, I beg you will put a notice to that effect in the *Gazette*, that we poor gentlemen of the ton may begin even now to gird ourselves."

"For shame, Cathcart." Lady Harringdon swatted at him with her fan. "Lady Margaret who just married is the last of my daughters, as you know perfectly well. This pretty young person is Miss Westbrook, a relation on Lord Harringdon's side. She accompanies me tonight as a prospective lady's companion, and I assure you she is not susceptible to such overblown flattery as you attempt. Miss Westbrook, this dreadful flirt of a man is Lord Cathcart."

"On the contrary, her ladyship is the dreadful flirt. I must scramble to keep up with her." He bowed over Kate's hand. "Can I persuade you into a dance, Miss Westbrook? Whether you're a companion or a marriageable miss is of no consequence to me, as I already have an eminently satisfactory viscountess. I simply pride myself on standing up with the prettiest girl at every ball."

Her heart lurched into a hasty cadence. This wasn't the invitation from a titled gentleman she'd pictured—she'd imagined an unmarried man with subtler manners—but it would be a distinction nevertheless. And if other men saw her dancing, then other invitations might follow.

Yet how could she accept? Lady Harringdon had been on the point of asking her to take Miss Smith about the room and help her catch a partner. She wouldn't be able to do that if she herself was dancing when Miss Smith returned.

She lowered her eyes to her hands, which sat folded in

her lap. "I'm deeply honored by your invitation, sir." Oh, she hated to pass up this chance, even for the sake of solidifying the countess's good impression of her. "But I'm here tonight by Lady Harringdon's goodness, and I—"

"A moment, please, Miss Westbrook." Her aunt's voice cut her off neatly. With her fan she waved the viscount away. "Will you please give us just a moment to consult, my lord?" The man retreated several steps; she snapped her fan open with such smart style as might reduce any sensible lady to tears of appreciation, and positioned it to screen her next words. "Have you any objection to dancing with him? He may flirt shamelessly, but he's harmless, and perfectly devoted to his wife."

"On my own account I shouldn't mind, but I'd meant to walk about the room with Miss Smith."

"I have a new assignment for you." *Assignment.* It had a very pleasant sound. As though she were some daring lady spy, and Lady Harringdon the mastermind who sent her out on missions. "You strike me as a persuading sort of lady. Do you think you can contrive to have him ask our friend for a dance, once your set is finished? He himself can be no prospect, but a first dance may put the machinery in motion, as it were. Other gentlemen may take note."

"Yes, of course." Here was an assignment entirely fitted to her abilities: if there was one thing in the world she knew how to do, it was to persuade gentlemen to her will. She needn't yet know *how* she would convince this viscount to dance with Miss Smith, to be sure that she would do it.

And if other gentlemen took note of her in the process, so much the better.

A country dance had begun some while since. They would have time to circle the room in conversation, waiting for the next set to form, and in that time she might accomplish a great deal. She nodded to Lady Harringdon, gave a single straightening touch to the pink ribbon woven through her hair, and rose from her seat to go take the viscount's proffered elbow.

Chapter Seven

"I HAVEN'T YET engaged a secretary, I should mention." Lord Barclay pivoted from the side table, where he'd been pouring a pair of drinks, and crossed the carpet to Nick's seat at the hearth, one glass held out in offering. "I'm used to doing things for myself, and not quite ready to hand over the management of any decisions to someone else. Even handing over my correspondence is a step at which I balk."

"I understand. I suspect it's a common condition for second sons." Nick took the glass, which held a finger's breadth or two of some honey-colored liquid that was doubtless beyond his ability to appreciate. "We grow accustomed to making our own way out of necessity, and then we get rather attached to the habit."

"Exactly so." The baron settled into the opposite chair, crossing his legs and propping one elbow on the chair's arm. "I do recognize that I shall have to eventually engage someone. I don't expect you to know yet whether you'd be interested in that post—we might discover our temperaments don't suit—but may I ask whether you entertain any political ambitions? I won't presume that every barrister does."

"I do, though I've fixed no firm date on their realization, nor clearly imagined the form it will take." He tilted his glass a few degrees back and forth, to catch the fire's glow on the amber liquid within. He wasn't ready to confide the strength of his ambitions to a man who might have a great deal of power over whether they came to fruition or not. "And I meanwhile find a considerable satisfaction in my present work." *On those occasions when work presents itself, that is.* "Were you always political yourself, or is it more a matter of wanting to do your duty by the title?"

"Truthfully, it's more a matter of having my eyes opened by my time in the Hussars. I grew up rather complacent, Blackshear, as I'm sure you may surmise by merely glancing about here." Indeed the library in which they sat was every bit as grand as the ballroom, in its way. Floor-to-ceiling shelves covered every wall, the expanse of books interrupted only by the open door, a pair of French doors to the terrace, and the marble fireplace. "I had polite ideas of the nation's good, as my brother Astley does, or as I daresay most men do, who haven't been exposed to much beyond their circle of privilege."

"I can see how the army would change that." Nick curled his fingers into a subtle grip on the chair's arm, to avoid fidgeting. All too well he knew the kinds of changes military service could effect in a man's way of thinking.

"Indeed. And even more so, the return to England, and the witnessing of what conditions are faced by returning soldiers who haven't got a proper pension and in some cases aren't equal to the demands of a steady situation. I couldn't long observe that without thinking it a disgrace, and thinking that our nation must do better— But do you not care for cognac?" He uncrossed his legs and leaned forward, ready to swoop in and take Nick's glass away. "Pardon me; I poured it without thinking to ask."

Cognac, then. He hadn't been quite sure. "No, I have no doubt it's splendid. I only got caught up in the conversation and forgot to drink."

"That's my fault." He got to his feet, grinning. "I get upon the subject of politics and I take the very air out of the room, or so Astley tells me. No intervals for a man to simply relax and enjoy his drink." While speaking, he made his way to the French doors and undid the latch to crack one open. "Voilà. Air. The marquess can reproach me with nothing now."

He seemed a remarkably good-natured man. Will had worn a sober, even distracted air in those months between when he'd come home from Belgium and when he'd announced his intention to fight a duel over someone else's mistress and to marry her if he survived. Whatever had affected him so in wartime had apparently left Barclay untouched.

He might make Miss Westbrook a fine husband. Nick took a sip of the cognac, just enough to anoint all the tasting parts of his tongue. It had a vague flavor of fruit mixed with wood, and it burned a bit when he swallowed.

Despite his teasing her about snaring a duke, he knew the odds were much against her, when she must go to parties as a mere companion-in-training. He ought to do what he could to put the baron in her way. He'd be doing a kindness to her father, too, if an attachment took hold between her and Barclay. With a worthy, respectable suitor, welcome in the Westbrook home, she'd have no need to attend any more of these parties. Mr. Westbrook could let go his worries over the danger of predatory lords.

A tiny protest came, a twisting in his chest. Mere cobwebs of old habit. As a friend, he wanted to see her happily married to some suitable man, and that suitable man was not himself.

At any rate, his plan already provided for a likely meeting between Miss Westbrook and the baron. "Let's speak a bit of the skills you foresee needing, to become an effective parliamentarian, and how I may be of service to you in acquiring those skills." He leaned forward, elbows on his knees, cognac glass balanced in the fingers of his right hand. "I'd recommend some study in the principles of persuasion—I can prepare some cases for you to argue before me—but before we come to that, if you don't mind, I propose we begin with the fundamental mechanics of speech. And for that, if you'll agree to it, I propose to take you to the same teacher with whom I myself studied."

"Mr. Blackshear asked you to dance with me?"

The viscount had cheerfully offered up this information as soon as they'd started their circuit of the room, and Kate didn't know whether to be grateful or galled.

"Don't be piqued with him. He feared you might be approached by unscrupulous sorts while he was out of the room and unable to protect you from their unscrupulous ways. It occurred to him that if you were dancing with me, you couldn't be dancing with anyone else, apart from briefly, during such exchanges as the figure of the dance requires."

"He has reason to trust you, I collect." She'd never met a friend of Mr. Blackshear's. She couldn't help being curious. It was difficult to imagine what he and Lord Cathcart had in common.

"An acquaintance going back to university days, and knowledge of my constancy to my wife. Speak of unscrupulous sorts, do you see that fellow who's eyeing you there, the one with the prodigious collar points? Don't dance with him if he asks." The flippancy went right out of his voice. "He's second in line for a dukedom, and Lady Cathcart tells me he's good looking, but he has a rotten reputation and I know for a fact it's deserved."

Well, *that* sounded a bit like Mr. Blackshear. And the information was intriguing, particularly as the man in question was one whom Lady Harringdon had pointed out as a suitable prospect to Miss Smith. She hadn't thought before of how useful a gentleman who kept abreast of these matters could be to a lady trying to make her way in society.

"Lord Cathcart." She fixed him with her most winning smile as they took their place in the line. If he was going to speak so bluntly, why shouldn't he welcome blunt talk in return? "I have an acquaintance who could profit from exactly that kind of advice. Since you're willing to dance with a lady of no distinction as a favor to a friend, I wonder if I can persuade you to dance with another lady, amiable and deserving and a perfectly delightful conversationalist, as a favor to me."

"BLACKSHEAR!" CATHCART beckoned him from a quarter of the way across the supper room, and broadened the gesture to include Lord Barclay as well. He had a pair of empty places at his table, which otherwise held the viscountess, Miss Westbrook, and her friend, though not, interestingly enough, Lady Harringdon.

Fine work, Cathcart. This was above and beyond what he'd requested, and all to the good. From even this distance he could see Miss Westbrook glowing at the distinction of sitting down with a titled husband and wife, for all the world as though she were a noble young lady with no questionable connections.

She glanced up at his approach and her smile went wider, her eyes sparkling like sapphires held up to a flame. He could almost feel a sharpening in Barclay's attention as that gentleman had his first full look at her, though perhaps he was merely imputing to the baron what he'd observed in so many male callers at the Westbrook house.

She did make a very pretty picture this evening. She wore a white gown with pink ribbons on the sleeves and tied round under the bodice, and a matching pink ribbon woven through her blond hair. Now that he was near her for the first time tonight, he could see she had her hair in some more-elaborate-than-usual arrangement. Mostly, though, he just saw her smile.

"Sophie, my dear, I think you'll remember Nick Blackshear; he was a year ahead of me at Cambridge." Cathcart stood, making the introductions while ushering Nick and Lord Barclay to the open seats. "Blackshear, I believe Miss Westbrook is already known to you; here is her friend Miss Smith." Between them they introduced Lord Barclay all around, and got him seated beside Miss Smith and directly across from Miss Westbrook. Nick took the place at her left.

Some mention of Parliament had occurred during the introductions, and it developed that Miss Smith had a brother in Commons. Barclay, having met several Mr. Smiths in that House, now set himself to puzzling out whether any of them was the Mr. Smith in question. Nick turned to his right. "My apologies," he muttered to Miss Westbrook under cover of the others' conversation. "I didn't expect the discussion to turn political so soon."

"You've nothing to apologize for." She smiled with such particular radiance that he knew Cathcart must have told her to whom she owed the dance. "I'm having a supremely enjoyable evening and I don't begrudge others' enjoying themselves as well. *You're* enjoying yourself, I hope? Your meeting with Lord Barclay went well?"

"I believe it did." He started in on his soup course. This was how they would enjoy themselves tonight and henceforward: privy to one another's ambitions, secret sharers in each other's triumphs. "He seems a very good man, the baron." He inclined a bit toward her and spoke under his breath. "An excellent candidate for snaring in your web, if you can bring yourself to make conversation about laws and elections and the social good."

"How little you know about snaring, Mr. Blackshear." She glowed with good-humored confidence. "Gentlemen don't want ladies who can converse on their favorite topics. They want ladies who can listen, wide-eyed. Let me demonstrate.

"Lord Barclay." She retracted her attention from Nick and sent it all across the table as the baron and Miss Smith finished their conference on the identity of that lady's brother. No trace of saucy manners remained: she was an innocent at her first rout, privileged to be sitting at a table with titled people. "What is it like in the House of Lords? We ladies, not being admitted, can only guess at all the pomp and ceremony."

Lord Barclay might be too seasoned a man to gape, but he did, unmistakably, absorb a heavy dose of her charm. He inclined his head to her. "In fact there is a deal of ceremony. More than I would have expected."

"A new creation has to dress in elaborate robes and carry in his writ of summons." Cathcart sent this intelligence up the table with evident relish. "Those are the best sessions, when someone new parades about and the rest of us can tell ourselves we never looked so foolish."

"Thank you for confirming my apprehension of how I looked. I felt like the worst sort of coxcomb." Barclay grinned at the viscount, and then at Miss Westbrook. "And it proves to have been a harbinger of how things would go on."

"Indeed?" She inclined forward by some, no doubt,

few degrees, reflecting his smile straight back to him. Anyone would think she'd come to this party entirely in hopes of hearing about the workings of Parliament.

"I'd supposed we'd spend our time addressing issues of national welfare." Barclay glanced around the table, too well bred to ignore the rest of the company in favor of the pretty girl opposite. "The alleviation of poverty, for example, or matters of health and disease, or perhaps some decisions having to do with import tariffs. But I swear last Monday we spent half the session hearing a petition on behalf of some gentleman in Southampton who believes his local magistrate is involved in some conspiracy to blacken his character and who wants the magistrate dismissed." He picked up his soup spoon. "I don't say such a man isn't entitled to a hearing, and to justice. But does that matter really require the attention of the full House of Lords?"

"There's a great deal of that sort of thing," Cathcart assured him. "Wait and see. Proclamations from the Prince Regent, votes in favor of giving official thanks to this or that set of people involved in a military action. It's in Commons, I think, where the real work of the nation is done. Am I correct, Miss Smith?"

"I do believe there's less in the way of ceremony, and fewer proclamations." Miss Smith, clearly, had never been informed that gentlemen preferred rapt attention to a thoughtful reply. Or perhaps the rules were different for a lady who wasn't setting her cap at a man. She angled herself to address the baron. "I expect you'll develop alliances in time with those members of Commons who share your concerns and positions. Then you can have influence with those men, and work with them on the issues that interest you. Poverty, I think you said?"

Barclay now spoke at some length, much as he'd done in the library, about the welfare of former soldiers and how he'd come to concern himself with the poor. He had passion and conviction, but also an air of reason; this combination would be much to his advantage as a speaker. He did need to learn the value of brevity, and the skill of choosing which phrases to emphasize. His breath originated from too high in his chest, as well. Granted he spoke at a supper table and had no need to project his voice, but it was a good bet he'd speak the same way on the Parliament floor.

"Do you suppose he might hire you as a secretary?" Miss Westbrook's soft voice broke into his thoughts. "Papa said he doesn't have one."

"It's too early to speculate on that." Nick reached for his wineglass. Uneasiness prickled just under his skin. To what extent had she and her father discussed this? Had they weighed and considered the likelihood that the Blackshear connections would present an insurmountable obstacle? Was that, in fact, what she was asking him now? His opinion on his chances of gaining a secretary post in spite of everything? "He's engaged me to help him with speaking. That's enough to thoroughly occupy me for the present."

"You'd take the post, though, wouldn't you, if he did offer? Surely it would be an advantageous opportunity for a man with an interest in politics." How quickly she abandoned the doe-eyed *naïf* act, now that she was speaking to him instead of to an eligible man with a title.

"To be honest, I don't know yet what I'd do. I shall have to give it all a bit more thought." *To be honest,* indeed. He couldn't speak honestly without broaching things he didn't want to discuss with her. *You and I both know there may be no such opportunity, once he's learned the facts about my family.* He couldn't, and wouldn't say that. Candor between him and Miss Westbrook could only go so far.

"I don't think I put it too strongly when I say it's the

shame of our nation that we should turn our backs on these men," the baron said, still speaking of soldiers, and Nick's glance connected for an uncomfortable instant with the viscount's.

Barclay's words must necessarily put them both in mind of Will. If he came to the point of telling the baron about his brother, he'd also have to tell him that he'd—well, *turned his back on him* was a pretty accurate way of putting it. Wouldn't that be a fine poetic absurdity, if he lost this man's good opinion and possible patronage not because of the family scandal, but because of his attempts to distance himself from it.

Nick went back to his soup. Soon enough he'd have to decide what to tell the baron and when, but he wouldn't put himself through that tonight. Instead he'd enjoy this congenial supper and gird himself for the hours ahead, in which he must loiter in the ballroom stealthily supervising Miss Westbrook and seeing whether he thought Lady Harringdon a fit chaperone. No doubt she'd have more invitations to dance, now that she'd been seen supping at the viscount's table instead of dutifully trailing after the countess. If Lady Harringdon granted her permission, Nick would have to be on guard against those ill-intentioned men he'd promised her father to protect her from.

Fortunately, her first after-supper dance went to Lord Barclay. From there she had another invitation and then another, to the apparent satisfaction of the countess. Clearly her aunt enjoyed the consequence that came with chaperoning such a sought-after lady. But it didn't bode well, that Lady Harringdon's head could be turned in this manner.

Nick took up first one station and then another from which he might observe both chaperone and charge, as the late night grew later and the rout rolled indefatigably on. He did consult his pocket watch a few times. He'd have been home in bed by now, if he'd had only himself to think of. And perhaps he did allow his attention to drift, now and then, to other quadrants of the room or even to the weightier world outside. Once or twice he left the ballroom as well. Not for any great length of time—only to escape the crowded room's heat with a sojourn to the more sparsely populated card room, or to the terrace to brace his lungs with a bit of fresh air. For the most part he was unswerving in his vigilance.

But *for the most part* was not what he'd promised the Westbrooks. And so he felt the alarm doubly, for their sake and his own, when at two o'clock in the morning he put away his watch, called back his thoughts from the details of a brief he'd got yesterday, and looked up to discover that Miss Westbrook was no longer in the room.

Chapter Eight

She wasn't in the dance. He would have seen her right away, if she had been. He'd been watching her pink ribbons and light-footed dancing all night; he could have picked her out with all the candles doused but one, so many foolish hours had he spent committing the details of her person to memory, but where the devil was she and how had he not seen her go?

Nick pushed away from his place on the wall and tugged at his cravat. She wasn't with her aunt. He'd glanced that way first thing, before making the thorough scrutiny of the dance that he'd known would not yield her. Nor was she idling with Miss Smith—that lady was dancing with a red-coated partner—or taking a turn about the room. She'd done both those things, as well as made a trip to the punch bowl, in the time he'd been watching, and he'd had no trouble finding her on those occasions.

The card room? But her path there, from the dance floor, would have taken her near enough to him that he would surely have noticed.

If she'd gone outside, though . . .

Already he was moving to the end of the room where the French doors stood open. What man had she been dancing with in this last set? Scrawny fellow. Brown coat. He hadn't looked at all like the sort who would try to lure a lady out of doors, and Miss Westbrook knew better than to be lured. Didn't she? Still, she might have felt unwell from the room's stuffiness and needed just a moment outside. If she had already been near the doors she might simply have stepped out instead of making the long walk back to ask one of her friends for help.

Speak of her friends, though, this certainly didn't improve his opinion of the countess as a chaperone. Even if her niece's disappearance should prove to be the innocent matter he hoped, it ill became her to be laughing as she now was, absorbed in whatever the lady beside her was saying and utterly unaware that her charge had gone missing. How was he to reassure the Westbrooks that their daughter would be well looked after at any future parties?

He slowed his pace, that he might not call attention to himself by an excess of visible purpose, and wove through a milling set of people before slipping through the open doors.

"I CONFESS IT astounds me that anyone could look at all that, once upon a time, and pick out the shape of a bull. I still cannot see the horns." There was a voice that a clever lady used for this sort of occasion: fascinated, a little at sea, thoroughly in need of some knowledgeable gentleman's help. This evening had been an excellent chance to practice that voice.

"Bear in mind they were all mapped out in a time of great superstition." Lord John Prior seemed an amiable man, if not quite the lofty prospect she'd hoped to meet tonight. Son of a duke he might be, but four elder brothers and a good number of nephews stood between him and the title. "People wanted to see recognizable shapes when they looked at the sky, and so they forced themselves to find a bull, a hunter, a set of twins."

"I don't see the twins at all."

"There." He stepped a bit closer to her. She could feel the nervous energy that ran through him when he came near. He probably didn't often get very close to ladies, with his gangly build and his unseemly preoccupation with stars. "There, and there." He lifted an arm to point, inadvertently brushing against hers. He backed up a step, doubtless affected by the contact. "And there and there are the bull's horns."

"Ah, now I see." She didn't. But all of this was practice toward making a conquest of some truly eligible man. Besides, Lord John was rather sweet in his bashful, star-studying way. He'd offered her his coat when she crossed her arms against the cold, and not made the least attempt to touch her beyond settling it on her shoulders. His manners ought to be rewarded. He could go home at the end of the evening with the satisfaction of having made a good impression on a pretty girl. Her own success tonight had left her in a generous mood.

"Modern astronomy is moving away from the shapes and pictures, I'm happy to say." She'd encouraged him. Now he was going to go on at length. "Now we live in an age of reason, we don't impose false patterns on what we see. We map out the locations of the various constellations, and note when they're visible in different parts of the sky, but we haven't that need to—"

"Miss Westbrook." She nearly jumped. She hadn't heard footsteps.

She turned—Lord John turned, too, with another awkward-looking step away from her—to find Mr. Blackshear. And also to find that they were alone on the terrace, but for one other couple at the far end. There'd been near a dozen people when they'd come out here; she hadn't heard them all go back inside.

Mr. Blackshear's gaze touched pointedly on the coat she wore. Then on Lord John's coatlessness. "Lady Harringdon has requested your presence. I'm to bring you back to her." He spoke only to her. Lord John merited no more than a curt nod that plainly said, *There'll be no further need of you.*

Humiliation sizzled down all her nerves, with outrage close behind. It was obvious what he thought he'd come upon. And therefore obvious what he thought her capable of, or what he thought her capable of falling prey to in her naivete.

How could he think such a thing? He'd been so friendly at supper, teasing her about snaring Lord Barclay in her web and talking at least a little about his own prospects. She'd felt as though they were comrades of a sort, each having managed to infiltrate this party and each looking forward to hearing about the other's successes. The look in his eyes now felt like a betrayal.

So did his actions. How dare he take it upon himself to come out here and spy on her, and shame Lord John in that way? Lady Harringdon had never sent for her. If she had, it would have been through some other emissary. All on his own, he'd decided he must go in search of her and jump to the worst possible conclusions about what he found.

She would not look at him. She pasted on the friendliest smile she could summon, and thanked Lord John for his kindness as she gave him back his coat. From the corner of her eye she could see Mr. Blackshear standing impassive, arms folded across his chest, no doubt congratulating himself on rescuing her virtue in the very nick of time.

She wouldn't speak to him. Yes, she would. With a final farewell of such warmth as might hopefully give any onlooker a lesson in manners, she watched Lord John go back indoors. Then she turned. "You had no right to do that." She kept her voice low. No one seeing them would think this was anything but an exchange of mundane pleasantries. "You know what my hopes were for this party. I confided them to you, and you encouraged me. How dare you embarrass me so, and drive away a gentleman on whom I'd been making a good impression?"

A lamp hanging a few feet to her right showed the progression of sentiment on his face as she spoke: surprise gave way to astonishment that quickly solidified into self-righteous anger. "Without doubt you made an impression, Miss Westbrook, but I can assure you it's not the sort you meant to make." He bit the words short, for discretion, and succeeded only in making them more vile. "Do you truly not understand what a man has in mind when he persuades a lady to seclude herself with him away from the company?"

"We didn't seclude ourselves." She gestured with an arm to show the wide-open terrace. "There were other people when we came out here, more than just that one couple. From where we stood, I didn't notice they'd gone." The jolly music of a reel filtered out from the ballroom, making a counterpoint to this awful discord that had slipped in between them. "It was warm and close on the dancing floor. Plenty of people have stepped out for air. Lord John happened to be my partner at the time and he was good enough to escort me outside."

None of what she said swayed him in the least. "Was the air nearer to the doors insufficient somehow? Did he give you some accounting of why it was necessary that he escort you all the way to this far corner, and why he must presume to wrap you in his coat?"

"In fact he did." She let her voice grow thinner, more brittle. "He wanted to show me some constellations."

"Oh, good God." He swung away from her for a second in an eloquent show of disgust. "If *that* isn't the oldest trick in the book; taking a lady out to gaze up at the stars."

He'd never spoken to her in anything like this horrid manner, and she'd never imagined she could be so furious at him. "You're speaking completely out of turn. Lord John has an interest in astronomy. If you'd bother to look up, instead of down your nose at me, perhaps you'd notice this is the spot on the terrace where your view is least encroached upon by surrounding houses." She hugged herself more tightly with her folded arms. "And he gave me his coat because he was kind enough to notice I was cold. As indeed I am now. I'd think you of all men would know better than to put a sinister construction on that."

She was sorry she'd ever worn his coat, with its plain soap smell. She was sorry she'd told him so much of her hopes. And at that moment she didn't care to speak to him anymore.

She made to march past him and he stepped into her path.

His gall was absolutely beyond anything. "I'm cold," she repeated, not sparing his face a glance. "I'd like to go inside. You've made your opinions of my actions clear. Anything further you say will be gratuitous insult." She was shaking, as much from anger as from the chill air.

"Fine." He caught her by the elbow and then she did look up, and his jaw was taut and his nostrils flared. "This way." Behind him was a set of French doors, slightly open, and before she could say a word, he whisked her through them into what proved to be an unoccupied library.

He'd lost his mind. Did he truly not see that taking her into this empty room was ten times more disrespectable than what she and Lord John had done?

"Listen to me." He rounded on her like a barrister pinning down a witness unsure of her story. "Left to my own wishes, I would not be here. I don't care for this sort of thing and there are a dozen interesting documents I could be reading at home."

"Then why don't you—"

"Let me speak, please. I need to say my piece and get us both out of here as quickly as I can." He did see the danger of being in this room, then. And he'd brought her in here anyway. "You must know your mother and father would never have permitted you to go to this rout but that they knew I'd be here to look out for you."

"I don't know that. I'm sure they were more amenable than they would have been if you weren't going to be here, but—"

"Miss Westbrook, I am *telling* you that." Impatience flashed in his eyes. "I made a promise to your father that I would stay for as long as you did, and keep you out of danger. Only then did he and your mother grant their permission."

That smarted. She'd known Papa must have asked him to watch out for her while he was here, but she hadn't known there was a formal promise, requiring him to stay so long, and she hadn't known her own attendance was contingent on his presence.

Cold air crept in through the cracked-open door. She turned and went to the hearth. She didn't know who to be angry with.

"Do you see that yours is not the only reputation you trifle with when you do careless things like letting a man of whom you know nothing lead you outdoors?" Mr. Blackshear clearly knew who she ought to be angry with. He thought she was the one at fault. "Think what would become of my credit with your father, if you were compromised under my watch." Behind her, she could hear him follow her to the fire. "His good opinion means a great deal to me. To lose that good opinion through someone else's actions would be a sore trial."

His words poked at her sympathy, shrouded up since the minute he'd come outside. Papa's good opinion was very worth having. She'd seen for three years how Mr. Blackshear prized it.

Also, there could have been some reference in his last words to the business with his brother. He knew what it was to lose something through someone else's actions. His brother's marriage had cost him his standing in society and, according to Papa, a deal of barrister work as well.

She turned to face him. His features in the room's lamplight showed more weariness than anger. In fact he looked thoroughly exhausted.

Sympathy stirred in her again. Perhaps they could both explain themselves and come to a civil understanding once more. "I wasn't aware your credit with Papa was at stake." She set her hand on the mantelpiece. "But I maintain there was nothing careless in what I did. No one can care more for my reputation than I do, and—"

He seized her wrist, putting a finger to his lips, and a second later she heard it, too: footsteps in the hallway. Panic plummeted through her, and then he moved with lightning speed, grabbing her around the waist, fairly dragging her with him to the space behind a sofa by the door. He pulled her down and they crouched side by side out of sight, her heart pounding as they waited for the footsteps to come in or pass by.

NICK HELD his breath. The door latch hardware made its small mechanical sound and the door swung open, thankfully blocking this newcomer's view of the space behind the sofa. Shoe soles rang brisk and purposeful across the few feet of bare floor before reaching the muted terrain of carpet. A tingling ran up his left arm, where an instant ago he'd seized Miss Westbrook by the waist.

Please, please take a book and go. If they were discovered it would mean ruin for her, or at the very least, marriage to a man she didn't want—that marriage entered into amid the smirks and whispers of everyone who heard how the bride and groom had been found crouching behind a sofa in an empty room.

A few private words in a corner of the terrace with Lord Scarecrow was nothing, nothing to this. For all the sanctimonious lecturing he'd given her on proper behavior, his own actions had put her reputation at far greater risk than hers had.

A scrape sounded on the hearth; that would be the screen dragged aside. Then came a rattle of iron against iron. The intruder must be a maid, come to put out what remained of the fire. Hope sprang up in his heart. She'd have no reason to linger. She could scatter or smother the coals, douse the lamps, and then walk a straight path back to the door, which still stood at an angle that should block her view of the space behind the sofa.

He stole a glance at Miss Westbrook, who sat with her knees drawn up, her arms bound about them as if to make herself as small and invisible as she could. *Take heart,* he would have liked to tell her. *We've a very good chance of getting out of this unscathed.* No thanks to him. He'd felt such fury, meeting with her self-righteous anger after how he'd worried for her—not to mention seeing her with that scarecrow of a Lord John after he'd gone to the trouble of introducing her to the baron—and he'd somehow or other completely lost his head.

He sent a hand to touch one of hers in mute reassurance, or perhaps mute apology. Her hand turned over and her fingers gripped his. In the shadows behind the sofa he couldn't read her expression, but the trembling in her fingers told him all he needed to know. She understood exactly what would be the cost if she was found with him here. There was nothing he could say or do that would reassure her.

A clanking sounded as the fire tool was put back; then the scrape of the screen on the hearth. A footstep or three, and the room dimmed as one lamp and then another went out. A faint light remained; that would be the maid's candle. Shadows slid across the wall suddenly as her shoes resumed their purposeful tread on the carpet.

Nick held his breath and wove his fingers with Miss Westbrook's. Ruin or reprieve, they would meet it together. Within seconds. Within heartbeats. Within the few remaining steps that would carry the maid from carpet to door.

There was a split second of awful illumination as the candle came to a place where its light fell over the sofa's back, and in that instant he could see that Miss Westbrook had her eyes shut tight. But the candle moved on without pause. Of a sudden it was on the other side of the still-open door, then the door was swinging closed, and an instant later the hardware clicked into place, a sound of such sweet finality as he'd never imagined.

He let out his breath, listening to the footsteps recede. "Good God." His words hung in the room's utter darkness. "Pardon my language. That can't have been more than two minutes, but deuced if it didn't feel like half a lifetime." Already he was getting his feet under him, disentangling his fingers from hers that he could properly help her to stand. "Now let's get you back to your aunt before anything else can happen to put your reputation at risk." He found a hold on her elbow and started to rise.

She tried to rise with him. She set one hand on the sofa's back and gripped his upper arm with the other, but she'd barely come up from a crouch before her knees gave way.

He caught her with both arms, just in time to stop her tumbling to the floor. She was shaking all over, like a shorn lamb caught in an out-of-season hailstorm. "I'm sorry," she said, and the two words bore an ocean's worth of mortification. "I don't know what's the matter with me."

"Nothing to be sorry for." Carefully he knelt, lowering her likewise to the stability of her knees. "Take a moment to recover yourself. It's no wonder your knees are weak, after such an alarm." If she were another woman, one with whom he claimed privileges of intimacy, he might have clasped her to his chest until the trembling stopped.

Instead his hands found their way to her elbows again as he eased his body clear of hers. "And please, let me be the one to apologize. I was a terrible hypocrite, taking you into a room alone to lecture to you on prudence and propriety. I wouldn't have soon forgiven myself, if . . ." But perhaps it was better not to voice their near-missed fate aloud. "At all events, we're out of it safely. No harm was done. You'll be well again in a minute, I'm sure."

He bent and pressed his lips to the crest of her forehead, lightly, in reassurance. It wasn't so forward as an embrace, and truly he wouldn't have done even this much but for the darkness of the room, and the grueling few moments they'd just borne together, and the fact that she was shaking, still, and gripping his coat sleeves like a woman in deep water who didn't know how to swim.

Her breath caught at the touch of his lips. Her grip on him changed, fingers spreading over his upper arms to hold on to him, instead of the fabric of his coat. He could feel, in the air between them, how her face tilted to peer up at him, though of course she wouldn't be able to see.

He'd stopped breathing, too. He hadn't intended . . . suddenly it didn't matter what he'd intended. Here she was, angling herself to him and waiting, unmistakably, for him to do whatever he was going to do next.

Don't. She's had a shock. She doesn't know what she's about.

Neither did he, altogether. He bent in. Slowly, to give her every chance to stop him. To give himself every chance to recover his reason and halt this.

His lips met with her cheek, encountered the firm, elegant structure of the cheekbone underneath. Her hands tightened on his arms. He felt her breath start up again, a ragged warmth ghosting against the underside of his jaw.

He stayed where he was for a moment, lips hovering a fraction of an inch from her cheek; chin and neck reveling in the caress of her exhalations.

He would have sworn on his soul that he'd stopped wanting this. And in truth he'd never, even in his most besotted days, wanted *this*. He'd pictured embracing her in a sunlit parlor where he might drink in her beauty between kisses, with a perfect understanding of what their future would be. He'd imagined a wedding night with all the candles lit, her body a lambent wonder atop the covers, her unguarded face telling him all the things she might be too shy to voice aloud. Not once had his daydreams wandered to wordless, heedless scandal in a pitch-dark room.

His hand traveled up her arm, kid against skin, kid against muslin, and then he let his fingertips brush up the side of her neck. She shivered again, and he knew this time it had nothing to do with fear.

Fool. Don't linger here. Get her on her feet and get her back to the ballroom. Yes, the responsible part of his brain was still in fine working order. No doubt it would whip up a fearsome and thorough reprimand in the time it took him to finish what he could not now refrain from starting. He set his palm to the corner of her jaw, and found her mouth with his.

IF SOMEONE walked in on them now, she'd deserve every last whisper of scandal and disgrace. Because Heaven help her, she'd wanted this. From the moment that door had clicked shut, leaving the room in darkness, she'd felt overpowered by sentiments she couldn't name—and then he'd kissed her forehead, and all the wild sentiments had coalesced into one simple primal thing.

This. Him. The feel of his mouth against hers. She held tight to his arms and let him tilt her face to an angle he liked better, and gave herself up to whatever came next.

It was the alarm, surely, the fright of her near brush with ruin that had loosened her hold on reason and shrunk her world down to the touch of his hands on her elbows, the ardent vibration of his apologizing voice, the familiar clean smell of his soap.

And now it was one dizzying sensation after the next. The smooth kid of his glove against her skin. His arm muscles bunching to fill her grip. The sound of his unsteady breaths in concert with hers . . . and the slow, thorough exploration of her mouth by his.

Or not thorough, really; not yet. This careful angling of his face and then hers, the delicate attention paid to every full place and every spare place across both her lips was just the beginning, she knew. No girl at school had ever been kissed, but Penelope Towne had a married sister who was apparently very forthcoming with details.

So she knew. Soon he would wish to impose his tongue

into her mouth, if she didn't stop him. And then his hands would roam, forsaking the elbow and cheek where they now rested in favor of improper parts and more improper parts. That would shock her, and charge her with the sudden strength to pull away and stop this madness.

She ought to stop it now, of course. She oughtn't to have let it begin. But his mouth on hers was an intoxication, a sweet, insidious liquor that left her light-headed and swaying, so that she had to feel about for a firmer grip on his arms.

She moved her lips, a bit. Surely a woman wasn't meant to just sit like a statue, accepting a man's attentions without any answer. So, though it made her feel both brazen and dreadfully unsure, she dragged her mouth, feather-light as she could make it, from one corner of his lower lip to the other.

He made a sound in his throat. It was unplanned, uncultured, unlike any utterance she'd ever heard from a man, and it struck up a hundred small fires in her. Maybe she wouldn't prevent the imposition of his tongue. Maybe she'd let his hands wander, especially if it meant he might make that sound again.

As though he'd overheard her thoughts, his left hand came away from her elbow. Her breath hung arrested as she waited to see where the hand would settle. Men started at the waist sometimes, Penelope had said, and worked their surreptitious way up the ribs. A crude man might go straight for a woman's derriere, and press her tight against him to gratify his arousal.

Mr. Blackshear's hand, clever and subtle, did neither of those things. It drifted to the side of her head, thumb on the sensitive hollow beneath her ear, and his kid-covered fingertips began to play, subtle as a whisper, at the back of her neck where her hair began.

Good Lord in Heaven. Penelope had said nothing of

this. Maybe it was a trick her sister's husband had never learned. Poor husband, then, and poor sister, because this exquisite touch at her nape, in tandem with the sly restraint of his kiss, was enough to liquefy her bones and evaporate her will altogether. She exhaled, and the breath came out as a sigh, languorous and wanton.

His own breath caught. His fingers stilled and his mouth paused in its artful siege.

Her heartbeat thundered in the silence. Now he would throw off his restraint. He would crush her to him. She'd feel his tongue and his teeth. He would lay her down on the floor and take such liberties as an experienced man knew how to take, and she would not offer the slightest resistance.

But he stayed as he was, fingers unmoving, mouth an agonizing half inch from hers. Then he settled his hands on her shoulders and tipped his face so their foreheads met. His upper arms, where she still clutched, rose and fell on a long breath.

"You see how easily these things can happen." His voice betrayed the effort by which he mastered himself. He would have liked to lay her down on the floor, she could tell. "Even a man with honorable intentions . . . Even a lady whose ambitions depend upon her virtue . . . Even two people who are no more than friends by daylight can fall prey to the influence of a secret dark room. That's why you must avoid ever being alone with a man in such settings. Even a man you deem trustworthy." His hands left her shoulders and he shifted all his weight away, perhaps back onto his heels. She had to let go of his arms.

"I'm not sorry." Almost certainly she would be, once the dizziness wore off and she was left to reckon with her own behavior. But before regret set in, she wanted him to know. "I'm not sorry this happened, Nick." She was all reckless courage now, and to use his name seemed only right.

"You will be. Katherina." He made her name into a sentence of its own, as if it were too rarefied to mix with common words. "If not this evening, then one day when you've met a man toward whom your heart inclines, and you wish he could have been the first to kiss you."

She couldn't muster up any reply. It seemed reasonable and probably true, what he said, and still she was a hundred miles from sorry.

And how did he know she hadn't been kissed before? Did he simply credit her with that much virtue, or had her response to him been tellingly inept? Her hand rose, reflexively, to touch her fingers to her lips.

"*I'm* sorry," he said, as though that could possibly be what she wanted to hear. "I owe you a thorough apology for my behavior, but I think it's better we leave this room without the delay that would entail. We've goaded fate quite enough for one night. Can you stand now?"

"Of course." She grasped the back of the sofa and let pride and self-preservation push her to her feet; no groping about to see whether he was offering her a hand. She might have liked another minute to recover her steadiness, but he was right in urging a prompt exit. Too, if they lingered, perhaps he'd take the opportunity to tell her at greater length how much he regretted having kissed her.

And even though regret was surely the correct attitude for both of them, and she would almost certainly arrive at that state herself before too long, it stung to see him so quickly recovered from the event that had turned her thoroughly inside out.

It's different for men. A reminder fitted to so many occasions. He'd kissed women before, she must recall. There was no novelty in it for him.

"I'll see whether there are many people on the terrace.

If not, you should be able to go back that way without being noticed." He was all business, planning the exact devices by which they would behave as though nothing had happened between them tonight. "I'll go by way of the halls."

"Yes. That will be prudent." Shame stirred in the pit of her stomach, preparing to rise from its inopportune slumber. She oughtn't to have told him she wasn't sorry. She oughtn't to have called him by his Christian name. That much, at least, she could already begin to regret.

She didn't say another word as he led her to the French doors; nor after he'd stepped out and come back to tell her the way was clear. Speech would only delay her further, and after all, what more was there to say? She whisked past him through the doors and took a straight path along the terrace, never looking back to see whether he watched her go.

Chapter Nine

He seldom thought of the day that he'd lost hope of winning her. As tales of romantic disappointment went, it had to be one of the most prosaic any man could claim. No one would ever buy tickets to see it acted out on stage.

Nick turned over in his bed. Sleep eluded him still. Partly because of an importunate erection that he would not, on principle, touch. Partly because what happened at the rout tonight had woken every memory of his foolish youthful hopes and mistakes, particularly the ignominious way it all came to an end.

He'd been calling in Gower Street for a month or so—he cringed to recall that he'd felt so sure, so soon, of his feelings for a lady he could scarcely have known, but thus it had been. He'd been six and twenty, in thrall to her beauty, his admiration no doubt mixed up with the regard he felt for her father and his infatuation with the family as a whole. At that time in his life he could imagine little finer than to marry a barrister's daughter, well spoken and lovely to behold, whose parents would smile upon his suit.

He'd always been careful with his shillings, but he'd laid out that morning for roses. A good big bunch of them, in a golden sort of yellow—he'd gone to four different market stalls before he'd found the right shade—reminiscent of her hair. And he'd written her a note, and copied it in his best hand on a pristine sheet of foolscap, expressing his regard for her and hinting at the hopes that such regard must necessarily engender. Quite a bit of effort he'd put into that note, arriving finally at an optimal balance of sincerity and circumspection: there'd be no danger of her missing his meaning, but also nothing to embarrass her, in the event his courtship was not welcome.

He hadn't been entirely stupid. He'd recognized the possibility of failure. But as he walked up Gower Street, roses in hand, recipient of approving smiles from every good-hearted passerby who liked the sight of a courting young man, that possibility seemed more and more distant, crowded almost to the border of impossibility by a prodigious bloating of hope.

Hope. He turned over again, lifting the sheets clear to avoid unhelpful friction. Well, why shouldn't he have been hopeful in those days? He'd been a handsome young man with bright prospects and a good family. She'd given every sign of liking him—only later had he been observant enough to notice that she treated every male caller with that same vibrant graciousness.

The ax had fallen with a swiftness that he'd eventually see was meant to be merciful. All four Westbrook daughters were in the parlor when he was shown in. Miss Westbrook's eyes fixed immediately on the flowers and she waited only for his smile, and his first step toward her, before springing to her feet and saying something about how pretty the roses were and how good it was of Mr. Blackshear to bring flowers to *them*. And before he could think of how to tactfully correct her, she plucked out his note and handed it to him, pretending to think it was a paper of his that had accidentally got mixed up among the flowers.

The rush of incredulity, as he took back the note, had not even left room for mortification.

"It's very vexing, isn't it, to have to make do with poor paper." That was the utterance most vivid in his memory. *Vexing.* She'd gone on to say something about how when she married a gentleman of rank and fortune, she would have linen-fiber paper for all her correspondence. By the time she'd finished saying it, his incredulity had made way for a breathtaking surge of humiliation. He hadn't known his paper was wanting in quality. To copy over his note on a fresh sheet had been a rare extravagance for a man of his means and habits. He'd been proud of the result.

He'd gone straight home and tossed his note in the fire. And even after he'd girded himself and resumed calling on the family, and found himself capable of friendship with her, and eventually put the embarrassment behind him, he'd never once pleasured himself to thoughts of her since that day.

It would just be pathetic, wouldn't it, spinning those fancies round a woman who'd made her lack of interest so plain. A man had to have a little pride.

I'm not sorry this happened, Nick. He shut his eyes against the memory. From the moment he'd watched her walk out of that darkened room, those words, the fervent voice in which she'd said them, wreathed round his other thoughts like a cat round his ankles, demanding notice.

I'm not sorry. She'd sounded like passion incarnate. So blazingly sure of herself. So utterly unhindered by shame.

He swept his palm across his stomach, a restless substitution for the act he would not commit. The muscles there were all rigid with tension, with unruly appetite.

She wasn't the only woman in the world who could be sure of herself and unhindered by shame. He knew several such women on an intimate basis. He ought to call on one. It had been too long. That was the real problem, now that he thought of it.

He opened his eyes and stared up at the ceiling. He'd lit a candle for reading when he'd gone to bed. He hadn't read a word.

God, the way she'd sighed when he'd worked his fingertips at the back of her neck! How far would she have let him go, drugged as she was by fleshly delight, her modesty lulled by the dark? What if he'd traced with his fingers down over the little rises and hollows of her vertebrae; feathered them across her collarbones; found his way under the edge of her bodice? A caress at the nape was nothing to what he could have shown her, given time and her acquiescence.

His palm felt damp against his stomach. His fingertips were creeping lower, into the narrow swath of hair that started at his navel and led downward. There'd been no lack of interest in her response to him tonight. *That* was the real problem. It was no longer a matter of spinning fancies round an unattainable porcelain princess. The air of pathos was gone. He had memories now, vivid recollections of how she'd felt and sounded and tasted. Two minutes' work, bolstered by those memories, and he'd be able to sleep.

He halted his fingers nevertheless. He couldn't give in to this. The kiss had been a single spectacular lapse, he'd told her he regretted it, and now he needed to behave in whatever way would make his words true. He needn't encourage any sentiments in himself that might make it more difficult to finally see her marry her marquess, or Lord Barclay, or Lord John Stargazing Scarecrow, or whatever man she eventually snared.

He threw off the covers and jumped out of bed, taking

his candle to the washstand. The water in the pitcher would be frigid at this hour. He poured a little into the bowl, then wrung a cloth and applied it, clutching up his nightshirt to undignified heights, gritting his teeth at the shock of cold. Serve his foolishness right if his bollocks shrunk all the way up into his groin and never came back.

But the chilly cloth did its job. Ten seconds of its noxious company and his appetites were doused to extinction. So at least he wouldn't have a private sin to recall, on top of the already awkward enough shared misdeed, the next time he faced Miss Westbrook.

Not to mention facing her parents. Christ. He let his nightshirt fall and tossed the washcloth into the bowl. It hit the china with a sodden *thunk*. He oughtn't to have needed the wilting effects of cold water, really. The consciousness of how he'd betrayed the Westbrooks' trust, how he'd perpetrated on their daughter the very sort of wrong he'd promised to protect her from, should have been enough to kill his ardor.

Well, at least they weren't likely to find out. He'd never breathe a word of the incident to anyone, and Miss Westbrook, with so much more to lose, would surely keep the secret just as close. In company—and henceforward, he'd be sure they saw each other only in company—they'd behave as though no such thing had ever happened. Then with luck, and perhaps a bit of time, it would be as if no such thing ever had.

MR. BLACKSHEAR had been right in his prediction. She was sorry. From the ends of her hair to the tips of her toes, she was sorry, sorry, sorry for having been so careless as to—

No. Kate curled her hands into fists and set her teeth, staring up into the darkness of her room. *Careless* made it sound like an accident that had happened while her guard was down. As if she'd had charge of Lady Harringdon's spaniel and turned her back long enough for the thing to run off. A matter of mere negligence, with no conscious wrongdoing.

She knew better than that.

She was sorry, from the unsettled pit of her stomach on out to all her restless limbs, for her part in—

No. Not *her part.* It was only half a repentance, if she took only half the blame. She flexed her fingers and curled them again.

He'd been the one to set his hand at her jaw and bring his mouth to hers, yes. He'd been the one to kiss, at first, and she the one to be kissed. But between that first friendly touch of his lips on her forehead, and the searing contact of mouth against mouth, she'd had ample opportunity to discourage him, and—

And no, even this was a dishonest way of recounting it. He hadn't meant that kiss on the forehead to lead to anything else. He'd had no intentions, no designs, that wanted *discouraging* by her. He would have waited, chaste and cordial, for her to regain her legs, if she hadn't caught her breath and tipped her face toward him and *willed* him, from some wild, foreign impulse, to put his lips on her again.

A half dozen small memories dove in like hornets. Her coarse, wanton sigh. *I'm not sorry this happened, Nick.* The clumsy eagerness with which she'd gripped his arms and dragged her mouth across his. His regret, owned frankly aloud while all her nerve endings were still pining for his touch. That long walk back through the ballroom, sure at every step that her eyes, her cheeks, her lips must make a plain confession to any onlooker of what she'd been about.

She brought her hands up to cover her face, to hide

from the memory hornets, and she let out a long, wavering breath.

"For Heaven's sake, what is it?" Viola's voice nearly spurred Kate out of her skin. "You may as well be over here jumping up and down on my mattress, for all that I'm likely to sleep."

"I'm sorry. I didn't mean to disturb you. I'd thought you were asleep." She had been when Kate had come in a little after four. Only Mama had waited up, and only long enough to see that she was safely home. She hadn't demanded to hear every last detail of the evening, and thank goodness for that.

"I was asleep, but I'm not now." A yawn sounded through the darkness. "Is something the matter? Did Lady Harringdon make you walk three paces behind her and forbid you to speak or meet anyone's eyes?"

"No. You're very unjust. She showed me a great deal of kind attention."

"Then what's unsettled you so? You're shifting about as if you had cake crumbs strewn across your sheets."

Kate slowly took her hands away from her face. The dark, she'd learned already tonight, had a nefarious way of making reckless acts seem reasonable. Now suddenly it pressed in on her with a new suggestion: *Tell her. Why not tell her?*

She could hear her own breath in the room's quiet. She could almost hear her heartbeat.

When she'd come back into the ballroom she'd felt as if she was viewing the guests and pleasant diversions through a pane of crazed glass. The modesty with which she impressed Lady Harringdon was but a fraudulent piece of playacting. Mrs. Smith would surely never let her daughter speak to Miss Westbrook again, if she knew the truth. She'd begun the evening feeling she'd finally found her place among people who spoke her language, and she'd ended it feeling utterly alone. Unworthy. Set apart from any chance of real belonging by her imprudent act, and all the necessary secrecy that followed.

"Kate?" Viola had sat up. All the irritation had fled her voice, its place taken by sisterly concern. "What is it? What happened?"

And all at once she felt the full weight of her daily burden, of being the only one in this house who went about measuring all her actions by how they might aid or hinder the family's respectability; by what they might mean for her younger sisters' prospects.

Or usually, rather, she measured her actions that way. Usually she kept respectability in mind. She'd finally staggered beneath that burden, and now she had a chance to step out from under it, for the length of a conversation at least.

"I kissed someone." She kept her voice low and gripped the counterpane in fistfuls. "At the party tonight, someone kissed me."

"What?" Viola's whisper shot across the room like an arrow in flight. "How could such a thing happen? Surely you didn't let a gentleman draw you away from the company, after Papa's warning. Where was Mr. Blackshear? He was supposed to guard against this."

They couldn't have this conversation across even the small distance that separated their beds. Kate slipped out from under the covers and padded over the carpet to climb in with her sister. She felt as if she were stepping into water whose depths she didn't know. She pressed her lips together, keeping the secret for one second more. Then she spoke. "Mr. Blackshear was there at the time."

Darkness prevented her from seeing the comprehension spread over Viola's face, but she could imagine it. It made a slow progress, like those outward-traveling rings that marked where a pebble had been tossed into a placid lake. Six seconds went by before the first ring lapped up against the shores of her sister's understanding.

"Mr. Blackshear?"

She couldn't blame Viola for her hushed, incredulous tone. The story was in every way preposterous.

Briefly it occurred to Kate to dart away from the truth. But she couldn't even begin to think of a credible lie. She took a breath. "Mr. Blackshear. Yes."

Vi, who'd remained sitting up, now lay down slowly. They'd shared a bed when they were small. Her sister's presence beside her, all space-claiming elbows, felt familiar and comforting. "I can scarce believe it of him." Not so incredulous now, despite her choice of words. Wondering, though, and more than half the way already to appalled. "He's always conducted himself here as the very pattern of honor and respect. I never would have guessed him for the sort of man who would turn a lady's trust to his unscrupulous advantage."

"He didn't. It wasn't—" The explanation stuck in her throat; she had to swallow and try again. "He's not that sort of man. He didn't take advantage."

"I don't understand. It *was* Mr. Blackshear who kissed you?"

"Yes. And he shouldn't have done it. He said as much himself. But it's not as though he'd schemed and calculated to bring it about. He'd drawn me aside to speak privately and we were nearly seen. It would have meant ruin. And somehow the fright of that predicament . . . and then the relief, when the danger had passed . . ." Words fell so pitifully short of conveying what that moment had been. "I was shaking, and a bit faint. He caught me at the elbows to support me when I couldn't stand. And then we were very near one another. And it was dark."

"He drew you aside to speak privately in the dark?"

Viola queried like a single-minded barrister, seizing those details that bolstered her grim reading of the events.

"He didn't plan what happened." Like the most stubborn of witnesses, never swaying from her story because she knew she spoke the truth. "I'm sure to my soul of that."

A brief pause, while Viola considered her sister's certainty, probably reviewed her own experience of Mr. Blackshear's character by way of corroboration, and tossed it all onto the scales against the bald fact of the transgression. "Very well, but that doesn't excuse him. Falling victim to the passion of the moment might not be quite so villainous as plotting a seduction, but it's still despicable. I cannot respect a man so at the mercy of his appetites that he would impose his attentions on a lady, even if the insult stops at a kiss."

"Viola." Here it came. The bombshell twist in her testimony. The step into deepest water. And yet she felt so strangely calm. "There was no insult. There was no imposition. If he was despicable, so am I."

"I cannot fathom your meaning." Vi turned on her side, as if to somehow read Kate through the dark.

"I wanted him to kiss me. I don't believe he would have done so, but that he sensed that I wanted him to. And I didn't stop him, either from starting or from carrying on. He was the one who stopped, at last, and said we oughtn't to have done it."

"Kate!" Up on one elbow now, her voice a scandalized whisper. "Are you in love with him?"

"I don't see how I could be. We've known him all this time. Surely if I were going to fall in love with him, I wouldn't have waited until now to do it." She'd asked herself this same question at length in Lady Harringdon's carriage on the way back home.

"It does sound . . . unlike what one hears about falling in love." The mattress sighed as Viola slowly lay back down. "Papa says when he first saw Mama it was like being struck by lightning."

"Yes." That was how love was meant to happen, one heard. "Of course it wasn't the same for her."

"No. She came to love him as she came to know him." They'd heard this story so many times, they could practically recite it in their parents' own words. "But that takes only a few weeks. Months, at the most. You've known Mr. Blackshear a great while longer than that."

"You see? It doesn't make any sense that I would be in love with him now. Besides, I wouldn't be in any doubt, would I? Surely I would know."

Viola mulled this over for several silent seconds. "I'm further than ever from understanding, then. Why did you let him kiss you if you're not in love with him?"

That was the very question with which she'd wrestled, once deciding that she was not in love. *Because I'm a wanton* had been the first, shameful answer, the self-condemnation that slithered in even before she'd stepped out onto that terrace to go back to the ballroom.

The longer she'd thought on it, though, the flimsier that answer had grown. Her sister, certainly, would not be satisfied with such a pronouncement. She'd demand it be justified and elaborated upon.

"I begin to believe, Viola, that there have been some major omissions in what we were taught of these things." Were these the words of a wanton? Maybe. They were no less true for that. "I, too, had always supposed that it was a man's part to kiss, and a woman's to permit or deny him. That men sought favors and women granted them, sometimes, for the sake of love. No one ever told me I might want to kiss a man for the sake of the kiss itself."

She could all but hear her sister chewing over this new and meaty thought. "You mean to say . . . it was pleasant," Viola said after a moment.

"Pleasant in the way I imagine strong drink must be." Part of her wanted to tell all the particulars: the heady sense of his nearness; the feather-light progress of his lips along hers; the various evidences of his enjoyment; his fingertips playing at the nape of her neck. But she was already betraying Mr. Blackshear a little by telling as much as she had. She would leave him this much privacy, at least. "And every bit as clouding to the judgment as drink. If he'd attempted anything beyond the kiss, I'm not at all sure I would have objected."

"You would have let yourself be ruined, even? Knowing a child could result?" Viola's voice went thin with amazement.

"I'd like to think I would be mindful of the consequences, and stop short of that point. But I risked grave consequences already, kissing him where we might have been discovered. I ceased to be a rational creature somehow. I'm ashamed to tell it. But so it was." A thought flitted in: how apt a word *unburden* was. Here she was, confessing her dark disgrace, and she felt lighter, looser in her shoulders and chest. "Are you terribly shocked at me?"

"Maybe a little. Surprised, at the very least." Vi spoke slowly, in the way she did when certain gears in her brain began their industrious turnings. "And yet why should I be? If men lose all their reason when their passions are engaged—and isn't that precisely why we're warned against allowing so much as a private interview with a man? Isn't that precisely the fancy upon which novelists like Mr. Richardson have spun so many tales?—then why on earth shouldn't that experience be the same for a woman?"

Bless her militant sister, so quick to absorb the shock, dispense with the shame, and begin shaping the whole experience into some new grist for one of her theories. Kate smiled into the darkness, pulling the covers up to her chin. "Maybe that's why I've never cared for Mr. Richardson's novels. Maybe I always suspected them to be full of lies."

"It's been a gross fraud perpetrated on our sex, I think. Richardson was but one in a vast army of charlatans. Why, every girl's mother is culpable, if she does not speak openly with her daughter on the subject of pleasure and passion. A girl taken by surprise, as you were tonight, could easily fall into disaster."

"I cannot judge reticent mothers very harshly, though." Kate yawned halfway through the thought. A warm drowsiness was settling in, now that she'd made her confession and been absolved of wantonness. "I'm sure they're wary of instilling a temptation where perhaps there had been none before."

"Then I shall have to do what they will not. Arm young ladies with true and comprehensive information. A separate pamphlet, I should think, in addition to the revisions I must make to my chapter on fallen women." She paused. "This may even call for some slight emendation to my thoughts on bodily integrity."

"I'm glad I told you, Viola." Those few words stood for a host of others. *Thank you for knowing something was wrong. Thank you for listening. Thank you for being the one lady of my acquaintance who could hear such a tale and find no cause for blame.*

"So am I, to be sure." Vi turned away on her side, taking most of the covers with her, as had been her habit in their youth. "I wasn't likely to find out the truth about kissing by any other means. And now I shall have a great deal of thinking and writing to do."

Kate stayed in her sister's bed. To be here, crammed alongside like children again, was a comfort. She could almost believe she was small still, innocent, years away from grown-up folly.

She breathed, slow and even, waiting for sleep. Facing

Mr. Blackshear again was going to be a mortifying trial. Dimly she knew that, even drowsing in the glow of Viola's ready exoneration. The prospect plucked at her thoughts and later thrummed along the edges of her dreams, distracting as gloved fingertips trifling through her ribbon-bound hair.

HE'D THOUGHT some, in the three days since the event, of what he might do to put her at ease. To reassure her that nothing would change between them; that he took all the blame for what had happened upon himself; that he'd already all but forgotten the particulars, up to and including *I'm not sorry this happened, Nick.*

She had apparently been mulling over the same matter, and decided on a facade of frivolous, impersonal gaiety. It hurt, somehow, to watch. He didn't like to be responsible for making her do anything false.

But here he was on his first visit to the house since promising her father to keep her safe from unscrupulous men, and his few incidental interactions with her had all the weight of the silk thread with which she was presently sewing some decorative thing. She sat on the sofa, Miss Viola beside her, their attention half occupied by their respective needlework frame and book, and half engaged by the odd exercise going forward at the hearth end of the parlor.

Though it wasn't so odd to the sisters, of course. They'd seen it enough times before.

Nick curled and uncurled his right hand fingers, flicking away the extraneous thoughts. "Ready?" He held up his paper where Lord Barclay could easily read from it. "Once more unto the breach, then."

Barclay stooped, caught up the buckets of coal at his left and right hands, and straightened. He drew in a breath, concentrating his attention on the paper. " 'Stiffen the sinews, summon up the blood, Disguise fair nature with—' Good Lord, that *does* make a difference."

"Do you feel how it brings the source of your voice down to just above your stomach?" Two rooms away, her words carrying effortlessly through two sets of open doors, Mrs. Westbrook paused in her regal pacing to deliver this query. Nick tapped the spot under his own ribcage for illustration before turning to watch her. "That's your natural source of speech," she went on. "If you want to be heard in the back rows without shouting, this is where you begin. Fierce articulation of your consonants will do the rest." She carried a walking stick with which she now made a little flourish. "Onward, and be mindful of where you take your breaths. 'Disguise fair nature . . .' "

Barclay nodded, wet his lips, and returned his gaze to the page.

"Disguise fair nature with hard-favor'd rage;
Then lend the eye a terrible aspect;
Let pry through the portage of the head
Like the brass cannon; let the brow o'erwhelm it
As fearfully as doth a galled rock
O'erhang and jutty his confounded base,
Swill'd with the wild and wasteful ocean."

This was their seventh time through the speech—Barclay had already whispered it, delivered it in conversational style, and articulated the whole with a wine cork clutched between his front teeth—and Nick suspected every person in the room could recite the final lines right along.

"Now set the teeth and stretch the nostril wide,
Hold hard the breath and bend up every spirit
To his full height. On, on, you noblest English.
Whose blood is fet from fathers of war-proof!"

"Splendid, sir. I believe every one of us is ready to charge off and fall upon whatever enemy you choose." She would have made an excellent leader of troops herself, Mrs. Westbrook. He could remember the pride that had welled up in him the first time he'd felt the full weight of her approval.

The full weight of her wrath must be equally formidable. He would surely feel it, and Mr. Westbrook's wrath as well, if they were to find out he'd put his hands on their daughter.

Maybe even worse than wrath would be their disappointment. *I'm not sorry this happened, Nick,* would be a poor consolation if his actions should lose him the good opinions he prized above all others

He flexed his fingers again to clear his thoughts.

Barclay dipped his head, acknowledging Mrs. Westbrook's praise. "You're very kind. I confess I feel a bit ridiculous, still, saying such grand words. I'd thought we'd be practicing with plain sentences."

"Count yourself lucky, Lord Barclay." Miss Westbrook was nearly sparkling with mischief and good humor when Nick turned to her. Her needle flashed busily on. "When Mr. Blackshear stood where you are now, Mama had him delivering one of Portia's speeches from the courtroom scene."

The baron, catching her mood, cocked a brow and grinned at Nick. "The quality of mercy is not strain'd?"

"Nothing of the kind." Mrs. Westbrook ventured a few steps into the intervening room; Nick could hear the smart tap of her walking stick. "If I'd assigned him that well-worn speech he would have plowed through it without pausing to get the sense of the words, just as you would if I'd set you the one about Saint Crispin's Day. I look for something with which the speaker must apply some energy to acquaint himself."

"Besides, that 'quality of mercy' business would never

do in a real courtroom. No judge would stand for it. I did the bit where she stipulates that Shylock cannot take any blood along with his pound of flesh. That's the sort of hairsplitting that warms a barrister's heart." Nick delivered this last line over his shoulder, with a smile meant for the Westbrook matriarch.

No, she didn't know what he'd done. He'd been reasonably certain Miss Westbrook wouldn't tell, and now he was sure of it—not because Mrs. Westbrook couldn't have dissembled on the matter, but because she wouldn't have. She would have confronted him straightaway.

"If I were a judge, I'd be more inclined to allow a lecture on mercy than to go along with that reasoning about the blood." Miss Viola spoke up, eyeing Nick rather severely. "There's no possible way to remove that much flesh without releasing some blood; therefore permission to take the blood is implicit in permission to cut out the flesh. It doesn't need explicit mention in the contract."

"Nevertheless, Portia succeeded in arguing the court round to her side." Miss Westbrook spoke lightly, hurrying the conversation away from the topics of blood and the cutting out of flesh. "Just as a barrister must often argue people away from their first reading of events, and just as Lord Barclay, I'm sure, will persuade other members of the House to see things as he does." She spoke with eyelids lowered, watching her fingers work away; only at the end did she glance up at the two men and smile.

The baron smiled back.

He liked her. As was to be expected. He'd met her at her most radiant, to be sure, all aglow with enjoyment at the ball, and to now observe her refined manners, set off by the unconventional family in which fate had placed her, seemed only to solidify the good opinion he'd formed that night. His smile creased his face hard enough to make the scar-crossed dimple appear.

Good. This was a triumph. Very easily the baron's response to meeting Miss Westbrook's family might have been a visible disappointment at finding that the pretty girl he'd met at the Astleys' rout was after all not eligible. But Nick had gambled on what he sensed of the man's deep fair-mindedness, and the gamble appeared to be going his way.

That was, Miss Westbrook's way. Which for his purposes was the same thing.

He took a half step back, twisting to address Mrs. Westbrook. "Should he go through it a second time with the buckets, or may he set those down?"

Sans buckets, Henry the Fifth urged his men to savagery again, and again, and another time after that, with attention paid to strategic pauses and the modulation of syllables. Nick kept his position, holding up the paper and occasionally offering his own suggestions.

She could see by his actions, couldn't she, that his intentions toward her were purely friendly? In the days since the rout, he'd had time to reflect on his behavior, from the moment he'd confronted her with Lord John through that point when he'd had his fingers at the back of her neck. The most unflattering motivations suggested themselves. Jealousy. Covetousness. A desire over which he had no control. Surely advancing her interest with another man was the best way to prove to both of them that he didn't have his own designs on her.

He rolled his shoulder, which had begun to tighten from his unvarying paper-holding stance, and took the opportunity to glance over to the sofa. Miss Westbrook immediately ducked her head and turned a look of fierce concentration upon her sewing.

Confound it. He couldn't stand to have her so uneasy in his presence as to alternate between acting false and frivolous, and refusing to meet his eyes. He needed a private interview. For all his virtuous resolve about seeing her only in company, he would have to find a moment during this visit to speak to her alone. A quick, frank acknowledgment of their mistake; an agreement on their resulting shared state of embarrassment, would surely be the way to put that event behind them, and set them on the path back to the unblushing friendship that would best suit them both.

SHEER STUBBORN pride kept her in her place on the sofa. The more she wanted to slink unnoticed along the wall until she reached the far open door, or lift a corner of the carpet and crawl underneath, the brighter she made her silly smile and the bolder were her flourishes with the needle and thread. Twice she pricked her finger and drew blood. Two *jots* of blood, to quote Portia's chosen term. Mr. Blackshear had been a very good sport about delivering that speech, back in his studying days. Some barristers-in-training balked at playing a woman's part, which was foolish of them as the role had been played by boys for years and years.

She peeked up to find that he'd finished flexing his shoulder and had returned his attention to Lord Barclay and his speech.

Had he always done these things? Moving his shoulder about, curling and stretching his fingers, cocking his head to one side or the other? Surely he had. But she noticed them only now, because each restless gesture woke some memory in her muscles and skin. And no sooner did her neck tingle at the flex of his fingers, or her own head want to tilt in answer to his, than she remembered Viola's all-too-aware presence beside her, and willed herself to smother her response.

This was the price paid by a lady who kissed a man.

She'd eaten of the forbidden fruit. She could not unknow the things she knew now. She could only hope the strength of that awareness would diminish over time, as indeed she trusted the mortification would fade and leave her able to face Mr. Blackshear with tolerable poise once more.

Again Lord Barclay chewed and spat his way through "hard-favor'd rage" and "the wild and wasteful ocean." He, too, was an excellent sport. Handsome as well. Not the handsomest man in the room, perhaps, but with his ready smile, his gracious manners, and a certain ineffable masculinity in his military bearing, he gave a lady much to admire.

She'd liked him already, from the supper and the one shared dance at Cranbourne House. He'd made effortless proper conversation during that dance, answering her questions on the house's history and never presuming to flirt. His conduct today, deferring to Mama's authority with such respect as surely few titled gentlemen would ever show an actress, could only improve what had already been her good opinion.

This was what she ought to be noticing: the merits of the one man present who had *Lord* in front of his name. She'd gone to the Astleys' rout determined to forge as many connections as she could with distinguished people. Whatever her intervening mistakes might have been, here, a mere three days later, was a baron in her parlor, cordial and ready to be charmed. What sort of fool would she be if she let this acquaintance slip through her fingers because her thoughts were all entangled with a man who regretted having kissed her and was no suitable prospect besides?

So when the speaking lesson had finally concluded and it was time for everyone to sit down and have tea, she leveled all her courteous conversation on the newer of their two guests.

There was everything to approve in him. Really, there was. For all his fine upbringing and military dignity, he evinced an agreeable modesty, and seemed altogether more interested in hearing about the Westbrook family than in speaking of himself.

His respectful manner to Mama continued unchanged, even though she no longer addressed him with a teacher's authority. He asked what parts she'd played, whether she preferred comic roles or tragic, and who she thought were the most promising of the modern playwrights. When Viola seized the opportunity—as she inevitably did—to put forth some political point relating to the plays of Mrs. Inchbald, he raised his eyebrows, nodded thoughtfully, and asked her to tell him more.

And though Kate stayed mostly clear of these conversations, confining herself to such pleasantries as seemed appropriate to a morning call with a slight acquaintance, he nevertheless smiled at her often and thanked her most particularly for the tea.

Mr. Blackshear thanked her as well—she'd remembered to make a separate pot of his bitter dark brew—and conversed with the family as congenially as he always did, though she sometimes caught him watching her with a troubled crease in his brow. Once, when she was up and tending to the teapot, he came to the table to replenish his own tea and said something about wondering whether the rain had stopped.

That was a subterfuge, and a fairly obvious one: he wanted her to go with him to the window at the room's far side, that they might speak privately.

She couldn't. Not only because Viola would be watching, and drawing conclusions. He would want to apologize again. He'd want to say what a mistake the kiss had been, and he'd want to assure her there'd be no danger, ever, of another such mistake. Probably he'd want to express his hopes for her snaring of Lord Barclay, as proof of his own disinterest.

She knew all that already. She didn't need to hear any of it.

"I do hope it will be dry by the time you must take your leave," was all the answer she gave, and then she took *her* leave, slipping away from the table and back to her seat as soon as she'd poured his tea.

He understood he'd been rebuffed. She saw it in his face when he sat down again. For the remainder of the call he wore a distracted air, and a slight frowning twist at one corner of his mouth.

And for the remainder of the call she felt sorrier than ever, wishing he could know, without her having to say so aloud, that she didn't blame him at all. And wishing she could notice his frown without igniting a hundred volatile memories, all having to do with his mouth.

Chapter Ten

"NOW THAT was an experience well worth this whole undertaking." Barclay settled in one corner of his carriage, dropping his hat on the seat beside him. He'd insisted that Nick accept a ride home, the rain not having abated. "The next time I attend a house party where someone proposes an amateur theatrical, I shall be ready to amaze the company."

"I'm sorry about the material." Nick sat in the opposite corner, steadying himself with his feet as the carriage swayed out into traffic. "I do remember you saying *Henry the Fifth* wasn't a good representation of what your time in the army had been."

The baron shrugged. "The reality of war would make a very poor play. There are great stretches of tedium such as no paying audience would stand for. And a man breathing his last rarely has anything poetic to say on the occasion. I prefer Shakespeare's version of things altogether."

The very few times Will had spoken of war, in the months after he'd returned to England and before he'd forsaken the family, he'd adopted a flippant tone not unlike Lord Barclay's. Nick had never known how to press past the flippancy, or whether he even ought to. If he'd been a better friend to his brother, a better listening ear, would Will perhaps not have felt the need to seek a connection with the woman for whom he'd then thrown everything away?

He took off his own hat, holding it over the straw-covered floor and tapping off the raindrops. "Would you say you were much altered by your experiences in war?" He frowned at the hat, to make it look as though he was primarily occupied by that matter and asking the question only by the by. The subject might be an uncomfortable one for his companion; he wouldn't add to the discomfort by watching for a response.

"Altered, yes. *Much* altered, though . . ." He was shaking his head when Nick glanced up. "Given what I've seen of some other men, I cannot say so. My alterations have mainly been of the benign sort, I hope. I suppose I took things a little more lightly before my military service. I told you—didn't I?—that my brother Astley has not been impressed by my recent political zeal."

"I should think political enthusiasm must be among the most benign sorts of alteration, as well as the least surprising. Who is more likely to concern himself with the good of the nation than a man who's just devoted several years of his life to that same concern? But perhaps Lord Astley simply regrets the loss of the brother he remembers; the one with lighter pursuits and preoccupations." He knew a bit about that sort of loss. He gave his hat a last shake and set it on the seat, eyes following the action of his hands all the way.

"I think he'd prefer I put the good of the family before that of the nation. I'm next in line for the marquessate, you know, and nearly from the moment I stepped off the ship he's been after me to marry."

From one uncomfortable subject straight to another: it was almost as though the man had somehow been privy to his thoughts during their time in the Westbrook parlor. He schooled his face and looked up. "Indeed?"

"He's ten years my senior and quite sure he'll predecease me, so he'd like to see me settled with a wife and, ideally, a son or two. Thus my presence at that rout. I believe he intends to compel my attendance at one social event after another this Season until finally I break down and offer for some lady, if only to silence him on the subject."

"You don't particularly wish to be married for your own sake, then?" Nick couldn't like the idea of Miss Westbrook marrying a man who'd offered for her only to silence his brother, even if her own approach to wedlock was at least that pragmatic.

"I'm sure I'll like to have a wife." The baron laced his fingers and stretched his arms out before him with a rueful grin. "However, I'd always fancied that thoughts of marriage followed upon meeting the right lady. I have difficulty reversing that sequence." He let his arms fall. "And you? No plans to renounce your bachelor state? Never found yourself tempted by one of the Misses Westbrook?"

Was this an attempt to discover the existence of a prior claim? In any case, his duty as her friend was clear. "No plans or temptations of recent date." Nick sat back and shrugged. "I'll admit to a brief, youthful *tendre* for the eldest Miss Westbrook, though that's little more than admitting to a pulse."

Barclay nodded, his grin gone wider. "To be sure, I would have doubted you if you'd denied the fact. Such beauty is exactly suited to a young man's taste. But I suppose you were in no position then to marry."

"No. And in the intervening years, we became more like brother and sister than a pair of possible lovers." The last word tasted of rank mendacity. He hurried to pile other, blander words upon it. "I suspect that's not uncommon, where habits of proximity do away with all the mystery a lady might have for a gentleman, and he for her. At all events, I look forward to one day celebrating her excellent match, and I'm sure she'll be just as happy for me on the day I tell her about the worthy lady who's won my heart."

"That sounds an admirable sort of friendship. You're fortunate."

Indeed it was an admirable sort of friendship, and indeed he was fortunate, or had been until everything had spun out of control for those scant few minutes in the Astleys' library.

She'd been so dreadfully uncomfortable when he'd tried to speak to her or even look at her today. He might, after all, have done irreparable damage to their connection. And for the first time the thought occurred to him: if she did succeed in marrying Lord Barclay, he might have to avoid them both.

He picked up his hat and tapped it over the straw again, just to have an outlet for a flare of desperate energy. He could never take a post as Barclay's secretary, in that case. He'd worked and waited so long for an opportunity like this one, and he might really have thrown it all away for the sake of an ill-considered kiss.

For the remainder of the journey to the Inns of Court they spoke of politics. And every sensible opinion the baron expressed—every proof of what good work a man who partnered with him might be involved in—drove further and further home the possible cost of his fleeting indulgence in a darkened room.

HE SEEMED to have stepped into some spiral of dire complications, and the next day brought another: an invitation to a ball at Lord Cathcart's house in Grosvenor Square.

Ostensibly the invitation issued from Lady Cathcart, who'd barely said a dozen words to him over the years of their slight acquaintance. However, the message scrawled upon it came in the viscount's slanting, careless hand.

Now you've shown yourself at one party, you cannot in decency decline to appear at another. . . . Don't tell me you'll have no one with whom to converse; my wife has neatly preempted that objection by inviting your Lord Fox Grey Holland Barclay, that the two of you may stupefy your unsuspecting dance partners with talk of reform. . . . Lady C. has also sent an invitation to your pretty Miss W., whose parents will no doubt wish to condition her attendance upon your own again, and I can scarce imagine you'd really like to disappoint—

Nick pushed the invitation away and got up from his desk to pace to the window that looked down on Brick Court. A lady sat on the bench near the sundial, probably waiting for a barrister to come down and speak to her, or to recruit a suitable chaperone with whom she could go upstairs. Unaccompanied women didn't venture into gentlemen's chambers, unless on errands of a most particular nature. Mrs. Simcox had come up sometimes, and Mrs. Marbury, too, though neither of them very recently.

He sighed and turned his back to the window, raking his fingers through his hair. No doubt Cathcart meant well. Perhaps he even thought to hasten the rehabilitation of the Blackshear name by setting the example—indeed, by prevailing on his wife to set the example—of acknowledging Nick. And if he was right, if even one respectable person in attendance should decide it was time to follow the Cathcarts' lead, and cease holding all Blackshears accountable for the transgressions of one, that would not only benefit Nick's own circumstances but might be a first step toward repairing the damage Andrew and Kitty had sustained. His elder brother and sister might begin to gradually replace the many connections they'd lost. By the time their respective children were old enough to marry, they might have a few decent prospects after all.

He folded his arms, resting his back against the strip of wall between the room's two windows. *All Blackshears accountable for the transgressions of one,* indeed. The truth was that he hadn't been able to think of Will, since the events of Tuesday night, without a suffocating sense of his own hypocrisy. His brother, at least, had not laid hands upon an innocent. Will hadn't taken advantage of a lady's feverish response to her first taste of passion.

You didn't do more than kiss her. And you stopped. You caught yourself in time, when you might have given her far more to regret than a kiss. Oh, but he hated the part of his brain that wanted to offer these pathetic self-acquittals. He'd never try anything so mealymouthed in a courtroom. *The prisoner may indeed have stolen the accuser's purse, Your Honor, but I beg you to base his punishment upon the fact that he didn't then follow her home and take all the money she had there as well.*

He pushed off the wall and went back to his desk, where he picked up the invitation. Little doubt of what reply he must make, but he needn't make it this instant. He pulled out the drawer in which he always stored documents that didn't require immediate attention, and found himself confronted by a paper that had languished there for some months.

Not that the paper took him by surprise. He hadn't forgotten about its existence. Why he hadn't thrown it away, when Martha had first sat down at this desk and made free with his pen and ink, he couldn't precisely say.

Proper ladies did sometimes venture alone into a barrister's chambers, after all. A sister given to imposing her will, for instance, might take it upon herself to call on her brother and prepare such an impertinent document.

He set down the invitation and lifted out the paper, which bore but two lines in his sister's hand, the greater part of the page being taken up by a rudimentary map. She'd drawn a set of tiny waves in the broad ribbon that curved left to right through her diagram, to identify it as the river—though the docks she'd sketched, protruding into that same ribbon, surely resolved the matter of identification without any need for waves.

He traced them with his smallest finger, the downward arcs and upward peaks meant to stand for moving water. They seemed such an odd embellishment, such a frivolity, so unlike the sister he'd known for all but the first five years of his life. But then, this wasn't the first thing she'd done that confounded all his expectations.

Nick sat back in his chair, palms resting on the desktop's edge, and closed his eyes. He didn't often permit himself the stillness to examine such matters, but . . . how, exactly, did he justify keeping the connection with Martha when he'd shut out Will? Oh, the superficial answer came readily enough: she and her husband had acted discreetly, committing their malfeasance in a quiet Sussex parish beyond the range of any ton gossips and then patching it over with a speedy marriage and besotted newlywed manners.

They'd brought no scandal to the family. The fact nevertheless remained that their first child, a daughter, had been conceived out of wedlock. Deliberately so. Martha couldn't claim to have been seduced, when she'd hired

Mr. Mirkwood for the express purpose of impregnating her.

Granted, Nick had made his disapproval plain. But a man of integrity would have cut their acquaintance. Or perhaps not cut Will's. A man of integrity would have done so many things differently from how he'd done them, it seemed of late.

He opened his eyes. In the middle of the map, she'd drawn an arrow pointing to a location on one of the docks, presumably the same site named at the top of the page.

There was no reason he couldn't go walking that way. He might just look about the area, so he'd have a picture of where Will spent much of his time. He needn't present himself at the establishment's door, and he certainly needn't prepare any words to say to his brother, or even make up his mind as to whether they ought to speak again. He could simply walk and ponder.

He rose, swiping up Martha's document and making a straight line to where his coat hung, that he might be out the door before he could think of a compelling reason to stay home. A word to Kersey across the hall, who agreed to take down the business of any callers in his absence, and he was free to walk out, past the sundial, past the now-empty bench where the lady had sat, out into the street and down toward the river.

I've had cause, in recent days, to give more thought to the questions of right and wrong behavior. Did he want to say that? Did he want to say anything? *I've done something of which I'm ashamed. I've jeopardized a connection—more than one connection—I'd be sorry to lose. And I cannot speak of it to anyone without imperiling a lady's reputation.*

He could, perhaps, speak of it to someone who lived beyond the bounds of the respectable world in which Miss Westbrook hoped to make her way. Not that he would allow himself to go to Will on so selfish an errand. If rapprochement between himself and his brother was possible, or even desirable—and really, a half dozen circumstances argued against it—then they would have a deal of talking to do on other subjects before he could indulge in the luxury of confessing himself.

So he hadn't the first idea, when he finally stood on the mapped-out dock, studying from a distance the weathered facade of what seemed to be the right office, what he ought to say or even quite why he was there. Only he'd walked all this way, following the directions his sister had set down, and to go back again after a mere bit of silent skulking felt like cowardice, of a sudden.

He shoved himself forward, hands in his coat pockets, one clutching Martha's folded-up map while the other tightened into a fist. Past a stack of crates that two men were passing down one by one to another two men in a wherry, past a clutch of seagulls squabbling over some rubbish they'd found on the dock, through the steady two-way traffic of people who had legitimate business there, he cut a path, heart protesting this decision with a series of dull thudding beats, until he'd set a hand on the door handle and, at more of a loss than ever for what to say, pulled the door open.

The office was a small one, and a good deal dimmer than the day-lit outdoors. A single lamp combined with the window in the building's facade to afford what illumination there was. And what illumination there was revealed at once that Will was not here.

Then, after a second or two of Nick's eyes adjusting, it revealed the three people who *were* here, and a more curious assemblage of three people he'd never seen in his life.

At his left, behind a table atop which he was arranging miscellaneous small items as he unpacked them from a crate, stood a brown-skinned man well over six feet tall. Straight ahead, with a pen in her hand and a ledger open on the desk before her, sat a fearsome-looking woman with a prominent nose. And to the right, his desk pushed up against the window and his visage thus flooded with unforgiving daylight, sat a figure who made the others look like exemplars of benign normalcy.

This man must have barely survived an encounter with fire, or possibly lye. Thick scars made up most of his face, from the scalp on down until they disappeared into his coat collar. His mouth sagged at both corners. He had but one complete ear, and very little in the way of hair.

Nick glanced away quickly, so as not to look as if he was staring, even as it dawned on him that this must be the man in charge. The advantageously located desk argued for it, as did a certain energy in the room that suggested the other two persons were waiting for that man to respond to this unexpected visitor. Indeed the brown-skinned giant had shifted his attention to his scarred compatriot. The woman kept her steady gaze on Nick, pen suspended an inch above her ink pot.

He cleared his throat. "I'm not sure I've come to the right place." He could look at the burned man now, since he was addressing him, without fear of seeming rude. "I'm looking for a William Blackshear. I was told he works here, or perhaps in one of the neighboring offices?" That Martha could have omitted any mention of their brother toiling alongside such an extraordinary collection of people seemed improbable, though not altogether outside the realm of possibility. It might be one of those things she judged to be of no consequence.

"Your skills of navigation haven't failed you, but you're unlucky in the time of your visit." The man sounded good-humored. It was difficult to tell, when his face gave no hint of his mood. "He's out aboard the ship at present, and we don't expect him back for another hour or so. Is it a matter with which someone else might be able to assist you?"

"No, no thank you. It's not to do with business." He'd pulled the door shut behind him, on entering, but hadn't let go the handle. His fingers flexed on it now, prepared to make a brisk withdrawal and leave these people to the industry he'd interrupted.

"Would you like to write a message for him?" The scarred man pushed up from his desk, waving a hand at the paper, pen, and ink there. "We'll see that he has it as soon as he returns."

"Oh, no, that won't be necessary. I'm sure I shall . . ." He made some vague gesture with the hand that wasn't gripping the door handle; something they might read for *I'm sure to encounter him soon enough,* because his scrupulous barrister's tongue was refusing to deliver that lie.

"Is something the matter?" That was the woman. She hadn't gone back to her writing, nor, from what he could tell, taken her gaze from him but for the span of an occasional blink. "Has something happened about which he ought to know?" She eyed him with an almost unsettling intensity, and as he set tongue to teeth to deliver yet another no, she added, "Something within the family? You're one of his brothers, I think."

"Yes." *How the devil did you know?* "That is, no, nothing's the matter. But yes, I am his brother." The words seemed to come out in the right order, for all that she'd taken him so by surprise.

There were two strains of Blackshear physiognomy, and he and Will came from opposite sides. New and slight acquaintances never drew a family connection between his light hair and his brother's dark; his symmetrical smile and Will's crooked; the composed features of one and the ready expressiveness of the other. Indeed the only thing that marked them as siblings was—

"You have the same eyes." She seemed to be reading his thoughts, though he could not make the slightest guess at hers. "Mrs. Mirkwood as well. You and she are very like." Abruptly she looked away, to the pen still poised above its ink pot. Perhaps she felt she'd said too much. Or perhaps she'd said all she had to say and now found no further use for him. She dipped her pen and tapped it with a forefinger over the jar.

He could feel the keen attention of the other two men in the room, and a glance either way showed them to be watching him with their respective aspects of curiosity—the scarred man's symptom being that he'd stayed half risen from his desk.

A thought occurred. It was scarcely conceivable, and yet conceive it he did. Only to dismiss it at once, because Martha would surely not have considered *that* to be of no consequence, would she?

He ventured another look at the woman with the pen, and the thought struggled back from its dismissal, even as a terribly ungallant part of him protested, *She couldn't have been anyone's mistress; she's not pretty enough.*

Self-disgust went swirling through his veins. He was as shallow as he was hypocritical. He, who liked to think he knew how to value a woman as a whole person instead of a pretty face and form.

He cleared his throat. "I beg your pardon, Miss. Madam." Her pen lifted from the paper and she raised her head just enough to catch his eye. "Is it possible—" This could be remarkably awkward, even more awkward than it already was, if he proved to be wrong. Nevertheless he let go the door and took a step forward.

"That is . . . might you perhaps be my sister?" Warmth crept up his throat to his cheeks. At the left and right peripheries the two men were watching, silent and still.

She straightened, fixing him with the full force of her gaze. "I'm Will Blackshear's wife," she said. "If I'm anything to you, that's more than we've been told." Without waiting for reply, she bowed her head to her work again, pen taking up where it had left off.

Her rudeness took his breath away. Literally, for a moment it seemed his lungs would not work, as he stood there, one step advanced into this room where he was not welcome, the warmth in his cheeks fanned to a raging heat that raced all the way up to his hairline. It was—and wasn't this rich!—strikingly similar to how he'd felt when Miss Mary Watson had addressed him before onlookers in the hallway at the Old Bailey, negligently invoking the subject of this same woman who sat before him now.

He glanced left and right, to find both men impassive—or the tall man impassive, at any rate. The other, for all he knew, might be thinking sympathetic thoughts that made no impression on the wrecked canvas of his face. But no, count him for impassive, too. Everyone here was loyal to Will. No one felt charitably toward this brother who'd cast him off. Why in God's name would they?

He found himself without the smallest desire to make answer to the woman's rudeness. She'd merely given voice to the self-dissatisfaction he'd been carrying about with him ever since the day he'd last spoken to Will. He might as well have conjured her for the purpose.

He stepped backward, feeling behind him for the door handle. He had to fumble for a second to find his grip. "Thank you for your time." His voice sounded like someone else's. "Good day to you all." Through the pounding of blood in his ears, and the creak of the door as he pushed it open, he couldn't hear whether anyone wished him good day in return. Not that it mattered. He got himself outside, swung the door shut, and left the place behind him, fists in his pockets, Martha's map wadded and crumpled until it took up almost no room at all.

Chapter Eleven

"IT DOES seem to be the viscountess's hand. She's stingy with the tails on her small *P*'s and *G*'s. You can scarcely tell them from an *A* or an *O*, but for knowing already what word she's spelling." Lady Harringdon sat in her corner of the sofa, Kate's invitation in one hand and her own invitation in another, to scrutinize them side by side. "Still, I suspect some prank on the part of her husband. He promoted you to her notice, didn't he, by having you girls sit with him at supper. He must have omitted any mention of your station. I expect she'll be none too pleased with him when she discovers she sent an invitation to a lady's companion."

"I'm not at all surprised that Miss Westbrook should have been invited." Miss Smith had called on her own today, Mrs. Smith being indisposed by headache. On the opposite sofa she sat very straight, hands clasped in her lap, clearly taken aback by the countess's remarks. "We all had such a pleasant time at supper." She threw a look to Kate, who'd taken a seat as near as she could to the dowager and had been reading to her from an *Ackermann's* while Lady Harringdon inspected the invitation. "I could tell you made a good impression on Lady Cathcart, and certainly on Lord Cathcart. I heard him remarking to his wife on your delightful manners."

Kate's heart warmed at the loyal kindness of Miss Smith, at Lord Cathcart's compliment, at his and his wife's generosity in inviting her to their ball; even at her aunt's befuddled suspicion of everyone's motives. The Harringdon House parlor made an altogether pleasant place to be today. She'd had to be presented to the dowager all over again, but her grandmother had twice remarked on her beauty and seemed to be enjoying the story she was reading aloud.

"You're a young, unmarried lady, Miss Smith, so I shall forgive a bit of ignorance." Lady Harringdon gave one last look to Kate's invitation, front and back. "But generally, when a gentleman remarks to his wife on the delightful manners of a beautiful girl with whom he danced at that evening's party, she does not respond by distinguishing that beautiful girl with an invitation to her own social event." With a flourish she set the invitations aside. "However, we shan't worry that Lord Cathcart harbors any sinister designs upon Miss Westbrook, as he prides himself so on his husbandly constancy."

"Do you recommend I accept the invitation, then?" She had every intention on earth of going to that ball, but a show of deference to her aunt's opinion could only be for the good. "I'd hate to be a cause of embarrassment to Lady Cathcart."

"By all means you must accept." The countess took up her fan, which had dangled from her wrist while she'd studied the invitations, and snapped it open. "You're not likely to ever have another such invitation, so seize it while you can, I say. Perhaps Lord and Lady Cathcart will learn they must review their guest lists together, to avoid any such mistakes in future."

"I still think it probable the invitation is entirely deliberate." What a good, noble-natured girl Miss Smith was, to dare Lady Harringdon's disapproval by making this defense. "The viscount knew Miss Westbrook was a lady's companion, and still invited her to his supper table. Why shouldn't the viscountess have known, and still chosen to invite her to this ball?"

"I seem to have lost the thread." The dowager Lady Harringdon spoke up, turning to Kate. "Is Cassandra going to a ball?" Cassandra was a lady in the *Ackermann's* story.

"No, my lady, I fear it's we who've wandered from the subject. I'll return to Cassandra now, if I may." She raised her eyebrows at her aunt, for permission.

Lady Harringdon nodded, with a smile of such approval as made Kate feel incandescent.

She read on about Cassandra, and hadn't quite finished the story when Lord Harringdon and the footman arrived to help the dowager to her room. The countess said they must come back in a very few minutes, and the footman withdrew. The earl, though, stood just inside the door, waiting and presumably watching her read. She couldn't see what was on his face, as she had to keep her eyes to the page. But when the time came for him and the footman to come help the dowager, he inclined his head to her and said thank you.

The small courtesy filled her with that same sense of triumph her aunt's nod and smile had roused. More than that, it stirred up a hopeful vision of the day she might sit in this parlor as an accepted member of the family, addressing the Harringdons as *Aunt* and *Uncle* and *Grandmother*, watching with pride and keenest satisfaction as Papa and his Westbrook relations rebuilt the bridges they'd demolished so long ago.

This was what she would have lost, if she'd been discovered in that library with Mr. Blackshear. This was why the kiss had indeed been a mistake. All her hopes depended on her marrying a man of high rank and good connections. She couldn't allow herself to forget again, not for so much as a minute.

She walked out with Miss Smith, and as soon as the front door had closed behind them, that young lady spoke. "I don't mean to be critical of Lady Harringdon. She's been most attentive to my mother since we lost my father, and I'm grateful for the interest she's shown in seeing me well settled. But I do wish she would more often choose tact over candor."

"I don't suppose she's ever had to learn tact." She liked Lady Harringdon, blunt manners and all, but she could certainly sympathize with Miss Smith. "And I don't think she truly meant to call you ignorant. Only to say that younger women don't know as much about marriage as do their elders."

"Oh, I didn't think anything of that remark. What disturbs me is her carelessness in speaking to you. Was it really necessary for her to say that your invitation must have been a prank by the viscount, that you're not likely ever to have another, and that Lady Cathcart is mistaken in granting you the consequence suited to an earl's near relation?" She knew, then, that Lord Harringdon was Kate's uncle.

"You're kind to take my part." They were walking up the square, in a northwest direction, and for a moment she kept her eyes lowered to the stones at their feet. "I don't mind, though, because she's right about the unlikelihood of the invitation. There are irregularities in my family that have prevented our being recognized in society, or by our nobler relations." She made her voice steady and smooth. She didn't usually go about offering this information to slight acquaintances, but with her relationship to Lord Harringdon already acknowledged, she would not try to hide the facts.

"I know. My mother told me, after we'd first met you." She halted in her progress up the street, suddenly, bringing a hand out from her ermine muff and laying it on Kate's arm to halt her as well. "And now I shall be guilty in my own turn of excessive candor." Equal measures of apology and unswerving resolve lit her blue eyes. "Do you have something suitable to wear to Lady Cathcart's ball, now that you'll be an invited guest instead of Lady Harringdon's companion? It occurs to me you might not own a true evening gown."

Miss Smith must have recognized the gown she wore to the Astleys' as the same one she'd worn when first calling at Harringdon House. Kate's pride gave an inward wince. "I haven't. I shall have to wear the same gown I wore at Lady Astley's rout. I'll change the pink ribbons for a different color and see if I can't borrow my mother's best shawl to make it more suitable for evening."

"Don't do that. You can borrow one of my gowns. We're exactly of a height, and near the same size, I think." Miss Smith's whole face shone with entreaty. "You could come to my house that evening, and we could go together to Berkeley Square to meet the countess, and then on to the ball. It would be a favor to me. I hate dressing for parties. It would be so much more tolerable with company."

The more Miss Smith piled on the protestations, the more glaring the fact: this was charity. She was pitying poor Miss Westbrook who didn't have a proper evening gown, and trying to do her a good turn.

Kate hesitated. She'd never been in the habit of accepting charity from other young ladies. Rather, she'd been the one to tell them what colors best became them and how to arrange their hair. She'd been the one whose friendship was sought after.

Yet they hadn't been friends, really, the girls with whom she'd associated at Miss Lowell's. At best they'd been like ladies-in-waiting, hanging on her every word of wisdom concerning the latest style of bonnet, or what novels a fashionable girl ought to read. And that had come only after a lengthy, determined campaign to make them all forget her curious parentage and see her on her own merits.

Miss Smith had glossed right over the question of parentage. In fact she'd known, even before the rout at Cranbourne House, and she'd nevertheless greeted Kate warmly and listened to her opinions on *Pride and Prejudice*. Was charity such a bad thing if it came with affinity and friendly feelings?

"You're so kind to offer. I'd like that very much." Kate felt strange and a bit shy, saying the words, but they sounded right.

Miss Smith beamed in answer, and for all Kate's worthy intentions she could not help the usual private observation concerning how the forehead and chin detracted from what was really a perfectly beguiling pair of eyes.

Well, she was in a position to do something about that now, wasn't she? There was no reason the charity in a friendship must go only one way. She hooked her arm through her friend's and started up the square again. "Have you given thought to how you might arrange your hair for the ball?" she said, and her mind was filling already with agreeable visions of scissors and comb and an artfully placed ribbon in just the right shade of blue.

"You may choose any of the gowns, as fancy strikes you, but I had a particular one in mind." Miss Smith—or Louisa, as Kate was now to call her—bustled about her dressing room three nights later with the unstudied poise of someone entirely accustomed to having a dressing room of her own.

And a bedroom of her own, for that matter. Kate had been introduced to three charming younger Smith sisters, but they proved to have their own quarters down the hall. No trace of sisterly presence intruded, either in the neatly arranged bedroom or in this anteroom, where the dressing table sat just where Louisa wished it to be and the gowns were all pretty, festive, and free from the depressing company of any grim-colored Quakerish garments.

Granted, it would take a great deal to depress the magnificence of the gown currently offered up for her consideration. It was made of red silk, the most vibrant shade of red imaginable, with no ruffles or flounces or ribbons to take one's attention away from the color and cut. The only decoration to speak of, if you could even count it as decoration, was a demi-train. She'd never worn a gown with a train of any kind.

She took a deep breath, clasped her greedy hands behind her back, and forced out the words courtesy demanded. "Wouldn't you rather wear that gown yourself, and be the one to make the fine impression?"

"To be honest, it's a bit bolder than I like. I don't mean it's not respectable. The neckline is entirely decent even without a chemisette. Only I didn't realize, looking at the pattern picture and the fabric separately, quite how it would come out. It draws the eye, you see, and I prefer to not have so many eyes upon me. Whereas I expect you're used to that condition." She smiled, not the smallest trace of envy visible. "Do try it on, at least. If it doesn't suit you we'll go through these others until we find one that does."

That settled it. If she had anything to say in the matter, Louisa would learn tonight just how enjoyable it could be to have many eyes upon her. "Thank you. I cannot imagine wanting to try on any other. But since you've deprived me of the pleasure of choosing by offering me a perfect gown on the first try, I insist you let me help you choose your own. And let me look at ribbons as well. I've been thinking since I first met you of how well your eyes would look with the right shade of blue nearby."

The next half hour passed in all the happy industry of putting on pretty clothes—with the help of a genuine lady's maid!—and then Kate exercised her talents in the matter of Miss Smith's toilette. There was indeed a ribbon in a felicitous indigo shade, of a width to make it a proper hair ornament and of such length that the trailing ends would flutter when Louisa danced. Better yet, there was a gown in a similar deep blue satin, and a necklace of dark sapphires, everything conspiring to bring out the color of her eyes. Best of all, the curls, when Kate sheared a few strategic locks of hair at the front, not only disguised the proportions of the forehead but fell and twisted in rather bewitching, unruly fashion. She looked suddenly intriguing and full of mischief; a lady Romantic; Byron's long-lost devilish younger sister.

"I'm not, though," she said when Kate had voiced the observation. "And I'm not interested in the attentions of any gentleman who would approach me in hopes of my being wicked—in hopes of my being *anything* I'm not."

"Mightn't a gentleman approach you under that misapprehension, though, and then, after some conversation, discover he likes your true character even better?" Kate had been standing to the left, arranging a narrow lock of hair to cover one of the hairpins that secured the ribbon. The maid—who ought really to have imposed a new arrangement on Miss Smith's hair long ago, on her own initiative—had gone off to dress Mrs. Smith, leaving them free to speak as particularly as they wished. Now Kate sent her attention to her own reflection in the mirror at the dressing table and made a minute adjustment to one of her sleeves.

The sleeves, short and gathered into puffs, sat wide as could be without falling off her shoulders. You could see almost the entire curve of shoulder into arm, echoing the curves of bosom framed and set off by the square-cut neck.

Louisa was right: it wasn't indecent. She'd seen just as much flesh—more, in fact—exposed on a number of women at the Astleys' rout. Still, she'd never been quite so conscious of her bosom before.

Well, she'd been fairly conscious of it in the Astleys' library, when she'd thought Mr. Blackshear might mean to put his hands there.

Mr. Blackshear would be at the ball tonight. He'd assured Papa of that, though that conversation had taken place somewhere about the Inns of Court. He hadn't been to the house since the day he'd been there with Lord Barclay. It felt odd to know she'd be seeing him again—and he seeing her, in such a gown.

"I suppose someone could make my acquaintance in the way you describe, but I'd prefer a gentleman who cared to know me even without being struck by my misleading looks." Louisa picked up the scissors from the dressing table and frowned at them, turning them over in her hands. "I wish there were other ways to find a husband besides these balls and gatherings where everyone is evaluating each other with thoughts of marriage already present. If I could come to know a man as a friend, first, without worrying over whether he was a good dancer, or whether I'd chosen the gown that best became me—if we could learn the turn of each other's minds; speak without any calculation of whether an opinion might diminish one's appeal to the other; if I could come to admire his good qualities, and he mine, without any thought of possession, then love, if it did come, would have the most solid foundation on which to rest."

"But . . . *could* love follow on such a beginning? Once you'd got used to thinking of him as . . . a brother, almost . . . it seems improbable you could ever be romantic about him. Or he about you." That wasn't how people fell in love. Indeed there'd be no *falling* at all in what Miss Smith described.

"I don't know. Have you read *Emma*?" Her friend looked up, setting the scissors aside again. "Mr. Knightley and Emma were very much like brother and sister for most of the book—indeed they were relations of a sort, his brother having married her sister—and still they fell in love. Don't you find that a terribly romantic idea? Love stealing in to overtake two people who'd believed they were merely friends?"

"It didn't steal in, exactly, though. At least not for Mr. Knightley." It seemed dreadfully important, of a sudden, that she dismantle Louisa's contention point by point. "He'd known for years that he loved Emma. I'm not sure one can even say love stole in upon her, so much as she matured over the course of the story to recognize what had probably been in her heart all along."

"Perhaps you're right. But I shan't stop wishing for a marriage in which I could know my husband had seen me first as a friend." Louisa peered into the mirror and fussed with her forehead curls. "When the romantic feelings ebbed, then, as I gather they generally do, we would still have the friendship to sustain us."

Kate's agitation all drained away, and for a moment she was simply speechless. What a miserable way for a young lady to think of marriage! How could you enjoy friendship with a husband who'd fallen out of love with you? Wouldn't you always feel you were picking at the stale crumbs of what had once been a banquet? Were you to stand by, perhaps, and wish him well as he took a mistress and lavished all his passion and affection on her? How could you—

She caught herself. She had no right to be appalled, she who was planning to make the loftiest match she could, without any interference from her heart. She who meant to lure a husband with her beauty, and see him shackled by marriage vows while he was still in the throes of foolish, unreasoning infatuation. He probably would take a mistress, her entrapped marquess, once the first flames of fancy had died down.

Well, she was prepared for that. She would console herself with thoughts of her sisters' consequence, and with a costly new gown or two. But Louisa's situation was different. She had a family of fair distinction and, by all appearances, a fine dowry. There was no reason for her to approach marriage with such pallid hopes.

Kate pulled up a chair beside her friend's, and sat. "Romantic feelings don't always ebb. I have reason to know. My father fell hard for my mother when he went to the theater one night and saw her on the stage. Even before they'd exchanged a word, he had it in his head to marry her. It sounds like the worst sort of youthful folly—indeed, so she told him in the beginning—but he'd made up his mind to attach her affections, and through perseverance and personal merit, he did." The story embarrassed her, usually, with its romantic excess, even apart from the embarrassment of the social mesalliance.

Louisa, though, did seem to have a romantic streak—even if her idea of romantic ran to Emma and Mr. Knightley—and would benefit by hearing how married love could endure. And she already knew the scandalous outline of the story and had sought Kate's society nevertheless.

She pressed on. "They've been married three and

twenty years now, and they continue to exhibit such affection for one another as must mortify their grown-up children." But oddly enough, having said the word, she didn't really feel mortified at all. Rather a warm sort of pride spilled through her, at the thought that her own parents could be a beacon of encouragement to a girl who owned sapphires and lived in South Audley Street.

She hadn't often been proud of that story. At Miss Lowell's she'd put all her energy into distancing herself from her origins, and cultivating a manner that might convince her schoolmates she'd sprung fully formed from the pages of the latest *Belle Assemblee,* free from any problematic relations. The effort had exhausted her some days.

"May I ask you something, Louisa?" She hadn't meant to broach this. But they were so near the topic already. She angled to face the mirror, and address the other lady through that protective distance. "Why have you been so friendly to me, knowing all along what my family is?"

Because I pity you. She dreaded to hear it, but she couldn't stand to wonder.

"I liked you when we met at your aunt's house." The girl's voice was all gentle gravity. "You were charming and well spoken, and I appreciated your observations relating to Sir George Bigby in particular. I was ready to hope we would be friends." In the mirror her face showed an absolute lack of guile or calculation, even with the devilish forehead curls. "What would it say of me if I were to change my opinion of you upon learning who your parents were?"

"Nothing very dire. Most people base their opinions of a young lady in large part on who her parents are. That you should do otherwise is out of the ordinary, I think you must admit."

"But it's not as though you're the daughter of pirates, or pawnbrokers." Here she went, warming to the argument, inclining her posture slightly and bringing more modulation to her voice. "People pack the theaters to see Mr. Kean. Mrs. Siddons was the toast of London in her day. For us to persist in telling ourselves that these are exceptions in an otherwise disreputable profession strikes me as more than a little absurd."

"Thank you for saying so. I wish more people thought as you do." Some people did, of course. Lord Barclay's respectful manner with Mama had lingered vivid in her mind.

"Well, that's what comes of having a political brother. Philip is forever on about this sort of thing. The importance of working people to the nation's health. The intrinsic right to dignity of every man. And so on. But is that the clock chiming? We'd better go see if my mother is nearly ready to leave."

Kate followed her out, thoughts churning along with the happy anticipation of the ball. How odd that twice now, since infiltrating the haut ton, she should have encountered such unexpected graciousness, and that neither case should have involved a gentleman stupefied by her beauty.

At least she was fairly certain Lord Barclay hadn't been stupefied. His courtesy, like Miss Smith's kindness, seemed more a product of an ideology that had been in place before he'd ever set eyes on her. If he did marry her, it wouldn't be a capricious act that he must sooner or later come to regret.

She couldn't help one more glance into a pier glass as she passed it. The gown might as well have been made for her, so splendidly did it accentuate the virtues of her form. And it did indeed have a demi-train, which couldn't but make a lady glide across the floor like royalty. If she was ever going to stun a man, or build upon the good impression she'd already made, then this night, when she'd arrive as a guest with her name announced and her looks polished to a dazzling glow, must be her finest chance.

Chapter Twelve

Miss Westbrook was late. Of all things. She was the one who wanted so fervently to spend her time at society parties; he was the one who'd passed up a relaxing evening of study in his chambers, again, because he could not be sure Lady Harringdon would look after her properly . . . and she wasn't even here.

Nick sidled along the wall until a pair of heavy-set gentlemen blocked him from the sight of Lord and Lady Cathcart, and then stole a look at his watch. That she would arrive, he did not doubt. Only it would have been nice if he'd known, ahead of time, that she didn't plan to be punctual. There were a dozen better uses he could have made of the half hour in which he'd been milling about, watching other people have what appeared to be a capital time.

If you'd been speaking to her, she might have told you she'd be coming late. The self-castigating part of his brain had been in rare form this past week. But he couldn't bear to see her so ill at ease in his presence as she'd been the day he'd visited with Barclay, so he'd stayed away. It was better for him, too, not to see her. The memory of that kiss would surely fade faster this way.

He pushed away from the wall and started a leisurely circuit of the room, his fourth since arriving. He turned two corners and came upon Lord Barclay, standing in conversation with an august-looking bespectacled gentleman. The baron caught his eye and waved him over.

"This is the fellow who's endeavoring to make a capable persuader of me," Barclay said after effecting the introduction with Lord Littleton, as the older man proved to be. "You ought to see him in court. Stirring speaker, quick on his feet, champion of the downtrodden, everything that's admirable in the legal profession."

"Ah. Your sort of man, indeed." A sudden acuity came to the man's gaze as he studied Nick. "Blackshear, you said. Are you a relation of Andrew Blackshear's, perhaps?"

His heart beat hard. Andrew wasn't political. Anyone acquainted with him must know him from social events or perhaps through his club, which meant they'd also be acquainted with the family scandal that had curtailed his appearances at such venues. "Indeed, he's my elder brother." He braced himself, and didn't look at Barclay.

Lord Littleton nodded, piecing matters together. "You have a deal to say to the baron, I expect, concerning what can be done for those men so altered by their service as to now be unfit for life among polite people."

And there it was, a sharp blow to the chest. Curse the man, he almost certainly hadn't even meant malice. He'd only drawn what seemed to him a logical conclusion, relevant to the conversation at hand. No doubt he never dreamed that this might be a subject on which Lord Barclay had been kept in the dark.

No matter. Littleton might as well have cackled and rubbed his hands together with villainous glee. Though Nick trained his gaze rigidly on the older man, he could feel Barclay's puzzlement, a peripheral disturbance like the rustle of leaves in a nearby tree.

He took a breath. "Not at all." A false briskness infected his words. "We've spoken enough to establish that we haven't any significant political incompatibilities. Beyond that I should consider it presumptuous to impose any of my opinions." He clasped his hands behind his back and raised his chin a jaunty degree to indicate a joke was coming. "And I prefer to confine my presumption to telling him he's not breathing properly, or refusing to be convinced by his well-reasoned arguments because he hasn't put his dramatic pauses in the right place."

Barclay and Littleton both laughed, with a gusto far outstripping the wit of the remark. "Quite right, quite right," Littleton said. "I'm sure he gives you opportunity enough for that." For good measure he asked the baron some question about his brother Astley, effectively sweeping all traces of the topic away.

Such a graceful, gentlemanly maneuver, a minuet figure impeccably executed by the three of them: without any open pronouncement, it was clearly understood that this subject would not be referred to again.

Lord. Could he possibly despise himself more? He must depend now on the baron's delicacy, hoping honor would prevent the man from later asking Littleton what had been behind that bit of awkwardness with Blackshear. A memory rose up of Will's wife, staring her harsh judgment at him. He'd been sure, once, of having a superior character to hers. Yet it was he who went about hoping people wouldn't discover the truth, and she who scorned society's opinion and stood up for his brother.

Somewhere in this morass of self-dissatisfaction studded with the fraudulent pleasantries he must occasionally contribute to the gentlemen's conversation, a word from elsewhere plucked at his consciousness. From the right, at the room's great doorway, in the butler's voice: *Harringdon*. Finally, Miss Westbrook's party had arrived.

He twisted to look. Probably not quite polite to the two men with whom he was ostensibly speaking, but damn it all, he knew better than anyone in the room what this moment meant to her—a grand entrance with her name called out—and, his own evening having already gone down the road of disaster, he could at least take some vicarious enjoyment in her triumph.

Besides, Barclay was turning to look, too. So she'd definitely succeeded in making an impression on the baron. Nick would do his best to be happy for her in that triumph, too.

Lady Harringdon blocked his view at first. Then a woman of middle years not familiar to him, and then a fetching young lady who proved, surprisingly, to be the same Miss Smith who'd sat across the supper table at Cranbourne House—he wouldn't have guessed it but when her name was announced he could see it was none other. She'd done something different with herself since he'd seen her; some rearrangement of . . . of . . .

Whatever he'd been thinking was gone all of a sudden, snatched from his grasp and whirled off like a feather on a blustery day, as Miss Smith stepped to one side.

"Miss Westbrook," the butler intoned.

He swallowed. That quickly, his mouth had gone dry.

Hell and fiery damnation, how could she continue to do this to him? Three years ought to buy a man some . . . well, not indifference; he wouldn't hope for that, but some aplomb, at least. *Ah, yes, I know those eyes; no novelty there. Yes, there's the hair to which I've long since grown accustomed, and the porcelain skin, too.* Granted he'd never seen quite so *much* of the porcelain skin. He'd never, to be specific, seen so much of her bosom, rising in curved perfection from the bodice of her gown, and suddenly his hands ached; he ached all over with ferocious regret that he had not touched her there when he'd had his one chance.

Get hold of yourself. Think how much worse your regrets would be now if you'd taken that liberty, too. And for God's sake stop gaping at her bosom like a damned schoolboy. He forced his gaze down, forsaking the view of flesh to instead fill his vision with the red, red silk that draped her. Where the devil had she been hiding this gown? Last week she'd been all delicate beauty in that pink-and-white thing she'd worn, like a visitor from some fairyland where ladies grew up alongside roses in the flower beds.

Tonight she was an incendiary device bewitched into human form. Not that the gown itself was necessarily provocative—the neck was no lower than was customary for evening—but the color invited eyes to linger, as milder colors did not. And once lingering, any eye that had a man's sensibility behind it must soon perceive the extraordinary merits of her figure.

His gaze traveled up again, pausing only briefly at the bosom before returning to the familiar face—and his breath caught. She was looking at him. Among all the titled and otherwise eligible gentlemen in this room, more than one of whom, he could now see, was craning for a look at her, he was the one on whom her glance had settled.

Instantly the glance flitted away, her cheeks gone pink.

Christ. She'd just seen him look her up and down, lingering at the bosom both ways. So, yes, he could despise himself more than he'd already done.

He forced himself to speak. "You ought to ask her for a dance." Here was one piece of penitence, muscling these words out to Barclay in a tone of casual good nature. "She won't know many people here. I'm sure she'd welcome a set with someone she can count as an acquaintance." The ladies were making their way into the crowd, apparently bound for some other part of the room.

"By that logic, oughtn't you to ask her? I should think a friend would be even more welcome than an acquaintance."

He shrugged one shoulder, hands still clasped behind his back. "Not on this occasion. She can dance with me whenever she likes." She'd never danced with him in all of three years. "I'll have the pleasure of hearing in minute detail about whom she danced with and what everyone wore, the next time I call at the Westbrooks' house."

"Ah." The baron grinned. "You didn't exaggerate, when you said you're like a brother in that family." He explained to Lord Littleton the connection between Nick and the Westbrooks, the role Charles Westbrook had played in introducing them, and of course the identity of the girl in red who'd momentarily captured their attention. Littleton pronounced her very fine.

That Littleton knew of the irregularities attending the Westbrook name, just as he knew what there was to know of the Blackshears, was clear from a slight increase in the gravity of his expression. He'd apparently resolved to be more circumspect on such matters now, though, because he made no remark. In fact when Barclay excused himself to go and secure one of Miss Westbrook's dances before they were all taken, the older man cleared his throat and tilted his head in an apologetic manner. "I fear I spoke out of turn, earlier. You've chosen reticence on a subject round which I would very likely choose reticence myself, were I in your place. I oughtn't to have assumed it was something freely discussed between you and the baron."

This was the opposite of gossip, this courteous apology from a gentleman—viscount? earl? marquess?—quite a few rungs above him. For all that, it carried much the same sting.

Nick bowed in turn. "Think nothing of it." He might have left matters there, but some perverse impulse spurred him to further speech. "Even had I been in the habit of urging my opinions on Lord Barclay, I'd have nothing to say on the topic of deranged soldiers. My brother is of sound mind and generally good judgment. His lapse, in the matter of choosing a bride, may have been spectacular but is certainly not without precedent among otherwise reasonable men. It wants no war-induced snapping of the mind for a man to fall under the spell of an unsuitable woman. English history provides examples aplenty of that particular frailty."

The fingers of his clasped hands tightened until he could feel the pinch of his nails. To defend Will against the charge of madness made him feel a little better, though he was skirting the edge of impertinence with Lord Littleton, who'd been gracious enough to apologize.

Littleton, slighted or not, was shortly called away by another acquaintance, which left Nick free to tour the room's perimeter once more, now with even less satisfaction than he'd found in the task on his first attempt. It might be a very long night, watching Miss Westbrook in her red gown and wondering how much longer it would be before Barclay learned what had been kept from him.

He took up a position beside one of the room's many decorative pillars, where he had a fair view of the dance—Miss Westbrook had already gone into the set with a gentleman he didn't know—and also, it developed, of Lady Harringdon holding court among the other matrons.

Devil take Andrew for not having been an earl, anyway. How long had it taken Lord and Lady Harringdon to recover all their consequence, once they'd cut off the Honorable Charles? A season at most, he'd wager. If the

Blackshears had only had a title at their head he might now be going about with Barclay, enjoying introductions to all manner of political men and beginning to build such a web of acquaintance as could later serve his grandest ambitions. Instead of standing by a post, avoiding any company, and playing chaperone-by-stealth to a barrister's daughter with too much beauty for her own good.

"I should find a place in the set and try to catch her eye, if I were you." The voice came unexpectedly from the other side of the pillar, startling him like a sudden flight of pigeons. "You don't show to best advantage at a pining distance."

"Mrs. Simcox." God, he hadn't seen her in months. "I had no idea you were here tonight." She was in excellent looks, too, all green and gold in her gown and jewels; all auburn in her hair. Her appearance, indeed her youth, had taken him by surprise the first time he'd met her. Ignorant as he'd been, he'd heard *widow* and imagined someone matronly, not a vibrant creature several scant years his senior and seething with wicked appetites.

"I've been in at cards for the past hour and more. I must have missed hearing you announced." She grinned her cheeky grin at him, waking all manner of pleasant memories. "And 'Mrs. Simcox,' is it? Am I not to be 'Anne' anymore?"

"I doubt your Mr. Stewart would appreciate my calling you Anne." In spite of good intentions he couldn't help falling into the rhythms of flirtatious speech.

"Mr. Stewart." She turned her face aside and sent a dismissive puff of breath through her lips. "You've been shut away in your chambers as usual, Blackshear, else you would have heard. Mr. Stewart got it into his head I must marry him. He got very tedious with it, and so I sent him on his way."

"Is that so?" He angled a bit farther to face her, and set his hand on the pillar between them.

"It's so." Her eyes took thorough note of his hand before flicking back up to his face. She set a hand of her own on the pillar, rather near his. "Has the widow Marbury had you all to herself these few months, or have you broadened your circle of acquaintances?"

"It's been a bit of a lull, actually. Mrs. Marbury followed your example in accepting a gentleman's respectable attentions, and as to new acquaintances, I don't seem to hold much appeal for the ladies of late."

"Because of the business with your brother, you mean?" With the hand that wasn't resting near his she made a contemptuous little wave. "Astute women care nothing for that, Nick. If anything, you've acquired an interesting frisson of disrespectability to go with your other charms. Which, as I recall in some detail, are considerable." Her gaze wandered down his form, with near as much effect as if she'd traced the same path with her fingers.

It had been too long since he'd enjoyed himself with a carefree sort of woman. He was weary—until this moment he hadn't realized just how weary—of watching his every step for the sake of a lady's innocence, and the friendship that had been between them, and the trust her parents had placed in him. He was tired of being the kind of man who reproached himself for a kiss.

He cleared his throat. "Unfortunately the charms you refer to are the sort a woman can only learn of through proximity. And the family scandal has made a formidable barrier to that."

"Nonsense. Ladies like a bit of scandal. Dewy young misses in red gowns like it best of all. Else they'd wear white, wouldn't they; or some innocent shade of pink." She'd turned while speaking; taken her hand from the pillar and maneuvered herself so that now she stood with her back to the thing, facing out over the dance, her shoulder but an inch or two from Nick's still-resting hand. "Depend upon it, she's aware of you." From this distance, she could drop her voice to its duskier range. "All the more since you began speaking to me. I do believe she'd counted you as a conquest, and now sees she was too hasty in that. Thus rendering you doubly intriguing to her."

"Anne, you couldn't be further from the truth." Laughter lurked just in back of his words. He'd forgotten how much he enjoyed this woman, even in mere conversation. "She's aware of me indeed, because we've known one another for years. I'm a friend of her father's, and I assure you she and I are long past the point where one might think to make a conquest of the other." Never mind how the sight of her in a red gown had conquered him nearly to his knees.

Mrs. Simcox turned her head to look at him. Her face was near enough that he could fancy he felt her breath. "She's seen you up close, then, and conversed with you, and still she has no interest?" Her right brow arched, an eloquent challenge to his assertion or perhaps a judgment on Miss Westbrook's soundness of mind.

"Why should she have an interest? She can converse with me to her heart's content as a friend, and whatever dubious gratification there is to be gained from a near view of me, our present connection affords her that as well."

"And she finds that sufficient? Conversation and a near view? But I was an ignorant girl once, too, with no idea that marital congress could be anything better than tolerable, and no notion of how to choose a husband who would make a wife's duty into pleasure." Her grin flashed again, teasing and altogether impudent. "Perhaps I ought to have a pointed word or two with your pretty friend, and see whether I cannot make her aware of you in a more particular way."

"You'll do no such thing." He took hold of her elbow. "Come and dance with me. I rely on the hope that standing in a line with respectable people at either side will force you to behave."

They danced, and all his knotted-up muscles seemed to loosen at the pure bodily pleasure of it. Or no, bodily pleasure was but one of the agents working upon him. Not only had he gone too long without a woman who risked nothing by being with him, but it seemed an age since he'd enjoyed the company of someone who knew all his secrets and thought them inconsequential. He ought to spend more time with such people—and now that her erstwhile suitor Mr. Stewart had gone on his way, he'd likely have the opportunity.

He glanced up to see Miss Westbrook and her partner coming down the line, and this time he was able to give her a proper, decent smile, his eyes never roaming from her face. He *would* enjoy her triumphs this evening, just as he'd intended, and if Mrs. Simcox's wicked mood held, he might even end the night with a triumph or two of his own.

WELL. MR. Blackshear did dance, after all. First with the auburn-haired lady in green who'd talked to him for so long and with such undisguised interest; then with a black-haired, full-figured lady to whom the first one introduced him. He spent the next dance laughing with the viscount at the far end of the room, and after that came a waltz and he danced it, with the auburn-haired lady for a partner again.

Not that she was keeping count. She was engaged in most of those same dances herself, and occupied all the while by making conversation with whichever gentleman stood opposite. Even now she might have been out among the waltzing couples, if a Captain Williams had

had his way. But to return to her chair, with all the modesty of a girl who would not dream of asking her chaperone for permission to waltz, had seemed the more effectual course. A lady did well to project a certain air of unattainability, that a gentleman could have the bracing pleasure of working to win her.

Someone ought to share that wisdom with Mr. Blackshear's auburn-haired friend. She would be embarrassed, later, when he grew weary of her too-attentive manner and forsook her to dance with more circumspect ladies, or perhaps to stand at the edge of the floor in solitude, as he'd been doing before she'd strolled up to engross him.

"I think a continuation of the tax upon income would have been the fairest approach." Lord Barclay's voice interrupted her thoughts. He'd danced the last set with Louisa and generously chosen to sit out the waltz in favor of keeping the ladies company. He would partner Kate for the next set. "But gentlemen of property had tolerated that tax with the expectation it would be retired at the end of the war, and I suppose there was a general fear that, extended once, it could easily become a permanent fixture." He bowed to Louisa, seated at his right. "Your brother would know more than I, of course, having been in Parliament at the time and therefore privy to the discussions."

"Yes, he had a great deal to say of that measure, as I recall." She achieved a fair degree of radiance in speaking on this topic, even if she didn't quite glow the way she did when debating over novels. "He said there was a sentiment, among those who opposed the tax, that our government ought to concentrate its efforts on reducing the public expenditure, and look for economies in its own operation."

"That strikes me as an entirely reasonable expectation for any government." Lady Harringdon, at Kate's left, apparently found herself equipped with as many authoritative opinions on this subject as on any other. "I wonder why it had to be brought up for debate at all. One hopes one's Parliament would not have been wasteful or extravagant in the first place."

The waltzing couples moved in a grand circle around the floor, and here came Mr. Blackshear and his lady friend in close hold, his hand high on her ribcage, her fingers settled on his right arm just below the shoulder. There was a place there, Kate knew, where the muscles sloped down and back up, a brief indentation between shoulder and bicep well fitted to a lady's hand. Even through a coat sleeve, Lady Auburn Attainable would have easily found that hollow, that mute invitation for her grasp.

To waltz looked very agreeable. Not necessarily to waltz with Mr. Blackshear, though he did lead his partner through the steps expertly and with some flair, his coattails flying out behind him whenever he had cause to make a quick pivot. He seemed to have some extra sense that told him how far away his neighbors were on either side, for he never glanced up to gauge the distance, as so many of the other men did. That much more attention did he reserve to spend on the lady who danced with him, her face tilted up toward his, her entire form submitting to his lead, telling him as plainly as if she spoke the words that she was his for the asking; that he could consider her as already attained.

Admittedly he did not look as though he would grow weary of her anytime soon.

Kate cast her eyes down in order to straighten her bracelets as the two passed by, not that either of them had noticed her on any previous circuit. The gold cuffs were tolerably straight already, but paired bracelets really ought to match, so she made a minute adjustment to the left one before allowing her gaze to float up again.

She could have been the one in his arms, if that had been what she'd wanted. She was reasonably certain of that. He'd been quite as taken with her in the beginning as any of Papa's young men, and by his own testimony he'd continued to feel an attraction to her, at least, even long after she'd brusquely disabused him of futile hopes. And then, of course, there'd been the testimony of the kiss. And . . . the way he'd looked at her tonight, when he'd first laid eyes on her in the red gown. She'd scarcely let herself think of it all evening; to do so felt like leaning down from a precarious perch to dip her fingers into a lake that might swallow her up.

She'd felt singled out, set on fire, seen in every part of her right down to the marrow of her bones. She felt dizzy even now, just remembering.

He, on the other hand, didn't seem to remember at all. Likely his brain was occupied with thinking ahead to the liaison that Lady Attainable would doubtless propose. Perhaps she was proposing it this minute, as they stepped through a different figure that required them to move side by side, his arm about her waist in what must feel, to the lady, like a proprietary hold.

Did she know that his brother had made a disgraceful marriage? Maybe that wouldn't matter to her.

"Indeed there was waltzing on the Continent, but I never did indulge." The conversation had rolled on without any contribution from her and apparently left the field of politics altogether. Lord Barclay was speaking around her to Lady Harringdon, answering a question Kate had somehow missed. "I see now the error of my ways. If I'd known it would catch on at home, and that I'd be granted a title, and expected to appear at places like Almack's, I would have made some effort to master the steps."

Title. Almack's. The words sounded beside her ear like miniature gongs, summoning back her straying attention. She had nothing to envy in the auburn-haired woman's state. Mr. Blackshear might acquit himself with distinction on the dancing floor, or in a darkened room, but a lady of purpose—a lady looking not for a few minutes of transitory pleasure but for a permanent improvement in the circumstances of her life—required more from a man.

She twisted to smile at Lord Barclay. He'd leaned in a bit while addressing the countess, and for a second, before he blinked and drew back, her face was quite near his. "I'm sure you made the best possible use of your time in those days." She packed all the warm admiration she could into her voice. "I've yet to hear of any man being granted a barony in recognition of his ballroom skills."

He blushed, and said something dismissive, which was what a gentleman did when enjoying flattery from a pretty girl. His glance even flickered to her bosom, now that she'd angled herself to present that virtue to his notice. Only for the briefest of instants, and as a kind of inadvertent masculine reflex—it wasn't such a look as a lady could feel in her marrow—but she notched the triumph nevertheless.

Beyond him she could see a slight wilting in Miss Smith's aspect. Louisa hadn't . . . formed hopes of him, had she? On the strength of a dance and the few minutes of political conversation they'd shared here and at the Astleys' rout? That seemed far from her professed ideal of a long-held friendship blossoming finally into love.

She'll have other prospects. You must make the most of what's before you now. Some streak of ruthlessness in her offered that advice. Kate didn't like to listen. But if she gave up any designs on Lord Barclay, she'd be passing up a gentleman who already knew the worst there was to know of her family and hadn't been at all put off.

She might find another such man, but until she did, it would be imprudent to discourage this one.

Besides, Louisa's wilting might have been but a reaction to the room's heat. Perhaps she'd even imagined the sight. She would find a private moment, later, to ascertain her friend's feelings, and then she could weigh the counsel of that ruthless streak. Though no ruthlessness would be needed if there'd been no wilting, which seemed more probable the longer she thought on it.

At all events, she was engaged to dance the next set with the man. To avoid conversing with him would simply be rude.

One more time she blocked out the sight of the waltzers going by. "Have you been to Almack's often, Lord Barclay? Is it true the lemonade tastes very like water?" She smoothed the skirts of the gown Miss Smith had so kindly lent her, and fixed the baron with a winning smile.

Chapter Thirteen

He could not doubt, by the end of the waltz, that Mrs. Simcox intended to have him in her bed that night. She'd never been subtle about such things, which in any man's opinion must be greatly to her credit. The looks she turned upon him, the deliberate lapses in conversation, the artful lingerings and trailings of her fingers whenever it was time to change a hold, all spoke of invitation. And he was entirely ready, after a drought of several months and too much thought wasted on Miss Westbrook, for that kind of invitation.

He bowed over her hand, when the music ended, and matched her for frankness. "Have you any plans for after this party, Mrs. Simcox?"

"Aren't you forward." But the twist of her smile, the coquettish tilt of her head, told him she didn't mind. "What will you do if I say I have made other plans?"

"I'll propose you give thought to changing them. I flatter myself I can offer you superior amusements to any you have planned." He let his smile sketch in a few details.

Wicked appreciation flashed in her eyes; she stepped backward, towing him by the hand still gripped in hers, to continue this conversation off the dance floor. "I have a counter proposal. Let's leave now."

The sheer flattering force of her desire swayed him, but he didn't quite topple. "I can wait." From the corner of his eye he could see Miss Westbrook—his responsibility—rising to ready herself for the next dance. "I'm sure you must be engaged for some of the later dances. I wouldn't want your disappointed partners on my conscience."

"Let me worry about my disappointed partners." She took another step back, as if to lead him right out of the room. "Besides, I thought gentlemen liked the idea of leaving bested rivals in their wake. I thought it added a layer of triumph to the assignation."

"For some men, perhaps. I prefer to not concern myself with other people of any sort, whether bested rivals or old lovers, when I'm in the midst of an assignation." He felt utterly disingenuous. What was he doing? He'd never had to resort to any maneuvering or artifice with Anne Simcox. They'd always been perfectly direct with each other.

A frown stole over her features. Her eyes narrowed and his heart sank. She slid her hand out of his grasp. "What are you not telling me, Blackshear? Has some young thing promised you her supper dance, and you're loath to abandon her?"

"You know my circumstances. You know no young thing's chaperone would countenance my being introduced to her charge." That didn't answer her question, and the fact wouldn't be lost on her.

She folded her arms and raised one eyebrow.

She deserved to be told the truth. Regardless of the cost to his hopes for tonight. "I am bound by a promise, but not that sort." He inclined his head to her and lowered his voice. "The young lady in red you saw me watching earlier—she hasn't much experience in society and I've promised her father I'll keep an eye on her. I cannot leave here until she and her party have gone."

"I see." Her glance veered away from him, doubtless to settle on Miss Westbrook. "You weren't really concerned, then, with disappointing those men to whom I might have promised my later dances."

"I'm sorry, Anne." He was. On his account as well as hers. "I oughtn't to have been less than frank. If not for my obligation to Mr. Westbrook, I'd have been out the door with you by now. If you will wait until I can leave in good conscience, you will have all my best and fullest attention. Trust to my word on that."

She brought her gaze back, the beginnings of a smile suggesting she might be placated. "We shall see. If no better prospect comes along, you may renew your offer at the end of the evening, or whenever your duty to your pretty friend concludes. But be advised I shall be looking out for more obliging men." She pivoted to leave, delivering the last words over her shoulder. "If I encounter someone agreeable, who comes and goes at his own command rather than binding himself with promises, then you mustn't count on my company."

It took her all of ten minutes to find that more obliging man. To add insult to injury, it was the same damned scarecrow of a fellow who'd started all the trouble with Miss Westbrook at the Astleys' rout. In promoting the claims of those men who expected to dance with her, Nick had unwittingly been advocating for this coxcomb.

The fellow led her out to their place in the dance, and, several figures in, acquired a look of such libidinous astonishment that Nick could not doubt what path their conversation had taken, or how it would all end up. Well, he didn't expect them to walk straight off the floor in the middle of the set; that came as a surprise. Mrs. Simcox threw him one look as they passed by, and an elegant shrug for emphasis—*What else could I do? You know my nature*—and there it went, his first chance in months to bed a woman. He could only watch them go, and then return to his loyal, steadfast, utterly unrewarding vigil over Miss Westbrook.

How had it happened that he'd come to this? Even having mostly outgrown his *tendre* for the lady, he still found his movements, his liberty, his amorous ambitions all constrained by her. He was effectively just as much in her thrall as he had been three years ago, when he'd had such youthful confidence in his luck, and such foolish hopes of her.

She tripped through the dance in her usual light-footed way, catching up her trailing skirts and bestowing such smiles and frequent laughter on her partner—Lord Barclay, it happened—as must have made him believe himself the cleverest, most fascinating man in this room or any other.

Nick leaned his shoulder into the nearest pillar and folded his arms. He oughtn't to blame her. She'd known nothing of his opportunity with Mrs. Simcox. She hadn't deliberately interfered. But he'd blamed himself so tirelessly since the night of the Astleys' rout, and sincerely grieved the loss of their easy cordiality, and now here she was laughing and capering as though the loss of his friendship suited her very well. It galled him to watch. And finally he could watch no more.

He retreated from the pillar to the wall, and struck out for the end of the room. Her virtue and reputation would be perfectly safe while she was dancing with Barclay; he could be certain of that. He would find a few minutes' respite in one of the parlors or a study where he could fully indulge his ill humor, and then he would return to finish out his commission.

And this would be the last such tour of duty. If his presence had proven beneficial to her, he was sincerely glad of the fact. But for his part he was done. He'd introduced her to a worthy man, and if she thought she could do better and wanted to cast about a bit more, that was certainly her right. Any parties she meant to attend in future, though, she would be attending without him.

A SICK FEELING in her stomach dragged her down like stones sewn into her hem. She put a proportional brightness in her smile, and danced with such sprightly grace that she might have been mistaken for a nymph in a pastoral ballet.

She could no longer pretend it was the heat that had made Louisa wilt. Her friend had grown quieter and quieter as Kate talked to Lord Barclay, and when they all took their places in the dance, Miss Smith had maneuvered to stand with her partner three couples down the line, instead of next to Kate and the baron.

Louisa's face betrayed no reproach. On those few occasions when their eyes met, she smiled, an expression of such brave artifice as reminded Kate . . . as reminded her of Rose, in fact, on the day of the knotted embroidery thread. But this time she was the source of the pain, and could not be its cure.

No, that last part wasn't true. She could discourage Lord Barclay with cool manners. She could spend the entire dance speaking of Louisa's virtues, and doing her best to promote her friend's interest.

"I've grown fond of living in London, to be honest," the baron said. She'd gotten him onto this subject, ushering him along from Almack's to the Houses of Parliament to his club, which was Brooks's, to Lord knows what else. She'd attended intermittently at best. "I'm not entirely without society in Kent—my property is near enough to Astley's that I can visit often—but I expect I'll miss all the vibrancy of the city, now that I've gotten so caught up in its life as I have."

He had an estate of his own. Even if he never succeeded to the marquessate, he had property in the country, and doubtless a good deal of consequence there. Could she really afford to discourage him before she'd had a chance to speak to Miss Smith and ascertain her feelings beyond the very last doubt? "I've always wanted to see Kent. For natural beauty, it's said to be one of the finest counties." She sounded as if she were angling to be taken there; perhaps installed there as a bride.

She was despicable. What did she think Louisa would tell her, that she couldn't already see for herself? And didn't a man as worthy as Lord Barclay deserve a wife who'd been drawn to him by affection and esteem instead of by a dispassionate reckoning of his holdings, his prospects, and what he could do for her family?

She pivoted, as the dance required, and saw again the empty spot where Mr. Blackshear had stood earlier.

Another sick pang sank her stomach. Miss Smith's unhappiness wasn't the only source.

He'd stood there with his lady friend, holding her hand for a pointed long time. Even a girl as sheltered and inexperienced in these matters as she, could not mistake the theme of their discussion. She'd had to avert her eyes.

And several eye-averted pivots later, she'd finally ventured a look and found they'd both vanished. She'd scanned the room, as discreetly as she could while dancing. They weren't here.

They might have gone to play cards, of course, but they certainly hadn't looked, in those few moments that she'd dared watch them, as though cards were on either one's mind. More likely they'd left the party altogether. Or found some convenient dark room.

Her hands curled into graceless fists, creasing the fine silk skirts. As if she hadn't already known reasons enough to not kiss a man! She might tell Viola to put it in her book: *Think how you'll feel when you see him pay marked attention to another woman. Think how you'd feel to know he was kissing her just the same as he'd done with you.*

But it wouldn't be just the same. With a woman like Lady Attainable, he wouldn't halt the proceedings and say he regretted having begun. His hands would go everywhere. Probably more than his hands. And he'd be grateful for the company of a worldly woman, one who knew the proper response to everything he did. He'd thank his lucky stars he wasn't with an innocent, ignorant miss to whose family he owed better behavior.

"You've been acquainted with Mr. Blackshear for some time, I think?" She nearly jumped out of her skin at the baron's words. He couldn't possibly know what was in her thoughts, and still, guilt flooded her.

"I suppose—well, yes." She shaped her face into a mask of mild unconcern. "He's been a friend of my family's for . . . three years now, I believe."

"I see. And are you likewise acquainted with his family?" Something in the expression of his face, the indirect quality of his gaze . . .

Suspicion darted through her, crystallizing into certainty on the way. He'd heard something. Some incomplete rumor of irregularity attending the Blackshear name, and he sought now to have it confirmed.

Her stomach twisted again. Lord knows Nick Blackshear had no claim on her loyalty, slinking off to amuse himself with another lady when he was supposed to be here, watching her. "We haven't the pleasure of acquaintance with his family," she said nevertheless. "We came to know him when he was studying with my father, and that has remained the basis of the connection."

"Ah, to be sure. I suppose that's generally the way, with professional connections." To his credit, he looked relieved to abandon the question, and ashamed to have asked.

Lord Barclay was a good man. He didn't deserve to be schemed upon, particularly not by a lady whose thoughts were more than half with someone else.

She would be cordial for the rest of the dance, because he also didn't deserve sudden, unaccountable coldness. Then for the remainder of the evening she would apply herself to determining whether any other gentleman here, those she was engaged to dance with and those who might yet approach her for a dance, could possibly be a real prospect. And only if she found no such prospects at all . . . well, even then she couldn't be sure what she would do. Better to concentrate her thoughts on finding other eligible men.

Fate, however, seemed determined to mock her virtuous resolve. She finished the dance, parted from Lord Barclay with a curtsy, and sat beside the countess to await her partner for the supper dance. Five minutes later he had not appeared.

"I fear he's discovered you're no suitable match." Lady Harringdon, as usual, saw no reason to spare her charge from her worst suppositions. "I did have an apprehension of this. The Cathcarts may think they did you a kindness with this invitation, but there's no kindness in exposing you to such disappointments."

Kate rearranged her skirts, declining to make a reply. The music hadn't begun, so the gentleman might yet prove her aunt mistaken. Couples were taking their places in the set, however, and with each new pair who stepped into line, her self-discontent wavered, reshaping itself into a discontent with her absent partner.

That she might sit out the supper dance, a wallflower in a lovely red gown, seemed more than a little ridiculous. She'd followed a charitable impulse in granting this dance to Lord John Prior, hoping to make up for his shabby treatment by Mr. Blackshear on the terrace at Cranbourne House, and she would regret her charity thoroughly if he proved to have deserted her.

Which she could not believe he would intentionally do. He'd seemed so polite and deferential. And whatever knowledge of her background he might have gained, there was no reason he should not *dance* with her. Certainly not when men of higher rank were doing so. He was but the fifth son of a duke, and she was, by all objective measures, the prettiest girl here. Some would say he was the lucky one in the pairing.

"At least you can take pleasure in the success of our little Miss Smith." Lady Harringdon fanned herself, the picture of serene satisfaction, and looked out to where that lady stood opposite her latest partner. "The change to her hair was an inspired idea. I don't believe she's sat down for a single dance besides the waltz. She'll owe you a great debt of gratitude, if her popularity leads to her making such a match as I've always hoped she would."

Guilt curled its tenacious fingers around Kate again. She couldn't sit and listen to praise for her kindness to Miss Smith. "Will your ladyship excuse me a moment?" She put up a hand to pat her hair. "Since my partner appears to not be coming, I think I'll take the opportunity to splash my face and see that my hair isn't coming undone."

"Very wise. Nothing to be gained by sitting conspicuous along the wall." The countess rose with her in a grand sweep of skirts. "For my part, I shall see how Mrs. Smith is doing at whist. You may find me in the card room when the time comes to go in for supper."

Here was another humiliation: she'd thought she'd go in to supper on a gentleman's arm, but now she must trail about as a lady's companion again, for all that she'd had her own invitation and been announced, and for all the impression she knew she'd made on her entrance in the red silk gown.

Or rather, she must go to supper as a lady's companion if she could not turn up her missing partner. He might yet be here, forgetting the time while he stared out the window at an arrangement of stars, or crouching behind a door somewhere because he hadn't the courage to tell her he'd changed his mind about their dance. Well, he'd better find his courage, or take prodigious enjoyment from those stars, because if he was in this house he had a reckoning coming. Never mind the washroom; she was going to find Lord John.

NICK HAD been in this room before. He could say that of most rooms in this house, granted. But this one, in particular, he remembered.

He and Will had come down to London with Cathcart one term holiday instead of spending the break at their quiet Cambridgeshire home. His brother and the viscount—not yet a viscount at the time—had got up to all manner of London nonsense, much of it involving drink, and had often ended the evening here, sitting on the carpet before the fire, obediently consuming the toasted bread and cheese Nick had pressed upon them in the interest of avoiding a poor head the next morning.

He sat back on the sofa, stretching his legs out toward the empty hearth. No fire tonight. No candles, either. He'd left the door open, to invite whatever light the hallway sconces could provide, and pushed aside the curtains to let moonlight in as well.

Not that there was anything he needed to see. The partial dim, with vague shapes of furniture in the shadows and paintings indistinguishable beyond their size and shape, suited him very well. The music rising from the ballroom pleased him better than it had when he'd been downstairs with the musicians in view.

He'd stayed here longer than intended. He knew because one song had ended and the next one begun. But he felt no inclination to return. Surely Miss Westbrook could keep out of trouble for the length of one more dance, at the end of which he'd drag himself off this comfortable sofa and go back downstairs to play watchful sheepdog for the last time.

A creak on the hallway staircase signaled some person's approach. He turned his head, without either sitting straight or unfolding the arms crossed over his chest, to see whether anyone would appear in the doorway. He needn't be formal for Cathcart, who would share his memories of sitting down on the hearth, and he felt a perverse defiance at the thought of any party guest intruding on his respite.

Slippers; that could be a lady or a gentleman. Not a servant. Softly but steadily over the hallway floorboards they came, a graceful lady or a slight and stealthy man. No, a lady, without question; the rustle of her skirts reached him. Too late it occurred to him it could be Lady Cathcart, whom he would not like to offend by slouching in her second-best parlor, and before he could make any alteration in his posture, a feminine shape slipped into view, peering into the room without entering, and it was not, after all, Lady Cathcart.

Of course it wasn't. Who else would it have been on this night but Kate Westbrook, apparently sworn to not only spoil his prospects but disturb his few minutes of badly needed peace?

Ah, but she hadn't expected to find him. He could see the surprise on her face.

Good God. Who *was* she expecting to find?

"Miss Westbrook." He pushed up from his slouch,

setting his elbow on the back of the sofa as he turned to confront her. "What the devil are you doing so far from the ballroom? I explained to you at the last party that your behavior has consequences for me as well as for you. Were you not listening?"

She started at his incivility, but he was thoroughly tired of being civil. His obligation to her had cheated him of what could have been an excellent night, and for all he knew, might have done permanent damage to his friendship with Mrs. Simcox. Now here she was on God knew what reckless errand, putting her reputation at risk again as though she'd learned nothing from their close call of last week. She'd surely earned a little blunt talk.

Only for an instant, though, was she taken aback. Her brow lowered as he watched, and her shoulders set. Shadows shifted across her bosom, and one small stubborn fraction of his brain took thorough notice of that.

The better part noticed her anger, and welcomed it. If she wanted an argument, she'd come to the right place. This conversation was long overdue.

THE SIGHT of him sent her stomach into knots that would do a sailor proud. The way he'd been sitting, with such defiant, sated sensuality, not caring whether she could guess what he and his lady friend must have been doing here no great while since. Then the presumption of his words to her, even without that context, simply took her breath away.

She forced in a breath, to replace the one he'd stolen, and willed her stomach calm. "Yes, you did lecture me about my behavior. I remember that. I also remember what happened subsequently, behind the sofa in the Astleys' library."

"I apologized for that. I regret it thoroughly. And it has nothing to do with the matter of what you're doing here, and why you looked surprised at the sight of me. You were expecting someone else, I presume."

"How do you dare to speak so?" She could hardly hear her own words for the blood pounding in her ears. "As if I couldn't deduce what your own business in this room has been." She shocked herself, giving voice to such thoughts. But she couldn't let his foul accusation rest unanswered.

And she apparently didn't shock him at all. His brows went up. His mouth twitched as though he found her very amusing. "What do you accuse me of?" He made a show of looking about the room. "Do you think I've hidden a lady behind one of these pieces of furniture?"

"Of course not." Really, how dare he invoke hiding behind furniture? "The fact there's no lady here now doesn't prove there was no lady earlier."

"I assure you my time in this room has not been nearly as interesting as you suppose." He held her gaze in silence just long enough to make her heart race. "And I ask again: what reason do you have for stealing away upstairs and looking into darkened rooms? I cannot imagine any respectable explanation."

"Not that I owe you any explanation at all, but my partner for the supper dance never came to claim me." She pulled herself tall. Confessing this to anyone would be unpleasant. Confessing it to Mr. Blackshear was somehow even worse. "I thought he might have wandered into one of the other rooms, as your own presence here testifies a gentleman will occasionally do, and I preferred to spend my time in search of him, instead of sitting down where everyone could see I had no partner."

"Why would he be in one of these rooms if he was engaged to dance with you? Surely you don't imagine he's deliberately avoiding you." His gaze skipped down and back up as he said this. He didn't leave her with that feeling of being consumed, as he'd done on her arrival tonight, but his eyes sent an unmistakable message: *What man in his right mind would not want to dance with you?*

"Not deliberately." She moved a step into the room. "Only I got the impression, last week, that he's scholarly and prone to distraction. He may have wandered into the library or some other room with books, and failed to notice the time."

"Last week?" He sounded as if he were at trial, closing in on a crucial piece of testimony.

"You met him at Lady Astley's rout. On the terrace. You were exceedingly rude. Lord John Prior is his name."

A disturbance crossed his face, centering in his taut mouth. She couldn't scry its meaning to save her life. He looked down at the sofa cushion and ran his hand along its front edge. "He's not coming." His glove against the sofa's fabric made a sibilance that snaked through the darkness. "Neither will you find him in any of these rooms. You may as well go back downstairs."

"I don't understand. How do you know?" She took another step into the room, edging to the left so that he'd see her from the corner of his eye even if he wouldn't face her.

He shot her a glance, considering, before tilting his head to study the sofa again. "He left the party. I saw him do so." He was very still, as though waiting in some suspense for her answer.

"He didn't say a thing to me."

"No, he wouldn't have." He paused, his chest rising and falling with a deliberate breath. "He left with a woman." He did look at her then. "I'm sorry to tell you so. But it's best, I think, that you should know what kind of man he is."

She felt behind her for a grip on the doorjamb. Here was all the humiliation she'd feared from staying in the ballroom, only worse than she'd imagined in that it was witnessed by a cold stranger who until very recently she'd counted as a friend. "I can scarcely believe it." Her cheeks burned and her voice came out a half whisper. "He didn't seem the sort." Let that teach her to think she was any judge of the characters of men.

"The lady, I assure you, is the sort. It wanted no predisposition from him." He glanced up again. "The development marred my evening at least as severely as it has marred yours, if that is any consolation."

Because it was Lady Attainable who had slipped out with Lord John. Of course. And it wasn't a consolation, it wasn't any consolation at all, to know that this was the reason for Mr. Blackshear's brooding in this remote room. He had, indeed, wanted more of that lady's company tonight. Maybe he would have brought her here if she had not preferred Lord John.

Or maybe . . . maybe it hadn't been a matter of preference. Maybe simple availability, and unavailability, had driven the lady's choice.

Good Lord. "You blame me," she said, letting go the doorjamb and stepping farther into the room. Suddenly his mood, his pointed incivility, made perfect sense. "You might have been the one to go with her, but for your obligation to me. You resent me for causing you to lose that opportunity."

"No," he said after a moment. He turned to face the fireplace in front of him, resting his hands on his knees. "Not really. I'm put out by the inconvenience, by the restriction to my coming and going, but I recognize I volunteered for this obligation. I recognize you aren't knowingly interfering with my . . . social prospects." He brought up a hand and dragged it over his face, from forehead to chin. "Forgive me. I oughtn't to be speaking to you on this topic. Forgive me too for my rudeness, and my language when you first appeared. I've had a trying night, and I forgot myself."

Here was an opportunity, maybe, for them to talk as friends again. It felt like a very long time since they had. "In what way has your night been trying? Besides seeing your lady friend leave with another gentleman, I mean." She'd had a trying night, too. She could almost certainly sympathize with his.

"The lady friend's departure is trial enough on its own, I assure you." Abruptly he rose from the sofa and went to lean one elbow on the mantelpiece. He stood in shadow now, and she couldn't read his face as well as she had. "She's an acquaintance of several years' standing, and I was enjoying her company after not having seen her for some months." He adjusted some object on the mantelpiece. She couldn't see it but it sounded like something made of china. "I met with a few other frustrations besides, but I shan't trouble you with those. Let us regret together the absconding of Mrs. Simcox with Lord John, and let that suffice."

Her feet carried her forward, almost without thought. "I wish you would trouble me." Where floor gave way to the bricks of the hearth, she stopped. Now they were both in shadow. "What are friends for, if not to hear each other's troubles, and share theirs in turn?"

"Do you have difficulties to share?" His head tipped forward in the dimness, as though to better read her across the four or five feet of space that divided them. "I presumed your evening to be a success. You looked to be having a fine time with Lord Barclay, when I saw you last."

He'd opened the very subject on which she might confide, if she felt so inclined. *I'm almost sure Miss Smith is fond of Lord Barclay. And she's been so kind to me. And I fear I may be capable of nevertheless pursuing him myself, with all my arts, if no better prospect comes along. I'm heartless, just as you've always said, and I'm altogether weary of being so. I'm weary of everything I am.*

But to say so would risk incurring his poor opinion, and it felt like a self-indulgence besides. She hadn't come to spill her troubles; she'd asked to hear his. And he'd unwittingly provided her with an opening on that subject, too.

"Nick." One foot, then the other, stepped onto the hearth. She settled a hand on the mantelpiece, which was the nearest she could come to closing the remaining distance and laying that hand on his sleeve. "You ought to know Lord Barclay asked me about you. He asked whether I was acquainted with your family."

"Ah." He half pivoted, putting his back to the fireplace. He faced toward the center of the room now, where moonlight mingled with the candlelight from the hall, rendering his features readable once more. "Yes, it stands to reason that he would." In the silence, he pressed his lips together. That was all he planned to say on the subject.

"Can't we speak of it?" The words crept out, low and three times as plaintive as she'd intended. She swayed a step nearer, gloved fingers trailing to a new hold on the mantelpiece. She might almost reach him now, with an arm extended. "You know I don't judge you. How could I? Knowing what you do of my own connections, you must—"

"No, Kate, we cannot speak of it." He stayed still, not facing her, but she could feel the way he shaped all his attention into a kind of shield, held up to stop her in her tracks. "I've nothing to say on the matter, and if I had, yours would not be the ear in which I'd choose to confide. Pardon me for saying so."

She blinked, and nearly had to fight back tears. Why should his statement come as such a blow? Why did she care whether he confided in her? He was right: she'd never given him reason to think of her as someone to whom he could turn in trouble. She'd been a friend of gossamer substance, teasing him when he was present at the house and scarcely sparing him a thought when he wasn't.

Scarcely sparing him a thought until recently.

This is the darkness acting upon you. Some part of her consciousness, still with a hold on reason, issued that reproof. *Darkness, and your memories of being kissed.* Also, memories of standing under the stairs with his soap-scented coat on her shoulders. And of his brisk capability on the courtroom floor. And of *Believe me, I've never for a moment imagined I was your brother.* If he hadn't put that knowledge in her brain, those other things might have passed unnoticed and the kiss might not have happened at all.

"Miss Westbrook?" She'd gone some time without speaking. She had perhaps been inching nearer to him in that time. No wonder he turned toward her, tilting his head to impose himself into whatever trance possessed her, and uttering her name in that wary tone.

"Yes," she said, because she had better speak before he resorted to snapping his fingers or waving a hand in her face. "You needn't tell me anything if you'd rather not. Only I thought perhaps I could be of some comfort to you." One more step, and there was no going back now. The unwinding skein of music, faint vibrations reaching her slipper soles a partial second before the notes reached her ear told her she yet had some time before she must appear for supper. She dropped her hand on his sleeve and tilted up her face, softening her eyes, her lips, her whole form into a statement of permission, while inside, her heart galloped like a racehorse under the whip.

Chapter Fourteen

Bloody, bloody hell. Of all the things he didn't need on this already ruinous night.

No dancing around it. He made his voice low, but forceful. "For the love of God, Miss Westbrook, what do you think you're doing?"

Her flinch ran all the way out to her hand. He felt the quick convulsion on his forearm.

Maybe he ought to have been gentler. Rejection of any sort must come as a harsh novelty to her. But he couldn't afford to let her proceed even an inch farther on this course. Dark as it was, the picture of her in that red gown hovered, ready to collaborate with her fumbling invitation and haul him into activities that would cost him his self-respect.

"I thought . . ." Her voice trailed off, and in the silence it was evident that she had *not* thought; that she'd assumed, without reflection, that she had only to signal her own inclination in order to rouse all his appetites to the proper pitch.

What could he do but laugh? It was terribly rude—guilt flicked its lash at him as she snatched her hand away—but what other earthly response could he make? Even his earlier rudeness, when she'd first entered this room, had not, after all, been misplaced. He'd suspected her of reckless intentions with a gentleman, and he hadn't been wrong. Besides, he needn't coddle her feelings, capable as she was of answering slight with slight.

"Forgive my not realizing you found the prospect so laughable." She could pass for an affronted queen dressing down her prime minister. "I do not recall your finding it so last week."

Good God. It was all too ridiculous. He felt in his pocket for a handkerchief and wiped his eyes. "Lord. She was right about you." Let that teach him never to doubt Anne Simcox again. "She was absolutely right."

"Who was right? With whom have you been discussing me?"

He wouldn't let her divert him. "You tucked me neatly away on your shelf of conquests, didn't you, and never gave me a thought until you noticed that your spell over me had begun to wane."

"That's not true." But he could hear the sting in her voice, the shame as she realized that it was, in fact, at least a little bit true.

"I would have courted you, you know. Honorably." She did know. Even without reading his note that day three years ago, she'd known damned well what was in it. She'd known what the flowers meant. "I would have given you every proper attention. And after the wedding, every improper attention as well. I would have done my utmost to be a good husband to you, not just a—" He waved his hand about, to show her this dark room in which they'd withdrawn. "There's a great deal more a man can offer a lady than a few illicit kisses in some secret room. I hope you'll be lucky enough to find that out one day. But I haven't the necessary feelings, anymore, for you to find it out from me."

He hadn't known how much he'd wanted to say these

words. They rolled forth like one of Henry the Fifth's more stirring speeches, albeit on a pettier subject.

He stepped away from the hearth. "I suggest you follow my example now, and return to the ballroom. If you plan to attend more parties in future, you shall have to do so without my surreptitious chaperonage. I find I no longer have the necessary feelings for that office, either."

He wouldn't even wait to see whether she followed. That was her own concern. He swung out past her, and—Good Lord, the gall of the woman!—was arrested by the sudden grasp of both her hands on his arm.

"I don't believe you." She stared up at him, eyes intent, whole face written over with reckless wanting. "I felt the way you kissed me. I saw the way you looked at me when I came into the ballroom tonight. You cannot convince me you haven't any interest at all."

"Katherina, it's *too late*. God above, does your vanity really extend so far as to blind you to the difference between partiality and simple lust?" A warning tocsin sounded in some inner recess of his brain: he truly, truly oughtn't to be speaking to her in this way. "I kissed you indeed, because that's what a man does when a woman offers herself on a platter."

"I didn't offer—"

"You bloody well did." She recoiled at the language; yanked her hands from his arm. His own hands shot out to catch her by the elbows. "And I had a good look at you in this gown because that, too, is what men do." He stood so near her now that he could look straight down at her uncovered bosom, and he did. She was breathing hard. "I'll wager nearly every man in the ballroom looked you over. But don't be so foolish as to take that for a sign of regard." He let go one elbow and skated his knuckles up her arm, catching the edges of her low sleeve in his fingers. "Every last one of them, I promise you, was calculating how to peel you out of this gown."

He might have blocked the slap, if he'd wanted. Plenty of time. Her eyes spelled out her intention plain enough to read by moonlight even before she jerked her hand into an awkward, clearly unpracticed swing.

He let it come. Her kid-sheathed palm connected with his cheek, knocking his head to the side and smarting just enough to goad him into one more expression of his resolute indifference: he seized her at the waist, pulled her roughly up against him, and brought his mouth down hard on hers.

HE WAS so angry. She could feel it in the hold of his splayed fingers against the back of her head, in the tongue that had thrust itself into her mouth without any coaxing or other preamble. His other hand, without so much as a by-your-leave, snaked round behind her and pressed her, by means of an utterly indecent grip, tight against him from the waist down. And this, too, was a way to make her feel every bit of his frustration, his disgust, his regret over the years he'd wasted in harboring such futile feelings for her.

She caught his coat in fistfuls, one at the waist and the other somewhere round back. His mood didn't frighten her, because she was angry, too: angry at his impertinence, angry at how craven she'd become, angry at the catastrophic timing that had brought her only now to realize she wanted him. Wanted him, and couldn't have him, not only because she had a grand plan in which a barrister with unfortunate connections had no place but because she'd missed her chance. His *tendre* had persisted like a stubborn desert plant, longer than it had any reason to, until finally withering for want of sustenance.

And then she'd noticed him. It was just as he'd said, just as some presumptuous woman had said to him. She was a shallow creature capable of wanting only those things that were beyond her reach.

Her eyes stung with tears she absolutely would not shed. She pushed up on her toes and sent her arms around his neck, to tell him she was equal to all the anger he had.

He understood. His hand flexed and resettled its grasp on her bottom, bolder even than it had been before, and his other hand came off the back of her head and found its way—her breath caught—found its way to her bosom, where he curved his palm over one breast as though it were his to do with what he wished. And then his kid-gloved fingertips traced the edge of her decolletage, and his thumb stroked over the silk, finding the shape of her nipple and rubbing it firm.

She nearly buckled to the floor. The kiss was no more than an expression of their anger; the hand at her bottom a mere impudence suited to their moods, but his thumb stopped her breath, stopped her brain, filled her insides with a million tiny shooting stars.

He felt the change in her. She could tell because he slowed and softened his kiss, teasing her lips with the tip of his tongue instead of shoving the whole thing inside. And this gave her room to answer, angling her head to encourage him, venturing her own tongue from her mouth into his.

He groaned. She could feel the sound in his belly, so close was her body pressed to his. "Katherina." He brought his mouth clear, rested his forehead against hers, just as he'd done in that dreadful moment last week when he'd told her they must stop. "We ought to stop." His thumb didn't stop, though, and crushed against him as she was, she could feel the evidence of how sorry he'd be to stop now.

"Yes. When the supper dance ends, we'll stop." His touch made her so bold. She let her eyes flutter open, and twisted against him like a cat seeking to be petted in the right place.

"You know this . . . this whole thing is impossible." His eyelids sank half shut, and his hand on her bottom tightened to bring her writhing more particularly against him.

He was right. Everything about this was impossible. Yet here they were, and in an evening when her every glance, every breath had been an act of artifice and calculation, this one thing with him felt raw and ragged and true. "Outside this room it's impossible, yes." She had to make him see. "Here, though, there's no reason why we cannot—" Her words ended in a gasp as he brought his forefinger together with his thumb and pinched her nipple through the fabric. There must be wickeder and better sensations than this, once the breeding organs were involved, but they were beyond her power to imagine.

His chest rose and fell with a great breath. He was succumbing. She knew it. "Will you come with me to the middle of the room?" He kissed her before she could make any answer. "Where the moonlight is stronger? Where I can see everything that happens on your face?"

She nodded, blood racing with equal parts triumph and apprehension. He loosened both his indecent holds on her and went to shut the door while she stepped away from the hearth, round the sofa to where light spilled through the window and made a ghostly path on the rug. The supper dance music filtered through the floor, suddenly poignant in its jolly innocence.

He turned the door handle before closing it, and turned it carefully back, to protect their privacy by preventing any sound from the latch. When he pivoted to face her, her heart swung about in her chest like the clapper of a bell, surely colliding with both her lungs. At this distance, where she could see the whole of him, there was no mistaking the fact that his body meant to do business with hers.

"Don't be afraid." He approached, each step as deliberate and sure as if they'd done this together a hundred times. "We haven't time to do anything irrevocable unless we hurry. And I don't ever like to hurry. Even without I cared for your virtue and your prospects, you're perfectly safe."

I'm not. I'm lost already. I'm as wrecked and ruined as a woman can be. "I know," she said. "I'm not afraid."

Then he was there before her, hands rising to find a hold on her upper arms, in the space between her bracelets and the beginnings of her sleeves. He stood, merely looking. At her face, he looked, and her nearly bare shoulders, and her decolletage, and the picture she made, top to toe, when he took a half step back to get that view.

"You're so beautiful," he said, hoarse with admiration, and for as long accustomed as she was to the fact, for as much as she'd grown to feel admiration was her due, his words made her shiver.

He touched his fingers to her chin, tipping her face up to win back her gaze, and leaned in the short distance to bring their mouths briefly together. Then he kissed her cheek. And her earlobe. And a place a little bit beneath her ear, from where he started to work his way down the side of her neck, unhurriedly, as though they had all the time in the world instead of the remaining span of one dance. "So, so beautiful," he whispered somewhere in between kisses.

Yes. She was. How clever of him, to put her at ease by repeating a fact of which she was most sure, and how crafty, to say the words in a way that made the fact sound wondrous and new. "Will you take off your coat?" She found his buttons with her fingertips. That would tell him, in terms palatable to masculine ears, that she liked the sight of him, too.

His fingers tangled with hers over the buttons. One hand only: he kept the other at her shoulder, and kissed his way back up her neck to her ear even as they got all the buttons undone. As though he couldn't bear to stop kissing her long enough to give his full attention to the coat.

He did pull away from her when the time came to shrug out of the sleeves and toss the coat over the back of the sofa. She put up a hand to stop him from coming back to her, and kept him there at arm's length while she made a survey of his coatless self. Waist, chest, shoulders; the arms half lifted, ready to reach for her; the simple folds of his cravat. Chin. Mouth. Eyes. All of it so familiar, and yet so strange.

She moved a step nearer and lifted her hand from his chest to his cheek, the one she'd slapped. She couldn't quite believe she'd done it, and yet she couldn't be sorry for it, either. Not when it had made him kiss her.

He smiled, as though he understood her thoughts. His hand rose and settled on her wrist, stroking up the kid leather until her glove gave way to bare flesh. The sofa, facing away, was a step or so behind him: he walked backward, towing her by his hold at her elbow, and sank to a perch on the sofa's back. "Come closer, Kate." He planted his feet apart to make room. And when she came closer, stepping into the fraught intimate space between his knees, he had to bend only a little forward to kiss her collarbones.

And then to kiss her bosom. Scarcely breathing, she followed his progress as he covered seemingly every inch of flesh the gown left bare. Across, a bit lower, and then back up again as though his very purpose was to drive her insane. His hands meanwhile swept up to cup her, and his thumbs, both his thumbs at once, commenced the same sweet wickedness through silk that he'd committed when they stood by the hearth.

She felt for a grip on his shoulder and splayed the fingers of her other hand on the back of his head. *Yes. Do that. Don't stop.*

He made a sound, when her hand tightened on his shoulder, but he didn't stop. His tongue came out to trace a path across the rise and fall of her flesh, and she wanted . . . oh, she didn't even know what it was she wanted; she didn't have the words.

But he knew. He lifted his head and watched her face, his eyes burning as his immensely clever fingers slipped one breast free of her bodice. Then he dipped his head and kissed what he'd exposed. "I've wanted to do this." His whispered breath on her flesh felt so dreadfully intimate. "God, Kate, you've no idea how I've wanted this." He kissed her nipple again, and this time he touched her with his tongue. Delicately, at first. Then less so.

She stood, not breathing at all now, paralyzed by shock and pleasure. The sight of him, head bent with such sinful, private purpose, her hand spread out over his close-shorn scalp as though to urge him on, stirred up strange, ferocious hungers in the pit of her belly and below. She wanted to caress him with infinite tenderness. She wanted to tear him limb from limb.

Want. The word was in her every thought now, and apparently in his as well. *You've no idea how I wanted this*. People got into trouble this way. Men and women threw away judgment, and their good names with it, because they lost the ability to think of anything but satisfying that aching want.

She sucked in a sharp breath, because she'd gone too long without one. He'd apparently only been waiting for such a sound: he took it for permission, and in a rush of movement too quick for her to parse, he had her off her feet, over the back of the sofa, and then flat on the cushions underneath him, part of his weight braced on his arms, the rest pinning her gloriously down. He took liberties with her bodice again, bringing the other breast out, and when he put his mouth to this one she could only pray he wouldn't try anything further, because she mightn't have the strength any longer to stop him.

He brought his mouth away and shifted his hips. "Put your legs apart." His voice was terse and intent.

No. Strength and good sense came roaring back from their slumber: she could not let this happen. It was different for him; it was just a diversion, but she'd have *nothing* if she gave away her virtue here. She squirmed to get out from under him, pushing at his shoulders, panic narrowing her throat. "No," she said, the syllable thin and high-pitched.

"Wait. Listen. Katherina. Wait. Trust me. Listen, please." Barely enough moonlight fell over the sofa's back to show her his face, drawn with urgent conviction. "I won't lift your skirts, I promise. I won't undo a single one of my buttons. Only let me be against you. Here." He flexed his hips, either to show her what was meant by *here,* or for the sheer animal pleasure of it. "Only for a minute or so. Only as long as you like it."

He looked so serious. As though everything in his world depended on her saying yes. That was how it was for men, according to Penelope Towne.

I don't have the necessary feelings anymore, he'd said. To stop him now would be a kindness. He wouldn't like to look back later and see how his base, ungovernable lusts had overridden both his judgment and the sentiments of his heart. Nor would she like to remember this incident with a suspicion that he'd spent on her only what he'd been cheated of spending on his auburn-haired lady friend.

"Only for a minute," she said nevertheless. She might

have regrets afterward, and so might he, but at least she didn't fear for her virtue. She knew him. If he said he wouldn't lift her skirts, he wouldn't. Of that she was resoundingly sure.

She moved her leg to give him the space he wanted. She'd supposed she might set that foot on the floor, the sofa being too narrow to otherwise allow much distance between her knees, but he had other ideas. He caught her leg behind the knee and angled it up and around, wrapping it behind his own leg. Her hips tilted with the action and he settled himself and resettled himself against her, studying her face with each adjustment as if he were expecting to see some particular—

Oh. *Oh.* Her breath caught in her throat and she could feel her eyes go wide.

"Good?" He didn't need to ask. The curve of his lips made perfectly plain that he knew.

She nodded. Her hands had convulsed on him, one clutching at the bottom edge of his waistcoat while the other curled around a fistful of sleeve.

"Good," he repeated, an affirmation this time. "Now hold on tight while I make it even better."

WITH ONLY a bit of twisting, and the involvement of one hand, he was able to get her nipple in his mouth again. She sighed, the smallest touch of voice in it; not quite a moan, but no matter. He'd have moans from her, too, in another minute or so.

He let her feel the whole broad surface of his tongue, slowly. She was so damn stiff against the softer parts of his mouth. He would have liked to see her with her bodice restored, her nipples hard and obvious through the silk, announcing to the world how he'd aroused her. For that matter he would have liked to send a hand up those skirts he'd promised not to lift, and find out if she was as wet between the legs as he suspected.

His hips rolled against her, and *there* came the first moan, frayed at its edges with the same astonishment her wide eyes had betrayed, in that instant when he'd found the right spot. He'd lay money that she hadn't ever learned where her best nerves were or what she could do with them. And much as he knew this was a prize he ought to leave to her husband—or hell, perhaps to her explorations and her own hand—he couldn't. His greed was too great, her moans too bewitching, the memory of his months of hopeless infatuation all too strong. Why shouldn't he take this compensation, and please her at the same time?

He put a purposeful rhythm into his hips, and sped up the work of his tongue.

SHE ARCHED and writhed and moaned, a raw, anxious sound reminiscent of a she-cat prowling for a tom. She would be ashamed, if he hadn't driven her past all such cares.

Penelope had said it could be pleasant, with a man who cared to make the effort. *Very pleasant*, she'd said, low and significant, because apparently her sister had married such a man and liked to speak of the fact.

But *pleasant* told you nothing. *Pleasant* was a warm spring day in a flower-filled meadow. *Very pleasant* meant especially pretty flowers, and a dry place to sit down in the grass. What word could possibly name the sensations that made your body seethe, shameless and desperate as a she-cat in season?

Her hands couldn't seem to find the right place to settle. His waist. His shoulders. The arm of the sofa, up above her head. "Nick." She wound her leg tighter, clamping his hips hard to hers. "I want . . ." She couldn't say it. Couldn't admit aloud to what she wanted, not when he'd promised only half a minute ago to keep her skirts down and his buttons fastened.

He raised his head, his eyes dark and all-seeing. "I know." His face dipped near and his mouth brushed hers. "Believe me, I want it, too. But we can't." He pressed his hard part against her, through the layers of detestable clothing, and rolled her nipple between fingers that had crept to her breast without her noticing. "Let me tend to you this way. You're almost there. I can feel it."

Almost where? She wanted to cry out in despair at her own ignorance, in fury at his refusal to seize the permission she was granting. She dug her fingers into the sofa's upholstered arm, one solid handhold as the rest of her raged, answering his every touch and demanding more.

"Good, sweetheart, good. Don't fight it. You're so close." He kissed her face all over, murmuring such meaningless words in between. Then he lifted his head to watch her. His gaze tracked from her face up her arms to where she gripped the sofa, and his eyes narrowed. He liked to see her this way.

She'd triumph in having pleased him, if she were capable of any thought so clear. But all was fierce sensation now, the industry of his fingers, his pressure between her legs; and her brain could only flash and spark ineffectually, like a pistol that someone had forgotten to load.

She thrashed against him, faster and faster as the pleasure built. He swore through gritted teeth; she didn't mind. She screwed her eyes shut and loosened her grip on the sofa to fling her arms round him, binding his whole body to hers as rapture came crashing over her, forceful and astonishing as a wild ocean wave.

Let it drown her. She didn't care. Let it sweep her out to sea, past the reach of any rescue. She didn't need rescue. She would stay right here, adrift and unrepentant for the rest of her days, because nothing else in life would ever again feel so right as this ruin.

For eight or nine different reasons, he should have been sorry. He wasn't. He lay still, feeling all her muscles go slack. His breaths and hers played a whispered duet in the otherwise silent room.

"Kate." He kissed her cheek. Would he ever be able to call her Miss Westbrook again? "Don't go to sleep. You've got to go back downstairs."

"When did the music end?" Her words came out a bit sluggish. Her eyes opened only halfway. She was too intoxicated, still, to feel any urgency about getting back to the ballroom.

"A minute or so since. No more. You'll be just in time for supper. But you mustn't linger." He eased himself off her as he spoke, and sank into a crouch at her side. "Do you mind if I put your bodice to rights? There's no mirror in here."

"Um. Yes. If you please." She struggled to a sitting position and he helped her get everything straightened away, bosom put back out of sight, shift in its proper place, silk smoothed over all. "Do you not mean to go to supper, too?"

"Eventually. But I'll need several minutes of very dull thoughts first, preferably while standing in a draft, in order to make myself presentable."

She puzzled it out, darting a not-quite-intentional glance below his waist to confirm her interpretation. "That . . . didn't happen for you, then? As it did for me?"

He shook his head. "A good thing, too. It's not so tidy an event for a gentleman as it is for a lady. Not advisable when one is wearing breeches." *Besides, I needed to keep my head so I could see every second of your pleasure,* he didn't say. *I'm going to recall it in vivid detail when I get home tonight. Two or three times at the least.* Certainly he didn't say *that.*

"Ah. I didn't know." She put up a hand to feel whether her hair was disarranged. She was gazing straight ahead now, embarrassment beginning to overtake her as the aftertaste of her climax faded.

"Kate, look at me." One more time he took her chin in his fingers. Here and here, he'd kissed her but a moment ago. "You may rely absolutely on my discretion and my respect for you. No one will hear of this from me, and there will be no alteration in my manners toward you. I hope you won't avoid me, or be ill at ease in my presence."

She nodded, her eyes not quite meeting his.

"We've done no worse than many, many young men and women before us. We did better than most, by leaving your virtue intact. There's no reason you shouldn't accept a marriage offer with a clear conscience, when the time comes, and no reason you and I cannot go on as we were. As friends, with a shared interest in keeping the knowledge of this event from ever coming to light."

He wasn't saying the right thing. He could feel her sinking deeper into mortification with his every word. She kept her eyes on his face, but with visible effort.

He let his hand fall from her chin, and picked up her hand from where it was restlessly smoothing a wrinkle in her skirt. "We're allies in this. Not adversaries. We've no need to be embarrassed before one another." Still he wasn't sorry, but he was beginning to see that he probably would be, if this awkwardness persisted—and why would it not? If a kiss had been enough to alter their friendship, why on earth should he expect that they could recover from an impropriety of this order?

"Thank you for saying so. I ought to go." She was all

but squirming to get her hand out of his; to get away from this conversation. She was right, too. He endangered her reputation with his selfish wish to get them back on easy footing before she left.

"Indeed you ought. Forgive my detaining you." He rose and helped her up, and no other words passed between them before she departed the room. And a gnawing sense of disappointment ultimately did just as much as Latin declensions and the chilly air by the window to render him fit for polite viewing once more.

SHE WENT to supper with Lady Harringdon, who was delighted to have an attendant again and thoroughly unaware of her having been gone from the ballroom for so long. No one, for that matter, appeared to have noticed her absence. So easily could a lady get up to mischief, without a zealous chaperone.

In small bites she consumed a polite portion of her tomato aspic, conversing as well as she could with the matrons among whom she and the countess sat, and trying not to wonder which of them had in her youth ever let a man take liberties. Trying even harder not to wonder whether each had experienced, within marriage or without, that unspeakable explosion of pleasure that echoed in her body even now.

Penelope Towne had implied a woman's enjoyment depended on the skill of the man. Thus there must be women, even long-married women, whose husbands had never brought about that private cataclysm.

Mr. Blackshear had done it so easily, without even removing his clothing or hers. Was that merely a testament to some sort of impersonal expertise, honed through practice with Lady Attainable and other worldly women? His attentions had felt expert, to be sure. They hadn't felt impersonal.

God, Kate, you've no idea how I wanted this. She carved out another neat forkful of the red-tinged quivering dish before her, but didn't bring it to her mouth. A lady could not wallow very deeply in the memory of a gentleman's stirring words to her when he'd said other, less-gratifying words as well. Concerning how it was too late now for her to return his affection, and assuring her of the propriety of her one day accepting some other man's marriage proposal.

"A passable aspic, no more." Lady Harringdon leaned close to issue this opinion in a confidential tone. "Lady Cathcart never would engage a French chef, even when the war ended. And here we have the fruits of her patriotism." She'd eaten but a quarter of her own serving, and pushed the rest about her plate as though to disguise the quantity remaining. "We shall hope for better from the succeeding courses, though we shan't hope for anything to rival what we enjoyed last week at Lady Astley's."

"Lady Astley's supper was very fine," Kate said, and wished she'd never gone to Lady Astley's. Wished she'd never indulged the hope of one day being Lady Astley, never set out to charm Lord Barclay, never caused pain to Louisa Smith.

She wished Mr. Blackshear had been the eldest son of a titled man, with spotless connections.

This whole thing is impossible. He'd told her nothing she hadn't already known, with those words. Why was the fact so much more troubling when he was the one to voice it?

She ate a forkful of aspic, and then another, because it was a point of pride that she show better manners than Lady Harringdon. Each bite went down like a lump of cold tar.

At the next table sat the Captain Williams who'd hoped to waltz with her. He was tall, broad, dashing, and elegant in his red coat and neat whiskers. She could not imagine ever writhing underneath him and making desperate she-cat sounds. Nor could she imagine doing so with any of the men who'd partnered with her tonight, Lord Barclay included.

She wouldn't have minded, before. She would have made the best match she could, and counted herself lucky if marital congress turned out to be sometimes pleasant. Her body would never have known itself to be deprived.

Now, her body trained its attention on the room's open door, keen and poised as a dog waiting for a stick to be thrown. And when Mr. Blackshear appeared, she felt it in her skin, in the hairs on the back of her neck, even before she glanced that way to confirm his arrival.

He didn't look as though he'd been up to anything improper. He'd restored his coat, of course, and . . . thought his several minutes of dull thoughts. No evidence of his arousal remained, unless you counted the fiery imprint his masculinity had left in her most private places. He looked like nothing so much as a barrister who'd been called away from the party on some professional business, and returned almost grudgingly to this frivolous affair.

He caught her eye and smiled, quick, encouraging, and not very intimate. *Don't worry,* said his expression. *Remember my promise. I'll never tell a soul, and you'll see no change in my manners toward you.*

To return his smile would be to ratify his version of events. To reduce their time upstairs to a quick animal dalliance, a fleshly misdemeanor from which both parties would naturally wish to disentangle and move on, unencumbered, with all possible haste.

She smiled, or at least warped her lips into the approximate right shape, before dropping her gaze to the aspic. What else could she do? She'd troubled him enough already, compelling his attendance at a party where he had few friends. From the corner of her eye she could see him glance about the room—neither Lord Barclay nor Lord Cathcart had an empty seat nearby, and did he even know anyone else in this company?—before taking a place at a table of young men who appeared to be well in their cups. Her heart hurt, watching him. He deserved better. In every particular, he deserved better than what he'd gotten from his association with her.

"Such a lovely gown, Miss Westbrook." Lady Waltham, the most resplendent, in gold-trimmed indigo, of Lady Harringdon's little circle, addressed her with a queen's lofty graciousness from across the table. "Have you seen this month's *Ackermann's*? I find the new styles altogether excessive in their layers and gatherings and embellishments, don't you?"

Some well-primed corner of her brain remembered how to converse on this topic, and so she did. Her heart ought to be doing a sprightly jig. This was what she'd wanted: to speak on such subjects with such women; to think of how she might charm her way into their drawing rooms, and from there into the notice of their marriageable sons. Now here she was, with events hewing so close to her many-times fondly envisioned course, and everything was wrong. Her triumph was built on a scaffold of lies, from the gaze she kept firmly averted from Mr. Blackshear, to her gracious acceptance of compliments for Louisa Smith's taste in gowns.

But she didn't know how to begin correcting the wrongs, so she only smiled, and gave her opinions on gatherings and embellishments, and secretly counted the minutes until the meal would end.

SHE DANCED with three more gentlemen after supper. None of them mattered. She tried four times to converse with Miss Smith, only to see the latter escape, on various pretexts, after the first few polite and superficial remarks. She went home, finally, and made her way to bed, only to have Viola ask across the room whether Mr. Blackshear had presumed to kiss her again.

"No." With that one syllable, she gave up all the comfort of confessing herself. The truth, this time, was too much to tell. "We did speak on the matter, though. We agreed we're both embarrassed, and thoroughly sorry, and are therefore in no danger of ever repeating the lapse."

"That sounds very sensible of you both." Vi's voice grew thoughtful. "Imagine how difficult it would be to have such a conversation with a man who wasn't a friend. I suppose you must count yourself lucky it was Mr. Blackshear with whom this happened."

"I suppose I must," Kate said, and she could not remember ever feeling less lucky in her life.

Chapter Fifteen

"A LADY DOWNSTAIRS to see you." Kersey leaned into the doorway long enough to communicate this fact, then swung away, unbuttoning his topcoat as he headed for his own chambers across the hall.

Kate was Nick's first thought. She hadn't strayed far from his thoughts all morning, to say nothing of the part she'd played there over a largely sleepless night. Hang what was left of his pride: he'd slaked his lusts to images of her; he'd lain awake wondering whether they'd compromised their relationship beyond repair; he'd remembered every compromising thing they'd done and he'd roused up a new set of lusts and slaked them all over again.

It couldn't be her downstairs, though—part of his brain was awake enough to recognize this—because Kersey knew her by sight. He wouldn't have announced her as merely "a lady." The same reasoning ruled out Mrs. Simcox, who would have been his second guess, because Kersey was well acquainted with the sight of her, too.

Nick pushed up from his desk and caught his coat on the way out. Just as well it wasn't Mrs. Simcox. If she'd come for some wicked daylight romp he would have had to turn her away, and he would never have been able to explain the reason.

Other possibilities flitted in and out as he descended the stairs. *Mrs. Westbrook* was the worst. So clearly he could envision her waiting on that bench, or perhaps striding back and forth before it, the terrible cast of her countenance telling him she knew how he'd betrayed the family's trust.

But it was another fearsome countenance that awaited him, when he pulled open the front door and stepped out into the chill morning.

Will's wife, of all people, sat on the bench. She'd twisted left to frown at the sundial, giving him a view of a stark, unfeminine profile. At his appearance she twisted back to glance at him, then returned to her study of the sundial.

Well, then. Apparently she hadn't come to tell him of some accident befalling his brother, or if she had, her phlegmatism was beyond anything.

He went to the bench and sat. Why bother with a greeting, or with asking her whether she'd like to come inside? She didn't like him, and he resented the corrupting intersection of her life with his. Whatever business had brought her here, they could discharge it without pretense of amity.

She didn't speak at first. The silence was surprisingly comfortable, if not quite companionable. He pushed his ungloved hands into his coat pockets, and waited.

From the corner of his eye he could see her shoulders rise. "I haven't come to apologize." She didn't turn to face him.

"I had no expectation that you would." Neither did he face her. Number Two Brick Court, with its illustrious past, was a more rewarding view than the back of her head.

"I mightn't have come at all, but I spoke to Mrs. Mirkwood on the subject and she said that I ought."

This, he could all too easily imagine. "My sister is inordinately fond of telling people what they ought to do."

"So I've observed." The smallest spark of kinship flickered between them. She must have felt it, too, because she relaxed her posture until she, like he, was facing straight ahead. "The first thing I want you to know, Mr. Blackshear, is that I love your brother. My attachment to him is fiercer than my attachment to life. I will never be capable of kindness to anyone who causes him pain."

"I'm glad to hear it. He's a very good man. He deserves that sort of loyalty." Every word of this was true.

"I don't say you ought to have done different, in regard to him." She dipped her chin to frown at the woolen muff that hid her forearms. "I was respectable, too, for a good part of my life. I know what rules you must follow. I didn't expect any of his family to keep the connection, once we married."

"It goes a bit beyond *rules*." The words tasted of pettiness and self-justification, but they, too, were true. "The connection has done damage to my practice. There are solicitors who decline to bring me cases now. I expect it will make an obstacle to the realization of my greater professional ambitions as well."

She nodded once, still frowning at her wool-blanketed hands. "I knew that was a likely outcome of our marriage. I knew your brothers and sisters would pay a price, too, in their social standing."

"As may their children. I have nieces and nephews who will like to marry one day, and will almost certainly face dimmer prospects than they would have if they brought no disreputable connection to the union."

"Indeed. I understood that consequence, too, and still

I could not give him up." She raised her chin, and angled her face to look at Nick sidelong. "I daresay you think if I truly loved him, I would have walked away and left him with his family intact."

Now he was the one to lower his gaze, fixing it on a spot some four feet in front of their bench, where the paving bricks were worn drab and dull-edged from years of purposeful barrister striding. He'd thought exactly that, once, that love ought to have prompted her to leave Will alone. Perhaps he knew a bit more now of how difficult it was to do such a thing, even with the other person's best interest at stake. He shook his head slowly. "That would have been an extraordinary sacrifice. I wouldn't presume to expect it of anyone."

"I did tell him, at first, that to marry me was impossible. I did try to refuse him. But I hadn't the heart to stand firm. He was determined, and I was satisfied that he should be. Partly for selfish reasons—my hopes of happiness were so slight before I met him—but partly, too, because he needed me." She twisted to face him fully, and he lifted his gaze from the bricks to meet hers. "You will have to take me at my word. I was as necessary to his life as he was to mine, and even if I'd been strong enough to sacrifice my own happiness, I would never, never sacrifice his."

He let one corner of his mouth pull into a smile, even as he dropped his attention back to the bricks. "He said almost exactly the same thing, you know. The day he told us what he meant to do. He said your happiness was his sacred trust, or something of that sort, and for your sake he couldn't give you up."

"He did?" She sounded genuinely surprised at the thought. "I never knew." In the silence, he could feel her examining this new proof of her husband's love and valor, like a fossil hunter turning over her latest find. "I'm glad to know that. Thank you for telling me."

"Think nothing of it." A breeze swept down Brick Court, rustling the tree branches, and he hunched his shoulders for warmth. He ought to have worn his hat, or maybe he ought to have invited her inside. Too late now. "I was never in any doubt of your devotion to Will, you should know. I won't pretend I welcomed the marriage, but I've always supposed he loved you and was loved in return." He cleared his throat. "I was sure of it on the day I met you, at the shipping office."

"Yes. That brings me to my other purpose in coming here. The other thing I want you to know." Now it was her turn to clear her throat. "As I said, I don't apologize for my incivility that day. I think you'll agree it's not very likely you and I will ever be friends. But my rudeness is mine alone. You mustn't think I express anyone's sentiments but my own."

Again he turned to look at her. Nowhere on her face could he spot any sign of urgency or beseeching, but the facts spoke for themselves. She'd come all this way from wherever she and Will lived, and sat down in conversation with a man for whom she did not care. Not for her own sake had she done these things.

"I can only think you had a reason for coming to the office." Her eyes never wavered from his. "Not, perhaps, an imperative reason, but a reason nonetheless. And surely that reason still stands. Surely I, and my rudeness, are not enough to turn you aside from what you meant to do that day."

What had he meant to do that day? He'd ventured down onto the docks with no clear purpose; with no idea of what he would say, if he and Will should meet. Only he'd been weary, after all these months, of not seeing his brother.

He frowned past her, at that confounded sundial reminding him about time and tide. "We lived in readiness for the loss of him when he was away at war." In his coat pockets his fingers flexed and curled. "When he came home whole we thought we could put away that fear. We were unprepared—I was unprepared—for the possibility he might be lost to us by other means."

"He won't come to call on you, as I've done." She got to her feet, and he understood that these were her concluding remarks. He rose, too. "He gave his word to stay clear of you and your elder brother and sister and their families. He doesn't break his word." She brought something out from the woolen muff, a folded paper that she must have been holding there all along. "This is our direction. You might make use of it, or you might not. I shan't tell him of this visit, so you needn't worry that he'll be expecting a letter. Only, whatever did possess you to seek him at the office last week . . ." She faltered slightly, and again the importunity of her errand showed itself despite her mask of composure. "I think that same thing might possess him, too."

Nick took the paper wordlessly. He put it in his pocket unread. And after she'd gone, disappearing round the corner into Middle Temple Lane, he sat back down on the bench and spent a good fifteen minutes staring out at nothing before he got up and went back inside.

ROSE DIDN'T appear at breakfast. She had a headache, Bea explained, and no appetite. She didn't feel well enough to go to lessons today.

"Did something happen at school yesterday?" Kate asked when Mama had left the room to see to Rose. Her heart was sinking already, and prepared to keep going all the way to the pit of her stomach.

Bea twisted her mouth, thinking. "Well, I played the piano for the dancing lesson because Miss Taylor who usually plays was home with a fever. That meant Rose didn't have me for a partner, and one of the other girls must dance with her, and several of them made a great show of their reluctance. I think it was Julia Lyon who was finally paired with her, and she sulked and slumped and made very little effort to keep up with the music. Will you pass the black currant jam, please?"

"Pity there's no caning at Miss Lowell's." Vi turned the page of her *Times,* not even glancing up. "That might teach those girls some manners."

Sebastian, engrossed in the *Gazette,* didn't make any remark or response at all.

Kate set the jar before her sister, noiseless and precise in direct proportion to her desire to heave it against the wall. How could everyone accept such an incident so calmly, as though it was but a routine irritation to which they all ought to be inured? Was she the only one who could see that Rose was not inured, and would never be inured? Was she the only one who understood how routine irritations, even petty ones, could wear away at a girl's well-being the way steady drops of water could gradually and irrevocably reshape stone?

Yes, of course she was the only one. Just as she was the only one to care about mending the rift between Papa and Lord Harringdon; the only one to feel the sorrow of a man's being a stranger to his own mother; the only one to whom it meant something that their unraveled family be knit up whole again. She alone had made it a mission to right those wrongs. Therefore she could not blame her failure on anyone but herself.

She poked at a kippered herring with the tines of her fork, but her appetite was gone. Last night had been one great, long chance to charm eligible men, and when she hadn't been frittering that chance away she'd been hurling it from her with all possible force. Indulging herself with thoughts of Mr. Blackshear, and then with Mr. Blackshear himself, when she might have been promoting her interest with some man whose rank could elevate her sisters beyond the reach of merchants' daughters and their nasty little pranks.

She'd spent virtually every day of her young womanhood in expectation of this opportunity. She'd planned and schemed and meticulously charted her course. How had she managed, in the space of two parties, to so utterly lose her way?

When breakfast was done she ventured up to Rose and Bea's room. Her sister lay abed, propped up on pillows, her hands folded atop the covers a few inches from an apparently discarded book. Kate went and sat down on the edge of the mattress. "*The Lairds of Glenfern?*" she said, picking up the book and turning it over.

"It's not very good. I probably won't finish it." She stared off toward the window, whose draperies had been pushed wide. On the bedside table sat a cup of something, doubtless a tisane Mama had ordered to be sent up. It had not, as far as Kate could tell, been touched.

She covered her sister's clasped hands with one of hers. "You haven't a headache really, I think."

Rose didn't answer for a moment. Then she shook her head, eyes still on the window.

Kate pressed her hand, to show she would listen but wouldn't demand that her sister talk.

Rose unclasped her hands and turned one palm up to lace her fingers with Kate's. She blinked several times. "I hate to be so weak," she said finally.

"You're not. There's no weakness in objecting to spiteful treatment."

"Bea told you about the dancing lesson?" Her face showed no sign of surprise. She knew better than to expect confidentiality from her sister.

Kate nodded. "Anyone would wish for a day away from that sort of nonsense every now and again."

"You didn't ever. Vi didn't. Bea doesn't. I'm the only one so cowardly." She blinked harder and bit her lip.

"You're not cowardly. You're only not as hardheaded as the rest of us. That's a virtue, not a fault. One day, when you meet the right sort of people, you'll charm them more thoroughly than any of us could ever do."

"I don't know why they dislike us so." She gave up staring at the window in favor of staring at a spot over Kate's shoulder. "I've done nothing to offend them. I've been as pleasant as I can. And I know Mama and Papa's marriage was irregular, but you'd think it had been a criminal offense. I'm sure a girl born out of wedlock, entirely ignorant of who is her father, could not be shunned any harder than Bea and I are."

"I know, dear. It's not fair or right or reasonable. But girls like that will always look for someone to shun, as a safeguard against being the one shunned. People secure in their own consequence aren't so mean." Her words felt trite and useless. Could she really offer no better consolation than these poor insights that Rose doubtless already knew?

Footsteps sounded in the hall, and Viola put her head in the door. "Someone's sent you a great bunch of flowers. Some gentleman from that party last night, I suppose. Do you want them brought to our room, or should they stay downstairs in the parlor?"

Kate's heart leaped and then sank again. Only one man at the party would know where to send those flowers. Well, two men—but she knew better than to suppose they might have come from Mr. Blackshear.

And indeed when the maid Patsy brought them up in a vase—to Rose's room, that they might have a cheering effect—tucked in among the rosebuds was Lord Barclay's card. Kate would have welcomed flowers from any other gentleman with whom she'd danced or spoken last night. She would have taken them as a reprieve, a signal that she might still correct her course and make the sort of match she'd intended. But the baron's roses loomed like an accusation, a reminder of all her missteps.

"He wasn't at all bad, for a peer." Viola studied the card, sitting on Bea's bed. "If you must marry a Lord Somebody, I suppose you could do worse."

"I sincerely doubt he wants to marry me." She leaned in to get a noseful of rose fragrance, and to hide her face from view. "He's met me all of three times. I'm sure he only meant to be kind, because he knows my situation and knew I wasn't likely to get flowers from anyone else."

"A man doesn't usually send roses just to be kind." Mama had come in with the maid and stood at the foot of Rose's bed. "You ought to give serious thought to whether you would accept his addresses. Your father would want to know what answer to make, if he should ask permission to court you."

The prospect—the very words—twisted her innards. *No*, she ought to say. *I've already thought about it and I cannot accept his addresses.* But the sight of Rose stopped her tongue. If she made a brilliant match, she'd be able to introduce her sister to some of those people so secure in their consequence that they never felt the need to claim it at others' expense.

She drew a breath. "I'll give it thought, then." It was as though she'd stepped into an intricate snare, and any move she made just drew it tighter. "Vi, did you still mean to walk with me to Berkeley Square? I'm expected there in half an hour."

SHE'D WISHED for flowers from some other man, and at Harringdon House she had them. Lord John Prior had sent a tasteless profusion of blossoms, along with a note apologizing for the sudden indisposition that had robbed him of the pleasure of dancing with her, to Miss Westbrook in care of Lady Harringdon.

"I do believe he mistakes matters." The countess, spaniel in her lap, looked over Lord John's note with delight. "He supposes I'm bringing you out as a marriageable young lady."

He mistook matters, surely enough. If he thought she didn't know exactly what sort of indisposition had led to his departure, or what physick he'd received for his pains, well, he was gravely mistaken indeed.

"I'm not sure there's necessarily any mistake." Louisa Smith's conduct simply put Kate to shame. Even with this new awkwardness between them, she was staunch in stepping up to challenge Lady Harringdon's slights. "He feels sorry for having had to break his engagement to dance with Miss Westbrook, and, not knowing her own direction, thought to send his bouquet to the lady with whom he's now seen her in company twice."

"If it had been a more modest bouquet, I might agree with you, Miss Smith." Lady Harringdon waved Lord John's note at the floral arrangement, which she'd had brought to the parlor that the two young ladies and Mrs. Smith might consider it thoroughly. "But these are the flowers of a man who means to impress himself in a lady's imagination. He's left nothing to chance, you see. Whatever might be Miss Westbrook's favorite color, she is assured of finding it here."

"Mistake or no, I think his regard for Miss Westbrook speaks well of him," Mrs. Smith ventured, sending Kate a kindly smile. She'd looked so pleased last night, when she'd seen Louisa turned out to such advantage. She must not know of the wilting that Kate had later induced.

"Indeed. And I'd say it speaks equally well of Miss Westbrook, who has proven that her manners and charm, at least, are worthy of a duke's son." Lady Harringdon handed back the note. "We shall have to take care to find you a position with an older lady who hasn't any wish to marry. No younger lady likes to feel that her companion outshines her with the gentlemen."

Kate folded the note to put away in her reticule. When she'd imagined stupefying a gentleman of rank, she'd supposed that the state of stupefaction would prevent him, at least in the beginning, from running off to engage in indecency with other women. Not to say Lord John was stupefied. But it was, indeed, an extravagant bunch of blooms. Perhaps he strove to assuage his guilt, and perhaps this was a representation of how he would go on with whatever lady he married. Committing indiscretions and paying penance in flowers.

"I'll own my taste in these things is old-fashioned, but I remain partial to a simple bouquet all of one color." Mrs. Smith nodded to her daughter. "I thought the roses Lord Barclay sent to Louisa were perfectly charming."

"Miss Smith, you sly devil." The countess trained the full weight of her attention on the other of her young callers. "You've been here five whole minutes and didn't breathe a word of this. Have you made a conquest, and what will this mean for Sir George Bigby? I insist you tell us everything."

Well. Apparently Mama had been wrong about what was signified by a man's sending roses, or perhaps Lord Barclay meant to court two ladies at once. Kate felt her fingers curling to grip the sofa cushions, in spite of her mightiest effort at aplomb. No sooner did she think she knew her circumstances, than something must change.

"There's nothing very much to tell." Miss Smith went pink. "A bunch of roses arrived this morning with his card." She threw one anxious glance to Kate. "We'd danced fairly early in the evening, and also spoken a bit before supper. He does make better conversation than many gentlemen."

"Better than Sir George, I think she means to say." Lady Harringdon looked around in satisfaction at the others. "I don't recall ever seeing you blush, Miss Smith, when speaking of the baronet."

What if she did just step aside, and leave Lord Barclay to Miss Smith? She could send back his flowers with some explanatory note. *It's clear to me you have a better prospect before you, and I suspect it's clear to you, too. I'm sorry but my heart is engaged elsewhere. I'm sorry but we just wouldn't suit.* Any of those explanations would do. Then she could live in hope that Lord John Prior would follow his garish bouquet with more attentions, and not too often make a wallflower of her while indulging himself in someone else's arms.

Somewhere in this dull meditation came the sound of footsteps in the hall; purposeful, urgent footsteps. All conversation trailed off at the appearance of Lord Harringdon in the doorway, pale and clearly distressed.

"The dowager Lady Harringdon has taken very ill." He spoke to his wife, not even acknowledging the guests. "Morland has sent for the physician. I'm going to have him send for all the family as well." He bowed, seeming only now to realize that he'd neglected to do so before, and as he came back up, his eyes connected with Kate's.

She was halfway to her feet, as indeed Mrs. and Miss Smith were, preparing to take an immediate leave. His gaze froze her. She felt every bit of his worry, as surely as if her heart took its rhythm from his. And she wanted—so, so badly she wanted him to ask her to send for Papa, but he didn't. "Ought I—" Her throat was parched and the words barely made a sound, and before she could try again he'd turned and gone.

"My apologies." Lady Harringdon rose, too. "I shall have a servant fetch all your wraps. Mrs. Smith, I'll have your carriage brought round." She hurried off, leaving them to wait for their cloaks.

Kate stood where she was, with nothing in the world to do but wait for her wrap and walk home. She still felt the echoes of Lord Harringdon's alarm in the middle of her chest. Everywhere else she felt numb.

"Miss Westbrook." Louisa stepped forward suddenly, hands clasped before her. "Kate. May Mama and I send our carriage to fetch your father?" She hadn't even asked her mother's permission. Her eyes were grave and resolute.

And now the numbness gave way to a crawling desperation. "You're so kind to offer. But even if he were welcome here, I don't know where to find him. If he's in a courtroom, he cannot simply leave. And I've no idea whether he's in a courtroom, or if so, which one he'd be in, or whether he's someplace else altogether." She'd never felt so helpless, so useless in her life. "And even if we do find him, I can't be at all sure that he'd want to come."

Louisa moved a step nearer. "He must have an office. We'll start there. If he's not in his office, someone there may know where he's gone. We'll ask everyone until we've found him." She reached out and took Kate's hands. "You'll feel better to be doing something than you would if you simply sat about."

Beyond her, Mrs. Smith nodded. Their generosity was almost too much to bear.

"Thank you." A footman came with the cloaks. She pressed Louisa's hands before releasing them, and bowed her head to Mrs. Smith. "Thank you both so much." She blinked back a few tears—she might have more need of them later—and hurried into her cloak.

THE CLERKS in Papa's office said he'd gone to meet with a solicitor, and gave her the direction. She and the Smith ladies arrived at that man's office to find he'd already left, and the solicitor hadn't any idea of his next destination.

"It wouldn't be his own office, or surely the clerks there would have said they expected him back soon," Miss Smith reasoned. Thank goodness for Miss Smith's ability to reason, because Kate's own had fled.

Papa could be anywhere. There were so many buildings in the Inns of Court, and so many rooms in each building. And for all they knew, he might have gone to see a solicitor who kept an office elsewhere, or to the wig maker's, or to any of a dizzying number of places. Where were they to start looking?

"I think we'd best try his office again," Mrs. Smith suggested. "Perhaps he finished this last appointment early and has gone back before the clerks expected him there."

Halfway back to his office, they ran into the Mr. Kersey she'd met the day she'd gone with Sebastian and Viola to see Mr. Blackshear in the criminal courts. Mr. Kersey hadn't seen Papa and had no way of guessing where he'd be, but he thought Mr. Blackshear might be of use, and lost no time in sending for him.

They were waiting with Mr. Kersey in his chambers when Mr. Blackshear came up the stairs, taking them two at a time. She'd never been so glad to hear anyone's footsteps, or see anyone come into view. He swung through Kersey's doorway in a swirl of robes, got them all resettled in his own rooms across the hall, directed Kersey to make tea, and asked her and the Smith ladies to tell him every detail.

What had happened, exactly? What did they wish him to tell Mr. Westbrook? Ought he to bring him back here, or could he take him straight to the Smiths' carriage? Where was the Smiths' carriage to be found? Where had they looked for him already? Did they all wish to wait here, or would they like him to order hackney cabs to take them home? With marvelous efficiency he got through all of this, and then he stopped in front of her. "I'll find him, Miss Westbrook. Don't worry. I'll take care of it." And in another swirl of robes, he was gone, and she heard the thump of his quick pace down the stairs.

It seemed a very long time before he returned, and he looked weary when he did. But he'd found Papa and sent him in the carriage, just as he'd said he would.

She was so grateful.

"Let's see to getting you all home now," he said, and he took care of that, too. A hackney took her home, where she told Mama what had happened, and waited on the bench in the entry hall until Papa finally came in.

A single look at him told her she'd been too late. Not only in finding him this afternoon but in taking the steps to reconcile him with his family. She ought to have . . . but she didn't know what she could have done differently. She'd been making her good impressions, little by little, with both Lady and Lord Harringdon. *Little by little* just hadn't been enough.

He sat down and put his arm about her, as he hadn't done since she was a child. She sagged against him. She couldn't cry.

"Kate," he said. She *would* not cry. "I grieved for her years and years ago."

"But she didn't die years and years ago." She understood his meaning perfectly well. It just wasn't fair to give up on someone who was still alive, and shared blood and so many memories with you. It wasn't fair to grieve for someone while she still liked to sit in the parlor for social calls, and hear stories read out of *Ackermann's Repository*.

"You're lucky to have the example of affectionate grandparents on your mother's side. Affectionate aunts and uncles as well. Not all families are like that."

She wouldn't speak of the letters. She couldn't admit to having read them. But there had been affection in Papa's family, once. Could it really die out altogether? "Was everybody there?" she said instead.

"Yes." For a moment he was silent. "Please don't imagine a tearful reconciliation around our mother's deathbed. There was nothing of the sort." He squeezed her shoulders and kissed the top of her head. "Be glad of your own loving family, dear." He stood, then, and went upstairs.

She didn't follow straightaway. When his footsteps had gone past the second landing she moved to the end of the bench against the wall, mere inches from where she'd stood side by side with Mr. Blackshear the day he'd encouraged her to go into ballrooms and catch a duke. And she wept, silently, for Papa and his mother, for her arrogant, hopeful plans of that day, for all the many things about which she'd been so very wrong.

Chapter Sixteen

Again he'd lain awake and thought about Miss Westbrook, but this time worry had kept his thoughts chaste.

He hadn't told her—nor did he intend to, ever—what effort had been required to persuade Mr. Westbrook to go to his brother's house and his mother's sickbed. He was the worst possible person to try to convince a man to overlook grievances with a brother, of course, but try he had, with every tactic of reason, every appeal to sentiment at his disposal. In the end he believed it had been the specter he'd conjured of Kate herself, pale and drawn as he'd left her in his chambers, that had finally convinced her father to make this gesture for her sake, if not his own.

Nick sighed, lifting his hat and scrubbing a hand through his hair, as he started up Middle Temple Lane on his way back to Brick Court. He hadn't bothered wearing a wig to breakfast, since he didn't have any appointments following. A part of him would like nothing better at the moment than to simply go back to bed. He might first make a visit to Westbrook's office, though, and learn about last night's outcome and how Miss Westbrook was faring.

His heart had fairly broken for her, seeing her in that

state. He'd known all about her pride in winning her aunt's notice, and the vanity that attended her relations with the Harringdon household, but he'd had no idea there was a genuine attachment to her grandmother. In fact he hadn't known there was a grandmother at all.

She'd been trying all along to patch up the estrangement in her father's family. Every time she asked one of those questions in the parlor or at the dinner table—*Are you sure no one on your side is musical? Perhaps our talent comes from the Westbrook line*—she'd been tilting at that same windmill. Someone ought to have told her that sometimes families broke apart and there was simply no way to mend them.

He sighed again, this time shoving his hands into his topcoat pockets. In the right one was the paper left with him by Mrs. William Blackshear. He hadn't even taken it out to read it yet, though until Kersey's messenger had found him with the news about Miss Westbrook yesterday, it had been the leading topic in his thoughts. Perhaps after he'd gone to look in on Westbrook he'd sit down and see what sort of note he might write, if he did decide he had something worth saying to Will.

He turned in to Brick Court, meaning to get his wig before venturing to call on Westbrook, and for the second straight day, he was stopped by the sight of a woman on the bench. A small, sad figure this time, wrapped in a cloak and facing him, or rather, the path from which she'd known he must appear, rather than making a study of the sundial.

He had nothing to learn, now, by going to call on Westbrook. Her face made everything plain.

"Kate." He crossed to the bench and sat. "Was it too late, then, when your father went to her?"

She nodded. Her eyes rolled skyward and her mouth compressed as she strove to hold back tears. "I think it was too late a long time ago. But I failed to see it."

"I'm sorry." He couldn't touch her. Not only because they were in public view and she had a reputation to protect but because things went so terribly wrong when he touched her. He kept his hands deep in his pockets. "You tried to do a worthy thing. I'm sure there's little consolation now, in thinking of that, but the consolation will grow in time. And your father will recognize the love behind what you tried to do."

In spite of both their efforts, her eyes glittered with tears, and now one spilled over and rolled down the soft plane of her cheek. She wiped it with the back of her glove. "I thought I had more time. I was proud of the progress I thought I was making. But I ought to have tried harder, instead of allowing myself to get so caught up in . . ." She waved her hand vaguely. "I've just made such a mess of everything, Nick."

"That's not true." His name in her voice touched him like a brief surreptitious kiss. He couldn't let her know that. "You're distracted by grief and disappointment at the moment, but that will ease. And then you'll see more clearly the things you've accomplished, and the things you can still accomplish. Trust me. You haven't made a mess of anything." He shifted, preparing to rise to his feet. "Come; I'll see you back to your father's office. You ought to go home and get some more rest."

She shook her head hard. "Papa doesn't know I'm here. I don't . . ." Of a sudden she was finding it very difficult to meet his eyes. "I said I was going to call on Miss Smith. And I walked down here on my own."

"To . . . tell me of your grandmother's death?" His whole body went still: if his blood could have arrested itself in his veins, it would have.

"Yes. And also to thank you for your help and kindness yesterday afternoon." She took a breath. *And also . . .* Her lifting intonation, the indrawn breath, an overall quality of suspension, made clear she had more to say. Her hesitation made clear she was finding herself short of nerve.

Inside one pocket Nick clenched his fingers, all apprehension. She'd come unchaperoned to see him, deceiving her parents as to her errand. She was distraught and doubtless wanting comfort, and filled with the recklessness that so often visited a person who'd been touched by death. He waited, not even knowing how he'd answer if his suspicions proved correct.

"I want . . ." She fixed her eyes straight ahead on Number Two Brick Court. Her throat rippled with a swallow. "I want to go . . . to your rooms with you. I want you to take me upstairs."

His whole body thrilled to her words, and to the low, determined voice in which she said them. He would not, must not, give his body the reins. "Kate." He made his voice as gentle as he could. "You're upset, and not thinking clearly."

"Wait, please." Now she directed her words to the bricks at her feet. "Let me make my case." She sat silent, her posture as taut as harp strings, until he nodded. "I am upset. I don't deny it. Not only about the dowager Lady Harringdon, and the loss of any chance for my father to know her again. Not only because I see how many mistakes I've made." Her hands clasped and unclasped in her lap. "I'm upset because I begin to doubt so much of the course I've chosen, and still, I don't see what else to do."

"I understand your distress. It's entirely natural, in such times, to seek the consolation of another person, and to want to flee from one's thoughts into pure sensation. It's eminently human to want to forget oneself in times of grief."

"But that's not what I mean." Her voice went lower still. Her cheek had flushed pink. "We will never have one another in marriage, Nick. You know of my plans, and how they have no place for you. Besides, you've said we don't suit. And that it's too late. And only recently . . . only recently have I begun to feel that as a loss."

His heart was pounding so hard that she must have heard it; his blood racing to predictable, futile destinations.

"Two nights ago at Lady Cathcart's ball, you said it wasn't so bad, what we did. You said it needn't alter our friendship." She brought her chin around until she was almost facing him. "Can we not do just that much again, and enjoy each other within the limits of what our respective plans allow, and . . . grieve, as much as it is appropriate for each of us to grieve . . . that our plans don't allow for more?"

God in heaven, she made it sound so reasonable. Like the act of two prudent, considering adults.

It was anything but. "Kate, we'd be playing with fire. Not only as regards your virtue. Indulging the sentiments you speak of will likely only lead to pain." Would. *Would* lead to pain, *if* they did it. Damn his transparent eagerness.

"I'm not afraid of pain. There will be pain in any case." Finally she raised her eyes, bright with unshed tears, to his. "I want to give you what I can of myself, and have what you will allow me of you." Her face was nearly scarlet, but she pressed on. "I know it's unwise. But it's what I want. And I hope there's a part of you that wants it, too."

There was. Not just the obvious fleshly part. He'd wanted her in his bed since nearly the first time he'd laid eyes on her. And he hated to send her away, fragile and thwarted, when he might have given her comfort, and bathed in the affection she bore him.

What if it *would* work the way she said? What if they could be together for an hour or two, eyes wide open to their idyll's necessary end, and go on afterward, their separate paths no more bitter than they already would have been?

In his pockets he curled and flexed his fingers. "This would have to be the last time, absolutely the last time, any such thing happened between us. I wrong your parents by doing this and I don't want to wrong them anymore."

"I know. I'm sorry. I never meant to make you go against your conscience. I've wronged you, too." Anything he said to her, in this mood, she'd find a way to twist into further fuel for her misery.

He could cheer her, though, and not with words. It wouldn't be a merry romp by any means, but he could take her mind from her cares for a little while, and find ways to coax a smile or two.

That did him in, really. If it had only been a matter of lust, he could have gritted his teeth and walked away, his honor and her reputation both unscathed. But the need to see her smile raced through him like a wildfire, scorching out the last pockets of better judgment.

"Very well." Deep inside him he felt something fall away, probably what remained of his self-respect. "One last time, followed by appropriate grieving. Let's go upstairs." He stood and put out his elbow. If someone was watching out the window, this much contact could still pass for respectable. As for things going wrong when he touched her, well, that barn door was surely flapping in the horses' wake.

SHE'D GONE up these same stairs for the first time not four and twenty hours earlier. Her heart halfway up her throat with worry, Miss and Mrs. Smith trailing behind, Mr. Kersey leading them with brisk purpose.

She hadn't noticed the details then. The balustrade, its

finish worn dull by years of trailing barrister hands. The wallpaper, a pattern of broad stripes in masculine red and dark brown. The sconce lamp at the landing, and the grime from smoke on the wallpaper above.

The staircase could scarcely make a starker contrast to the William Kent masterpiece at Harringdon House, or remind her in blunter fashion that she did not belong in Nick Blackshear's world.

You could belong here if you wanted to. A rebellious voice inside her piped up. *You could choose to be the kind of lady who belongs here instead of the kind who belongs in ballrooms.* She let the thought slide through and away.

At the door to his chambers he paused. "You're sure?" He spoke just above a murmur, despite the fact that they'd passed nobody on the way up, and the door across the hall from his was closed. His eyes searched hers for signs of second thoughts.

She was more sure than ever. How did any woman do this with a man who had not already been a friend? Imagine a wedding night in which one's husband claimed his due despite having only the smallest, most formal acquaintance with his bride. Imagine giving yourself to a man who didn't know how to read you; who wouldn't even think to look for hesitation in your eyes, because he would not alter his actions in any case.

"Quite sure." She lowered her voice, too. "And you?" Friendship was no friendship at all if it went only one way. He'd had qualms over the advisability of this course, and if he'd come to regret his assent during the journey upstairs, she must honor his change of heart as he was prepared to honor hers.

"I might have a reservation or two." The curve of his lips invited her into a joke. "But I fear I've passed the point of being able to properly heed them." He pushed the door open and tilted his head to usher her in.

She might not have noticed the details of the stairway yesterday, but she'd had time enough in his office to weave all the furnishings, the rug and the draperies and the papers atop his desk, into her tapestry of distress. Her stomach went heavy as she stepped into the room and saw all those objects again.

"Come." He must have understood because he was quick to shut the door, quicker still to grasp her hand and draw her through a doorway to a small sitting room, and from there into the bedroom. He dropped his hat, topcoat, and gloves on the floor. Then he closed the door, put his back against it, and gathered her into his arms.

He didn't kiss her. He only held her there, spreading his fingers over the surface of her hat to tip her head gently onto his shoulder, and the next thing she knew she was crying.

She hadn't expected to cry. She'd wept already, last night, for everything she had to grieve. But something in the way he held her . . . his arms enveloping her and urging her to lean all her weight on him . . . his stillness and patience and solidity . . . made her feel, for the first time in a very long time, that she had nothing to calculate or strive for. Here, she needn't do anything but *be.*

She'd nearly forgotten what that felt like. The stinging sweetness of it welled up and out in tears.

"This is the first time you've had a near relation die." He spoke softly. He wasn't asking a question, because he knew this fact about her.

"Yes. Though she wasn't truly very near. Not like a mother and father." Mr. Blackshear—*Nick,* rather; surely in this room, on this occasion, she could think of him by his Christian name—had lost both his parents years before she'd ever met him. She couldn't even remember the occasion of his saying so. It was just one of the many things she knew, as he knew so many things about her.

"Near enough that you're grieved by her loss. That's

all that matters." He lifted her chin and looked down at her, his eyes shining dark as the dregs of that horrid strong tea she liked to tease him about. He kissed her, carefully and with great solemnity, where a tear made its haphazard way down her cheek. He found a tear on her other cheek and kissed that one, too. With one hand he captured the ribbons of her hat and drew them loose.

He was going to take liberties. She'd asked him to. She'd come all alone to his rooms for that purpose, risking her reputation and possibly her heart. *Playing with fire,* he'd said. Yes. She needed to do that, for reasons she couldn't altogether name.

Her hat came off and her cloak followed. "Come with me to the hearth," he whispered, his breath tickling her ear. "Let me build up the fire and make the room warm."

"You don't have to." She found her brazen courage and held it fast. "We can go to the bed."

"The bed can wait." With his thumb he wiped another tear from her cheek. The look in his eyes told her there'd be no point in arguing. "Come to the hearth."

She followed and sat down on the bricks to watch him build the fire. He went about it with the quiet competence of a man who lacked for servants and had learned how to manage routine tasks on his own. From a metal box he took a handful of small sticks that he laid one by one in the glowing embers, and when they'd caught flame, he added a larger piece of wood and then a larger one yet, until at last he had a proper fire.

When she married, she would never see her husband do this. Some maid or maids would be responsible for all the household's fires, and she and the man she married would sit in tasteful chairs at a comfortable distance from the flames. Never side by side on the bricks.

Nick set the screen back in place and looked at her over his shoulder. "What is it?" A smile hovered at his lips. He must notice how intently she watched him.

"Nothing. You're so kind to make this fire for me."

"It's for me, too." The smile settled in and stretched. "If the room is cold, I can't in good conscience remove as much of your clothing as I'd like."

"Ah." She dropped her gaze to the floor. "I didn't . . . Last time we kept our clothes on." They'd had to, of course, not having the leisure to do otherwise. But everything had worked perfectly well that way.

"Kate. Sweetheart." He ducked low, to catch her eye. He looked as grave as she'd ever seen him. "I want you to be comfortable in this. I'll put you at ease in whatever way I can. But please don't ask me to leave your clothing on."

He'd been so solicitous until this moment, succumbing to her proposition, offering her the chance to change her mind, wiping her tears. She'd almost believed him to have put away his own needs and wants entirely.

"You mustn't suppose that I'm selfless. I'm not." His hand crept across the bricks between them and his fingers closed on a fold of her skirts. "I'll see to your pleasure and consolation, but I mean to see to mine as well. And I've spent too much time imagining undressing you to pass up the opportunity now."

She shivered, in spite of the heat from the fire. This was what she wanted. This was why she'd come here. His desire would meet with and match hers, and she would lose herself, forget herself, be consumed in the resulting conflagration. This one time, she would defy every stricture of her existence, all those careful rules that had failed her. If doing so unnerved her, so much the better. She raised her chin to look at him directly, and set to tugging off one glove.

"Not yet." He caught her hands in his. "I can wait." His smile told her he sensed every bit of her unease. "Let's give the fire a little time to warm the room." He pulled her to him and kissed her.

He bent her to his will without even trying. The more proofs he showed of his restraint, of how willing he was to curb his own desire for the sake of her ease, the more room she found for her own appetites to run loose. Ten minutes of kissing, with the fire's warmth stealing gradually out into the room, and she had all the nerve she needed. She broke off the kiss, and turned her attention to unfastening his cravat. This time she wouldn't let him stop her.

THANK GOD. It had begun to seem possible that he might die of balked lust. He'd wanted to do this as carefully as he could, with all the tenderness her fragile state—not to mention her inexperience—deserved. But he'd hoped, deep down, that a point would come when she'd hunger for something other than tenderness and care.

His cravat brushed deliciously over his neck as she drew it loose. She stared for a moment at the triangle of bared skin, where the collar of his shirt fell open. One hand lifted and a forefinger ventured over his skin, tracing its way through the hairs on his chest. Her eyes rose to meet his. She took back her hand and turned away, wordlessly presenting the buttons that fastened her gown.

The rest happened in something of a flurry. Buttons, hairpins, coat and waistcoat, petticoats, boots here and shoes there, shirt pulled over his head, and the infernal delay of the corset. But at last they faced each other, he in nothing but breeches, she in shift and stockings.

The stockings, he intended to leave on.

"One more time, Kate." With effort he addressed this to her face. Her shift was cobweb thin and her nipples stood out against the fabric. "Are you quite sure you want to do this?"

She nodded, looking slightly dazed and more than a little distracted, in her turn, by his naked torso. She wouldn't have seen a shirtless man before.

Well, she'd have ample opportunity to make an examination. He scooped her into his arms—God, she felt good against his bare skin—and bore her off to the bed.

Laid atop the counterpane, bathed in pale midmorning sunlight, she looked like she'd materialized straight out of one of his wickedest dreams. When her shift came off, his brain might simply combust.

So he'd make do without a brain. "Will you take off your shift?" He walked round to the other side of the bed, unbuttoning his breeches as he went, and shoving them off without ceremony before climbing onto the mattress. She'd sat up to remove the shift, twisting away out of modesty or perhaps to heighten the suspense. Her ribs expanded with a quick breath before she dropped the garment, turned, and lay down facing him.

Hellfire and bloody damnation. Who was the fellow in the Greek myth who'd created the first woman? Prometheus? No, that wasn't it; she'd been created as punishment for Prometheus, hadn't she, but for some reason delivered to his brother instead. In a box—or no, that wasn't right either; she'd *opened* a box and all sorts of plagues had flown out, and if she'd looked even one-tenth as enticing as Kate Westbrook did at this moment, her husband would have laughed at the gods and told them they could send this kind of punishment any time they liked.

"Kate." He brought his eyes to her face. She'd turned pink, watching the progress of his gaze. "Have I any sparks coming out of my ears? Smoke, perhaps?"

Her brow creased and she shook her head.

"I fear for my brain. I can't seem to properly remember the story of how the first woman came to be."

"She was made out of a rib of the first man. She ate a

fruit she shouldn't have eaten, and it cost her everything good in her life."

"She must have been sorry to have eaten that fruit." He reached out a hand and skimmed his first two knuckles over her arm, from shoulder to the bend of her elbow to her sensitive inner wrist.

"She was sorry for the consequences, I think." She shivered as he stroked her wrist. "That's not the same as being sorry for the fruit."

"She was lured into it, wasn't she? Unscrupulously persuaded."

"She chose it." Her fingers closed about his, where his knuckles had crept from her wrist to her palm. "The persuasion was all her own."

"I see." He threaded his fingers with hers and gave her hand a squeeze. "I'm not going to venture to your side of the bed, you know, or allow you onto mine, until you've looked at me."

"I've been looking at you all this time. At your face, as is polite when two people are speaking."

He brought the forefinger of his free hand to his lips and drew it across, sealing them. *We're not speaking now.*

Her cheeks went pinker, but she looked. She freed her hand from his and reached across to touch, again, the hair on his chest. From there her fingers worked their way down to the bare planes of his stomach, and then to the place where hair started up again. Her gaze followed her fingers, and her mouth pursed with what might be unease, or just thorough attention. She made a brief survey of his legs and feet before returning to the area of chief concern.

"It's . . . imposing." Her brows edged together. "Is it large, as compared to others?"

"Sweetheart, how would I know?" He would not laugh at her, though her question did tickle his sense of the absurd. "Men don't go about measuring them against one another."

"It's not something on which any of your lovers has ever remarked, then?" Her eyes flicked back to his face.

He shrugged. "I presume women make those remarks to their lovers as a matter of course. They're not to be seriously heeded."

She frowned at him, clearly unconvinced, and returned her apprehensive attention to the region below his waist.

"Don't worry. Large or not, it isn't going to go in you, remember?" In fact he had certain hopes that might render this statement less than perfectly true, but no need to concern her with that matter quite yet. Not until he'd done a few things to put her in a less bashful, more amenable state. "Here." He rose to a partial crouch and piled the pillows against the headboard. "Let's get you sitting part of the way up so I can proceed."

Her eyes went wide even as she let him prop her on the pillows in the middle of the bed. "Proceed with what? What are you meaning to do?"

"Worship you." He swung his body over hers, hands to either side of her, one knee between her legs. "The way the first woman's husband surely worshipped her."

"What way is that?" Shock or shyness or maybe even lust squeezed her voice down to something near a whisper.

"I wasn't there at the time so I can only guess." He kissed her, sweeping his tongue over the seam of her lips. "But I feel certain it involved the tasting of forbidden fruit."

Chapter Seventeen

She would have liked to tell him, as he sank his head to her breast and sucked her nipple brazenly into his mouth, how comically unfitting was his choice of image. Far from being forbidden, her breasts seemed to fancy themselves a kind of fruit that ripened expressly for him. From the moment he'd stopped her removing her gloves and pulled her into that kiss, her nipples had gone hard against her layers of linen, making a faintly embarrassing proof of how much she wanted him—how much she wanted him to do *this* in particular, to flick his tongue against her in the most exquisite fashion and then to suck her with punishing strength.

Those were the things she might have liked to tell him, had she been capable of forming words.

She put a hand on the back of his head, and one on his broad shoulder. To watch him felt inexpressibly sinful, but that must have been his intention in propping her up this way, and if it pleased him to be watched then that was what she would do. As he saw to her pleasure, so would she see to his. He would know how she wanted him, even if nothing could come of it.

He switched to the other breast and her thoughts went spinning into disorder again. She squirmed, her body wanting to lie flat, and wanting him to lie down on top of her. Two nights ago he'd done so and it had been that pressure, against a secret, sensitive place, that had combined with this fiery bliss to build and build until culminating in that apoplexy of pleasure. Did he not mean to do that now? Was it too risky, perhaps, for his naked manhood to be so near her naked maidenhead? She squirmed again, this time curling her fingers for a tighter grip on his shoulder.

He let go her nipple and raised his head just enough to meet her eyes. Now was when she ought to speak; to ask whether he couldn't do what he'd done last time, if they were very careful and perhaps even put a sheet between them, but something in his eyes stopped her words before they were halfway formed. He lowered his head and kissed her again, this time between her breasts, where she was not particularly sensitive, and from there in a steady trail toward her navel.

An image formed of what he might mean to do and her breath froze, half in and half out. To watch his downward progress was more than she could dare, so she closed her eyes and followed with desperately acute other senses; the flat of his palms pushing her thighs apart, the creak and shift of the mattress as he brought his second knee between her legs, the warmth—oh, God, the warmth of his breath against her most private parts just before he followed with his hot, wet tongue.

She filled her lungs on a gasp that must surely have been audible from two floors away, and clapped both hands over her mouth. The sensations forked through her body with lightning-strike precision and a devastation to match. She jerked, as someone struck by lightning would, and took one hand from her mouth to scrabble behind her for a grip on the top of the headboard. Ecstasy was beginning its furious approach, much more rapidly than it had done on the sofa two nights before, with no mercy for her sensibilities or decorum.

Then all at once it was gone. His mouth had left her; his tongue had abandoned its worship; and in the time it took her to blink her eyes open and feel the first stirrings of outrage, he'd moved up the bed to where he knelt, straddling her half-propped-up form, his male member stiff and adamant before her.

"I warned you I'm not selfless." He caressed the side of her head, his thumb tracing the shell of her ear. His eyes were so dark with appetite that he might have been a different man. "There's something I'd like you to do. Perhaps you can guess it."

Even a day ago, if someone had told her men and women did such things, she would have recoiled at the thought. But he'd roused her hungers to an unruly pitch. And from the very core of her being she felt a need to please him, to see him driven wild, and to know she'd been the one to do it. "I can guess, generally." She took her hand off the headboard and found a place to settle it on his hip. "But I'll need direction. I don't know precisely what to do."

"Kissing makes an excellent beginning." Again his thumb went round her ear. "In particular the kind of kissing that employs the tongue."

Audacity flashed through all her nerves. If she was going to do this, she wasn't going to do it by halves. "What if I wished to skip the beginning, and go directly to what will drive you out of your senses?"

"Take it in your mouth, as far as it will go." He was speaking almost before she'd stopped. "Be careful not to scrape me with your teeth. Make use of your tongue, and don't worry about being gentle." He'd been so ready with that answer, he must have been hoping against hope she'd ask.

He loomed over her, up on his knees, not nearly as shy

about watching as she'd been. With the hand that wasn't at her ear he took hold of his member, bunching back some of the skin and steadying it to receive her attentions.

She took it in gradually, because it felt so strange and because she needed a few seconds to work out how to protect him from her teeth. Part of it fit. Not all. She was fairly certain those lovers who'd remarked on its size had been telling the truth.

An inconvenient despondency woke, at the thought of his other lovers. But she had no right whatsoever to be jealous, when he'd been willing once to give her his heart. So she wouldn't allow jealousy, or the despondency under whose cloak it stole in. Every bit of her attention would go to his pleasure, and most particularly to the exercise of her tongue.

"God, that's good." The path of his voice told her he was looking down at her, though she kept her own eyes closed. "Keep doing it just like that." His hand left her ear and she heard it grip the headboard. His hips started moving, slowly, drawing his manhood most of the way out and then easing it back in. The hand that still gripped his bunched skin was moving as well, bringing pleasure to as much of him as wasn't in her mouth. She couldn't say *Let me do that* with her mouth full, but she put her hand over his until he understood and gave way.

He swore, in a whisper. His breath was coming in pants and his hips had begun to move a bit harder, faster. "Wait." His whole body shuddered with effort. "Wait. Stop. Just for a minute."

She'd heard these commands before, but she knew, this time, he wasn't going to say they oughtn't to be doing this. She parted her lips and let him draw himself out.

"I'm going to lie down. Then you can start again."

His eyes gleamed with urgent purpose. "I want you on hands and knees above me."

She moved over to give him room, and moved down the bed to where he wanted her.

"No." He caught her arm. "The other way. Hands down there, knees up here."

She ought to have left blushing behind by now, but her face went furnace-hot as she grasped his intent. He must have forgotten his promise to make this easy and comfortable for her. Only the most shameless women would be capable of . . . what he proposed.

No, that wasn't true. A woman determined to please a man, to lose herself and forget herself as thoroughly as was in her power, could be capable of it, too. She took a deep breath and turned herself, easing one hand across and then one knee, letting him guide her hips to where he wanted them.

"Listen." He paused in his adjustment of her position to address her. "There will come a point when I'll tell you to stop. And you must take your mouth off me at once. Yes?"

"Yes." She had a vague idea of why. In any case, this wasn't the moment for discussion.

"Good. Now return to driving me out of my senses, if you please. You've made an excellent start."

To be atop him this way, naked and splayed and so dreadfully exposed to him, felt shocking and frankly wrong. If she paused to reflect on her position, she'd grow too mortified to continue. She must marshal all her thoughts on the task before her, and concentrate her attention on his body until she forgot the existence of her own.

That proved easier said than done. In fact it proved impossible. From the instant he brought her private parts into contact with his mouth, she was deeply, ferociously aware of her body and of each diabolical thing he did to it.

And strangely, the shame receded. She bent down and took his male organ into her mouth, using her hand to slide back the skin as she'd seen him do, and all she wanted in the world was to be able to match him for wickedness. As crudely, lasciviously as he tasted her, just that crude and lascivious would she be with him. She took more and then less of him into her mouth, mimicking the rhythm of his hips from before, and she squeezed and stroked with her hand, that every inch of him might be gratified.

He groaned, thrillingly, arching underneath her. His tongue worked faster and she twisted against him, whether to escape the torment or to demand more she couldn't say. It didn't matter. Nothing mattered anymore but the advance of pleasure, gaining speed and power like a cart hurtling down a steep grade, and all at once it had her in spasms, gasping around his flesh, haphazard in her attentions, in such a state of divine distraction that she almost missed hearing his command to stop.

He rolled onto his side, as she brought away her mouth, and had his release. With the hand that still grasped him she could feel the pulsing that would have delivered his seed into her womb, had he been inside her. He hadn't wanted to inconvenience her mouth with that. Though now he'd have to launder his counterpane.

Thus came back the real world, one mundane concern at a time. If only it wouldn't. If only she could stay in their delirious little world for two, past shame, past sorrow, hiding away from all the reasons they could not be together.

A clock chimed in one of his outer rooms as the pulsing in her hand slowed and ended. She let go and eased herself away from him, off him, slipping free of the hands that, after tightening on her hips with his onslaught of pleasure, had finally relaxed their grip.

She knelt on her side of the bed. He lay with his back to her, breaths expanding his ribs at a pace that suggested he needed more time to recover.

So did she. In fact it seemed possible, kneeling here naked, her privates still tender from his attentions, the taste of him lingering on her tongue, that she might never recover at all.

"KATE." HE lay on his side, still in the place where he'd ended when he'd twisted away from her at the moment of climax. Probably he ought to turn and face her, but he didn't. "We've told each other reasons why we cannot be married."

"I remember them." She hadn't lain down. From her voice he knew she was sitting or kneeling, and facing him.

"We've never spoken of the strongest." He closed his finger and his thumb on a wrinkle in the counterpane.

"Nick. You don't have to speak of it."

"I know. And I know that you've known for some time. But I want to have it said, out loud, between us."

"I'll listen." The mattress shifted as she lay down.

He took a breath. "I have a connection that would discredit you and your family." He couldn't stop there. He had to own the details. "My brother married a Cyprian. A gentleman's mistress. A woman who made a profession of lying with men. Not a year ago, he did this."

Her hand fell light as a snowflake on his arm, settling in the place above his bicep. "When did you last speak to your brother?"

That wasn't the question he'd expected, but he was ready to answer. "Last spring. The day he told us of his plans. I know the marriage did take place because one of my sisters continued to know him. Also because I've seen his wife." The next set of words jostled about on his tongue, waiting to be spoken or swallowed back. But why shouldn't he say anything he wanted on this occasion, knowing it would be the last of its kind? "There are days I wish I'd continued to know him, too. More such days, as time goes on."

The mattress shifted again and she pressed herself to him from behind, her arm slipping over his waist, her breath on the back of his neck. "Would he welcome a reconciliation? Would he be willing to speak to you?"

"I think he might." He turned over to face her, resting a hand on her hip. She looked remarkably serene and unashamed, for an innocent who'd just been drawn into an act of gross debauchery. "Are you encouraging me to speak to him? I'd always imagined you'd be put off by the scandal."

"I was, when I learned of it. I fully approved of your action in cutting him off. Only . . ." She frowned at his bare shoulder as she pieced together her plea. "Having so recently seen a family estrangement carried to the grave, I cannot help thinking that, if one or both of you would like to mend things, then perhaps you ought to try." Again she met his eyes. "I want you to be happy. All else seems secondary to that."

He kissed the tip of her nose. "I want you to be happy, too." That was why he would only watch, and wish her well, when in a little while she got up and left his bed forever. Never mind how profoundly right she looked here, naked but for the stockings, hair tumbling over the disarranged pillows, her whole body limp and supple with satisfaction. "What do you mean to do, hereafter? Do you have hopes of an offer from any of the gentlemen you've met?" He needed to speak of this, to remind himself of what her future would be. Or more to the point, what it wouldn't be. "Lord Barclay certainly seems to think highly of you."

She sighed and sank her forehead against his shoulder. "I don't know what to do. I doubt myself in everything. I wish . . ." She went silent, as though she'd only now realized she didn't know what words should follow. "I wish things could be different."

So do I, Kate. He wrapped her in his arms and kissed her. For mute comfort, at first, because he had no words that could make anything better for either of them. He kissed her face, kissed her ears, lingered at her mouth.

She was going to leave. When they finished kissing, or when she grew concerned about how long she'd been gone from home, she was going to get up and ask for his help with her stays, and she was going to put on her many layers of clothing and go home. And he was going to let her go, because he wanted her to be happy and her happiness wasn't here.

"Kate," he whispered. He couldn't stop kissing her. He couldn't let her leave yet. "I'm so glad you came to me today." He rolled her onto her back and eased on top of her. He was hard again. It was as if his body knew she'd be going, and had to plead for another chance with her while she was still here.

"I'm glad, too." She clung to him, her arms lashed tight around his back. "Do you remember when you said I'd wish another man had been the first to kiss me?"

"I think so." He kissed his way down her neck. His arousal was demanding attention and he was losing his ability to converse.

"I never will. I'll never be sorry for what we've done. I'll always be glad I did these things first with you." She squirmed under him, and suddenly the head of his cock met with her soft, wet privates.

"Sweetheart, be careful." He started to shift himself

away, and only when she caught his shaft in her hand did he realize she'd meant for that contact to happen.

"Nick." She looked him in the eye. "Please."

His breath caught and for a moment his lungs forgot how to work. Outside the closed window and two stories down, indistinct laughter sounded as people passed by in the Middle Temple Lane. Her hand tightened gently, encouraging him. Her eyes were dark with need.

A part of him wanted nothing more than to bury himself in her that instant. Another, more conscientious, part spoke up. "We can't. I can't ruin you. I can't ruin your prospects."

"You've ruined me already in every way that matters. You know you have."

He closed his eyes. He couldn't . . . "It's not that simple. You'll have a husband . . ." But even he didn't believe her eventual husband had greater rights to her body than she did herself. "It wouldn't be pleasant." That was a better argument. He opened his eyes. "It's not comfortable the first time, for a woman. It hurts. You may bleed."

"I know. I've heard of that. I don't mind." The hand that wasn't on his cock stroked up and down his back. "I told you there will be pain in any case. I'm not afraid."

"It might be worse than you expect. I don't want you to remember that, when you remember this day."

"Please," she said again. "I'll have to do this for the first time with someone. If it's wonderful, I want it to be with you. If it hurts and I need care and comforting, I want it to be with you."

Damn her barrister blood. If there was ever an occasion on which he needed to not be out-argued, it was surely this one. But he had no answer for her, besides the answer his body could give.

He drew in a big breath. "Stop me if it's too uncomfortable, or if you have a change of heart for any reason." He waited for her to nod her assent, and then he set himself at her entrance and pushed, slowly.

He'd never done this with a virgin. He wasn't sure what sort of resistance there would be. He braced himself for something blocking his way, for something tearing, but it felt rather more as if he was stretching her, gradually, to accommodate him.

She'd sunk her teeth into her lower lip. The skin had gone white all around her mouth.

"Is it too much?" He made his voice as soothing as he could. "Do you want me to stop?"

She shook her head. "I'll tell you if I need you to stop. Don't ask again."

So he didn't. He pushed a little more, and a little more, and finally he was well inside her. He kissed her, in case she needed care and comforting, and he drew out a few inches and thrust, gently as he could.

It set his brain on fire.

"It doesn't hurt too much?" Was he not supposed to ask that, or just not supposed to ask if he should stop? His poor burning-up brain couldn't remember the rules.

"It hurts a bit." Her face was pale and determined. "But not too much."

"Take heart. I can promise you this won't last long." She was so absurdly tight about him. He kissed all over her face as he moved in and out, trying not to go too deep or too hard. The pleasure built in him with merciless speed—thank goodness she had no experience against which to measure his performance—and within a too-short time he was pulling out of her to spill into the sheets.

She stayed a little while after that. After being deflowered. Damned if he was going to send her home without placating her sore places by means of some thorough, luxuriant kissing. She liked that, and it kept him from thinking too hard about what he'd done. Only after he'd helped her back into her clothes and seen her safely downstairs, outside, and on her way home; only when he came back to his bedroom and looked at the rumpled linens where she'd been, did he feel his sanity returning, bringing with it a colossal portion of regret.

Chapter Eighteen

No doubt Mr. Blackshear was sorry now. What honorable man would not be, after sending a lady home debauched and deflowered? Never mind that she'd been the one to talk him into bed and then into her body. He'd find a way to shoulder all the blame, telling himself he ought to have resisted.

She was so glad he hadn't resisted.

"The next corner is where we turn." She'd made Rose walk a long way. She'd felt so restless coming home this afternoon, transformed and unfit for any of her usual daytime occupations, and the walk to fetch her sisters from school had made her more restless still. When Rose had wished to go to the shops in search of a certain shade of purple embroidery silk, she'd been quick to offer her company. Then halfway through that errand she'd realized she had an errand of her own.

"They must be very good, to have given Papa the use of their carriage. They do know all about our family?" Rose, having been at Miss Lowell's all day, didn't know that Kate was already supposed to have been in South Audley Street this morning. She'd see nothing to question in this visit.

"They do know. And yes, they are very good." Miss

Smith had been good from the start. Kind, generous, tactful, loyal, and, as of yesterday, downright noble. And while Kate herself might fall woefully short of the standard her friend set in personal merit, she at least knew how to appreciate nobility when she saw it. And how to pay that quality its proper tribute.

I don't know, she'd answered when Mr. Blackshear asked what she meant to do in regard to marriage. It was still true. She didn't know what she would do. But she did know now what she would *not* do. And that was a start.

Louisa sat with one of her sisters in the Smiths' drawing room, and as Kate and Rose were shown in, she came to her feet and crossed the room to meet them. "I'm so sorry about your grandmother." She squeezed Kate's hands. "Mother heard from Lady Harringdon this morning of the loss. We've been thinking about you and your family all day."

Kate made her apology for calling outside of at-home hours, explaining that she'd wished to thank Louisa and her mother at the earliest opportunity for their very great kindness of yesterday. Introductions followed: felicitously, the Smith sister present was fifteen-year-old Caroline, and not only did she wish to see the embroidery silk when that errand was mentioned, and to know for what project it would be used, but the book she'd set aside at their entrance proved to be a novel that Rose had recently read.

Louisa prodded her sister to show the younger Miss Westbrook the house's library, and to see whether there were any books she might like to borrow. Then, with the younger girls gone from the room, the elder two could speak with perfect freedom.

Kate took the chair nearest Louisa's place on the sofa. Her friend waited, too well-mannered to broach the obvious questions—*How is your father? Was he welcomed when he arrived at Harringdon House? Was he sorry to have gone?*—but making a quiet show of her willingness to listen, and her equal willingness to let the subject go untouched.

For now, it would be the latter. Other subjects took precedence.

"Are those the roses Lord Barclay sent?" A bunch of them, creamy white, stood in a crystal vase on a table at the sofa's other end.

"Oh—indeed." She hadn't expected that question, and was clearly set off balance. "I think Lady Harringdon made a deal too much of that, yesterday. Myself, I never supposed he meant anything by them but simple cordiality."

"They're very pretty roses." Her own were pale pink, and equally pretty. She could sit about and wonder how to interpret the fact, or she could impose the meaning most advantageous to everyone. "I would be surprised if cordiality were all he meant to express with them."

"I don't know." Louisa made a brief study of the carpet, color blooming in her cheeks, before she raised her anxious eyes once more. "He was friendly at the Cathcarts' ball, but didn't display such marked attentions as would suggest any purposeful sentiment." Indeed, because he'd been too busy dividing his attentions between a congenial lady who shared his interest in politics, and a mercenary beauty using every art she possessed to try to gain his notice. She couldn't think back on the night without shame.

"Louisa, I'm going to be dreadfully frank. I hope you don't mind." Yesterday, she would have balked at speaking so. Today, having already done things ten thousand times less proper, she didn't waver for even an instant. "I've hoped to make a marriage that can elevate my station, confer on my sisters the consequence of good connections, and advance my family's return to respectability. Lord Barclay, because of his title and the generous regard he's already shown my family, struck me as an excellent prospect for a husband. I did attempt to promote my interest with him, for those pragmatic reasons."

Louisa nodded. She could not fail to notice that all of this was being related in the past tense.

"But observing you with him that same evening, I began to see how very well you two would suit one another. And I'm nothing but delighted to see evidence of his preference for you." If that preference was not yet fact, it would be, soon enough. The pink roses probably represented what roses from men had always represented, with her: a temporary succumbing to her superficial charms. The white roses testified to the good sense that prevented him from discounting Miss Smith's merits and compatible mind in favor of mere coquettish beauty.

"I'm not at all convinced there's a preference." Louisa's shoulders settled, slightly, as though she had not quite been able to relax in Kate's company until now. "But I'll confess to you I do think highly of him. Please don't tell Lady Harringdon." Her smile, confiding and hopeful, lit her eyes brighter than any blue hair ribbon could.

"I shan't breathe a word." She ran a finger across her pressed-together lips. Mr. Blackshear had made that same gesture in bed, when he'd insisted she look at his naked form. With her whole body she remembered.

She felt a bit light-headed, and not only from the memories of this morning. She'd just let go of something for which she'd schemed nearly as long as she could remember. She wasn't likely to find another marital prospect as fitted to her ambitions as Lord Barclay. Not soon, at any rate. Perhaps not ever.

And yet she didn't feel any disappointment. Rather

she felt a sense of satisfaction at her own accomplishments. She was the one who'd cut Louisa's hair, and made her look so pretty for the Cathcarts' ball. She would encourage her in cultivating Lord Barclay's attentions, and perhaps find a way to prod Lord Barclay as well. She had a talent for these things. She might find some of the same gratification in realizing someone else's romantic prospects as in realizing her own.

"If I may follow your example of frankness, I believe there must be many gentlemen for whom your merits will outweigh whatever reservations they might have in regard to your family." Steadfast, idealistic, good-hearted Louisa. If the baron didn't fall for her he was the biggest fool on earth. "I hear often from my brother of how society is changing in this respect. I feel sure you'll make a marriage that will answer all your hopes, and in the meanwhile, you and your sisters may count on whatever advantage the friendship of my family can confer."

"Thank you." Kate slipped the words past a tightening in her throat, and lowered her eyes to where her hands sat folded in her lap. She'd imagined the renunciation of Lord Barclay as a sacrifice whose reward would come in the knowledge that she'd done the right thing. She hadn't expected any benefit beyond that.

But when the younger girls came back from the library, Rose's face aglow and three volumes clutched in her hands, and when, as they started home, her sister reported that she'd been invited to bring her needlework when she came to return the volumes, so that she and Caroline could have a good look at each other's projects, a thought took shape that had somehow never taken shape before.

Perhaps some of what she'd hoped to attain through marriage could, after all, be attained by other means. Friendship—maybe even a double friendship with Louisa and Lord Barclay, if everything in that quarter went as it ought—could lend its own kind of consequence. There might be invitations to social events, for her sisters as well as herself, and with no required pretense of intending to be a lady's companion. There might be real, open cordiality between her family and this one. There might be a friend for Rose.

Altogether, she might not have made quite as much a mess of everything as she'd thought. In fact, she might have achieved some very worthwhile ends.

Arriving home, Kate met with yet another unlooked-for triumph: a letter on heavy ivory-colored paper, franked, the date and signature on the outside nearly illegible. This time, though, the letter was not for her.

"It's as close to an apology as I imagine I'll ever have from Edward," Papa said over dinner. "From Lord Harringdon, that is." He nodded to Kate, to Sebastian, to Viola, to the younger girls. "Your uncle."

Never before had the earl been "your uncle" or been referred to as "Edward," as far back as Kate could remember. This, too, was something won at least in part by her efforts.

Viola, predictably, was unimpressed. "I should think the person to whom he most owes an apology is our mother." She turned to Mama. "I don't suppose he troubled to send a letter to you."

"No, but it would be odd if he did, considering we've never been introduced." No queen, no duchess, no countess could hope to match the grace and nobility with which Mama delivered this reply as she carved out a bite-sized morsel of her poached haddock.

"What did he say, if it wasn't an apology?" This was really Papa's business and nobody else's, but Kate couldn't help asking. "And does he mean to recognize you again? And what about Mama?"

"It's too soon to know what will happen." Papa, too, went on cutting his fish. "Too soon to know even what

I wish to happen. Twenty-three years is a long time for someone to be absent from your life, and you get accustomed to doing without him." His eyes connected with hers. He was talking about his mother, too, and how twenty-three years of distance had eroded his ability to grieve for her. "And Viola is right in bringing up the insult to your mother. I cannot allow any reconciliation that doesn't include her, and make some acknowledgment of how she was wronged."

"You needn't concern yourself with that." Half the table separated Mama from Papa, and still she managed to sound as though they were speaking in private. "I've lived my whole life without Lord Harringdon's approval, and never felt the lack. What matters is what will make you happy. It's reasonable to suppose a truce between long-estranged brothers might have that result."

I want you to be happy. All else seems secondary to that. Countless things conspired to make Kate think of Mr. Blackshear. She'd told him to speak to his brother, and he'd kissed her on the nose and asked who she might marry.

"As to what he said, Kate, much of that will remain between me and him. But some I can share, and I suspect this will be of particular interest to you." Papa smiled down the table at her. "You were right in some of your suppositions. Lady Harringdon's attentions to you were the result of my brother's wish to do something for this family, no doubt to assuage his guilt over having cut us off so long ago. He also said his wife is very pleased with you and pronounces you a credit to your Westbrook blood. Oh, and here's what came as a surprise to me: I find it was through Edward's doing that Lord Barclay was referred to me, when he put it about that he'd like a barrister to help him study speech."

Even before she'd had her note from Lady Harringdon, then, the earl had been thinking of Papa, looking for small, inconspicuous gestures he could make; ways he could reach out and benefit his brother's family. And still, yesterday when he might have asked her to fetch her father to the dowager's bedside, his courage or his brotherly feeling had failed him.

And then he'd had another chance. By her own doing—and Miss and Mrs. Smith's, and Mr. Blackshear's, with help from Mr. Kersey—Papa had come anyway, and Lord Harringdon had decided to write this letter. Thus a person progressed toward a worthy goal, it seemed, a step forward and a step back and the occasional intervention of other people to guide him back the right way when he'd stumbled off the path.

She shifted in her chair, and felt a sharp reminder of how she'd stumbled off her own path that morning. Lain down in a gentleman's bed and got up again without her virtue. It felt like something someone else had done, a whispered report at which she pursed her lips and shook her head. It also felt like the only logical outcome of her three years' acquaintance with Mr. Blackshear. As though from the moment they met, they'd been making their haphazard way toward that culmination.

What will you do, hereafter?

I don't know. I wish things could be different.

She reached for her glass. "Mr. Blackshear owes a debt of gratitude to Lord Harringdon then, doesn't he, for this opportunity with Lord Barclay?" Singular, how everything wove itself together, or rather, how it had all been woven together from the start.

"I shouldn't advise him to send a note of thanks." With visible gusto Viola seized this new opportunity for disapproval. "I doubt the earl bothers to open any mail from a gentleman who has a profession, and no title in his lineage."

Vi didn't even know the worst. Lord Harringdon certainly wouldn't welcome any correspondence from a man with Mr. Blackshear's shocking connections. Perhaps even Lord Barclay would find the matter too unsavory, once he learned of it, and thus would end all Mr. Blackshear's hopes of political opportunity.

Maybe not, though. Society was changing, Louisa had said. Lord Barclay had already proven himself extraordinarily fair-minded in regard to her own connections. Surely if there was a man capable of overlooking the unfortunate marriage in Mr. Blackshear's family, and judging Mr. Blackshear strictly on his own merit, the baron was that man.

She stole a glance at the long-case clock. Mere hours since she'd left his rooms, and all she wanted was to see him again, and tell him of all that had happened since they'd parted, and hear what had happened with him. But if he blamed himself for her ruin, it might be a great while before his next call here.

I wish things could be different.

She'd been a coward. *I love you,* she ought to have said. *Help me have the courage to choose with my heart. Tell me I'm strong enough to bear a descent in station, and clever enough to help you make your way back up.* He might have answered, as he'd done once already, with that gentle explanation about her not being the right sort of woman to stand at his side. But at least she'd know she'd been brave enough to ask. Brave enough to be honest.

Never mind. She would count herself lucky in his friendship, and hope for at least the beginning of reparation with his brother, if that was what Nick wanted. Without reference to herself she would wish for his happiness, because that was what you did when you loved someone.

* * *

He'd imagined, ignorantly, that a footman would answer his knock. And that he'd consequently have a minute or so, the time it took to climb the stairs, in which to orient himself to his surroundings and make his last small preparations for this meeting that still felt a bit ill-advised.

But it was Will himself who stood there when the door swung back, his cheerful, unguarded expression suggesting he'd just stepped away from an amusing conversation and felt equal to whoever or whatever he might find on his doorstep.

He'd always had the most ridiculously readable face. His brows now lofted a quarter inch and came back down: that was surprise. The laughter left his eyes like a candle blown out. No anger or coldness came in to take its place; instead he looked curious, and ready to see where this unexpected twist in his day's narrative would lead. "Nick." At the sound of his voice, it suddenly felt like only yesterday that they'd last spoken. "Come in."

"Do I intrude?" But Nick was halfway over the threshold already.

"On my glittering dinner party with all the leading lights of the ton? Hardly." Will shut the door behind him. "We do have company, but nothing on which you need fear intruding. Take off your coat and come upstairs."

Cathcart was Nick's first thought; *Martha* was his second. His third thought was that Will seemed remarkably at ease considering one of the siblings who'd cut him off had just appeared at his door after nearly a year of silence.

As Will led the way upstairs, Nick made a quick, discreet survey of the surroundings. He'd never had cause to call on anyone in the Hans Town neighborhood before, and hadn't known what sort of house to expect. *Modest* described it fairly well. The stairs, from what he could see, were in good repair, and the wallpaper was bright and not peeling. No signs of squalor; nothing dingy; but the house was undeniably small and the serving staff must have been minimal, if none of them counted it among his duties to answer the door.

You could never bring Kate Westbrook here. God, the impudence of his unbidden thoughts! He wasn't intending to bring her anywhere, and besides, who was he to make that judgment? Cathcart was a viscount; Martha was the wife of a baronet's heir, and neither of them turned up their noses at visiting this house. After everything he'd seen of Miss Westbrook in recent days, could he really think her so superficial by comparison?

He followed his brother round the landing and along the hall to the first of two doorways, which opened on to a drawing room. There, side by side on the sofa, sat his grave-faced younger sister and the forbidding Mrs. Blackshear. "Lydia," Will said, advancing into the room. "Allow me to present my brother Nicholas. Nick, this is my wife, Lydia Blackshear."

He nodded, and Mrs. Blackshear nodded back. Her face showed nothing—he was used to that after two meetings—but an invisible thread of understanding ran between them. He wouldn't be here now if she hadn't shown up on the bench in Brick Court yesterday morning with a slip of paper and a roundabout encouragement.

"Nick, it's so good to see you." Martha struggled, still, with social niceties, but she did attempt them with some spirit. "I hope you won't use up all your conversation on Will while I'm out of the room. Mrs. Blackshear and I were just preparing to go upstairs, that she could show me her new gown."

"Indeed." Will's wife rose, with Martha a hair behind. "You'll excuse us, I hope. I've been waiting some time to show Mrs. Mirkwood this gown." The two filed out,

Martha pausing to grasp Nick's hand and fix him with a look of fervent feeling, briefly, before snatching back her hand and hurrying flush-faced from the room.

He oughtn't to laugh at his sister, certainly not at a show of heartfelt emotion when for too many years she'd been stolid to a fault. And indeed it seemed at first that he would successfully suppress the laugh, even though the idea of Martha eager to see anyone's new gown had a layer of absurdity all its own.

But he happened to cross glances with Will, who likewise was fighting a tide of laughter, lips pressed together, eyes glittering with hilarity, and all at once they might as well have been eight and ten years old again, side by side in the church pew and jabbing one another whenever Reverend Roberts uttered any word that could be tenuously associated with a bodily function.

He laughed. Not out loud; their sister deserved better than to overhear and feel mocked, even affectionately. Everything was so ridiculous, though—his and Mrs. Blackshear's stifled animosity, the clumsy maneuvering that had left him and Will alone, his very presence here in the first place—that he needed the relief of collapsing onto the now-vacant sofa and giving vent to his mirth.

Will laughed, too, sinking into a chair at right angles to the sofa and burying his face in his hands. For nearly a minute they gave themselves up to silent merriment, and by the end of that minute much of the awkwardness between them had simply evaporated. The habits of over twenty years, it turned out, could trump the habits of the last nine or ten months.

Will wiped his eyes, and nodded toward where the women had gone. "She hasn't got any new gown, you know."

"I suspected as much." Nick sat back, relaxing a little into the sofa's corner. He lowered his voice to a stage whisper. "I don't think she likes me."

"No?" His brother grinned, smug in the knowledge of his wife's fierce affection. "Well, she didn't like me either at first. So I wouldn't give up hope yet." He looked so comfortable here in this too-small drawing room, settled into circumstances much humbler than those in which he'd grown up. "In the meantime you can console yourself with Martha's surfeit of sisterly affection."

"That damnable Mirkwood; he's gone and altered her almost beyond recognition." This wasn't really true, but he wanted to speak strongly about something, and the man who'd debauched his little sister into marriage was as good a target as any. "You weren't here during her first marriage, but she was every bit the sobersides she'd always been. Only when this fellow came along did she start doing unaccountable things, and behaving in the way you see now."

"I don't fault her for it, or fault her husband either. Love makes us all do unaccountable things." Will leaned back and crossed his ankle over the opposite knee. "I'm nothing if not evidence of that fact, and I expect one day you'll learn it by your own experience."

Nick might have made any number of replies. A jibe, for example, taking aim at younger brothers who presumed to lecture to their elders about experience. More abuse heaped on Mr. Mirkwood. A swift change of subject.

None of them came to hand. With the tremendously unaccountable act of this morning on his conscience, and a confusion of sentiments that might, under close examination, parse themselves out to something like love, he could only sit silent.

"Ah." Will propped his elbows on the arms of his chair, and steepled his fingers. "I wondered if something had happened, to prompt this visit. Will she have you, or do your connections make too great an impediment?" His brows lowered in worry. He'd apologized, the day he'd announced his decision, for the cost he'd known the rest of the Blackshears would bear.

"It's not even . . ." Nick waved a hand vaguely. "I hadn't any intention of asking her. It's not the sort of . . ." What the devil was he trying to say? He let his hand fall. "It's all confoundedly complicated."

"Isn't it always?" His brother studied him a moment, features etched with wry sympathy. "You'd better tell me the whole story. What's her name, and where did you meet?"

So he told the story, feeling more than a little selfish and ungracious as he did. He ought to be spending this call in asking how Will got on, or perhaps in speaking directly about their estrangement and whether they might come to be friendly again. He oughtn't to be violating Kate's privacy by recounting, even in the most nonspecific terms, what had happened between them.

He couldn't help himself. The words spilled from him like water from an overturned jug. Who else was he to tell, after all? He wasn't on confiding terms with any of his associates or friends, and as to family, he couldn't possibly discuss such matters either with his sisters or with upright, unfailingly correct Andrew.

Will, though. His younger brother had some acquaintance with human frailty, and felt no need to register his dismay or disapproval, instead proceeding straight to practical questions. Was there any chance he'd gotten her with a child? Might she come to regret the act, once the fog of grief had lifted? Might she tell her parents? Did his income even permit him to marry?

The realization arrived somewhere in the middle of this unsentimental sorting through of facts and possibilities. Not like a lightning bolt illuminating what had been a pitch-dark room; more like a gradual thaw that wiped the frost from a window, so the objects on which he'd been looking out all along took on a clarity that had not been there before.

He had to ask her to marry him. Not because there might be a child—having taken the usual precaution, he was fairly sure there wouldn't be—nor out of guilt for having ruined her, or fear of her parents' wrath. Not even because of the same heady infatuation that had informed all his hopes three years before.

He had to ask because he could not bear to picture her sinking her head on another man's shoulder to confess all her self-doubts. He couldn't bear to imagine a time when she'd make only polite conversation with him because teasing and sparring with a gentleman ill became a lady who was someone else's wife. He couldn't bear to let some other man be the one to hear her hopes and ambitions, her victories and her setbacks. And he couldn't bear to tell his own to any woman but her. "We don't suit one another at all, though. We could scarcely be more ill-matched." He hadn't meant to speak the words aloud, yet there they were.

"That hasn't stopped you being friends." Will made the observation quietly, drumming his fingers on the arm of his chair.

"No, it hasn't." Without protest he'd watched her walk away this morning because he wanted her happiness above all. When he ought to have asked her outright if there was any chance her happiness could trace its path through him. "In spite of all our unsuitability we've managed to be friends." *So maybe . . .*

Of course it wasn't that simple. His precarious income, even supplemented with what he might draw out of his savings, wouldn't stretch to silk gowns and linen-fiber paper. His connections would moor her in a level of society far from the one to which she'd aspired.

But he'd asked what she intended to do, and she

hadn't said, *I hope for an offer from Lord Barclay,* or, *I'll marry the first man of noble name who wants me.* She'd leaned her head on his shoulder and wished things could be different.

Things *could* be different. Some things could. He and she, chiefly, could resolve to be different. They could allow some alteration to their respective long-held plans. They could put their faith in each other and go forward.

"You're contented here, Will, aren't you?" He gestured around the drawing room. "Your wife as well? You find these quarters sufficient, and you don't mind that you're not received anywhere?"

"I won't lie. I feel your absence from my life, and our elder brother's and sister's absences, too. And I continue to regret that my marriage has brought difficulty to you." Will frowned at his fingers, drumming once more on the chair's arm, and stilled them. "I don't regret anything else, but neither would I recommend this life except in extraordinary cases. Lydia and I . . . have both had such experience as prepared us to appreciate a small house and a few friends. The sacrifice would be greater, I expect, for someone who was not so prepared."

It wouldn't be easy, he meant. Prudent, in that case, to choose a bride who didn't limit herself to easy undertakings.

Besides, their circumstances needn't be quite this modest. He did have some money. If he drew out of his savings he could manage a reasonable house, well staffed. He must push the possibility of buying land a few years further off, but he could do that. He knew how to be patient. Very, very good things did come sometimes to people who were willing to wait.

He grinned. He probably looked like a royal idiot. Probably sounded like one, too, with this report of his doings and the hints of his injudicious hopes. No, worse than an idiot, he probably sounded like a scoundrel and a colossal hypocrite, ruining an innocent and confiding the fact to the man he'd high-handedly cut off as a too-scandalous connection.

But there Will sat, watching him with a grave crease in his brow, every bit as concerned for his welfare as he'd have been if they'd remained friendly all these months.

Nick stretched his legs out before him and rubbed his hands through his hair. One day, when he felt their connection was sufficiently repaired, he'd ask what sort of experiences had prepared his brother to bear these reduced circumstances. Perhaps he'd even be on such terms with Will's wife as to learn her history, too.

For now he just went on grinning, satisfied down to his bones with the decision to come here today. "Christ, I'm glad you didn't die in that duel," he said.

He'd been waiting a long time to say so.

BY THE end of his visit Nick had managed a bit of cordiality with Mrs. Blackshear, on the subject of budgeting for a house and staff, and that was enough to go on with. Their relations might gradually improve.

One hurdle remained, before he could address himself to Kate, and it was no small one. But the visit to Will and his wife had given him practice in speaking frankly and confessing his wrongs, so the next morning, when he went to call on Lord Barclay at his home in Charles Street, he was as ready as he could be.

"I was wrong in not being honest with you from the start." He sat across the desk from the baron, in a dark-paneled study with a bay window through which sunlight streamed, and did his best to keep from picturing what it would be like to work in this pleasant space. Sorting through correspondence. Researching any measures currently under discussion in Parliament, and preparing summaries for Barclay's use. "I wanted this opportunity, and any subsequent opportunities, very much. And so I balked at telling you what you had a right to know, and were all but certain to find out sooner or later by other means. I don't attempt to defend my lack of candor; only to explain the process of thought that lay behind it."

Barclay nodded. "That accounts for what Lord Littleton said to you at the Cathcarts' ball. I did notice, and wonder." He'd been reading through some documents when Nick was announced. They lay scattered across his desktop, fairly crying out for the strong organizing hand of a secretary.

"To be sure. I apologize for putting you in that position. You oughtn't to have had to hear rumors from someone else." He took a breath. "And I may as well tell you now that I called on my brother yesterday, and intend to acknowledge him henceforward."

The baron rubbed his knuckles along his jaw, studying Nick with a thoughtful expression. "You must know that will make your political ambitions more difficult to realize."

"They would have been difficult already." He lifted one shoulder. Really, he was almost at peace with this. "I disowned Will when he announced his intention to marry, and I find I might as well have continued to know him, for all the good it's done me. I don't get nearly the work from solicitors that I used to. Nor do I receive social invitations, beyond a very few. I expect it will be *more* difficult to advance if I own the connection, yes. But not so much more difficult as to dissuade me."

Barclay studied him in silence for a moment. "I'd make a poor example of integrity, wouldn't I, if I ended our partnership because of this connection and meanwhile represented myself as an advocate for returned soldiers?"

"Perhaps. But you could also end it because you object to my having turned my back—those were your words, I recall—on one of the men whose welfare you particularly champion. Or you could judge there to have been too much deception for you to retain trust in me."

A grin cracked across the baron's features. "A barrister through and through, aren't you? I advise you to stop before you come across a reason that compels me."

Hope, his constant loitering companion of late, was quick to parse the sentence: Barclay had not yet heard a reason that would compel him to terminate their arrangement.

"The truth is, Blackshear, I don't pay enough attention to these things to be much concerned. Your name wasn't known to me the way it was to Littleton, recall. And I can't imagine that studying speech with a gentleman whose brother married a woman of poor reputation will really put a blight on my own name. Even a secretary whose brother married such a woman seems unlikely to do damage to my respectability." He paused for a breath, filling his lungs all the way to the bottom as Mrs. Westbrook had taught him. "But I'll require candor, henceforward, particularly if I'm to consider you for the secretary post. I'll rely on the man in that position to be honest with me, and never shrink from telling me what he suspects I won't like to hear."

And there was a cue if ever Nick had heard one. He sat straighter and took a prodigious breath of his own. "In the interest of honesty, then, I must correct an impression I've given you on another matter. Regarding Miss Westbrook." The safer course of action would have been to speak to Kate first, because, depending on her answer, he might have had nothing, after all, to confess to the baron.

On this matter, though, he'd lost all taste for safety. "I fear I misled you as to the nature of my feelings for her.

In my defense, I can only say I misled myself as well." His heart beat like a resolute church bell as he put all his ambitions at risk one more time. "We're friends, as I told you. That much is true. But I've realized very recently that I've been in love with her for quite some time."

Chapter Nineteen

Once before, Mr. Blackshear had come calling with flowers. She couldn't regret that she'd rejected him that day. She could certainly wish she'd been more graceful in how she went about it, and less injurious to his pride. He had recovered, though, and they'd gone on to enjoy three years of coming to know each other, to esteem and appreciate each other, in that rare freedom conferred by the absence of weighty hopes and expectations.

No, she would never regret that she hadn't encouraged him then. Because here he was now, stepping into the drawing room with an elegant arrangement of lilies and carnations, and even if the flowers proved to not be for her, she could appreciate them as an expression of substantial, abiding regard rather than the impulse of a young man's fancy for a pretty girl.

"Blackshear." Papa rose from his place by the hearth and went to meet him. "I'm glad you called. I've been wanting to express my thanks for all you did, two nights ago."

Mr. Blackshear bowed his head. "I'm sorry for your loss. I heard the news, and wished to extend my condolences in person."

The flowers weren't for her, of course. She'd known it

was unlikely they would be, and still she could not help a pooling sense of disappointment as the bouquet went from Mr. Blackshear's hands to Papa's, and then to Mama's.

"Sit down, please." Mama spoke over her shoulder, already on her way to the bellpull. "I'll ring for tea. Shall I have cake sent up as well?"

"Please don't go to that trouble. I haven't any need of tea." His gaze settled on her, not on Mama, as he spoke, and her pulse began pounding with the force of a brawny housemaid cleaning a rug even before he said his next words. "I do, however, have need of a private interview with Miss Westbrook, if you'll grant me permission."

For an instant there was silence, broken only by someone's quick indrawn breath. Rose's, it must be, since she was sitting somewhere behind and to the left and the sound did seem to have come from there. But this, the matter of the breath and who'd drawn it, was perhaps the least important of all the things that Kate could possibly perceive in this moment.

"Kate?" That was Mama. The single syllable said, *Do you want this?* Because she wouldn't leave the room—none of the family would—if it meant leaving Kate to a conversation she did not welcome.

The world seemed all but overflowing with people's kindness and benevolence of late, and still, the goodness of her family, ready to close ranks around her even against so beloved a friend as Mr. Blackshear, sent a new current of warmth through her heart.

"I'd like to hear what Mr. Blackshear has to say." She'd imagined one day being solicited for an interview by a gentleman of whom she had hopes. She'd practiced, before her mirror, half a dozen different attitudes for granting consent, finally settling on a serene nod and bare hint of a smile such as could heighten his hopes while still keeping him in suspense.

Lord, what a self-satisfied fool she'd been, and how ignorant of what this moment would really be like! Not once had it occurred to her that the man in question might be a near acquaintance who could see through all her artifice. Not once had she suspected she'd no more want to play a part before him than before her family, and that she'd voice her permission in matter-of-fact, conversational tones.

He nodded to each Westbrook as they filed from the room, and when only he and she were left, he crossed over to the sofa and sat next to her, angling himself to face her and laying his arm atop the sofa's back. "Kate," he said. He looked at her for a moment; then glanced away to the ceiling and dragged a hand over his face. "I find I don't know where to begin."

"It doesn't matter where you begin. The ending will come out the same."

"Will it?" He ventured his hand across the space between them, and traced the curve of her ear. She couldn't suppress a quick, vivid memory of the last occasion on which he'd touched her ear like that, and what she'd been doing at the time.

"It will. I can tell you the ending now if you like."

He shook his head, smiling, and let his hand fall. "I'm a barrister, remember, and a would-be politician. I'm afraid you have to sit through the speech."

But there didn't turn out to be a speech, exactly. He found her hand and wove his fingers with hers, and told her about how he'd gone to call on his brother yesterday. Then he listened while she told about her visit to Louisa. They exchanged accounts of a meeting with Lord Barclay and Papa's letter from Lord Harringdon, commending one another's achievements and rejoicing in good fortune. They might almost have had this same conversation with the family present, but for his thumb tracing circles in her palm, and the undisguised affection with which he looked at her.

"I can't promise you a grand house, or the life to go with it." He slid right into this subject, without having proposed or even declared himself in love with her. As though he was eager to skip all the ceremony and go straight to the business of building a shared life. "We'd probably begin in some place comparable to this one, and have to watch our pennies for a few years while I save up to buy land. Would you mind that?"

She wouldn't. That was the odd thing. She'd dreamed for so long of marrying into a life of consequence and ease, as ladies always did in books. Suddenly that sounded dreary beyond imagining. What did you do all day, once you'd married Mr. Darcy? You could rearrange the paintings at Pemberley only so many times.

If she married Mr. Blackshear, though, she would have a role to play in his success. She could institute such economies as would accelerate his savings and hasten the day he could become a landowner. She could listen as he described his cases, and ask questions that might prepare him for arguing in court. And once he began to make political acquaintances—she might prevail on Louisa to arrange some introductions through her brother—she could meet those men, too, and charm them with her conversation, as a good politician's wife was supposed to do.

"Where have you gone?" His voice twisted with teasing fondness; he took her chin in his fingers to turn her face to his. "I can see your mind is running like a rabbit ahead of the hounds, but I have no idea where it's taking you."

"Don't laugh, Nick, but I think it might suit me very well to be a political hostess, and in the meantime, to strive with you toward that end." His face, as he listened, made her want to confide in him for the rest of her life. "All these years I've pursued social status with such industry, and lately it's become more and more clear to me that I kept at it because I enjoyed the industry, and the challenges, at least as much as I longed for the goal itself."

"I fear you'd have to let go your hopes of social status indeed, if we married."

Finally he'd said the word. It shimmered between them, bright as a lake on the hottest day of summer. She smiled, foolishly, and so did he.

"I'll never entirely let go those hopes. In fact I intend to be the most sought-after political hostess in town. But I can wait." She'd have Louisa to acknowledge her, after all, and perhaps the pleasure of watching Papa and Lord Harringdon come to be friendly again. "However, I'm not as patient in all things as I am in this. We've been left alone for nearly as long as a decent private interview should last, and you have yet to come to the point."

His mouth twitched with laughter as he unwove his fingers from hers and brought both his hands up to cradle her face. "Believe me, it's by heroic effort on my part that this interview has remained as decent as it has. And you know the point, imperious chit. I want you to marry me." His words thrilled her to the core, even if they told her nothing she hadn't already known. "We're all wrong for each other and I only love you all the more for that." His fingertips had roamed to the back of her neck and found her hairline there. The sensation might have seduced her out of her senses, if she hadn't already been sure of her reply. "You told me you knew before I began how this would end. May I hope it ends in your saying yes?"

"You may hope whatever you like. But this, in fact, is how it ends." She lifted her hands to his jaw in her turn, and drew him down near, and kissed him.

Epilogue

THE WEDDING breakfast was a beginning. Wedding breakfasts usually were, of course, and indeed this one celebrated the commencement of their married life. However, it also sketched a tentative outline of how their two families would fit together. And how Nick's own might come to be whole once again.

A beginning called for small steps rather than large, and so they'd been careful to not put Mrs. William Blackshear too near to Kitty or Andrew. If that woman thought to spend the meal in undisturbed solitude, however, well, she'd come to the wrong wedding breakfast for that.

"It occurs to me a woman who is engaged as a gentleman's mistress enjoys many of the same privileges as would a wife, with the very great advantage of personal independence." Miss Viola had scarcely touched her food, so engrossed was she in questioning the exotic creature whom it had pleased Fate to bring into the family. Every now and then some snatch of her conversation reached Nick's ears. "She controls her own money. She owns her clothes and her jewels. She may end the arrangement when it pleases her to do so."

"True, but so may the gentleman." Mrs. Blackshear—

one of three Mrs. Blackshears at the table, now that she and Andrew's wife had been joined in that name by the bride—kept her voice low, darting a glance around to see how far she was overheard. "He'll generally settle a sum on her, but it might not be enough to provide for the rest of her days. There, a wife has the advantage. And certainly a wife's children have every advantage over the children of a mistress."

"Ah. Legitimacy and inheritance. I'd forgot about that." Miss Viola adjusted her spectacles, frowning as she digested this amendment to her impression of a mistress's advantages.

Kate, seated at his right, glanced up at him, her merry eyes and tight-pressed lips making clear that she, too, was listening to the highly irregular discussion at the table's far end.

"You see what a service I've done, bringing my connections into your family?" Nick lowered his voice to a murmur. He had a hundred and ten things to murmur to her later, once breakfast was eaten and everyone had gone home. He hadn't touched her, beyond a kiss or two, in the weeks since the proposal. "I expect Miss Viola will have enough material for a whole new chapter, by the end of this meal."

"I don't doubt you're right. Heaven help us all." She'd been anxious, he knew, about the introduction to Will and his wife, but when the time came she met them with a well-rehearsed poise, and an underlying graciousness that put him to shame. She would be his ally in putting his family back together. She did have some practice in that pursuit.

He glanced up the table to Mr. Westbrook, speaking to Andrew's wife, and from there he took a moment to look around at the various conversations that had sprung up, thanks in part to one enjoyable evening in which he and Kate had drawn diagrams and conferred over who should sit where. Here was Mrs. Westbrook, discussing some aspect of hunting with Kitty's husband. Here Mr. Mirkwood, who had some fondness for music, bent his head to ask questions of Miss Bea. Directly across the table sat Lord Barclay, dividing his time between Will, on one side, and Miss Smith, on the other—Kate had ideas of promoting a match between the baron and her friend. Stoic Martha sat by distractible Sebastian, neither of them needing much in the way of conversation. And Miss Rose, by his and Kate's agreement the most generally pleasing and dependable Westbrook, served as family ambassador to Andrew and Kitty.

She'd giggled when they told her she had the very important assignment of creating an excellent impression with the most exacting of the Blackshears, but she'd agreed to do it and appeared to be doing a fine job.

Not present, needless to say, were Lord and Lady Harringdon. They'd sent their congratulations and said Miss Westbrook must bring her husband to meet them one day, and that much was more than Nick had expected.

This was what a beginning looked like. Some prospects would come to fruition, and some would probably not. But for now, he had the luxury of immoderate, unchecked hope.

"Mrs. Blackshear." It would be a long time before the novelty of so addressing her wore off.

"Yes, Mr. Blackshear?" How many times, over the course of their acquaintance, had he looked at her and thought she'd never been more beautiful? Yet she truly had never looked lovelier than she did today, in a sky blue silk gown that had been a betrothal gift from her aunt and uncle. Nick couldn't wait to take it off her.

"I'm so glad you didn't accept my addresses three years ago."

She laughed, but it was a knowing laugh. She understood him precisely. Love meant more when it followed upon a thorough knowledge of the other person, flaws as well as graces, small charms as well as large, scandalous connections and all.

For two people so ill-suited, they fit together remarkably well.

"I'm glad I didn't accept you, too," she said, and under the table she fit her hand into his.